Acclaim for ~~The Bird In~~ the Bamboo Cage

'I've been completely swept away by *The Bird In The Bamboo Cage* . . . it transported me utterly – vivid, heart-rending and so, so beautiful. I loved it'

> Jenny Ashcroft, bestselling author of
> *Beneath a Burning Sky*

'Touching and timely . . . inspired by real events during the Second World War'

> *Sunday Times Culture*

'Above all this is a novel about human courage, generosity of spirit, and the power of friendship. I was hooked from first to last page'

> Gill Paul, *USA Today* bestselling author of *The Secret Wife*

'A well-researched book exploring a slice of little-known history during World War Two, with a terrific feel for the period and perfectly attuned to the language of the times'

> Dinah Jefferies, bestselling author of *The Missing Sister*

'Stunning . . . Based on an incredible true story, *The Bird in the Bamboo Cage* is immersive, moving and utterly unforgettable'

> Catherine Ryan Howard, bestselling
> author of *The Nothing Man*

'A great read . . . beautifully written . . . That it is based on real events only serves to make the tale more powerful'

> Liz Trenow, bestselling author of *Under a Wartime Sky*

The Bird in the Bamboo Cage

Hazel Gaynor is an award-winning, *New York Times*, *USA Today*, and *Irish Times* bestselling author of historical fiction, including her debut *The Girl Who Came Home*, for which she received the 2015 RNA Historical Novel of the Year award. *A Memory of Violets* was a WHSmith Fresh Talent pick for spring 2015, *The Girl from The Savoy* was shortlisted for the 2016 Irish Book Awards, and *The Lighthouse Keeper's Daughter* was shortlisted for the 2019 Historical Writers' Association Gold Crown award. *The Bird in the Bamboo Cage* was shortlisted for the 2020 Irish Book Awards Popular Fiction Novel of the Year, and was a national bestseller in the USA, where it is published as *When We Were Young & Brave*. Hazel's work has been translated into seventeen languages and is published in twenty-three countries to date.

Hazel is co-founder of the creative writing event, The Inspiration Project. Originally from Yorkshire, she now lives in Ireland with her husband and two children.

To keep up to date with Hazel and her books, please visit www. hazelgaynor.com and connect with her on social media:

🐦 @HazelGaynor
📘 @HazelGaynorBooks
📷 @HazelGaynor

Also by Hazel Gaynor

The Girl Who Came Home: A Novel of the Titanic
A Memory of Violets
The Girl From The Savoy
The Cottingley Secret
The Lighthouse Keeper's Daughter

With Heather Webb
Fall of Poppies
Last Christmas in Paris
Meet Me in Monaco
Three Words for Goodbye

The
Bird
in the
Bamboo
Cage

HAZEL GAYNOR

HarperCollins*Publishers*

HarperCollins*Publishers* Ltd
1 London Bridge Street,
London SE1 9GF

www.harpercollins.co.uk

HarperCollins*Publishers*
1st Floor, Watermarque Building, Ringsend Road
Dublin 4, Ireland

First published by HarperCollins*Publishers* 2020
This paperback edition published 2021

3

A catalogue record for this book is available from the British Library

ISBN: 978-0-00-839367-0

Set in Sabon Lt Std by
Palimpsest Book Production Limited, Falkirk, Stirlingshire

Printed and bound in the UK by
CPI Group (UK) Ltd, Croydon CR0 4YY

MIX
Paper from
responsible sources
FSC
www.fsc.org
FSC™ C007454

For Damien, Max, and Sam –
my favourite story of all.

'Girls! Imagine that a battle has taken place in and around your town or village . . . What are you going to do? Are you going to sit down, and wring your hands and cry, or are you going to be plucky, and go out and do something to help?'
Agnes Baden-Powell, co-founder of the Girl Guides

'The caged bird sings
with a fearful trill
of things unknown
but longed for still
and his tune is heard
on the distant hill
for the caged bird
sings of freedom.'
Maya Angelou, 'Caged Bird' from
Shaker Why Don't You Sing?

Contents

PROLOGUE

NANCY

Oxford, 1975

We didn't talk about it afterwards. Not to loved ones, or to neighbours who stared at us from across the street, or to the newspaper men who were curious to know more about these lost children, returned from the war in China like ghosts come back from the dead. We quietly packed it all away in our battered suitcases and stepped awkwardly back into the lives we'd once known. Eventually, everyone stopped asking; stopped staring and wondering. Like our suitcases gathering dust in the attic, we were forgotten.

But we didn't forget.

Those years clung to us like a midday shadow, waiting to trip us up when we least expected it: a remembered song, a familiar scent, a name overheard in a shop, and there we were in an instant, wilting in the stifling heat during roll-call, kept awake at night by the ache of unimaginable hunger. I suppose it was inevitable that we would talk about it in the end; that we would tell the story of our war.

I'm still surprised by how much I have to say; how much I remember. I'd assumed I would only recall odd scraps and incoherent fragments, but it has all become clearer despite being ignored; the memories sharpened by distance and time. Now, when I talk about my school years in China, people only want to hear the parts about occupation and internment. That's the story everyone wants me to tell; how terrible it was and how frightened we were. But I also remember the smaller, simpler moments of a young girl's school days: smudged ink on fingertips, disinfectant in the corridors, hopscotch squares and skipping games, the iridescent wings of a butterfly that danced through the classroom window one autumn morning and settled on the back of my hand. I want to tell that side of my story, too.

Perhaps part of me wishes I could go back to the time before; that I could appreciate those quiet, inconsequential days before everything changed: giggling into our hands when Miss Kent's back was turned, grumbling to Sprout about lumpy porridge, turning cartwheels with Mouse on the golden sands of the bay, exchanging secret whispers in the pitch dark of the dorm. Unprepared for what lay ahead, we clattered thoughtlessly on through the careful precision of school routine – breakfast and prayers, assembly and lessons, tiffin and supper, Sibling Saturday and Empire Day – wildly ignorant of our privileges; and of how much we were about to lose.

Our war arrived quietly, two weeks before Christmas, settling over the terracotta roof tiles of Chefoo School with the first of the season's snow. Safe in our beds, over one hundred boys and girls slept soundly, oblivious to the events happening at Pearl Harbor over five thousand miles away; unaware that the ripples of conflict were racing across the Pacific toward us.

I was ten years old that winter. Brownie Guides was my favourite part of the school week, and my feet still couldn't quite reach the floor when I sat on the edge of my bed . . .

PART ONE: OCCUPATION

Chefoo, Shantung Province, China

1941–1943

THE GUIDE LAW: A GUIDE IS LOYAL

This does not mean that she thinks her friends and
family and school are perfect; far from it. But there is a
way of standing up for what is dear to you, even though
you admit that it has its faults.

NANCY

China Inland Mission School, Chefoo, December 1941

'We've been contacted by your parents, Nancy,' Miss Kent said, arms folded across her rose-pink cardigan as she stood beside the window. 'I'm afraid you won't be spending the Christmas holidays with them after all.'

Her words seemed to echo off the wood-panelled walls of the principal's office – a small suffocating room that smelled of linseed oil and bad news – so that I heard them again and again. *You won't be spending the Christmas holidays with them after all.* I wanted to cover my ears. I didn't want it to be true.

I stood in the middle of an Oriental rug, the pattern worn away by years of children coming and going to receive bad news, or the sharp end of the principal's tongue. I looked up at my teacher, and couldn't think of one word to say.

'Your mother sent a letter each for you and Edward,' Miss Kent continued. She held out an envelope, addressed to me in my mother's elegant handwriting. I stared at it. 'Well?' she prompted. 'It won't read itself.'

Reluctantly, I took the envelope, opened it, and removed the letter. The scent of English lavender bloomed around me as I read.

I'm so desperately sorry to disappoint you again, Nonny, but your father insists it's too dangerous for us to travel with the Chinese and Japanese armies still fighting. Besides, the roads are in a desperate state after the recent landslides. You should have seen the rain! I'm sure you'll have wonderful fun with your friends. I can't wait to see you, darling. How you must have grown!

I imagined Mummy at her writing desk, the sun on her face, her pen poised in mid-air as she composed the next sentence. I imagined her more often than I saw her.

Since starting my first term at the school two years earlier, my parents' missionary work had taken them from the China Inland Mission compound at the International Settlement in Shanghai all the way to Ch'ing-hai Province on the other side of the country. Hard winters, landslides and the Sino-Japanese war had, in turns, prevented them from travelling back to Chefoo; back to me.

Seeing my eyes fill with tears, Miss Kent offered an encouraging, 'Come along now. Chin up.' She studied me through her round wire spectacles. The grey eyes that peered at me, often so serious, carried a hint of an apology, as if she somehow felt it were her fault that I would spend another Christmas away from my parents. 'Better to be safe than sorry,' she concluded. 'And think about all the displaced Chinese children and refugees who are benefitting from your parents' missionary work.' She gave a little smile. 'And at least Dorothy and Joan – or should I say, "Sprout and Mouse" – are staying, too, so that's something, isn't it?'

She hadn't used my friends' nicknames before. I suppose she did it to make me feel better.

I held the sheet of writing paper to my nose. 'It smells of her,' I whispered. 'Of lavender. Her favourite.' I tucked the letter into my pinafore pocket and wiped a tear from my cheek. 'She likes the smell of sweet peas, too. And roses. She doesn't care for lily-of-the-valley though. It makes her sneeze.' My mother had become a collection of such memories; scraps and fragments I rummaged through. 'I really did want to see her, Miss. Ever so much.' I pushed my hands into my pockets. 'It isn't fair.'

I hadn't meant to say the words out loud. Self-pity was not a trait to be admired, and homesickness was considered 'sentimental nonsense'. We were often reminded how disappointed our parents would be to learn that we were thinking only of ourselves, but still, it *was* unfair that I couldn't see Mummy, and I didn't care that I'd said so.

Miss Kent asked me to join her at the window. We stood for a moment, side by side in silence. I wondered if she might place a comforting arm around my shoulder, but she kept her arms folded and looked straight ahead.

'What do you see outside?' she asked.

I reached up onto my tiptoes. Beyond the window, several school servants, dressed in their uniforms of cropped black trousers and a white blouse with knotted buttons, were busy with various tasks. 'I can see Shu Lan carrying a basket of laundry. And Wei Huan, with a rake and broom . . .' I trailed off as we watched them work.

Wei Huan, one of the school gardeners, had helped us with our Gardener badge for Brownies that summer. He called us his 'Little Flowers'. Shu Lan was less friendly and wasn't very popular among the girls as a result. If we interrupted her before she'd finished tidying our dorm, she would shoo us away with her hands, and mutter things at us in Chinese.

'Perhaps it isn't fair that Shu Lan has to carry that heavy basket, full of our dirty bedsheets,' Miss Kent said. 'Or perhaps it isn't fair for Wei Huan to sweep up the leaves that we walk over and kick into the air, for fun.'

I thought about my amah, one of many 'little mothers' at the Mission compound in Shanghai, who'd helped with domestic chores while our parents carried out their missionary work. Having our own servant had been a novelty when we'd first arrived from England, but I hardly noticed them now. I certainly didn't think about all the work they did to make our lives more comfortable.

'We might see them as the school's servants, but that's just their job,' Miss Kent continued. 'They're also somebody's daughters and sons, and no doubt they also receive disappointing news from time to time, and wish they could see their mothers more often. Life isn't always fair for them, either.'

When she was cross, Miss Kent spoke in a way that reminded me of brittle twigs snapping underfoot on autumn walks. I pressed the toe of my shoe against the skirting board and felt my cheeks go red. Without giving me a ticking-off, she'd done exactly that.

'We all have to make the best of the circumstances we are given, Nancy,' she continued, as she turned to face me, her expression softening a little. 'All things considered, I'd say we have plenty to be grateful for. Don't you?'

I nodded, and bit my lip. 'Yes, Miss.'

'Then we won't need to discuss things being fair or not again, shall we?'

I shook my head and took Miss Kent's handkerchief from my pocket to wipe my tears. The embroidered letters EK and HE had started to fray a little, but the fabric still carried the scent of roses and kindness, just as it had when Miss Kent had first given it to me.

She let out a funny little gasp. 'Gosh! So that's where it went.'

'You gave it to me on the boat, remember? When we left Shanghai.' I thought about the promise she'd made to Mummy, to keep a special eye on me during the journey to Chefoo. Miss Kent had given me the handkerchief to dry my tears as I stood beside her at the railings. I'd waved madly to Mummy until she'd eventually disappeared beneath a sea of colourful rice-paper parasols held by elegant ladies sheltering their faces from the sun. 'I'm sorry, Miss,' I said as I held the handkerchief out to her. 'I should have given it back.'

She hesitated before closing my fingers around it. 'It's yours now. Let it be a reminder that there's always somebody worse off, no matter how rotten things might seem.' She let her hand rest on mine for just a moment before folding her arms again. 'Now, run along.'

I forced a smile as I left the office and set off down the corridor.

'And pull your socks up, Nancy Plummer,' she called after me. 'It's impossible to feel cheerful with socks sagging around your ankles like bread dough.'

I added Mummy's letter to the collection I kept in the tea caddy beneath my bed. It was almost full of letters and other special things that reminded me of her: a button from her coat, a photograph of us standing outside our house in England, the eye of a peacock feather I'd found in the Pleasure Gardens in Shanghai. Simple mementoes of time spent with her; precious treasures while we were forced to be apart.

Even my best friend, Sprout, couldn't cheer me up as we got ready for Brownies.

'It's not the end of the world, Plum,' she said, using my nickname, as she tucked a strand of wispy blonde hair behind her sticky-out ear and made herself go cross-eyed to make me laugh. 'We'll have plenty of fun. And you'll see her in the spring.'

Sprout – given her nickname for being skinny as a bamboo stalk, and much taller than the rest of us – was from Connecticut, in America, which made her fascinating to me, a freckled English girl who'd grown up in the Sussex countryside and enunciated everything in Received Pronunciation. Sprout spoke with a lovely loose confidence that I envied and admired. Out of nearly two hundred children who attended the school – mostly British nationals, a dozen or so Americans, and a handful of Canadians, Australians and Dutch – Dorothy 'Sprout' Hinshaw was the funniest, and most interesting person I'd ever met. She was also very good at getting herself into trouble. I often wished I could be more like her: more American and carefree.

For once, I wasn't in the mood for Brownies that evening. I tried not to let it show as we stood in our Fairy Ring and said the Brownie Promise because, as Sixer of Pixies, I had to set a good example to the rest of the girls. As we recited the familiar words, I really did promise to do my best and serve my king and country and help other people, but a flush of shame rushed to my cheeks when I promised to love my God. I wanted to, very much, but I had an awful lot of questions about Him that nobody could ever answer, mostly about why He never answered my prayers to see Mummy. To make up for it, I squeezed my eyes shut extra tight as we said the Amen.

I'd been a Pixie since joining the 2nd Chefoo Brownies in my first term. We were one of two Brownie Guide packs, and several Girl Guide and Boy Scout groups at the school. I'd worked hard for Golden Bar, and the interest badges I'd sewn onto the sleeve of my tunic – Booklover, Thrift, Musician, Gardener, Collector and, most recently, First Aider. Every badge earned was a source of immense pride, each one a step towards becoming a Girl Guide. I was especially proud of the second yellow stripe I'd been awarded recently to signify my appointment as Sixer.

Our Guide leaders, Miss Kent and Miss Butterworth, were

known as Brown Owl and Tawny Owl during our meetings. They were different at Brownies. Less strict. It was part of the reason we all enjoyed it so much.

'We'll be doing Christmas paper craft this evening,' Brown Owl announced when we'd all sung our Six Songs and she'd finished inspecting our hands, nails and hair. 'I've asked Shu Lan to help. I'm sure you will all make her feel very welcome.'

We always admired the intricate 'window flowers' Shu Lan made and hung at the dormitory windows every spring as symbols of good fortune and happiness for the new season. She called them chuanghua. We watched in awe as she started to make delicate paper snowflakes with the same skill and precision. We did our best with our scissors, but our snowflakes were simple and clumsy, while Shu Lan's were as beautiful as the real thing. Only Mouse managed to make anything half decent.

'That's ever so good,' I said, offering her an encouraging smile.

Joan 'Mouse' Nuttall – nicknamed because she was always so quiet – muttered a 'Thank you.' I felt a little sorry for her, although I'd never admitted it to anyone. Like a doll you've grown tired of playing with, most of the time I forgot she was there.

'You make many folds, and then, very carefully cutting,' Shu Lan explained as we all started again with a fresh piece of paper.

Sprout's sister, Connie (who was ever so grown up, and styled her hair just like Princess Elizabeth) had once told us that Shu Lan, and some of the other servants, had come to Chefoo as refugees from the city of Nanking, where something terrible had happened a few years ago. She wouldn't say what the terrible thing was, only that it was something to do with the Japanese Imperial Army, and that lots of Chinese people had died rather horribly. I tried not to think about it as I watched Shu Lan make her paper snowflakes. I found her fascinating. She was so beautiful I had to force myself not to stare, because that was rude.

Apart from the local fishermen we often saw at the bay, and

the occasional rickshaw puller rushing past the school gates, the school servants were the only Chinese people we saw regularly. When the wind blew in the right direction, we could hear the bells from the Buddhist temples, and from the upstairs dormitory windows we sometimes watched the little hongtou sampans on the bay, and the graceful junks with their bamboo sails spread wide like enormous wings. At harvest time, we liked to watch the farmers and their water buffalo working in the fields, traditional bamboo hats shading the farmers from the baking sun, the women pulling the ripe plants from the ground, often while carrying their babies on their backs. That was the China I'd imagined when I'd looked in Edward's atlas before we'd left England; the China I'd been so excited to visit. Part of me wanted to climb over the school walls and run through the rice fields; to know what life was like for a ten-year-old Chinese girl.

While we worked, Miss Kent asked Shu Lan to tell us about her great-great-grandfather, an imperial metalsmith who'd made beautiful jewellery using feathers from kingfisher wings.

'The feathers are placed close together, to look like enamel,' she explained. 'The jewellery is very delicate.' She described the elegant aristocrats – wives and daughters of emperors – who'd worn the treasured pieces. I enjoyed the story until we learned that the kingfishers were captured in nets, their feathers taken from them while they were still alive in order to preserve their beautiful blue colour.

'But that's cruel,' I said.

'And yet it is a Chinese tradition, and a highly valued skill,' Miss Kent countered. 'We can't simply dismiss things that are unfamiliar to us as cruel, Nancy. We must learn to understand, and respect.'

Even so, I was relieved when Shu Lan explained that the activity was now illegal. We finished our snowflakes in silence.

* * *

That night, I dreamed of lost things and of kingfishers trapped in a metalsmith's net. I was still dreaming when I was woken by the sound of an approaching aeroplane. The dormitory was dark as I crept out of bed and tiptoed to the window. The floorboards were cold. They creaked beneath my bare feet.

As I opened the shutter, a Japanese plane flew low over the school chapel and headed out across the bay. In the distance, a line of soldiers marched toward a truck. The Japanese army had occupied the city of Chefoo a year before I'd arrived at the school, so I was used to seeing the soldiers coming and going on operations against their enemy. We understood that Britain wasn't at war with Japan, so although it was unusual for one of their planes to fly so close to the school, I hardly gave it a moment's thought and turned my attention instead to the fat snowflakes tumbling from the sky. I pressed my forehead to the glass, delighted by the spectacle.

I watched until I began to shiver from the cold and climbed back into bed. I pulled the sheets up to my nose, wrapped my arms around myself, and listened to the soft patter of snow at the window. I imagined Mummy lying awake somewhere too, remembering a time when we'd watched the snow together, missing me so much that her bones ached. I wished, more than anything, that I was with her and not stuck at school, and hoped I really would see her in the spring.

But wishes and hopes are fragile things, easily crushed by the marching boots of enemy soldiers.

ELSPETH

I rose before dawn, my sleep disturbed by the prospect of the difficult conversations the morning would bring, and by Japanese soldiers roaring past the school gates in their noisy trucks until the small hours. While I knew they posed no threat to a western missionary school, I didn't care to be so close to other people's disputes, especially when it kept me awake half the night and left unsightly bags under my eyes.

I washed and dressed and made my bed, hospital corners precisely tucked in, the eiderdown smoothed of any unsightly creases. A cursory glance in the mirror left me wishing I could remove the lines from my face as easily. I missed the Elspeth Kent I used to see in the reflection; the carefree young thing who'd smiled for a week when Harry Evans asked her to dance. I hoped I might still find some scraps of her in England. Stitch her back together. Make Do and Mend. After all, wasn't that what the Ministry encouraged?

The decades-old floorboards creaked and cracked beneath my shoes as I made my way along the corridor and downstairs, past trophy cabinets and the many proud moments of the school's

16

history. Once outside, I took a moment to glance toward the waters of the bay and then hurried on across the courtyard, beneath the branches of the plum trees, to the old stone chapel. My footsteps echoed off the flagstones as I walked to the altar and bent my head in prayer before settling into a pew. I sat in silent thought, remembering the wedding day that had been cruelly taken from me, and the other I'd walked away from. I was six thousand miles away from home, and still they haunted me: the man I should have married, and the man who had nearly taken his place. Ghosts now, both of them.

Pushing my memories aside, I took my letter of resignation from my pocket. I'd agonized over the words for so long they were imprinted on my mind. *It is with much difficulty, and after a great deal of personal anguish and reflection, that I must inform you of my intention to leave my position at Chefoo School and return to my family in England . . .* For weeks it had idled among the pages of my Girl Guide Handbook. I would give it to the principal of the Girls' School after assembly that morning, and confirm my intention to return to England on the next available steamer from Shanghai. There was no reason to delay further, although the prospect of telling Minnie Butterworth – my dearest friend on the teaching staff –wasn't quite so straightforward. Calling off a wedding and travelling halfway around the world had been easy in comparison.

I sat in the chapel until the cold got the better of my faith, and made my way outside to discover a soft blanket of snow had fallen. It was a perfect winter morning, still and calm. I stood for a moment beneath the arched lintel of the chapel doorway, admiring the quiet beauty and the deliciously plump flakes. Across the courtyard, Shu Lan, was already busy with her day's work. She paused to listen to the distant toll of the Buddhist temple bells. I listened too, imagining that they were saying goodbye. China was almost invisible beneath the western sensibilities of Chefoo School and its privileged offspring of missionaries and diplomats, so much so that I sometimes forgot I was in China at all. The temple bells and the snow-covered branches of the plum and gingko trees were a timely reminder of place, and that as the seasons moved on, so must I.

A smile laced the edge of my lips. Finally, I would set in motion the wheels that would lead me back home. But the heavy drone of an approaching aircraft interrupted the delicate silence, and saw my smile quickly fade.

Instinctively, I stepped back inside the chapel doorway and tipped my face skywards, shielding my eyes against the swirling snow. I brushed a stray curl from my cheek as I watched the aircraft pass directly overhead. I stared up at the distinctive red circles painted onto the wingtips, and tracked a stream of papers that tumbled from the rear of the craft before the pilot banked sharply over Chefoo harbour, and disappeared into the rose-tinted snow clouds.

When I was quite sure it had gone, I brushed snow from the bottom of my coat, and grabbed one of the papers as it fluttered toward me through the frigid air. I stood perfectly still as I read an English translation of the front page of a Japanese newspaper: *We hereby declare War on the United States of America and the British Empire. The men and officers of Our Army and Navy shall do their utmost in prosecuting the war* . . . I skimmed over the full declaration, my hand raised to my mouth in dread as I reached the signature, *HIROHITO*, and the distinctive chrysanthemum emblem of the Japanese Imperial Seal.

I leaned against the chapel wall to steady myself as the world seemed to tilt a little to one side.

It had happened then, just as we'd feared.

Britain was at war with Japan.

I immediately made my way back to the school building, my footprints sinking deep in the snow as I scooped up as many leaflets as I could. Across the courtyard, beneath the plum trees, I saw Shu Lan doing the same. We paused and looked at each other for the briefest moment before resuming our collection. As I turned the corner, I caught a glimpse of an eager little face peering out at the snow through an upstairs dormitory window, warm breaths misting the glass. Nancy Plummer. The sight of her set my mind racing. What would the declaration of war mean for the children with their parents already thousands of miles away? I sighed as I searched for the ocean in the distance. Perhaps it wasn't too late. Maybe I could take a rickshaw to the harbour and set out for Shanghai later that morning.

When it was time for morning assembly, I slipped into the back of the packed hall, beside Minnie, who towered above me.

She tapped her wristwatch. 'What kept you? It's not like you to be late.' If she noticed the fear and worry in my eyes, she was kind enough not to say anything.

Minnie had been at the school almost seven years. We hadn't hit it off at first, my natural pessimism and faltering faith rather at odds with her stoic optimism and steadfast devoutness, but we'd recognized something familiar in our Northern sensibilities, not to mention the silent shame that surrounded women like us – surplus women, society's problem – whatever term was fashionable at any given time. Despite our differences, we'd become the greatest of friends.

'I'm not late,' I replied, fussing with the bun at my neck which was all asunder.

Minnie narrowed her eyes at me, poised to ask more, but the rousing strains of 'Imperial Echoes', the accompanying theme music for the popular Radio Newsreel programme on the BBC Overseas Service, emerged from the wireless cabinet, and we all jumped to attention. I was relieved to be spared an interrogation. At that moment I was held together by the smallest fragments of resolve. It would take only a fraction of Minnie's gentle kindness to set me off.

The hubbub of conversation subsided as the introductory music reached the final bars and we waited for the announcer's smooth English accent. His steady delivery made even the worst news palatable to the very youngest ears, and had become another reassuring constant I'd come to rely on while I was so far from home.

'*This is London calling in the Overseas Service of the British Broadcasting Corporation. Here is the news, and this is Alvar Lidell reading it.*' Goosebumps ran along my arms. I laced my hands and cleared my throat, prepared to react appropriately to whatever he was about to say. '*Japan's long-threatened aggression in the Far East began tonight with air attacks on United States naval bases in the Pacific. Fresh reports are coming in every minute. The latest facts of the situation are these: messages from Tokyo say that Japan has announced a formal declaration of war against both the United States and Britain . . .*'

An audible gasp rippled around the room. Minnie grabbed my hand.

'Oh, Els! It's happened. We're at war with Japan.' To hear her say the words out loud made everything horribly real. 'We're enemy aliens.'

I shushed her, a little too brusquely, as I strained to hear the rest of the broadcast.

'*Japan's attacks on American naval bases in the Pacific were announced by President Roosevelt in a statement from the White House . . .*' the announcer continued, calmly relaying details of sustained Japanese bombing raids on an American naval base in Pearl Harbor, Hawaii, with significant casualties reported. '*President Roosevelt has ordered the mobilization of the United States army . . .*'

The words settled ominously over the room as I observed

the faces of my colleagues, watching closely for their reactions: Mr Collins, our ever-reliable headmaster; Amelia Prescott, all the colour drained from her usually ruddy cheeks; Ella Redmond, stoic as ever; Tom Martin, the Latin master; young Eleanor Yarwood, a recent addition to the teaching staff at the Prep School, and on and on. Even the boys' PT master, Charlie Harris, was lacking his usual disarming smile. Everywhere I looked, a familiar face concealed the true emotions the announcement had stirred. We hid it well, but we all understood that Japan's declaration of war against Britain changed everything. Missionary school or not, we were now the enemy, and we were in danger.

That winter had seen an unusually high number of children remain at school for the Christmas holidays, one hundred and twenty-four, in total. Just over a dozen staff and a handful of missionaries had also stayed, a few through choice, but most due to the Sino-Japanese war which made long journeys across the country too dangerous. The irony was not lost on me that danger had found us anyway.

My first instinct was to locate the girls from my class.

'What are you doing?' Minnie asked, as I reached up onto my tiptoes and began muttering under my breath.

'Counting,' I replied. 'I can't just stand here. I have to do something.'

For all their similarities, honed by the strict routines of school, it was the girls' individuality I'd come to enjoy: Joan Nuttall, nicknamed Mouse, crippled by shyness but growing in confidence recently; Dorothy Hinshaw, nicknamed Sprout, the resident class clown, bursting with potential if only she would apply herself; and good-natured, ever-reliable Nancy Plummer, Plum to her friends, whom I'd recently appointed as Sixer of Pixies in the 2nd Chefoo Brownies. Nancy wasn't the most natural leader, but was more than capable when given a nudge, and I was pleased to see her rise to the challenge. Despite being warned by several of the teachers about having favourites, the undeniable truth was that I'd grown fond of these three girls. I saw a little of myself in each of them: my past, certainly, but they also held a tantalizing sense of the present, and of a future full of possibility.

Aside from Joan, Nancy and Dorothy, Winnie, Agnes and Elsie were also present. Alice, Mary and Barbara had returned to their parents in Shanghai and Hong Kong. Bunty Browne had left for Australia only two days ago to rendezvous with her parents, who were already on furlough. I wondered how significant those last-minute decisions, and my own indecision, would prove to be. With the children's parents dispersed all over China, reuniting them would be challenging, if not impossible. If I'd once felt uncertain about making an impromptu wharf-side promise to Lillian Plummer to keep a special eye on Nancy, I wondered what on earth that promise might mean now. Wherever Lillian Plummer was, I could feel her, urging me to keep my word; to keep watch over her daughter.

As the seriousness of the announcement began to sink in, the children turned to each other, wide-eyed. Some were upset, while others were excited to finally find themselves part of the war they had read and heard so much about. Some of the boys practised their *rat-a-tat-a* machine-gun noises as the rising drone of speculation and conjecture filled the room.

'You don't think Japanese soldiers will occupy the school, do you?' Minnie whispered, voicing my own fears. 'What if they come roaring through the gates in their awful trucks and fly their flag over the cricket pitch? I can't stop thinking about Nanking.'

Neither could I.

The atrocities committed by the Imperial Japanese army in Nanking had preceded my arrival in China, but the horrific massacre of thousands of Chinese civilians was so shocking it had left a deep and painful scar. I knew that many of the school's servants had seen family and loved ones brutally murdered, many women enduring the very worst indignity at the hands of the soldiers. The word rape was too ugly to speak out loud, but it had certainly occupied my thoughts whenever I'd seen the soldiers beyond the school gates, and it troubled me greatly now. While none of us wanted to think about the possibility of the horrors of Nanking ever happening again, the question on all our lips was not *if* soldiers would arrive at the school, but *when*. I hoped Minnie hadn't noticed the tremble in my hand.

'Well, let's hope for the best,' Minnie continued. 'I'm quite sure a western missionary school won't be of any interest to them, and children have a wonderful capacity for bringing out compassion in people, don't they? Besides, the British Navy will be on top of things. They'll send a warship to evacuate us and we'll be repatriated and tucking into goose and all the trimmings before you can say "Merry Christmas, Mister Scrooge." I wouldn't be at all surprised if they weren't already en route.'

It was typical of Minnie to look on the bright side. Not for the first time, I found her optimism rather naïve and misplaced and I had to bite my tongue to prevent myself saying something unkind as an awful sense of dread settled in my stomach. It was the same feeling I'd woken up with on the morning of my wedding day.

In the end, calling it off was the easiest decision I'd ever made. The sun had just risen, spiderwebs draped across the hedgerows like lace veils as I'd walked up the lane to Reggie's mother's house and calmly explained that I couldn't marry him after all. He wasn't surprised. He knew he wasn't the man I wanted to spend the rest of my life with. That man, Harry Evans, was buried beneath the collapsed mine he'd worked in all his adult life, and the vibrant young woman who should have married him and lived a quiet life with our children asleep in their beds and washing dancing on the line, had been buried with him.

'God save the King,' Minnie whispered as the broadcast came to an end.

My fingertips brushed against the envelope in my pocket. *It is with much difficulty, and after a great deal of personal anguish and reflection, that I must inform you of my intention to leave my position at Chefoo School and return to my family in England* . . . I imagined my words slipping from the page, unwritten, unseen, irrelevant now.

'God save us all, Minnie,' I replied. 'God save us all.'

Immediately after assembly, we were called to an emergency meeting in the staff room.

'I will assess the local and international situation with Mission HQ and await further instruction,' our headmaster explained. 'We have one hundred and twenty-four children in our care, comprising ninety British, three Canadians, five Australians, two South Africans, eighteen Americans, three Norwegians and three Dutch. The preservation of the children's faith, safety and education must be our utmost priority until assistance arrives, and, in the meantime, it's business as usual.'

Everything else, including my plans to return to England, would simply have to wait.

After the short meeting, we returned to our respective classrooms.

I smoothed any signs of worry from my face and walked the eleven steps to the front of the classroom, just as I had yesterday, and the many hundreds of days before that. I tapped my metre rule three times against the desk, and cleared my throat, twice. Routine and discipline sustained me in many ways, but especially on days like this.

The simmering noise of the girls' chatter fell away as they

stood behind their desks, the scraping of chair legs against the floor setting my teeth on edge.

'Good morning, class,' I announced.

'Good morning, Miss Kent.'

Like a well-rehearsed song, there was a distinct harmony and tone to the exchange, but the girls' response that morning was understandably sombre.

'Hands together for prayers.'

When the children had closed their eyes tight, and I was certain nobody was peeping, I crumpled Emperor Hirohito's declaration into a ball and tossed it into the wastepaper basket beneath my desk. I placed my resignation letter inside the China Inland Mission Bible in my drawer. The pages fell open at Joshua 10:25. *Joshua said to them, 'Do not be afraid; do not be discouraged. Be strong and courageous.'* Not for the first time, I wished the words meant more to me than they did.

I joined the girls in prayer, focusing on the singular truth I'd clung to all these uncertain years: that every decision I made, whether right or wrong, whether people criticized or admired me for my choices, took me closer to the place, and the person, I was meant to be. As the girls' bright voices filled the classroom, I closed my eyes and absorbed the simple familiarity of the moment: chalk dust on my fingertips, the pool of winter sunlight against my cheek, the sounds of singing and instruction drifting along the corridors. Routine and discipline. The glue holding me together while the world was falling apart.

We were halfway through the Lord's Prayer when the soldiers arrived.

NANCY

Our prayer puttered to a stop, and the classroom fell silent.

I opened my eyes and reached up onto my tiptoes to see what all the commotion was beyond the snow-speckled windows: the loud rumble of trucks, raised voices, doors slamming.

Miss Kent followed my gaze, all the colour having drained from her face. For a moment, the world seemed to stop, unsure of what to do with us next, until Miss Kent clapped her hands and cleared her throat.

'Face the front, children,' she instructed. 'It appears our new rulers have arrived. But that's no excuse for incomplete prayers. Start again, please. Our Father . . .'

But another loud noise outside pulled everyone's attention back to the window. The low winter sun glinted against steel helmets and short swords that hung from belts. Khaki-coloured jodhpur-like trousers ballooned over the tops of glossy knee-high boots that stamped roughly across the fresh snow. I was too shocked to do anything but stare. It wasn't the soldiers themselves that was so shocking – we'd seen them plenty of times before – it was the fact that they were here, in our school, trampling all over Wei Huan's lovely flower beds.

'They're spoiling everything!' The words came out before I could stop them. I clapped my hand over my mouth and glanced at Miss Kent, expecting a reprimand. When none came, I added, 'Wei Huan will be so upset. They're squashing the China roses. His favourites.'

Miss Kent started us off in the Lord's Prayer again. I squeezed my eyes shut, swallowed hard, and pressed my knees together to stop them shaking.

'Our Father, Who art in Heaven . . .'

There was an unusual wobble to Miss Kent's voice. Even when we joined in, our combined voices couldn't drown out the noise that was now coming from all directions. As we reached the part where we forgive those who trespass against us, an almighty commotion started up in the corridor outside the classroom. I opened my eyes a fraction and glanced at the door.

'For Thine is the kingdom,' Miss Kent continued, raising her voice another level until we joined her in the final words.

'The power and the glory, Forever and ever. Amen.'

A long pause circled the classroom as we waited to see what would happen next.

Miss Kent stood at the front of the room, her cheeks as pale as chalk dust. I couldn't remember the classroom ever being so quiet. Even Sprout was silent. She'd recently returned from a spell in the San with instructions to take Nurse Prune's awful cough medicine. I glanced toward the door again as another loud bang came from the corridor, closer this time. Any moment now they would burst in, I was sure of it. Agnes started to cry, which set off Winnie, and then Elsie beside her. I looked at Mouse, who stared at the floor. At the back of the room, Sprout smothered a cough with her hand.

'You can sit down,' Miss Kent announced, finally finding her voice. 'There's nothing to be afraid of.'

Miss Kent rarely smiled in the classroom so I knew the smile she gave us that morning was the sort of 'we must be brave' smile adults use when they're trying to pretend something awful isn't happening. As I smiled back at her, the classroom door flew open, swung roughly back on its hinges and banged against the bookcase which fell forward with an almighty thud, spilling its books everywhere as two soldiers marched through the door. Their long boots squeaked against the polished floor as they positioned themselves on either side of Miss Kent's desk, their dark eyes fixed on the wall at the back of the classroom where the map of the British Empire hung below a painting of King George VI. A third, older man, arrived and stood stiffly in the doorway.

'School is now the property of Emperor Hirohito,' he said, his voice harsh. 'I am Commander Hayashi. You obey my orders. All children. Come.' He waved a heavy-looking bamboo stick in the direction of the corridor.

We all looked at Miss Kent.

'Form a neat line beside the wall, girls,' she instructed, her voice as steady and calm as if she were about to lead us out to the bay for a spot of exercise.

We did as we were told. Nobody said a word.

With one soldier at the front of our line, and one bringing up the rear, we filed out of the classroom. I stared at the world map as I passed it, remembering how I'd borrowed Edward's atlas before we left England and traced my fingertip around China's vast coastline, wondering what it would be like to live somewhere as mysterious and exotic as the Far East. I'd seen so little of the real China, the China beyond the missionary and school compound walls, that I still didn't know the answer. As

Commander Hayashi marched ahead, leading us to the assembly hall, I wondered if I ever would.

Most of the other children were already gathered in the hall by the time we arrived. I looked around for Edward and was relieved to see him with his friend, Larry, and some other boys. I waved when I thought he was looking, but he didn't wave back. I let my hand fall to my side, embarrassed for having waved at all.

'I don't think he saw you,' Sprout whispered as she squeezed my hand encouragingly. 'Connie never waves when she sees me. She doesn't like to be seen with her little sister now that she's all grown up and wears a brassiere.'

I told her to shush before she got into trouble for talking.

'Wait here,' Commander Hayashi ordered. He pointed his bamboo stick at us and then at the soldiers guarding the door. 'Guards see everything.'

'What an awful man,' Sprout said when he'd gone. '*You come here. You wait there.*'

Her imitation of him made some of the girls giggle nervously.

Miss Kent overheard, and was quick to scold.

'I do *not* want to hear such insolence again, Dorothy. Not from any of you,' she snapped. I'd never seen her so cross. 'We will show the soldiers the same courtesy and respect we would show any visitor to the school. Do you understand?'

'Yes, Miss,' we chorused.

'Good. Now, sit down in a circle. Nancy will start you off in a game of "I Went to the Shops". I'll be back in a moment.'

She crossed the hall to speak to some of the other teachers as I started us off in the memory game, but nobody could concentrate on the shopping list we tried to memorize. We only got as far as onions, sausages, buttons and blue wool before Winnie got in a terrible muddle and couldn't even remember onions. She started to cry, which made me want to cry, too. I bit my lip to stop myself.

Miss Kent soon returned to explain that Japanese Shinto priests wished to perform a ceremony at the sports field. 'They would like us all to wait here until the ceremony is done. Then I'm sure we'll be able to return to our classrooms.' She fiddled with the St. Christopher that hung from a slim gold chain at her neck. 'How about a few rounds of "This Little Light of Mine" and "Little Peter Rabbit" while we wait?'

The songs distracted us for a while and, when we'd finished, the Latin master from the Boys' School led us all in a rendition of 'Jerusalem'. I thought it rather brave to sing something so patriotic, but the guards at the door hardly seemed to care and didn't stop us. Like a perfectly hemmed seam, our voices fit neatly together, boys and girls, teachers and children, all stitched together as one. When we sang, it felt as if nothing could harm us, so we kept singing, one song after another, until we were nearly hoarse and the younger children grew fidgety and tired.

'Are you frightened?' Sprout whispered as we played a game of Cat's Cradle with a piece of wool she'd found in her pocket.

'A bit,' I admitted. 'Are you?'

She nodded as we moved our fingers to make the intricate patterns from the wool. 'A bit.'

Despite the teachers assuring us there was nothing to worry about, it was impossible not to be wary with stern-looking soldiers guarding the door and others marching about outside and shouting commands and instructions at each other. It was all so different from the usual calm routine.

Sprout lowered her voice and grabbed my hand. 'But imagine what a story we'll have to tell when we're rescued. We'll be famous Chefusians, like the children who were captured by Chinese pirates on their way to school a few years ago.'

'I'd rather not be a famous Chefusian,' I said with a sigh. 'I'd much rather be spending Christmas in the Western Hills with my parents.'

I wondered what my father would say when he heard the school had been overrun by 'the Japs' as he called them. He certainly didn't have anything nice to say about them whenever I'd heard him discussing the Sino-Japanese war with Edward.

I couldn't stop thinking about the fact that we shouldn't even have been at the school when war and the soldiers arrived. We should have been with our parents, wrapping Christmas gifts and singing carols. It made it all seem so much worse.

The morning dragged on. We waited for hours in the cold assembly hall and still the headmaster didn't come to tell us it had all been a mistake and we could return to our classrooms and carry on as normal. Several of us needed to use the toilet. Miss Kent told those of us who couldn't hold it any longer to follow her.

'The children need to use the conveniences,' she announced to the taller of the two guards. Miss Kent looked especially short beside him. I noticed how she held her head high to add an inch or two. 'The. Toilet.' She pointed at us, enunciating her words slowly and clearly, as grown-ups do when they're not sure the other person understands.

The soldier looked at us without moving a muscle. We stared back, jiggling about like tadpoles, all of us bursting. He eventually seemed to comprehend the situation and waved us along.

'Hurry,' he said, as Miss Kent shepherded us past, making sure to stand between him and us. 'Quick, quick.'

I stared at his sword as we marched past.

In the girls' toilets, notices in Japanese writing had been stuck to the sinks, the mirrors, the doors, even to the bar of soap. We all spent a penny as quickly as we could and followed Miss Kent back to the assembly hall. We passed a soldier who was sticking more notices to the classroom doors and to trophy cabinets along the corridor.

'What is he doing, Miss?' I whispered.

'They're taking what is not rightfully theirs, Nancy,' Miss Kent replied, stiffly. 'But we won't stand in their way. They are, after all, only things. They can't put a notice on us, can they?'

As we passed Miss Butterworth's classroom, Miss Kent stopped suddenly. The door was broken at the hinge and I could hear a soldier shouting orders inside.

'You can jolly well shout all you like, young man, but you will *not* place one of your notices on *my* desk.'

I recognized Miss Butterworth's voice, although it sounded strained, and much louder than usual.

I knew I shouldn't look. Like the blind beggar who'd died at the end of our street in Shanghai, I knew that if Mummy were there she would tell me to cover my eyes and look away. *There are some things little girls aren't meant to see, darling. Best not to look.* But the temptation to peer into the classroom was too great. I looked, and immediately wished I hadn't. I saw the soldier raise his arm. I saw him punch Miss Butterworth in the face. I heard the clatter of books and chairs as she stumbled backwards and hit her head against the edge of the desk. And I heard the panic and fear in Miss Kent's voice as she ran forward, screaming at the soldier. 'Stop! Stop it! Leave her alone, you brute!'

Despite the many things I couldn't understand that morning, I knew, with absolute certainty, that in those few horrible minutes, everything had changed. It didn't matter that we were a Christian missionary school, or that our fathers were well respected and our mothers well dressed. In the end, our parents' occupations, our nice homes and clothes, the language we spoke and the colour of our skin, didn't make any difference. We were at war now. Chinese, British, American, Dutch – we were all the same.

We were the enemy.

ELSPETH

The soldier stared at Minnie, who was huddled in a lifeless heap on the floor. He laughed, kicked a book out of the way and bent down to where I was crouched beside her – part nurse, part shield. He angled his face toward mine. I flinched at his nearness and prepared for the worst.

He placed his notice, slowly, deliberately, on the desk.

'This desk now belongs to the Japanese Emperor,' he whispered, his mouth so close to my ear that I could feel the nauseating warmth of his breath against my skin. 'This *school* now belongs to the Japanese Emperor.' The cold menace in his words turned my stomach. 'What is your name?' he asked.

Minnie groaned and tried to sit up. I told her to stay still.

'Your name!' he shouted, his question now an order; his language clipped and terse.

'Elspeth,' I replied, desperately trying to conceal the tremor in my voice. 'My name is Elspeth Kent. And yours?'

He smirked, either impressed or insulted by my response, I couldn't tell. 'Trouble,' he replied. 'You can call me Trouble, Elizabeth Kent.'

'Elspeth,' I corrected. '*Elspeth* Kent.'

He burst into a sneering laugh as he stood up and kicked another book out of the way. '*Elspeth* Kent,' he repeated, mocking my British accent as he stalked from the room like a satisfied lion after a kill. '*Elspeth* Kent.'

'He's gone, Minnie,' I said, as I helped her sit up. Her lip was bloodied and horribly swollen. 'It's all right. He's gone now.'

'Don't let the children see,' she whispered. Her eyes were full of pain and fear and humiliation. 'Not like this. Take them back to the hall.'

The girls were crowded around the broken door, too horrified to speak, too shocked to look away. It was typical of Minnie to think of everybody else. The selflessness of the gesture nearly broke me. I blinked away my tears, determined not to let the girls see how afraid or upset I was. Nor Minnie, for that matter.

'I can't leave you,' I said. 'I'll send Nancy to fetch someone.'

'No, Els. Take them back. Please.'

Despite my reluctance to leave her alone, I knew she was right. I propped her against the wall and folded my cardigan to make a pillow for her to rest her head against.

'You're to stay right there,' I said.

'I can't go very far, can I?' she replied, nodding toward the corridor where soldiers were prowling up and down.

'I'll be as quick as I can,' I promised.

'Els,' she whispered, as I stood up. 'Is it very bad?'

I shook my head, although it was. I wrapped my hands around hers. 'You'll live. I'll fetch some ice for the swelling. Don't move.'

It was a very subdued group of children I shepherded back along the corridors. I was glad of their silence, relieved to be spared the difficult questions that were inevitably thundering through their minds and for which I had no reasonable answers. Everything was happening and changing too fast, and there was no time to gather my thoughts.

The four girls were keen to share the awful news about Miss Butterworth with the others. The story quickly developed from one soldier to two, and from a punch in the face to a barrage of bamboo sticks, and a raised sword. The girls had poor Minnie practically dead by the time I'd explained to Eleanor Yarwood what had actually happened.

'I ought to get back to her,' I said, as I glanced at the door. 'I hate to leave her.'

The young teacher urged me to go. 'Will Almena . . . be all right?' she whispered.

'I'm sure she's had better days, and she must have got a terrible fright, but she'll be fine when I've patched her up and she's had some rest,' I assured her. I hoped I sounded more certain than I was.

Eleanor Yarwood nodded. She knew I was trying to make the best of a bad situation and didn't press for more.

'Give the girls a riddle or two to work out,' I suggested. 'They're awfully good, really. I'll be as quick as I can.'

By the time I'd fetched ice from the kitchen and made my way back to Minnie, she'd moved from where I left her. Somehow, she'd managed to pick up the books and fetch the first aid kit from the supply cupboard where she kept spare knickers, music stands, and glitter for Christmas decorations. She was sitting on one of the children's chairs. It was far too small for her and I could have wept at the indignity of it all, but somehow I managed to pull myself together.

I folded my arms and tutted my mock disapproval. 'I thought I told you not to move,' I chided. 'You're a terrible patient, Almena Butterworth.' I smiled encouragingly.

Her face was milky pale, her usually rosy cheeks bleached by shock. It was so unimaginably awful that it was Minnie – a teacher who'd given so much to the school, and who treated everyone with such care – who'd been subjected to such a dreadful ordeal.

36

'I couldn't just sit there,' she said. 'You know what I'm like.'

'Yes. I do.' I patted her hand. It wasn't her awful shiner I found so upsetting, but her quiet determination not to make a fuss. 'You're a stubborn old goose. Let them put their notices on everything if they want. A desk can be replaced. You, dear girl, can't.' Minnie was like the big sister I'd never had. I wanted to throw my arms around her and give her a hug, like my brother Alfie always had whenever I fell in the lane and grazed my knees. But Minnie wasn't family, and besides, affection wasn't something that came easily to me. 'Let me take a proper look,' I said. 'Where does it hurt?'

'Where *doesn't* it hurt might be the easier question to answer.' She managed a small smile and then winced. 'I'm sure it looks worse than it is.'

It looked absolutely ghastly. Her eye was already bruising badly, but I didn't want to say so. 'He gave you a pretty decent wallop, all right.' I dabbed carefully at her face with disinfectant, apologizing for the pain of the sting.

'It was silly of me to stand up to him, but while it might only be a desk today, what, or who, will they lay claim to next?'

'Let's not think about that,' I said, and I meant it. The girls seemed suddenly exceptionally young, and horribly vulnerable.

I wrapped the ice in a tea towel and placed it carefully against Minnie's eye. 'That'll have to do for now. Let's get you into bed with a nice cup of tea.' I helped her to her feet and put my arm around her shoulder for support. 'Good job we've had all that practice in the three-legged race. I think we could win it this year, don't you?'

She let out a little gasp as her shock turned to tears.

I'd never seen Minnie cry. I very much hoped I never would again.

*   *   *

The day that had started with the beauty of snowflakes in a chapel doorway, and my determination to finally put in place my plan to leave China, ended with threatening notices being posted at the gates declaring that the school was *Under the Control of the Naval Forces of Great Japan*. The plane I'd seen that morning flew intermittently over the school throughout the afternoon, banking over the harbour and tracking back across town, a steady stream of leaflets falling from its belly to join the still swirling snow. I wondered what was happening beyond the school walls, what other acts of violence were being witnessed by innocent children too young to know that such cruelty was possible, or to understand why. Worse still, the school wireless had been confiscated by the soldiers and removed from the assembly hall. Our last connection to the world beyond the school walls was now in the hands of our enemy.

So much had happened in so short a time. By nightfall that evening, the alarming news spread among the teaching staff that our headmaster, Mr Collins, was missing. Nobody had seen him since the emergency staff meeting following the BBC broadcast, and we were all desperately worried. My concern only grew when Shu Lan stopped me on the stairs to tell me she'd seen him being taken from his house in the school grounds.

'They take him away, Miss Elspeth. On Commander Hayashi's motorbike,' she explained. 'I see from the laundry room. We hide.' She trembled as she spoke. 'I'm very afraid, Miss Elspeth. I remember Nanking,' she whispered.

'Did the soldiers . . . hurt you?' I asked. I couldn't bring myself to say the word.

She took a deep breath and dipped her head in the smallest excruciating acknowledgement. 'They take the city first, and then the farms. They murder my father and my brothers. The women . . . they keep.' Her eyes held such pain. 'You do not understand.'

She was right. I couldn't possibly comprehend what she had seen and endured, but that didn't stop me from wanting to help her.

'The British government will be aware of the situation here,' I said, keeping my voice as measured as possible. 'We expect them to send help very soon.'

I reassured her as best I could, and advised her to tell the servants to stay in their accommodation for the time being, but we both knew there was very little that I, or anyone else, could do to stop the guards if they decided to satisfy their urges. I'd seen how quickly they could turn violent, and already regretted drawing attention to myself from the soldier who'd called himself Trouble. I would be less vocal from now on.

After lights out, when the children were safely in their dorms, a group of six teachers – myself, Eleanor Yarwood, Amelia Prescott, Ella Redmond, Charlie Harris and Tom Martin – met in the staff room. I'd assumed we would try to make some sense of the day, and agree on a plan of action, but Charlie surprised us all by revealing that he was in possession of a home-made radio.

'I managed to keep it hidden from the soldiers when they searched our rooms earlier,' he whispered as he showed us a rather rudimentary piece of equipment. It appeared to be nothing more than a block of wood with a razor blade, a safety pin, and some wires stuck to it. 'I'm not sure it still works, but it's worth a try.'

'Are you sure about this?' I asked, terrified of the consequences should one of the soldiers discover it. 'Perhaps it would be safer to forget you ever had it.'

Either nobody heard me, or everyone disagreed with me, because Charlie proceeded to tinker with the wires.

'I was an electrician, and a mechanic, before I was a PE teacher,' he explained. 'I made this last year. It was just a bit of a hobby really, but maybe it will turn out to be of use after all.'

'Is it working?' I asked, my eyes fixed on Charlie as he pressed the headset to his ear, his brow creased in concentration as he strained to hear a signal.

'Got it!' he whispered after an interminable wait.

I could hear a crackle and the faintest of voices, intermittently fading in and out.

We sat in silence, all eyes on Charlie as he listened carefully to the broadcast he'd picked up. Through agonizing fragments, we learned the shocking news that Pearl Harbor hadn't been the only target. The Forces of the Empire of Japan had also launched an attack on British and US naval ships in Shanghai, and had taken control of the International Settlement there. Terrible assaults had also been launched on the British Crown Colony of Hong Kong, and brutal bombing raids on Singapore and Malaya had left many dead and hundreds injured. All three countries were now under Japanese control, with restrictions and house arrest imposed on all western nationals. The situation was far worse than any of us had imagined. The war had escalated quickly, and dangerously.

Gradually, we shared our thoughts and concerns, but we soon began to go around in circles, asking more questions than we had answers for.

Charlie returned the makeshift radio to a hollowed-out book of cricketing rules.

'I got the idea from a spy film,' he explained, evidently rather pleased with himself.

'Make sure it's very well hidden,' Tom advised. 'Information is our best ally now. With knowledge comes power. That little radio could be crucial.'

'I think I'll turn in,' I said, in an attempt to bring things to a conclusion. 'It has been a rather difficult day.'

'I don't know how anyone is expected to sleep with all those soldiers prowling around,' Miss Yarwood remarked. 'It's horribly unsettling.'

Charlie Harris suggested we all push a heavy piece of furniture against the door. 'Not to cause alarm,' he added. 'But better to take precautions. Be Prepared, isn't that your Brownie motto, Elspeth?'

'Lend a Hand,' I corrected. 'Be Prepared is for the Girl Guides and Boy Scouts.'

'Well, I suggest we use all the mottos and furniture available,' he added. 'And I suggest we meet again tomorrow evening to see what other developments have occurred. I suspect this is just the start of it. I'm afraid we should prepare ourselves for more bad news to come.'

'What sort of bad news?' I asked, wondering how much worse it could get.

He smiled, thinly. 'Let's wait and see what tomorrow brings. In the meantime, let's all try to get some sleep.'

Weary, and deeply troubled by the day's events, I bid everyone goodnight.

Before I turned in, I checked on Minnie. She was propped up against her pillow, a book lying face down on her lap. Her eye was the size of a golf ball and the colour of blackberries.

'Can't sleep?' I asked as I peered around the door.

She shook her head. 'Every creak in the corridor has me springing up like a startled cat.'

'That's understandable, considering.'

'How are the children?' she asked.

'Tremendously resilient,' I said as I stepped further inside. 'They're approaching it all as a rather thrilling adventure, and we're not discouraging them. Most of their talk is about the great fleet of British naval ships on their way to rescue us. Edward Plummer is quite the expert on the matter. Or a dreadful show-off, perhaps. I can never quite decide.'

'Do you think they will?' she asked. 'Rescue us.'

I tugged the wrinkles from my cardigan. 'Of course. And if they don't, we will jolly well rescue ourselves. I always suspected my Girl Guide skills would come in handy one day. All those knots and signals and lessons in self-defence? No better time to put them to use than during a war.'

Minnie smiled wearily. 'I'm not sure we can knit or knot our way out of this one, Els. I'm afraid we're in rather a pickle, aren't we?'

I plumped her pillows and smoothed her eiderdown. My silence was all the answer required.

The sound of boots marching beneath the window made Minnie flinch again.

I took her hockey stick from the wardrobe. 'Here. Put this beneath the covers.'

'Whatever for?'

'Protection. A quick swipe with that will see them off. You're a dab hand with a hockey stick. Didn't you tell me you were county champion, 1924? Those soldiers won't stand a chance.'

Minnie ran her fingers over the handle of the stick. 'Lord help us if we have to resort to women defending themselves with hockey sticks.'

I wished her a peaceful night. As I turned off her light, she slid the hockey stick beneath the eiderdown all the same.

My mind raced as I walked back along the empty corridor. I hardly knew where to start, or what to think about first: the declaration of war, the arrival of the soldiers, the violent attack on Minnie, the troubling disappearance of our headmaster. I'd spent so much of the day reassuring everyone else that I'd hardly had time to think about myself. Not for the first time, I missed having someone to share my troubles with at the end of the day. I missed having someone to reassure *me*.

As I did every night, I stopped to check on the girls before

I retired for the evening. I leaned my head against the door-frame and studied the dozen peaceful faces nestled among the crumpled bedsheets. It was one of my favourite parts of the day. To see them all sleeping meant that I, too, could finally rest. No questioning hands in the air. No need to scold or encourage. I could be Elspeth, and not Miss Kent. But in the moonlit silence that winter night, I felt something other than relief as I stood at the dormitory door. I felt a fierce need to protect the girls from the dangers that now lurked within Chefoo's proud walls. Nothing was certain anymore and, without their parents to protect them, that job fell to us, their teachers. The prospect terrified me.

As I carried on to my bedroom, I thought about how close I'd come to leaving Chefoo, how fateful my hesitation in delivering my letter might prove to be. What was there waiting for me at home anyway? An empty bed. Regret. A headstone bearing his inscription: Harry Daniel Evans. The man whose name I'd so often imagined as my own. So many times I had written it down. So many times I'd smiled at the whispery feel of it on my tongue: Elspeth Evans. It fit so perfectly. *We* fit so perfectly. But like a favourite dress regretfully outgrown, I'd put away the life I'd once worn so well. Nothing would ever suit me like Harry did. Nothing else worked.

My bedroom at the school was furnished exactly as it was when I'd arrived two years ago. Nothing added, nor taken away. In many ways, I'd always considered my position as temporary. The China Inland Mission had offered a place for me to escape. It was never intended as a place for me to stay. A painting of Christ still hung above the bed, a Bible sat on a lace doily on the bedside table, a Wedgewood vase stood on top of the chest of drawers beside the window, empty now of the fragrant sprigs of peach blossom Shu Lan always placed in it at the start of spring.

As I kicked off my shoes, I noticed an envelope beside the vase. Even amid the chaos of the day, the morning post had made its way around the school. I immediately recognized my mother's precise black copperplate. She didn't write often, and not without good reason. I opened the envelope with trepidation and sank down onto the edge of the bed as I absorbed her words.

Dear Elspeth, I'm so sorry to have to tell you that Alfie is reported as missing. He was last seen in North Africa . . .

Like the snowflakes that had melted against my outstretched hand beside the chapel that morning, my brother, Private Alfred Kent, had disappeared. I read the letter again, unable to fully grasp what it meant. Keys went missing, and stockings and slippers. Not dear Alfie. Please, not Alfie.

I wept without shame.

War had found me in the place I had run from, and the place I had run to.

There was nowhere left to hide.

NANCY

A week after the soldiers had burst into our classroom, the snow still lay thick on the ground, and our headmaster, Mr Collins, was still missing. Sprout dared me to ask Miss Kent about him after choir practice.

'Well, Nancy, I'm sure he's busy talking to the authorities,' she said when I finally plucked up the courage to ask. 'Nothing for you to worry about. Everything will be back to normal soon.' But she looked away when she spoke, and Edward said looking away from someone when you're talking to them was a sign of fibbing.

'Watch out for it, Nonny,' he warned as we walked around the courtyard. We were both wrapped up against the cold in our best wool coats and school hats, but the tips of my ears were freezing. 'All sorts of fibs are told when there's a war on. It's called propaganda. I read about it in a book from the library.'

'I don't like the way they stare,' I whispered, as we passed close to one of the soldiers. We'd nicknamed him Charlie Chaplin because he never said anything, unlike the others who always shouted at each other.

'They only stare because they're as fascinated by us as we are by them,' Edward said. 'I bet they've never seen freckles before. Or ginger hair. We're as foreign to them as they are to us.'

I'd never thought about it that way, and supposed he was right.

'Humbug?' He held out a crumpled paper packet. 'It's my last one, but I don't mind.'

I felt lucky to have the sort of brother who gave me his last humbug, and not the sort who pulled wings off flies and stood on spiders, like Winnie's horrid brother, Alex. I took the humbug and let it rest on my tongue, savouring the sweet buttery-mint taste.

'Make it last,' Edward said.

'Why?' I mumbled.

He looked at me before ruffling my hair. 'Just do.'

Sibling Saturday – when the boys and girls were allowed to mix for a while – went ahead even though Japanese soldiers now seemed to be in every part of the school grounds. I was always glad to spend time with Edward, and especially glad of him given our current predicament. I liked that he called me Nonny, the way Mummy did. It reminded me of being at home in England, butter dripping onto our fingers from warm bread, and the gold carriage clock ticking away the minutes on the mantelpiece.

Edward knew all sorts of interesting facts about the war and talked a lot about the Navy coming to rescue us, but it was bitterly cold and I was glad when the bell was rung to signal that we should make our way back inside. I hung my coat on the peg in the corridor. I would need a new one soon. My arms were already sticking out below the cuffs.

The assembly hall wasn't much warmer, and I wished I'd kept my coat on. Edward and I sat together on a gym bench, and his best friend, Larry Crofton, soon abandoned his own sister and came to join us. Sprout and Winnie thought Larry was ever so handsome and went red whenever he looked at them, but to me he was just Edward's spotty friend. I didn't understand what all the fuss was about.

'Shove up, Nance,' he said as he squashed in between us. I shuffled to the right of the bench and nearly fell off the end. 'Do you think the Navy will really come and rescue us, Ed?' he asked.

'Absolutely. Churchill won't see a group of British school-children deprived of their Christmas goose.' Edward always spoke with such confidence, as if he were part of Churchill's War Cabinet and knew this for a fact. 'He'd never live it down. Imagine the stories they would print in the newspapers. Bad for his image.'

'But how will they even know what's happening all the way out here in China?' I asked. 'How will the government know we're being held captive?' In the past week I'd often thought about the map of China in Edward's atlas, and the tiny little peninsula where Chefoo School was based. It felt so very far away from Churchill and London.

Edward smiled. 'Oh, they'll know all right. The China Inland Mission HQ in Shanghai will have alerted them. Besides, the government knows everything. They have spies and all sorts of secret intelligence. They won't leave us under enemy guard for long. It isn't the British way.'

For once, I didn't mind Edward showing off. I was glad that someone seemed to know what was happening. The soldiers had already confiscated the big wireless cabinet, and had also banned production and circulation of the school newspaper, so we really didn't have the foggiest what was going on beyond the school walls. Sprout said we were probably better off not knowing.

'Even if the Navy do come to rescue us, the guards won't let us go without a fight,' she said as she shoved in beside me.

Sprout, Winnie, and Mouse had made a beeline for us as soon as they'd seen Larry sitting beside me. 'We're prisoners now. Enemy nationals.'

Edward scoffed at the notion. 'Most of the so-called guards are part of the puppet regime. They're only there as a deterrent. If push comes to shove, they'll be about as useful as melted ice.' Sprout shrugged. She didn't say anything else. 'There's a former British naval base not too far up the coast at Weihaiwei,' Edward continued, enjoying the little audience that had gathered. 'The Navy still patrol the waters there. Their aircraft carrier *Eagle* is the pride of the fleet. It would be quite something if that came to our rescue. And anyway, we're not prisoners,' he added. 'David Balfour was a prisoner in *Kidnapped*. We're just "temporarily inconvenienced". Master Harris said so.'

The idea of being part of a dramatic rescue was quite exciting, but one thing still worried me.

'If we are rescued in a secret operation and taken away from the school, how will our parents know where to find us?' I asked. 'What if it's safer for us to stay where we are than it is for us to leave?'

Nobody had an answer for that. Not even Edward.

The attack we'd witnessed on Poor Miss Butterworth (as she was now generally known) remained a favourite topic of conversation among us. Her face was still horribly bruised and looked like a rotten old apple.

'I wouldn't have let the soldier put a notice on the desk either,' Sprout said as we made our beds that evening. 'Miss Butterworth was terrifically brave to stand up to him. Still, if they can do that with their bare hands, imagine the damage they could do with those bamboo sticks and swords they carry around,' she added.

'I wish you wouldn't say things like that,' I said. 'I'd rather *not* imagine it, thank you very much.'

'There's no point pretending it isn't happening, Plum. We're the enemy now.'

Sprout sat cross-legged on her bed, having given up on the hospital corners we were trying to master as part of our House Orderly badges for Brownies. Brown Owl had made it look easy during her demonstration. 'Forty-five-degree angles. Neat folds and smooth top sheets.' But it wasn't easy and most of us couldn't get it right at all.

Beyond the window, we could hear the familiar shouts of 'Yah! Yah!' coming from the sports field which the soldiers now used for military training and bayonet practice. We'd nicknamed their drills 'Yah' drills, because of the noises they made as they lunged at each other.

Mouse came over to my bed. She'd finished her hospital corners and offered to help me with mine since I'd got into such a muddle.

'Miss Kent says we have to look on the bright side,' she offered. 'The soldiers will still be out there, lunging at each other with their sticks, whether we cry into our pillows or laugh our heads off.'

Sprout looked at me, and I looked at Mouse, and we all burst out laughing because it was so unlike Mouse to be so outspoken.

But with the guards at the gates and soldiers marching about with swords swinging at their hips, there weren't too many bright sides to be found, whichever way you looked at it.

Despite the soldiers patrolling the school grounds and taking over our meeting room, Miss Kent insisted that Brownies would go ahead as usual. Nothing really felt usual anymore, but it was a nice change from all the talk of war.

We were instructed to meet in Miss Vincent's music room. After tidying away the music stands, tambourines and triangles, we sang our Six Songs and said the Brownie Promise. When Brown Owl inspected our hands and uniforms, I was pleased to get a special mention for my neat fingernails. Mouse was complimented on how neatly she'd tied her scarf. I smiled at her and whispered, 'Well done.'

'Tawny Owl and I are aware that several of the older girls amongst you are eager to fly up to Girl Guides, and are ready for new challenges,' Brown Owl announced as we sat in our Sixes. 'As a result, we plan to form a new Girl Guides patrol after Christmas.'

The announcement caused a great deal of excitement. I couldn't wait to fly up to Girl Guides and sew my Brownie Wings badge onto the sleeve of my blue shirt. My nut-brown cotton dress, which had fallen well below my knees at my first meeting of Brownies, was now on the short side, and my once-bright buttercup-yellow scarf was faded from the sun and too many boil-washes. I couldn't wait to wear the blue Girl Guide uniform instead. 'We'll look just like the royal princesses,' I whispered to Sprout. 'They're members of the 1st Buckingham Palace Company. It was formed especially so they could become Girl Guides.'

Sprout thought it was funny the way I always went on about the Princesses Elizabeth and Margaret. They didn't have princesses in America which I thought was an awful shame.

'In preparation for the new patrol, you should all read the Girl Guide Handbook, and learn your new Promise and the Guide Law,' Brown Owl continued. 'You'll also need to know your knots, and the history of the Union Jack and other flags, ready for the investiture ceremony. We would also like you to come up with ideas for the patrol name and emblem.'

As we worked on our ideas, and drew pictures of the

wildflowers and birds we'd each chosen for the emblem, we sang rounds of 'Kookaburra', and 'Oh You'll Never Get to Heaven', and for a while I felt content and forgot all about the war and the disappointment of Christmas without my parents.

Brown Owl then told us how Brownies and Girl Guides in Britain were being awarded special War Service badges.

'They're doing their bit for the war effort,' she said. 'Knitting socks and mittens and balaclavas to send out to the troops, collecting sphagnum moss which is used to dress wounds, singing in the bomb shelters to keep everyone's spirits up, and collecting cotton reels, and other household items the Ministry has a use for. Those living in the country are also helping with the evacuees,' she explained. 'Some of the city children have never seen cows and sheep before and find country life quite strange. It must be very difficult for them being parted from their parents.'

'I suppose we're a bit like evacuees, aren't we,' Sprout remarked. 'Except we see water buffalo and cranes instead of sheep and cows.'

Brown Owl smiled. 'Well, I rather think we've been a little less disrupted, Dorothy. And thankfully there's no need for gas masks here.'

As ever, we were reminded that no matter how strange or challenging our own situation, there were always others dealing with much worse. I felt for Miss Kent's handkerchief in my pinafore pocket and recalled what she'd said to me as we'd sailed away from Shanghai harbour. *We must always look forward, Nancy, never back. Eyes on the horizon, that's the ticket.*

I was distracted during the rest of the meeting. I couldn't stop thinking about the Brownies and Guides back in Britain and wished we could do something to help the war effort, too.

'They're all doing brave and important things,' I said as we tidied up. 'All we're doing is cutting out snowflakes for the windows, and drawing pictures of kingfishers and primroses.'

Winnie Morris disagreed with me. As usual.

'Who'd want to be stuck in an Anderson shelter with a stinky old gas mask waiting for the air-raid sirens to sound the all-clear. I'd much rather be here, away from Hitler's bombs, thank you very much. Even with soldiers at the school gates.'

I hated to admit that she was right, but it probably was better to be in China, even if it meant being away from our parents, and that birthdays and Christmases came and went without so much as a candle to blow out or a stocking to hang on the fireplace.

'Excellent work tonight, girls,' Brown Owl said as the meeting came to a close. 'It has been a very difficult week, and I'm pleased to see you're all putting your best foot forward and getting on with it.'

We stood together in a circle to sing 'Brownie Bells' to end the meeting. The melody really did have the rhythm of church bells, the tone moving up and down, like a gentle chime. '*Oh Lord, our God / Thy children call / Grant us Thy peace / And bless us all / Goodnight, Goodnight.*' The final two goodnights were sung soft and slow, the last note spreading around us like the warm glow from a fire. We finished by saying, 'Goodnight, Brown Owl. Goodnight, Tawny Owl,' even though Tawny Owl (Miss Butterworth) wasn't there.

Brown Owl replied with, 'Goodnight, Brownies,' and for a moment, despite the war and the stony-faced soldiers outside, I felt that nothing bad would happen as long as I had my friends beside me and good thoughts in my heart.

But, as I was starting to realize, things change very quickly in a war and, where one moment can make you feel safe and hopeful, another can just as easily make you feel terribly alone and afraid.

As we made our way back to the dorm, Sprout grabbed my hand, and I grabbed Mouse's, and we swung our arms wildly back and forth as we skipped along the corridor. It wasn't possible to be homesick and worried all the time, and it was nice to forget about the seriousness of everything for a while. But we came to a sudden stop as we saw Shu Lan waiting at the dormitory door, and walked the rest of the way. I presumed she'd come to tell us off about the mess we'd left it in but, as we got closer, I could see she was dreadfully upset.

'What's the matter?' Sprout asked. She was always so forthright. Sometimes she sounded a little heartless, although she didn't mean to.

'I come to say goodbye.' Shu Lan kept her gaze fixed on the floor as she spoke.

'Goodbye?' Sprout turned to face me, a smile spreading across her face. 'We're going home, Plum! The Navy must be here! Edward was right!'

Shu Lan shook her head. 'You will stay. I go.'

Sprout's excitement faded, and mine with it.

'Where are you going?' I asked.

'All servants must leave. Soldiers' orders. We go back to our villages and farms.' She looked afraid as she spoke, but a hesitant smile formed on her lips. 'I miss you. Chefoo is my family.'

Before we could say anything else, she turned and rushed off down the corridor, her long plait swinging down her back.

We walked into the dorm without saying another word. The rest of the girls, having caught up, followed behind. A small gasp from Sprout broke the silence as we stood together in the middle of the room. A paper lotus flower had been placed on each of our pillows, and the windows were decorated with dozens of delicate paper snowflakes.

I let go of Sprout's hand and sank onto my bed. My legs dangled over the side, my feet still not quite able to reach the floor. For the first time since the soldiers had marched into the school, I understood just how serious the situation was. I closed the shutters over the window, pausing for just a moment to watch the snowflakes that danced and swirled in the dark, but the sight of them didn't fill me with excitement as usual. It only made me envy their freedom.

That night, nobody whispered into the dark after lights out. We lay in silence with our own worries and fears. I closed my eyes and searched through my memories, looking for Mummy among the crowds on the wharf, but all I could see was her dress fading from view until she was a blue dot, and I was all alone, sailing out of Shanghai harbour toward an uncertain future.

I was a feather, cruelly plucked from its wing. A kingfisher, trapped in a metalsmith's net.

THE GUIDE LAW: A GUIDE'S DUTY IS TO BE USEFUL AND TO HELP OTHERS

If it is a question of being a help to the rest of the world, or a burden on it, a Girl Guide is always to be found among the helpers.

ELSPETH

The awful news that the servants had been ordered to leave the school was shared at the staff meeting that evening.

'It's a worrying development,' Charlie Harris admitted. 'For them, and for us.'

'Are they being taken somewhere, or will they be allowed to go back to their families?' I asked.

'I'm afraid I don't know,' he confirmed. 'Let's hope it's the latter.'

'Yes, let's hope for the best,' I replied, although I couldn't help but fear the worst.

'We'll have to make arrangements for managing the chores,' Minnie added, practical as ever. I was glad she was now feeling well enough to join our daily staff meetings. 'Perhaps Elspeth and I could work out a roster? We should include the children, where possible. Our Brownies will certainly be keen to lend a hand. With all hands to the pump, I'm sure we'll manage.'

But would we manage? The servants had kept everything

running smoothly at the school, from lighting the lamps at dusk to cleaning, gardening, cooking, and any number of other chores we probably weren't even aware of. Whether we chose to acknowledge it or not, we'd taken them for granted. I was ashamed of how easily I'd become accustomed to having servants; how quickly I'd forgotten my sense of unease as the rickshaw puller had transported me from Chefoo harbour, his bamboo hat bobbing up and down as he ran on like a faithful packhorse.

After the meeting, I went to find Shu Lan. Teaching staff didn't usually mix with the servants, let alone visit their accommodation, but we were living through curious times, and nothing about our situation was usual anymore.

'You are to leave us,' I said, when I found her. 'I'm so sorry. Is there anything I can do to help?'

Shu Lan was a very private young woman. The events in Nanking had left her understandably wounded and distrustful. Her reluctance to interact was often mistaken for rudeness and she wasn't much liked among the teachers, or the children. But I saw a strength in her that I greatly admired.

She kept her eyes down as she spoke. 'Yes, we go.'

'Where?' I asked, aware that she didn't have any immediate family to return to. 'Where will you go?'

'To my cousin's farm, not far from the school,' she said, eventually lifting her gaze to look at me. 'She has a baby coming. She will be glad of my help.'

'And Wei Huan?'

She smiled shyly at his name. I knew they planned to marry in the spring. That much she had told me in a rare moment of confidence.

'To his brother,' she said. 'In the spring, we travel to his uncle, in Weihsien. Near Tsingtao.'

The names and locations meant nothing to me. Despite living in China for two years, I'd travelled no further than Chefoo.

'I will keep telling the children your stories,' I assured her. 'So that they will know about your country, and your culture.'

'You are a good woman, Miss Elspeth,' she said. 'You will keep the children safe.'

I only wished I could be so sure.

She asked me to wait a moment as she stepped inside the accommodation block.

'For you,' she said, as she returned and pressed a book into my hands. 'The Sanzang. Buddhist scriptures. I mark the pages for you.'

I took the small leather-bound book from her. 'Thank you. I will treasure it.'

She shook her head. 'Don't treasure. Learn.' She pressed her hands to mine. 'Take it inside, like food for the spirit.'

I promised I would.

We exchanged polite smiles that barely concealed our despair. What else could we do? Despite the awful circumstances we found ourselves in, the boundaries of servant and teacher, of west and east, prevailed.

The news about the servants' expulsion was soon followed by more worrying developments.

'There's something I think you should all know,' Charlie announced at the staff meeting the next evening. He hesitated before he carried on. 'I had a quiet word earlier with one of the more sympathetic guards. He told me Allied civilian enemies of Japan are being sent away.'

I couldn't get used to the idea that *we* were the Allied civilian enemies. Such words belonged in spy novels, not to someone like me.

'What do you mean?' I asked. 'Sent away where?'

Charlie took a deep breath. 'To so-called Civilian Assembly Centres. Otherwise known as internment camps.'

I loosened the top button at my collar as all the air seemed to be sucked out of the small staff room. We'd heard about Jews being rounded up in Europe and taken to Nazi-run work camps in Poland and Germany. Some reports suggested that children were separated from their parents, and husbands from their wives. I couldn't believe we might find ourselves in a similar situation.

'Where are these . . . camps?' I asked.

'Most appear to be in various locations around Shanghai. There are also several large camps in Hong Kong.' He paused. 'And there's one other. In northern China. In Weihsien.'

I repeated the name. 'Wey-shen.' It was familiar to me, but I couldn't remember why.

'I don't wish to alarm anyone, but it would certainly be possible for us to be moved there in a few days by boat and train,' Charlie added. 'I think we should be prepared.'

'Surely they wouldn't uproot the entire school,' I remarked. 'There are over a hundred children here! It would be a logistical nightmare.' The awful thought also occurred to me that if we *were* moved, how would we ever let the children's parents know where we were?

'Quite apart from which we're British citizens,' Minnie added quietly. 'Teachers. In a missionary school! They wouldn't put us into some dreadful camp.' She looked around the room, her eyes wide. 'Would they?'

The answer lay in the silence that settled over us like ash from a dying fire.

I went to bed early that evening, eager to be alone with my thoughts. I sat for a while, reading over my mother's letter, wondering where on earth Alfie was. Part of me hoped his patrol had been captured and that he'd been taken to a POW camp. Better that than the far worse alternative.

After turning out the light, I lay awake and listened to the haunting hoot of an owl beyond the window, searching for his mate in the dark. I followed his call, letting my memories stray through the night, to happier times when I'd placed my cheek against Harry's chest as we'd danced. I'd told him I could hear his heart beating.

'What's it saying?' he'd asked.

I pressed my ear to his shirt and listened to the rhythmic beat. 'I think it's saying you love me.'

I felt his smile before he dipped his lips and whispered in my ear, 'I think it's asking you to marry me.'

The following day, our small army of cooks, cleaners, amahs, gardeners, groundsmen and boatmen were rounded up in the Boys' School courtyard. The snow had been cleared by the soldiers and piled up in great drifts beside the school buildings. Commander Hayashi and the more senior guards shouted orders at the servants, using their bamboo sticks to push and prod anyone who didn't move quickly enough. I noticed that the soldier who'd struck Minnie and called himself Trouble was always the first to use physical force.

'Why must they always be so rough,' Minnie asked. 'Is it really necessary?'

She stood beside me as we huddled together for warmth. Her eye was finally starting to heal, but I knew she felt every one of those rough prods as if the stick were prodding her.

'It gives them a sense of power,' I said. 'They're nothing better than a group of school bullies. I'd like to give them a piece of my mind.'

'Well, I hope you won't,' she replied, giving me one of her looks. 'We both know what happens when one talks back to them.'

I sighed, and patted her hand. 'Of course I won't. But, still. I'd very much like to.'

I was surprised by how upset I was by the servants' departure. They were part of the fabric of the school; as much a part of our days as assembly and prayers, tiffin and supper. Theirs were the familiar faces we passed in the corridors, the voices we heard speaking in the local tongue, the only regular contact we had with a people whose country we had made our home. We'd quietly shared their celebrations and grief, triumphs and despair, albeit from a distance, and I suspected I wasn't the only member of staff to have formed something of a personal connection with one or another of them.

As Wei Huan moved forward to join the line, he paused beside me.

'I miss Chefoo School very much,' he said. 'I miss the children.'

'And they will miss you,' I replied. I reached for his hands, pressing my unspoken shame and apology into the landscape of hard work I felt in his rough skin. 'We will all miss you,' I added. 'The school will not be the same without you.' I hoped he knew how much I meant it.

'Where will you go, Wei Huan?' Minnie asked.

'To my family, here in Chefoo. In the spring, we travel to my uncle's farm, near Weihsien. We have good prospects there.'

My mouth felt as if it was stuffed with sawdust as I recalled Charlie Harris mentioning the internment camp at Weihsien. I couldn't think of anything to say.

'I have gift for you.' Wei Huan pressed a small square of folded cotton into my hands.

Surprised by the gesture, I folded back the neat corners of the little parcel. 'Nine sunflower seeds!' I smiled. 'Thank you.'

'In Chinese culture, nine means everlasting. Eternity. We grow anywhere,' he said, 'with strong roots.'

I pressed a hand to my heart. 'You are a good man, Wei Huan. I will take care of them.'

He offered a hesitant smile, made a small bow and walked on to join the group already assembled in the courtyard.

'You! What did he give you?'

The loud voice made me jump. I turned to see Trouble stalking toward me, his face cold and emotionless until he recognized me.

His thin lips curved into a knowing smirk as he slowly pronounced my name. 'Elspeth Kent.' He carried a menacing air of arrogance and authority. 'What did he give you?' he repeated.

I placed my hands behind my back. 'Nothing. Just some flower seeds.' Those small grey seeds suddenly felt like the most important thing in the world.

'Show.' He tapped my arm firmly with his stick, his sentences becoming clipped as his anger increased.

Heart pounding, I unfolded the cotton parcel and held out my hands to show him the seeds. 'Sunflowers. For the garden. Not opium.'

He flicked his fingertip roughly over the seeds, sending one tumbling to the ground beside the wall. I bent down to pick it up but his boot found it first, deliberately grinding it into the frozen earth with his heel before tossing his spent cigarette on top of it. As a final insult, he spat on the place where the seed had fallen. He tipped my chin toward him with the end of his stick, laughed, and returned to the group of servants.

'What an absolute brute,' Minnie whispered.

I took a moment to compose myself before I stood up. 'That seed is all of us, Minnie. He just showed us how insignificant we are; how easily he might stamp any one of us into the ground with the heel of his boot. "Brute" is too generous a name for him.'

Minnie let out a sigh. 'I will pray for him tonight. For all of them.'

A ball of anger and frustration burst inside me.

'He doesn't deserve your prayers, Minnie!' I snapped. 'None of them do. Besides, all the prayers in the world won't make them leave. Prayers won't bring an end to the war, or to this damned invasion. Prayers can't bring back our loved ones, can they?'

I hadn't meant to speak so honestly, or to raise my voice, especially not to Minnie, but all the emotions I'd kept carefully hidden these past weeks – years, even – rushed out like air from a punctured lung, and left me breathless.

Minnie stared at me, shocked by my outburst, but before she could say anything the servants began to walk through the school gates, one line for the men, one line for the women. I swallowed a knot of emotion and pushed the handkerchief with its seeds into my pocket, wrapping my hand around them as if they were the most precious of jewels.

A spectacular winter sunset lit up the sky as the servants departed, tinting everything a fiery red. In different circumstances, I would have admired it, but I couldn't find any joy in it today. It made me think of Harry. I could picture him so clearly, standing in front of his easel, adding layers of colour to get it just right. Painting was his escape from the colourless world he entered every day, his brushes and paints allowing him to restore colour and beauty to his world after a day spent underground in the pitch dark of the colliery mine. 'I'll paint you every day, when we're married,' he'd joked. 'I'll paint you first thing in the morning, and late at night. My very own sunrise and sunset.' I imagined his fingers like brushes against my skin until I realized it was Minnie, looping her arm through mine.

'Let's get inside,' she said. 'I'm freezing.'

'I'm so sorry, Minnie. I . . .'

She shushed me before I had a chance to apologize for my outburst. 'No need to say anything. I think we could both do with a cup of strong sweet tea, don't you?'

But I couldn't stop thinking about how cruelly Trouble had

trampled the sunflower seed into the ground, and there wasn't a cup of tea strong or sweet enough to ease my concerns.

The gaps left behind by the servants' quiet efficiency clung to the school as keenly as the frosts that decorated the windows.

'Who'll do all the servants' work now, Miss?' Joan asked quietly, as she took the pile of Christmas carol books from my desk to hand out to the others. 'They did such a lot for us, didn't they?'

The way she launched into the question made it clear the girls had been discussing it among themselves. No matter how much we tried to protect the children from the worst of our situation, or how much we tried to brighten things up with optimism and stoicism, the truth was never far away.

'That's a very good question, Joan,' I replied. 'And the answer is that we will do the work ourselves, of course. We'll roll up our sleeves and get on with it. And we'll make a jolly good go of it too, I'd say. In fact, Tawny Owl and I have already agreed that you can all count the additional tasks towards your House Orderly badges.'

The girls were always keen to earn another badge and as Joan returned to her seat she whispered it to Nancy, who whispered it to Winnie, and so on and so on, until the news reached Dorothy, who wanted to know why everyone was talking about badgers, which made them all giggle. It was the first time I'd heard the girls laugh since the soldiers arrived. For once, I didn't stop them.

I fetched Pearl S. Buck's *The Good Earth* from my desk drawer, hesitating for just a moment before I removed the Japanese notice that had been placed on the cover. I felt a small thrill of rebellion as I sat down and opened the book. The girls were soon intrigued by the story of Wang Lung, and his wife, O-Lan, a former slave, and their struggle to survive amid poverty, famine and war. I hoped the book would stir an interest in

Chinese culture in the minds of these privileged western children who, fortunately for them, had never known a life of poverty and servitude.

While our experience of life under Japanese guard was still very new and none of us knew what worrying development the next day might bring, one small relief was that the guards seemed rather disinterested in us. The violent attack on Minnie had left us in no doubt that their presence brought plenty of danger, but – on the whole – they seemed content to let us carry on as normal, or as normal as things could possibly be.

As temperatures dropped further, concerns for the servants who'd left the school heightened. Long before the events of Pearl Harbor, Shu Lan had told me that local farmers were suffering terribly under Japanese occupation. Rice and wheat harvests were taken by the soldiers for a fraction of the price they would normally sell for, and any fish and meat also had to be given up. Those who had pigs had slaughtered them, salted the meat, and hidden it in cellars beneath the courtyards of their homes.

'Could we somehow send food parcels out to them?' I suggested to Minnie when I discussed my concerns with her. 'I'm sure we can spare enough to help.'

She thought it was a good idea. 'But how? One enemy helping another. The guards would never allow it.'

'Unless there's a way to secretly send food parcels over the wall,' I suggested. 'Avoid the guards completely?'

'Goodness, Els. That sounds awfully daring and dangerous.'

It did, but if it worked, it would be worth the risk. 'I'll talk to Charlie about it at the staff meeting,' I added as I smoothed the edge of her eiderdown and wished her goodnight. 'He seems to be rather good at things like that.'

'Things like what?' Minnie asked.

'*Espionage!*' I whispered as I closed the door behind me.

My bedroom was especially cold that night, my breath as visible as the guards' cigarette smoke that trailed behind them as they patrolled the corridors. It was the coldest December I'd experienced since arriving at Chefoo. The clear seasonal change was one of the things I'd come to enjoy most about China, the marked progression from the fragrant calm of spring to the warm rains of summer, the cool crisp mornings of autumn to the piercing chills of the winter snows. As the warmth of the day's weak sunlight leached away after dark, I thought about the damp grey summers in Yorkshire and promised myself I would never complain about them again, when – if – I ever got back.

Once I'd washed and dressed for bed, I pulled my steamer trunk out from beneath the iron bedstead. My fingers were cold and I fumbled as I unbuckled the latches. Inside were the starched skirts and blouses and neatly darned stockings I'd already packed in anticipation of my return to England. I blew out a breath and lifted them up, shaking out the creases and hope I'd packed among them, just as I had on my first evening here. Next, I took out the books I'd brought with me: *The Pilgrim's Progress*, my Girl Guide Handbook, *Little Women*, a battered copy of Pearl S. Buck's *The Good Earth* and Isabella Bird's *The Yangtze Valley and Beyond*. Books before comfort had seemed like a wise packing principle at the time, but I sorely regretted leaving my favourite woollen blanket behind. I'd imagined and hoped for so many things as the Blue Funnel Line steamship had carried me east from Liverpool to Shanghai – a new life, a new purpose, the excitement of getting to know a new culture and country. If England had felt distant after three weeks at sea with a cargo of Lancashire cotton, it felt impossibly far away now. I thought of everyone I'd left behind there: my mother and Alfie, Auntie Gert, Phyllis at the post office, poor jilted Reggie, Harry.

I unfolded my map of China next. It was still as creased as just-washed linen, having been well-studied in the weeks leading up to my departure from England, and scrutinized several times a day during the long journey at sea. With my fingertip, I retraced my journey from Shanghai, around the tip of the Shantung Peninsula (Dragon's Beak as I now knew it was known to the locals), past Haiyang and Weihaiwei to the picturesque port of Chefoo, perched on the southern edge of the Gulf of Chihli on the north-eastern coast of the Yellow Sea, over five hundred miles from Shanghai. I thought about the final thirty minutes of bone-shaking transfer by rickshaw with Amelia Prescott, the formidable Prep School principal, and how she'd sat beside me, chatting effusively on about the proud legacy of the Chefusians and advising on the daily windmilling of one's arms to prevent unsightly sagging. It all seemed so strange and distant, as if it had happened to a different person entirely.

I folded the map back up, pushed the trunk beneath the bed and walked to the window where I stretched the challenges of the day from my tired limbs. My gaze settled on the curve of the bay just visible in the distance, the water silvered by a generous yule moon. The ocean had always given me great comfort. To know that the waters that had carried me here could take me back to England anytime I wanted had offered a reassurance I hadn't expected to need. Only now it felt as if the ocean was the thing holding me in place, rather than the thing that might set me free. I froze, mid-stretch, as a line of guards marched beneath my window, the rhythmic goose-step of their boots matched by the heavy thump of my heart. I stepped back and pulled the shutters closed with a snap.

Kneeling beside the bed, I said a prayer for Alfie, willing him to be alive wherever in the world he was, praying for him to find the strength to endure whatever circumstances he now faced. I finished with a prayer for all the brave boys fighting the Nazis in Europe, and for my mother, and for Minnie and the girls, and for Shu Lan and Wei Huan, and finally – as always – I prayed for Harry. Whether my words were founded in habit, or came from a place of genuine faith, I wasn't sure.

Before I climbed into bed, I opened my Girl Guide Handbook. I took out the envelope, pulled the single page from inside and read over my words. *It is with much difficulty, and after a great deal of personal anguish and reflection, that I must inform you of my intention to leave my position at Chefoo School and return to my family in England . . .*

I'd written the letter so full of determination, pleased to be taking control of my future rather than letting others twist and bend it like one of Shu Lan's paper flowers, but I'd let it linger for too long. The time I thought I'd had in which to make difficult decisions had been washed away with the last of the autumn tides. Now, the things I hadn't said would remain unspoken. The words I'd so carefully written would remain unread.

Without hesitation, I tore the letter into tiny fragments, pushed open the window and scattered the pieces, like snowflakes, into the darkness. I watched them drift away on the wind. I was staying now, for better or worse.

Unable to sleep, I opened the book of Buddhist scriptures Shu Lan had given me and read a passage she'd marked and translated into English. One line, in particular, stood out: *The price of freedom is simply choosing to be; liberation is in the mind.* I held tight to the words, gripped my hockey stick beneath the bedcovers, and waited for the sun to rise. While nothing much was certain anymore, that, at least, I could depend on.

NANCY

Despite our teachers' best efforts to carry on as normal with school routine, there was nothing normal about seeing soldiers everywhere. They seemed to multiply overnight and take over another part of the school every day. They mostly kept their distance, but I was wary of them and their snarling dogs. Edward warned me about the one who called himself Trouble; the one who'd hit Poor Miss Butterworth. 'I don't like the look of him, Nonny,' he said. 'Make sure you're on your best behaviour whenever he's around.'

Sprout came up with nicknames for some of the other soldiers. She said it made them seem less serious. Home Run was named for being the best baseball player, and Charlie Chaplin because we'd still never heard him speak. Home Run was one of the few soldiers who didn't stare at us when we walked past, so I wasn't especially worried when our rounders ball landed at his feet during a game Miss Kent had suggested we play to keep warm. Mouse had hit the ball with a terrific wallop, sending it as far as the Prep School wall. She got past all four bases before Home

Run picked the ball up and threw it back to me in a perfectly aimed looping arc.

'Thank you,' I called as I caught it, and then covered my mouth with my hand, afraid I would get into trouble for speaking to him. Thankfully, nobody had noticed.

'Babe Ruth!' he called back, smiling. 'Good catch!'

I smiled back before I ran over to the others.

'What was all that about?' Sprout asked as we walked back inside together when the game had finished.

'What was what about?'

'Talking to Home Run. I saw you.'

I was grateful for the colour in my cheeks that hid my guilty blushes. 'I only thanked him for throwing the ball back. He called me Babe Ruth!'

Sprout wasn't impressed. 'Don't be fooled, Plum. They're all horrid. Every one of them. I saw Trouble kicking his dog yesterday until it howled in pain.'

'Well, he's a brute,' I said. 'They can't all be that bad.'

She laughed. 'Yes, they can. We're their enemy. It's their job to be bad.' She looked at me seriously as we hung up our coats. 'You trust people too easily. He'd just as quickly throw us all into prison as throw your ball back.'

Our status as enemy nationals became even clearer when Commander Hayashi issued everyone with an armband to declare our nationality. The letter 'A' for American was stamped onto some of the armbands, 'B' for British on others.

'You must wear at all time,' he ordered from the top of the stepladders he used whenever he addressed us as a group.

Sprout did a marvellous impression of him when we were in the dorm and the teachers and soldiers couldn't hear. She stood on her bed and borrowed Winnie's spectacles and had us all in fits of giggles as she mimicked his stern commands, but nobody laughed when the armbands were distributed.

'They might as well put one of their notices on us and declare us the property of the Great Emperor of Japan,' I said as I pulled mine on with a sigh.

One of the American girls put hers on upside down by accident.

'Look at that,' Sprout said, covering the middle bar of the A with her finger. 'It looks like a V for Victory.'

When the guards weren't looking, some of the other American girls turned their armbands upside down so that their 'A's also became victory Vs. I thought it was wonderfully rebellious and brave of them, until Miss Kent noticed and scolded them. There was a sharp edge to her voice that I hadn't heard before.

'You are silly foolish girls,' she snapped, insisting they turn their armbands the right way up immediately. 'I do not want to see such insolence from any of you again. Do you understand?'

We all said, 'Yes, Miss,' and stared at the floor because Miss Kent's cheeks had gone bright red, and that meant she was really very cross.

While we knew better than to complain to the teachers, in the privacy of the dorm we grumbled to each other about the armbands, and everything else that was changing.

'Did you see the ugly stable block they're building across the tennis courts?'

'And the way they trample all over Wei Huan's flower beds.'

'Edward says they've absolutely ruined the cricket field with their baseball matches.'

'Don't you think it's odd that nobody's mentioned the head-master?' I said as I watched the soldiers march past the window. 'He's been missing for ages now. Somebody must know where he is.'

'I suspect they do know, but aren't telling us,' Mouse replied. 'I hope they haven't taken him somewhere awful.'

'Like where?'

She shrugged. 'I don't know. I just hope they're not being cruel to him, wherever he is.'

We were all ever so worried about him. Sprout said she wished she could tell the soldiers what she really thought of their silly orders and poor manners.

'I'd like to point a stick at *them* and see how they like it.'

I made her promise not to, on Brownie's honour. Sprout had a knack for getting herself into trouble, and I couldn't forget Miss Butterworth being punched in the face. It was too awful to imagine the same thing happening to my best friend.

'It wouldn't make any difference anyway,' I said, 'even if you did tell them what you thought of them. Besides, you're supposed to be concentrating on getting better, not planning a mutiny. Christmas will be doubly awful if you're in the San again. It isn't the same when you're not around.'

She dug her elbow playfully into my ribs. 'I'm not going anywhere.' She nodded toward the window and the guards at the gates. 'You're stuck with me now. Like it or not.'

And, despite the seriousness of the situation, I smiled. If I was going to be stuck anywhere, with anyone other than Mummy, I would choose Sprout every time.

As the days came and went, I started to lose hope about being rescued. Even Edward didn't sound quite so confident about the arrival of the British warships.

'They're not coming, are they?' I said, as we trudged around the courtyard together. 'They're going to leave us here forever.'

'Maybe not forever,' he said. 'But it might take them a bit longer to get here than we thought. And if not, we'll have to rescue ourselves.'

He gave me a serious look and, although I didn't know exactly what he meant or how we were ever going to manage that, I trusted him to know the right thing to do.

The dorm was especially cold that night – whether from the snow, or a lack of wood for the fires, I wasn't sure – and I dressed for bed quickly, flinching as my frozen fingers brushed against my skin. We slept in dorms of eight, with two older girls – the prefects – sleeping at each end of the room, and the younger children in the middle. Sprout was still coughing quite badly, so I plumped her pillow to make her more comfortable. She complained of being cold, so I gave her my blanket, too.

When she was comfortable, I took the tea caddy from beneath my bed and pulled out the first letter Mummy had sent after I'd arrived in Chefoo. It still carried a trace of her favourite perfume, English lavender, and as I held the page to my nose, savouring the scent, I pressed the memory of her onto my heart, like the wildflowers I picked from the kaoliang fields and kept between the pages of my Bible.

Hello darling,

I'm writing this from the desk in your bedroom at the Mission compound. It is so quiet without you, but we are very proud of you, and know you will have the most wonderful time at Chefoo School. It will be strange at first being so far away from home, but you'll soon get used to it. I expect you'll be so busy you'll hardly have time to miss us at all! I can't wait to hear all about it when we see you again in the spring. I hope you'll join the Brownies and learn all the marvellous songs. We can sing them together when I see you. I still remember them! 'Brownie Bells' and 'Taps' were always my favourites.

Be a good girl for your teachers, and don't forget to say your prayers before bed, even when you're too tired to kneel up straight. Above all, remember the Lord is always listening, and that those who have faith will never be alone.

With all our love to you, and God's blessings. Be brave, darling.
Mummy and Daddy
xxx

I knelt beside my bed and said my prayers before climbing beneath the covers. As I lay in silence, I thought about how she'd said the Lord is always listening, and I whispered one more prayer, to keep her safe wherever she was, and to let her know that I was being brave and thinking about her. I imagined her arms tucked around my waist as I leaned my head against her chest. I imagined her until she became as real as the patter of snowflakes at the window, and I curled up under the blankets and covered my sobs with a pretend cough.

As she did every night, Miss Kent stopped at the dorm to check on us after lights out, but that night, she stepped into the room, rather than just looking in through the door as she usually did. I heard her neat footsteps cross the room, and stop beside my bed.

'It's perfectly normal to miss people, Nancy,' she whispered when she saw that I was still awake. 'But remember, they are with us all the time, watching over us, even when they're very far away.'

I peeped out from beneath the covers. 'Thank you, Miss.'

She dipped her chin in a brisk nod, patted the bedcovers encouragingly and tugged a crease from the top blanket before she took one final turn around the room and closed the door behind her. Maybe I'd imagined the tears in Miss Kent's eyes, but the thought of it made me wonder if a grown-up could miss her mother, too. Perhaps we were all missing someone; all waiting for the fighting and wars to end so we could see them again.

Long after the other girls had settled down, Sprout was still fidgeting in her bed beside mine.

'Can't sleep?' I whispered.

'No,' she replied.

'Me neither.'

We were both silent for a moment.

'Plum?' she whispered, eventually.

'Yes.'

'Did your mother ever kiss you goodnight?'

'Every night,' I replied, smiling at the memory. 'Did yours?'

There was a long silence. 'No.'

It was one of the saddest things I'd ever heard.

I lay still for a few minutes before I pushed back the covers, placed my bare feet on the cold boards and tiptoed the few steps toward Sprout's bed. She was just visible in the moonlight, her hair painted silver against her pillow.

I leaned forward and kissed her on the forehead. 'Goodnight, Sprout,' I whispered. 'Sleep tight. See you in the morning.'

I was about to step back into bed when she said she was still cold.

I hesitated for just a moment, grabbed my doll, and climbed into Sprout's bed, tucking in tight beside her and pulling the sheets and blankets right up to our chins.

'Is that better?' I whispered.

'Yes. Sleep tight, Plum. See you in the morning.'

Huddled together like sardines, we fell asleep with our arms wrapped around each other and our cotton nightdresses tangled around our legs. It was the best night's sleep I'd had in ages; the sleep of those who feel safe, and warm.

I would think about it often in the long months ahead.

ELSPETH

With everything changing so quickly, the headmaster still missing, and my mother's letter an awful constant reminder that Alfie was also missing, I was desperate to do something to feel that I was in control. So, despite the threat of reprisals should we be found out, I mentioned my idea of the food drop to Charlie Harris.

'Even a small amount could make a big difference to the local farmers and their families,' I said. 'And we should have enough to see us through until we are rescued, and repatriated.'

'I suppose we can't expect others to put themselves in danger to help us if we're not willing to do the same for our neighbours,' he agreed. 'The servants were loyal for so many years. It feels only right that we help them now, especially during the season of goodwill.'

With Charlie's encouragement, I raised the idea at the staff meeting that evening. The soldiers were used to our get-togethers and didn't seem overly suspicious of us, although I was still twitchy every time we met, and felt as though we all had a sign on our backs saying 'UP TO NO GOOD'.

The food drop was approved by everyone, although it was agreed that we should refer to it as 'Operation F' in case the soldiers got wind of what we were planning.

'You can't be too careful,' Tom Martin warned. 'Best not to give anything away.' Tom was the Latin master in the Boys' School. Usually a very quiet and unfortunately dour fellow, as ex-military he had rather come into his own since the arrival of the soldiers. 'I already have an arrangement in place with one of the farmers, as it happens,' he announced, much to our surprise. 'We meet at the wall beside the sports pitch so that he can pass on news of any Allied developments. I will do the necessary.'

Two days later, we met again to finalize the plans.

'Righty-ho then. Let battle commence!' Tom unrolled a large sheet of A3 paper, onto which he'd drawn a detailed plan of the school buildings and a series of dashed and dotted lines indicating where people were to be positioned. He tapped the side of his nose conspiratorially. 'X marks the spot for the rendezvous.'

I glanced at Minnie, who'd got a fit of the giggles and had to pretend to blow her nose to hide her amusement.

It had certainly become a far more complex operation than I'd anticipated when I'd first suggested it. Tom was evidently thriving under the challenge. His plan was to lower the food parcels over the wall at the far end of the sports field. This was the boundary furthest from the guards, and led directly into the kaoliang fields, so there was plenty of cover to protect those retrieving the parcels. Whatever punishments the guards might hand out to us if they found us passing food to our Chinese friends, the consequences would be far worse for their hated enemy.

'If we're careful, we shouldn't get caught,' Tom added, apparently reading my thoughts as he rolled up his plan.

'Was anybody thinking that?' I asked, glancing at my colleagues.

Charlie leaned forward and smiled encouragingly. 'I suspect we all were, but fortune favours the brave. Isn't that right, Miss Kent?'

I took a sip of anaemic tea. 'Absolutely, Master Harris.' My spoon dropped against my saucer with a clatter. 'And it's quite all right to call me Elspeth,' I added.

Before drawing the meeting to a close, Tom asked if there were any questions.

'Just one,' I said, putting down my teacup and saucer. 'I wondered where I'll be positioned during the *manoeuvres*. I don't believe you mentioned me.'

Tom looked surprised. 'Well. No. I didn't mention you. This isn't a job for a woman, Miss Kent. I'd rather assumed you would be positioned beneath your eiderdown, fast asleep.'

I took a deep breath. 'Yes. I thought as much. But . . . well . . . since this whole thing was *my* idea, I'd assumed I would be rather more part of the action end of things than the sleeping end of things. Perhaps I could assist with the job of lookout? Two sets of eyes are better than one, after all.'

I felt the heat rise to my cheeks and wished everyone would stop staring at me, Minnie especially. Her teacup was suspended in mid-air. When nobody said anything to suggest otherwise, it was agreed that I would also report to the music room at midnight. I was instructed to dress in my darkest clothing.

Minnie was still agog as we walked back to our bedrooms.

'I say, Els. That was quite something. I had no idea you were planning to get involved.' She looked worried. 'I rather wish you wouldn't.'

'I had no idea I was planning to be involved either, but I found it infuriating the way Tom went crashing on with his *manoeuvres* and taking all the credit. Women need to take a stand sometimes, even if we *would* rather be fast asleep beneath our eiderdowns.' I stepped into my room. 'I'll give you a full debrief first thing tomorrow. Sleep tight.'

I doubted very much whether anybody would get any sleep. Espionage and good deeds were all very well, but they didn't exactly make for a restful night.

Fortune did indeed favour the brave, and luck was on our side. The moon was hidden behind a curtain of thick cloud that night, leaving the school bathed in perfect darkness. It had been agreed that our best chance to make a dash for it was just after midnight, when the guards changed shifts and often dallied over a cigarette or two.

Bundled up in as many layers as I could comfortably wear while still being able to run if necessary, I crept downstairs and out through the kitchens where Tom and Charlie were already waiting. To my surprise, Eleanor Yarwood was there, too.

'What on earth are you doing here?' I whispered, urging her to go back inside immediately.

'I'm making a stand, Elspeth. Besides, I couldn't let you go scampering about in the dark on your own with Tom and Charlie. I'm coming with you. Like it or not.'

I didn't like it but, evidently, her mind was made up.

Between our party of four, we carried the food parcels toward the sports field where Charlie retrieved a length of rope he'd concealed there earlier. He proceeded to tie intermittent reef knots to secure the parcels in stages.

We huddled against the wall then, waiting for the signal from Tom's contact. My heart thumped so hard I was certain the guards would hear and send their dogs to investigate.

After a few minutes, the cry of a pond heron broke the silence. '*Khaaa. Khaaa.*'

Without speaking, Tom indicated that was our signal. Hoisted up by Charlie, he expertly tossed one end of the rope over the wall where it found its accomplice. All we could do then was sit tight, and wait, and keep watch over the darkness of the sports field as the rope tightened and slackened in turn as the parcels were untied. After a short while, there was a sharp tug on the rope and Tom and Charlie pulled together to haul it back over the wall.

The deed was done.

Coiling the rope deftly around his arm, Charlie motioned for us to start walking back, but as we did there was a break in the clouds and one of the dogs set up a ferocious barking. We fell to the ground, keeping as low and still as possible, our faces pressed against the frozen earth as an arc of distant torchlight swept across the darkness in front of us. I held my breath. What was I thinking, coming out here, putting myself, and others, in danger? This wasn't a game, or a spy novel. It was real life, and we were only schoolteachers who didn't know the first thing about war.

After what felt like an eternity, the barking stopped, the light disappeared, and everything became dark and silent again. Hesitantly, we stood up.

'That was a close one,' Charlie whispered. 'Gets the old ticker going, doesn't it! Right, let's get back, quick sharp.'

We scuttled across the sports field, keeping as low as we could. I was never more grateful to see the entrance to the school. Once inside, we didn't hang about, dispersing like oil in water, eager to get back to our rooms before the soldiers suspected anything.

Charlie pressed a piece of paper into my hand as I turned to go. 'This was tied to the rope when it came back over the wall.'

My name was written on the front. *Miss Elspeth*.

Without stopping to ask any questions, I hurried back to my bedroom and closed the door. Too afraid to switch on a light in case I drew the attention of the guards, I fumbled in the dark, placed the letter beneath my pillow, and climbed into bed fully clothed. I was restless and anxious, disturbed by every creak and crack from the dark corridors and empty classrooms. The sounds I'd once found familiar and comforting, I now didn't trust at all. Beneath the bedcovers, I gripped the handle of my hockey stick. It wasn't much, but it offered some small reassurance at least.

I woke at first light, relieved to have navigated the rest of the night without incident.

I pulled back the shutters to lend the room some light, and took the note from beneath my pillow. I guessed who it was from before I broke the seal. Inside was a delicate paper kingfisher, and a paper lotus flower. On a scrap of paper, the words, *Rise from the mud, and bloom* were written. The intricate folded shapes held such kindness and simple beauty that I couldn't help but smile. They were an important reminder that even while the world was at war, it was still possible to touch someone's heart; still possible to think of others. I hoped Shu Lan was safe. I couldn't bear to think of her suffering again as she had already suffered once before.

I put the papers onto the bedcovers and walked to the window. Outside, a couple of the guards – Home Run, and the silent one the children called Charlie Chaplin – sat quietly beneath the plane trees where I'd read to the girls that summer. I wondered if they knew how deeply their intrusion had affected us, if they understood that without dropping any bombs, they'd destroyed, just as violently, the sense of safety and harmony that had always existed here?

Before I'd arrived in China, I hadn't really thought about what it would mean to teach the children of missionaries and diplomats. I was just pleased to get the position, and to be leaving the suffocating claustrophobia of home. It wasn't until the end of my second term when I'd fully understood that the children could be separated from their parents for months on end, or how uncomfortable that would make me feel.

A number of the children had now been apart from their parents for two years or more, and none of us could offer any firm reassurance as to when they would see them again. For some, it was too much to bear. They'd become withdrawn and morose, too young to understand why their parents had chosen to put the work of the mission before them; too polite and well-behaved to complain. As their teachers, we saw how much the children struggled and suffered, we heard their stifled sobs and calmed them down after a nightmare, and yet their mothers and fathers saw only the well-educated, well-presented children they came to collect whenever their work allowed. The contradiction didn't sit well with me, and as I stood at the window, watching the two young soldiers talk quietly to each other and share stories of the photographs they pulled from their pockets, I dared to wonder the unspeakable: that Japan wasn't the only enemy. Perhaps the status and privilege that had taken Chefoo's children thousands of miles from home were as much to blame for the situation they now faced: separated from their families; cut off from the rest of the world.

I thought of Lillian Plummer, and the impromptu promise I'd made to her on the wharfside in Shanghai. She must know by now that the school was under Japanese guard. As Charlie had proven with his makeshift radio, and Tom with his secret contact, despite Japan's occupation of China, there was always some way to get information. Was Lillian desperately waiting for news, or was she confident in our ability to manage the situation? I thought of my own agony in not knowing where Alfie was, and not knowing how to help him. Was the agony of prolonged separation from a loved one worse than the finality of death? I'd known both, and I didn't have an answer.

I closed the shutters, and turned away from the window.

I didn't have an answer for any of this.

NANCY

Nobody talked about the fact that it was nearly Christmas. Even when we had our final rehearsal for the Christmas carol concert, and sang my favourite, 'O! Holy Night', I didn't feel excited. If anything, the fact that it was nearly Christmas only made me feel sadder about everything being as it was and not as it should be.

The teachers put on a good show of everything going along quite nicely, and did their best to jolly us along with games of winter rounders and brisk walks to the bay. Miss Kent and Miss Butterworth found clever ways to make challenges and games from our chores: who could make their bed the fastest, who had the best hospital corners and who could fold their clothes the neatest. We became so good at making our beds and keeping the dorm tidy that I wondered why we'd ever needed Shu Lan and the other servants to do it for us.

After a busy day of lessons and exercise and doing our share of domestic chores, we fell into our beds exhausted, too tired to talk about the usual silly things, like who we would marry, and how many children we wanted to have. We always remembered to say a prayer for our liberation, no matter how tired we were, but although I said the words and the Amen along with the others, I wasn't absolutely certain God was listening. Mouse said that with the whole world at war, there must be so many people saying so many prayers that He couldn't possibly have time to answer them all.

'Don't you wish you'd gone home for Christmas, Mouse?' I asked as we walked to breakfast together. Sprout had been sent back to the San because of her cough, so I'd paired up with Mouse instead. Her hand was bony and cold in mine. It felt like holding a bundle of frosty sticks.

'I don't really mind. I prefer being here,' she mumbled. She kept her gaze fixed on her scuffed shoes. Sprout said Mouse's eyes looked like they'd fallen too far into her face and might disappear entirely if she wasn't careful. I just thought she looked unbearably sad all the time.

'Don't you miss your mother though?' I pressed, prepared to do most of the talking. 'I miss mine terribly. I sometimes get a pain in my tummy when I think about her. Sprout calls it a Mummy Ache! She says the funniest things, doesn't she!'

'My mother died when I was a baby.'

I stopped walking. I wasn't sure which was worse: to discover that Mouse's mother was dead, or to realize it had taken me two whole years to find out.

'Gosh, Mouse. That's awfully sad.'

She shrugged. 'Not really. How can you be sad about someone you never knew?'

I didn't have an answer for that. 'But there must be photographs of her? And what about your father?' I hardly dared ask if she had any brothers or sisters I'd never heard of.

'He's busy with his work at the embassy in Shanghai. I'm only a nuisance to him when I'm at home.'

I tightened my grip on her hand as we walked on. 'Why didn't you say anything before? About your mother?'

She hesitated for a moment before she turned to look at me. 'Nobody ever asked.'

We walked the rest of the way to the dining room in silence.

I didn't have much of an appetite that morning, which was just as well. Another thing that had changed since the soldiers had arrived were the reduced portions at mealtimes and no second helpings.

'I didn't think we'd see rationing quite so soon,' Edward said when I mentioned it to him. 'But it's sensible of the teachers to be cautious. Just in case.'

'Just in case what?' I asked.

'In case we're here longer than anyone is expecting.' He looked ever so serious when he spoke.

'How long is longer than anyone is expecting?'

He glanced at me and shook his head. 'Wars can go on for years, Nonny. I'm afraid we could be here for a very long time.'

It wasn't like Edward to be so gloomy. It made me feel all prickly and sad.

We were all gathered in the assembly hall, where several of us had turned the PE benches upside down so we could practise our gymnastics. Me and Mouse spent an hour pretending we were on the beam in an Olympic competition. Mouse was very good at it, but I wobbled off more than I stayed on.

'You'll have to keep practising if you're ever going to make the British team,' Edward teased.

He had his sights firmly set on being an Olympic runner, like his hero, Eric Liddell, who'd won gold at the Paris Olympics and, by funny coincidence, now worked as a missionary in northern China. Edward had once asked Daddy about him in a letter home. *Have you come across Mr Liddell on your travels?*

If you do, would you tell him I'd very much like to meet him one day.

But Edward didn't go on about Mr Liddell or the Olympics that afternoon. Even Larry Crofton couldn't cheer him up. He went off to talk to some of the other boys instead.

'I still believe the Navy will come to rescue us, Edward,' I said as I watched Larry saunter across the hall in that ever-so-confident way of his. 'I suspect they're just terribly busy with the other bits of the war.' I offered him a mint imperial to cheer him up.

He smiled half-heartedly and ruffled my hair. 'Where'd you get the mints?' he asked. 'Not from Home Run, I hope?'

I stared at a gap between the floorboards, my answer written all over my face.

'You're such a silly girl, Nonny. I told you not to talk to him.'

'But he's one of the nice ones,' I said. 'He wants the war to end, and to go home, just as much as we do.'

Home Run had shown me and Mouse a photograph of his children, who were the same age as us. He'd told us he missed them, and his home near the ocean. He sometimes gave us a piece of fresh fruit, or a few sweets, as long as we promised not to tell the others, or our teachers.

Edward wasn't convinced that any of the guards were nice. 'Just be careful,' he cautioned. 'I don't trust him. I don't trust any of them.'

Whatever Edward thought, I didn't believe Home Run was a bad man, or the same as all the other soldiers. If I believed that, what hope was there for any of us?

ELSPETH

'Penny for them?' Minnie said as we took a stroll around the cricket pitch, closely watched from a distance by Trouble and his minions. 'You're awfully quiet today.'

'Sorry, Min. I'm tired, and I have a thumping headache.'

'Is it your Alfie?' She lowered her voice as she spoke, the way we all did whenever we mentioned news from home, which wasn't often. Since the outbreak of war in Europe, we'd learned to avoid discussing anything that might provoke an emotional response, as if it were an infection we might catch if we got too close.

I nodded. 'How did you know?'

'I always know.' She smiled. 'You might think you're a closed book, but I know you better than you think.'

'It's like he's disappeared off the face of the earth, and I'm stuck here and can't do a thing about it.' I couldn't hide the fear and frustration in my voice.

'Try not to worry, Els dear.' She placed her hand on my shoulder. 'I'm sure he's safe and well. Chin up, eh.'

I smiled thinly, grateful for her concern and reassurance, but

I couldn't share her optimism. Alfie's absence worried me greatly, and my concern only increased with each day that passed without any word from him, or my mother.

With letters from home no longer reliably getting through to us, we were as starved of news and information as we were of a decent meal. When we listened for the faint crackle of a signal on Charlie's radio, it felt like listening for the splash of a stone dropped into a deep well. Each night, we dropped our pebbles of hope and listened for an echo, for news of an Allied victory, or something to let us know our loved ones were safe or, at the very least, to give us hope.

'I just wish I could be out there, looking for him, demanding some answers from the Ministry, but what can I do, stuck here, with *them* watching our every move?'

I was beginning to resent Chefoo School and all its privileges. I shouldn't have even been there. I should have been sitting in the puddle of winter sunlight at the kitchen table back home in York, sharing a pot of tea with my mother. I should have been waiting for the rattle of the milk van down the lane, and the squeak of the front gate as the postman called. I should have been picking snowdrops from the garden and walking by the mill race and watching the minnows in the shallows by the riverbank.

'I'm sure Alfie's worried about you, too. He'll be ever so proud when he hears about all this,' Minnie added. 'It's not everyone can say they have a sister in China, making a jolly good fist of things, despite being under armed guard.'

Would Alfie be proud? Or worried? He was the only one who'd encouraged me to come to China. All anyone else had said was, Why China? Why leave Yorkshire at all? But not Alfie. He'd put his arm around my shoulder and said, 'Why not? What have you got to lose?' Plenty, as it turned out. I had plenty to lose.

'Are you hoping to hear from anyone?' I asked, to change the subject. 'From home?'

'Not especially,' she replied. 'Mother was never one for letter-writing. She's a woman of very few words.'

'And there's nobody else who might write?'

Minnie picked up her pace a little. 'No. There's nobody else.' She pushed her hands into her coat pockets. 'Come along. We'd better get back.'

As Christmas approached, a dozen children were confined to the San with coughs and chest infections brought on by the cold weather. I hated to see any of the children poorly, but it was especially hard around Christmas time. Dorothy Hinshaw's cough bothered me particularly. The child hadn't been in full health since she'd returned from a holiday to the coast with her parents that summer.

The most senior school nurse, Eve Walsh (known rather cruelly as 'Prune' to the children because of her wrinkled skin), wasn't happy with Dorothy's health either.

'I'd like to see an improvement soon,' she said. 'She usually bounces back much faster.'

Nurse Eve was a temperate soul and a very sensible, practical woman. I liked her a lot, and was very glad she was with us, along with two other school nurses. I had a horrible feeling we would need their experience more than ever in the weeks ahead.

As part of our roster for the day-to-day running of the school, I'd volunteered to assist in the Sanitorium when required.

'It was always assumed I would go into nursing,' I said as I helped to organize and count the medical supplies. 'My mother was a nurse with the British Red Cross, and my great-grand-mother trained as a Nightingale. She served under the great lady herself in the Crimea.'

'Really! Gosh. That's quite the thing.' Nurse Eve frowned as she rummaged through boxes of medicine bottles and sterilizing fluid. 'So why didn't you? Become a nurse? I'd say you'd have been rather suited to it.'

I marked the tally for calamine lotion, camphor and gauze on my sheet as Nurse Eve called them out to me. 'I'm not really sure. Stubbornness, probably. Determined to do something different to prove to my mother that I didn't always have to follow her plan for me.'

'Teaching is an admirable profession. She must be very proud of you.'

I laughed. 'I don't think my mother has ever been proud of me. I'm afraid I'm rather a perpetual disappointment to her. When the idea of nursing was abandoned, she suggested I become a shop girl in a department store, like my cousin. Mother thought it was quite refined, as far as shop work goes. "*They wear evening dresses in the afternoons, Elspeth.*"'

Nurse Eve chuckled as I imitated my mother. 'Well, I'm glad you didn't become a shop girl,' she said. 'It would be a shame if a talented teacher like you spent her days serving silly posh knickers to silly posh people.'

'Thankfully, I've never paid much attention to what my mother wanted me to do. The department store was destroyed by a Nazi bomb last December. My cousin was killed. It could so easily have been me.'

Nurse Eve turned to look at me as the now familiar shouting of bayonet practice started up outside. 'It could still be you, Elspeth. It could be any one of us, at any time.' She closed the cupboard door and stood up with a sigh. 'Let's hope everyone's in good health this winter. There's just about enough to see us through the usual coughs and colds, but if there's an outbreak of a more serious infection . . .' She shook her head as we moved on to organize the linen cupboard.

'What about using traditional Chinese medicine?' I suggested. 'Wei Huan told me they use ginseng, cinnamon, liquorice and something called wolfberry.'

She laughed and said it sounded more like a list of ingredients for a Christmas cake than medicine. 'I shouldn't scoff,' she added as she placed her hands on her hips and let out a weary sigh. 'If we're here for the foreseeable, cinnamon and liquorice might be our only option.'

I couldn't sleep that night. I lay awake in the dark, thinking about our dwindling medical supplies. With the Shanghai International Settlement now under the control of the Imperial Japanese Army, we were completely cut off from all financial and supply support from Mission HQ. At that evening's staff meeting, Minnie and Eleanor had also reported that food supplies were worse than we'd thought. I didn't understand how stock had dwindled so quickly. Although deliveries from Mission HQ in Shanghai had become increasingly unreliable in recent months, held up by bad weather and the many checkpoints established to deliberately cause disruption across the country, and while rationing back home had also seen imports from Britain stop some time ago, we'd still believed we had sufficient supplies to see us through several months. We'd even done one more food drop over the wall, after which we'd decided it was probably best to leave it for a while, in case we aroused suspicion.

Certain the two women had miscounted, and unable to rest until I'd checked, I threw on my slippers and housecoat, and crept from my room. My hand lamp cast disconcerting shadows against the walls of the long corridors as I made my way down to the kitchens.

I heard the whispers before I saw the three men, helping themselves to our food.

Heart in my mouth, I ducked behind a cupboard, covered the

lamp with my housecoat and crouched down low. I couldn't see their faces, but I could tell from their clothing that they weren't Japanese guards. My first instinct was to shout at them and scare them off, but I held my tongue and kept as quiet as I could, afraid of what they might do if they discovered a woman alone in her night attire. I pushed the thought from my mind, gripped the collar of my nightdress and pulled the belt of my housecoat tight around my waist.

I hardly dared breathe as I watched them fill two straw baskets with our provisions. I thought about the children asleep upstairs, already going to bed hungry each night. My fear quickly turned to anger. This was wrong. It was all wrong.

I was about to scream for help when they turned to leave, and I saw a face I recognized. Wei Huan. Except, it wasn't the Wei Huan I knew, the man who had so carefully tended the school gardens, and always had a smile for the children. This man's face was hard and anxious. This man was afraid and hungry, prepared to do anything to help his family. I stayed where I was and let the three of them pass as I tried to steady my trembling hands.

When I was sure they'd gone, I hurried back to my room and climbed beneath the covers. I lay awake for hours, wrestling with my conscience. Had I done the right thing in letting Wei Huan go? To my shame, I knew only what little Shu Lan had told me about how Japan's occupation of China had affected the population, but I knew that while our struggles were only just beginning, theirs had been ongoing for years. Were their needs greater than ours? Our older boys, especially, had started to complain of being hungry, and I'd noticed they were becoming listless, lacking the energy and calories their growing limbs needed. Not for the first time since the soldiers had marched into the school, I realized how shortsighted we'd been to believe we were somehow immune from the reality of war. For a group of adults whose roles as Guide and Scout leaders often led us to talk about the need to Be Prepared, we found ourselves severely lacking.

As night turned to dawn, my torment over the stolen food led me back to other decisions and indecisions in my life; moments when I'd hesitated instead of acted. Like a chain connecting my past to my present, it all linked together, leading me to this exact moment in a sparse little bedroom in China, lit by a blue December dawn. I closed my eyes and thought about Alfie, willing us both to find the courage to endure the circumstances we found ourselves in.

The thieves returned the next night, relieving us of more of our meagre supplies, and also taking some of the girls' winter coats from their hooks in the corridor. When it was discussed at the staff meeting, the consensus was that it must be the local farmers.

'There's no other reasonable explanation,' Minnie said. 'The soldiers are kept so well fed by their superiors I don't see why they'd need to steal from us. It must be the farmers. It might even be some of the school servants, in which case I can't be angry. I'm sure they're starving out there.'

I almost admitted what I'd seen, but I couldn't bear to betray Wei Huan, so I kept the secret to myself, my guilt a little assuaged by Minnie's refusal to condemn the thieves.

'And what about the coats?' Eleanor Yarwood asked. 'How will the children keep warm without them?'

'The Ministry in Britain issued instructions to parents for keeping their children warm last winter,' I offered. 'My mother wrote about it in a letter. She has a couple of evacuee children staying with her. She was advised to wrap a layer of newspaper next to their skin, and to dress them with two extra layers beneath their pinafores. A woollen vest, preferably. We could repurpose wool from any spare gloves and socks.'

'Ah yes. Make Do and Mend,' Amelia Prescott added. 'Housewives can turn their hand to anything these days. Darn, alter, unpick, re-stitch, cover holes with patches, turn men's clothes into women's and vice versa. It's a terrific idea, Miss Kent.'

'Mending and repurposing isn't the difficult part,' I said, rather more curtly than I'd intended. I found Amelia's relentless vigour and good cheer increasingly overbearing. 'It's the making do we have no comprehension of. I have a horrible feeling our hardships are only just beginning.'

'Either way, it looks like Christmas dinner will be a rather frugal affair,' Minnie sighed. 'More trimmings than goose.'

She looked tired and drawn and her hair had lost some of its shine.

I leaned my head wearily against her shoulder. 'Trimmings it is then, Mister Scrooge.'

We both laughed, quietly at first and then louder, until we were both bent double, tears streaming down our cheeks, and then the others, infected by our laughter, started to laugh too. There was nothing amusing about the situation at all, but it felt good to laugh. Who could tell if our tears were from mirth or despair? Nobody knew. And nobody asked.

On Christmas Eve, the temperature continued to plummet, along with any hope of being rescued in time to spend Christmas with our families. The final acknowledgement that our prayers hadn't been answered and that the children wouldn't be reunited with their parents was too much for some of them to bear. Their resilience and fortitude had been thoroughly tested over the past few weeks, and despite all the optimism and certainty that we wouldn't be left under Japanese guard for more than a few inconvenient days, we had been proven wrong. Worse still, we had let the children down.

I felt completely helpless as I stopped at the dormitory door that night to check on the girls, most of whom were still wide awake. Whispering after lights out was tolerated a little longer on special occasions. There was, after all, a lot for the children to discuss.

'Nancy Plummer! Dorothy Hinshaw!' I whispered. 'That's enough talking now. Go to sleep.'

'I can't sleep, Miss,' Nancy whispered back. 'I can never sleep on Christmas Eve.'

I walked over to her bed, my footsteps making the boards creak as restless bodies sent bedsprings pinging all around the room. As I tucked the stiff blankets around Nancy's body, it struck me how the girls always looked so much smaller in their beds. Too small to be spending Christmas away from their parents.

'Shall we say "Taps"?' I whispered. 'Would that help?'

Nancy wriggled beneath the starched sheets and blankets, delighted to have my attention to herself as we sang together, our voices feather-like whispers in the dark. As we sang, the others joined in.

'Day is done / Gone the sun, / From the lakes, from the hills, from the sky! / All is well / Safely rest, / God is nigh.'

As the final note faded into the darkness, I stood up straight and tugged a final crease from Nancy's blanket.

'Goodnight, Brown Owl,' she whispered.

Like a breeze on the surface of a pond, that one whisper set off a ripple as the others echoed Nancy's words, and a gentle chorus of 'Goodnight, Brown Owl' filled the room.

Even I couldn't deny the surge of compassion that swelled in my heart.

'Goodnight, Brownies,' I whispered. 'Happy Christmas.'

As I closed the door and walked to my bedroom, it dawned on me that perhaps this was why I'd come to China; why life had led me here, at this time of war and great uncertainty. I was here to step into the shoes of all the absent parents. I was here to watch over these temporary orphans of war. I was here to become the mother I'd always hoped to be. Only now that the opportunity presented itself, I found myself full of fear and doubt.

A low winter sun settled above the distant mountains that Christmas morning, painting the sky in shades of violet and pink as we led the children across the snow-covered pathways to the chapel for the Christmas service. I'd never seen a sky more peaceful, or beautiful, and never wished more that I were somewhere else, and hadn't seen it at all.

'Merry Christmas' greetings were exchanged with a mixture of hope and despair, our good wishes caught on frosty breaths that drifted skywards before being carried away, across the rice fields and the ocean. How easily our words found freedom.

As the bright melody of the children's voices sent the carols soaring up into the rafters, I noticed a number of the guards standing quietly at the back of the chapel. I wondered if they heard the hope and innocence in the children's voices; if they understood the sentiments of peace and goodwill to all men.

As we led the children back to the school for a morning of games, the guards stood aside to make room for us to pass. Only one stepped forward, blocking my way as I made to walk through the chapel door.

Trouble.

He stared at me, his dark eyes intense and yet expressionless; the now familiar sneering smile at his lips.

'It is Christmas, Elspeth Kent,' he whispered. 'The British give presents. Do you have one for me?'

I was deeply uncomfortable beneath his scrutiny. 'I don't understand?'

He laughed. 'All women have a gift for men.' He flicked the end of my skirt with his stick.

I swallowed hard, desperately trying not to show any sign of intimidation or fear.

'Is everything quite all right, Miss Kent?'

I turned, relieved to see Charlie over my shoulder.

'Go,' Trouble hissed, clearly annoyed by the interruption. 'I will take my gift another day.'

As he stalked away, I stood, rooted to the spot.

'What was all that about?' Charlie asked. 'Was he making a nuisance of himself?'

I fussed with my gloves and the buttons on my coat because Charlie's eyes were so gentle and kind compared to Trouble's, and every bone in my body wanted to tell him everything – about the sinister threats, and how desperately afraid of him I was.

'Just passing on Christmas wishes. Isn't it marvellous how the Christmas spirit touches everyone?'

Charlie smiled, although there was a hint of concern in his eyes.

'Indeed,' he conceded. 'And a very merry Christmas to you, Elspeth.'

'And to you,' I replied. 'God bless us, every one!' We looked at each other for a hopeless moment, full of what-ifs and maybes. 'We'd better get back,' I said. 'I'm in charge of pin the tail on the donkey, and, so far, I have neither donkey, nor tail.'

We made the day as happy as we could for the children, and somehow provided a reasonable Christmas dinner. Minnie even unearthed some Christmas puddings that had been made months earlier and were absolutely delicious. But no matter how jolly we tried to make things, or how staunchly the children ignored their stomachs' growls of hunger, it was hard to ignore the fact that there was more plate than food. Still, the children were easily distracted by a few games, and went to bed as happy as could be expected.

I thought about Christmases at home in England, and how we'd gathered around the wireless to listen to the King's Christmas message. It had always struck me as remarkable that our Sovereign's faltering words could find their way into our sitting room in Yorkshire. We'd listened to the Christmas speech every year since George V had first addressed the Empire across the wireless on Christmas Day, 1932. One year, when our wireless wasn't working, we were invited to the Evans's, the new family who'd moved in at the end of the street. I hardly heard any of the speech that Christmas Day, distracted by Harry's knee occasionally knocking against mine. He asked me to the local dance that New Year's Eve, and asked me to marry him exactly a year later, on the stroke of midnight. I said yes, and yes, and yes! I loved him then, and I loved him still, just the same. I missed him no less than when I'd only just lost him, but I also heard him gently reminding me that I had a different life now, new responsibilities, and that I had to pull my socks up and get on with it.

I wished, more than ever, that I could sit beside Harry once more and listen to the King's words of comfort and reassurance. I closed my eyes, permitting myself a quiet moment to remember loved ones far away. Wherever Alfie was, I hoped he'd heard the King's Christmas message, and that he saw how brightly the stars shone that Christmas night. It was as if they shone for us all; bright beacons of hope in the dark.

I would often look at the stars in the long months ahead, remembering our first uncertain Christmas under occupation, and wondering when we would ever see our last.

THE GUIDE LAW: A GUIDE SMILES AND SINGS
UNDER ALL DIFFICULTIES

It has been scientifically proved that if you deliberately make your voice and face cheerful and bright you imme-diately begin to feel that way . . . 'as cheerful as a Girl Scout' ought to become a proverb.

ELSPETH

1942

O ur first year under Japanese guard felt like many more. As the first disruptive weeks had turned to months, and months began to reach toward a year of occupation, my greatest fear was no longer the soldiers at the school gates, but the awful possibility that we'd been forgotten.

We shared our concerns at our nightly staff meeting, ever more conscious of our remote location, and the thousands of miles between us and Churchill's War Cabinet. Our initial confidence in being rescued had gradually diminished until the possibility was barely mentioned at all. Sketchy reports of Allied and enemy progress in Europe and the Pacific reached us in unreliable fragments relayed through Charlie's increasingly temperamental radio, and, while our hopes were lifted by news of Allied successes in the South Pacific during the Battle of Coral Sea and the Battle of Midway, which had inflicted significant damage on the Imperial Japanese Navy fleet, still we waited for a liberation that didn't come. War raged on and, as it did, we each fought a very private battle of our own courage and faith.

Thankfully, our resilience and optimism fluctuated in turns, so we never all lost hope together. No matter how helpless things seemed, there was always someone around to offer a bolstering word or two. Charlie was a rock of immense practicality and sense, and, as ever, Minnie was my trusty stalwart. She'd also become my roommate after we'd settled on an arrangement to top and tail in my bed.

'I was wondering if, perhaps, it wouldn't be awfully strange if we were to, well, bunk up together,' she'd said out of the blue one day as we folded bedsheets. 'I know we have to put on a brave face for the children, but I can't settle at night. Even with my hockey stick, every time I hear a noise, I think it's one of them coming to . . . you know.'

All the women in the school feared the unspeakable. The ghosts of Nanking hung heavy around Chefoo's walls and, while Trouble hadn't spoken directly to me again since his sinister talk of Christmas gifts, I was always on high alert whenever he was around. I agreed to the idea instantly. Minnie snored like a walrus, and her cold toes pressed into my elbow, but it was oddly comforting all the same.

In early February, a couple of months into our occupation, our flagging optimism had been rewarded with the return of our headmaster, Mr Collins. While he wouldn't (or couldn't) say where he'd been, it had clearly affected him profoundly. He was worryingly thin and grey-faced when he addressed us at assembly.

'While many of our privileges and liberties have been curtailed, our captors cannot prevent us from learning, or improving our minds. School exams will continue as planned in the months ahead,' he announced. We all listened in awe, admiring his gentle strength and humility. 'I know I can rely on you all to study hard, and I am confident that you will carry the good name of Chefoo School with you as you go forth into adulthood.'

Some of the older girls and several teachers began sniffling into handkerchiefs pulled hastily from cardigan sleeves and skirt pockets. The headmaster's return provided a welcome boost to morale, not to mention enormous personal relief to those of us who'd been so desperately worried about him.

'I hear we have a new Girl Guides patrol, Miss Kent,' he said as we walked back to our classrooms.

'Yes. We now have eight proud members of Kingfisher Patrol,' I replied. 'It's been a welcome distraction for them.'

'I'm sure it has. And I believe the girls have been quite industrious in their efforts to help around the school.'

'They've been marvellous. I'm not sure what I would have done without them.'

He smiled. 'I'm quite sure it is the other way around. Keep going, Miss Kent. They're relying on you.'

Winter made way for a fragrant spring, when the plum trees burst into flower and brought a much-needed sense of renewal and hope. But spring, in turn, melted away beneath the fierce heat of a summer sun that saw us wither and wilt like the flowers in Wei Huan's neglected gardens.

As I turned over the parched soil, Minnie came running from the direction of the Boys' School, her arms flapping madly.

'Elspeth. Quickly! Come and see!' She was out of breath when she reached me.

Before I had time to respond, she grabbed my arm and dragged me along behind her.

'What is it? Have the Navy arrived?' I asked the question out of habit rather than any real hope that it was true.

'Pish. Don't be silly. Just come and see, will you!'

Too hot and weary to resist, I let her drag me along until she came to a sudden stop beside the south-facing wall of the Boys' School.

'Look!' She pointed at a small green shoot in the ground.

'Is that it?'

'Look closer!' She folded her arms, evidently delighted with herself.

I bent down to take a closer look. Two healthy green leaves spread out from the top of the shoot, like hands ready to catch a ball. On the ground beneath lay the husk of a small grey seed. I picked it up.

'A sunflower seed. It can't be possible.'

Minnie crouched down beside me as we peered at the tiny little seed husk in the palm of my hand. 'It grew, Els,' she whispered. 'It found a way. Isn't it marvellous!'

The sunflower seed Trouble had cruelly stamped into the ground had grown in the very spot where it had fallen. I brushed my fingertips across the fragile green leaves. The sight of that tiny shoot gave me more strength and hope than any prayer ever had. I thought of the words on the scrap of paper from Shu Lan. *Rise from the mud, and bloom.*

The resilience of that little flower, and all that it stood for, finally saw me crack. I sank onto my knees and wept without embarrassment or apology. Minnie wrapped her arms around me, and held me like a child.

Over the following weeks, the girls cared for the sunflower as if it were the most precious thing in the world. In many ways, it was. They sang to it and watered it and supported it with pea canes when it grew taller. As it followed the sun and outgrew even the tallest girls, that single neglected sunflower came to represent the struggle and resilience of us all. In full bloom it was magnificent. Within its bright face, and its quiet determination to thrive, I saw every one of us, and I knew that we, too, would somehow prevail.

The Bird in the Bamboo Cage

Autumn in China was an artist's dream. As the leaves on the maple and gingko trees turned, the mountains burst into nuggets of rich golds and dazzling reds, and long beams of amber sunlight reached like fingertips across the bay. Everything was clearer beneath the autumn skies: crisp edges, rich colours and a temperature far kinder to hair with a natural curl than the sticky humidity of summer.

Apart from the changing seasons, time passed in a blur of sameness, but one constant barometer of progression was the children. Even war couldn't hold back what nature intended, and they continued to grow, upwards and outwards, and every-which-way. Most of my girls had, by now, reached their eleventh birthday. One or two had already started their monthlies, which had caused great consternation and a degree of personal intimacy I hadn't anticipated when I'd accepted the teaching position here. Thankfully, there were adequate supplies for the situation, albeit helped by the fact that the adult women and older girls washed their napkins, many of which had, by now, seen better days. Boys who'd sounded like boys a year ago now spoke in much lower tones, and soft downy moustaches adorned many a top lip. Charlie Harris and Tom Martin taught the boys how to shave.

At least we had a semi-reliable food supply now with Red Cross parcels making their way through to us, albeit intermittently, and Commander Hayashi having reached some sort of arrangement with Mission HQ in Shanghai. Portions and standards of meals still weren't back to what we were used to, but we knew better than to complain. Somehow, we made the best of things, even when the best was really quite awful.

Life under occupation brought daily challenges and unexpected difficulties, but our focus remained firmly on the children, and we did everything we could to retain an air of normality for them. Our weekly meetings of Brownies and Guides had become an essential part of that normality. We all found strength and comfort in the camaraderie and routine it provided; a reassuring constant amid such unpredictability. As promised, we'd formed our new Girl Guide patrol, and the older girls of the 2nd Chefoo Brownies were now proud members of Kingfisher Patrol. Nancy's suggestion for the patrol name had been voted the most popular, and the girls had all carefully embroidered the patrol emblem onto felt badges that were now neatly sewn onto the shirt pockets of their Guide uniforms.

'Why a kingfisher, Nancy?' I'd asked at the end of our first meeting of the summer term. 'I never got around to asking you.'

'Because of Shu Lan's story, Miss. Because we're trapped, like the kingfishers in the metalsmith's nets.'

I was touched that she'd remembered Shu Lan's story, but the sense of entrapment was rather desolate.

'Perhaps we could think of it another way. That rather than being trapped, we are simply waiting for the right time to fly away.'

She liked that idea. 'Did you know that female kingfishers are more colourful than the males?'

'I didn't, although it doesn't surprise me. Us girls are often more colourful.' My playful wink brought a smile to Nancy's face.

At our next meeting, I gave her the paper kingfisher Shu Lan had sent to me. 'Shu Lan would be very pleased to know you remember her stories about China. I think she would like you to keep this.'

'Thank you, Miss. It's ever so pretty. I'll put it with the rest of my special things.'

There were moments when I was glad to have stayed in China, despite the circumstances, and standing as Guide Captain, beside my Lieutenant, Minnie, listening as the girls solemnly recited their Guide promise and laws, offered a rare moment of gratitude each week. I'd been so proud to watch our Brownies 'fly up' to become Girl Guides, and loved to see them all turned out so smartly each week in their blue skirts and shirt blouses, dark blue felt hats and knotted neckerchiefs.

Most heartening of all, the girls had elected Joan as their patrol leader. Like a December rose, she'd bloomed over the winter, thriving while many of the more confident girls had wilted under the long months of occupation. Electing someone who wasn't the most popular girl, but who would value the responsibility the most, was a sign of the girls' increasing maturity. In the months since their investiture, they'd all worked hard and were almost ready to progress to Second-Class rank, after which they would be able to start earning their proficiency badges. Minnie and I had already agreed that Self-Defence and Ambulance badges would be a priority.

But, as I'd come to realize about life during a war, nothing stayed the same for long. Just when you thought you'd adjusted and adapted and found a way to cope, the situation changed.

It was a bright autumn morning when Mr Collins was summoned to a meeting with Commander Hayashi. We were all anxious while he was gone, remembering his long absence once before. But he returned quickly, and called an emergency staff meeting.

'I'm afraid I have some rather alarming news.' He cleared his throat and fiddled with his tie, his face pale and gravely serious. 'Our school is to be taken over entirely, to be used as a training base for the Japanese Navy.' He paused, before continuing. 'All staff and children will be moved to a new location. We are to make immediate preparations to leave.'

NANCY

'We've been instructed to leave the school with immediate effect,' our headmaster announced. 'We will all be relocating to another school in Chefoo, at Temple Hill, about three miles across town.'

A stunned silence drifted around the assembly hall as we absorbed the shocking news that we were to leave our school. Sprout reached for my hand.

'I expect you all to be helpful and patient while we make the necessary preparations,' the headmaster continued. 'You are each to pack your belongings. Wear as many clothes as you can, and pack the rest into your trunks and cases. We leave first thing tomorrow morning.'

'Tomorrow!' I was so shocked I couldn't stop myself blurting it out.

After all the wondering and imagining, after all the talk of dramatic rescues, we would leave Chefoo School and our Japanese captors, only to become prisoners at a different school, with different soldiers guarding the gates. It was far from the thrilling midnight liberation we'd hoped for.

'Why do we have to leave, Miss?' Sprout asked when we returned to our classrooms for the morning's lessons. I was glad to see Sprout almost back to full health, although Nurse Prune was keeping a close eye on her to make sure she took her medicine and had plenty of rest.

Miss Kent did one of her funny little sniffs and pushed her spectacles onto the bridge of her nose. 'The school is to be used as a military base for the Japanese Navy. There's no need for alarm, girls. We will set ourselves up at the new location, and school routine will continue as normal there.' She paused, giving her words time to settle so that we might try to make sense of them. 'Are there any other questions?'

I put my hand up.

'Yes, Nancy?'

'Will Miss Butterworth be able to take the kitten?'

Miss Kent was surprised by my question. 'Well, yes. I don't see why not. We can't very well leave the kitten behind, can we?'

Miss Butterworth had found the kitten in a patch of wildflowers behind the San, the only one alive in a litter of six. The mother cat was nowhere to be seen, so Miss Butterworth had rescued the little orphan and kept her in a bed of old newspapers and scraps of wool in a drawer in her bedroom. We'd christened her Tinkerbell after the fairy in the story of Peter Pan. We were sometimes allowed to play with her, and we all adored her.

I sat on my hands to make sure I didn't ask any more questions because Miss Kent looked ever so weary and I suspected she wanted to get on with packing and organizing for the big move rather than answering questions about kittens.

'I'd rather stay,' Sprout said sulkily as we packed all our belongings into our large school trunks and smaller cases. 'Even with the soldiers marching about and our silly armbands, I'd rather stay here.'

I agreed. None of us wanted to leave unless it was because the war was over and we were on our way to be reunited with our parents. Chefoo wasn't just our school; it was our home. Leaving now was as unimaginable as staying under Japanese guard had once been.

'Maybe they'll let us come back when they've finished their training, or whatever it is they're doing,' I said. I didn't believe it, but it felt like the right sort of thing to say.

'What I'd like to know is how our parents will know where to find us,' Sprout continued.

I'd been wondering the same thing. When we'd first arrived in Shanghai, and Mummy had taken me and Edward shopping along the Bund, she'd told us that if we ever got lost, we should stay where we were, rather than go wandering off. 'That way, I can retrace my steps to find you,' she said. 'If you go wandering around, how will I ever know where to start looking?'

'I'm sure the headmaster will write to them,' I said. 'Or Mission HQ. They won't move us and not tell our parents where we are.'

Sprout raised an eyebrow. 'We're in the middle of a war, Plum. It's not exactly easy to get in touch with people.'

Mouse put her hand up, and then put it immediately down again as she remembered she wasn't in the classroom.

'What is it, Mouse?' I prompted.

'I just thought we could maybe leave some clues about where we're going. Or not. It doesn't really matter.'

For someone who didn't speak very often, when she did, Mouse always made it worthwhile. We agreed it was a good idea, and spent the last few minutes before lights out scratching our names, and the date, and the words 'Gone to Temple Hill' onto a loose floorboard beneath Mouse's bed. It felt like a very clever thing to do. Like something a Girl Guide would do to Be Prepared.

As darkness filled the room after lights out, my imagination started to wander, my head occupied with the prospect of the day ahead. I thought of all the times I'd imagined leaving the school, my trunk beside me in the rickshaw as I set off to spend the holidays with Mummy and Daddy. I'd imagined the sway of the ship as we sailed around the peninsula, and my excitement when I saw Mummy waiting on the wharf. She would be wearing her favourite blue dress and would say how wonderful it was to see me, and how terribly grown up I was, and I wouldn't say a word, but just sink into her arms and inhale the lovely lavender warmth of her. Leaving the school felt like leaving Mummy all over again. I still remembered the sickening sense of dread as I'd stepped aboard the boat in Shanghai.

It was now three years since I'd seen her. The scent of English lavender had faded from her letters, the paper worn so thin from where I'd folded and unfolded it that it was almost falling apart. Afraid that they would disintegrate entirely, I'd stopped reading them. I was especially disappointed that Mummy hadn't written since our occupation, when other parents had. Letters from home were few and far between, and hopelessly outdated when they did eventually arrive, thanks to the intervention of the Red Cross. Edward said the guards intercepted all the mail and censored the letters, and that Mummy had most likely written, but her letters had got lost. I wanted to believe him.

Sometimes I couldn't quite grasp her image in my mind, as if I were looking at her through ripples in water. It had often been said how alike her I was. The same heart-shaped face, the same petite nose, the same hyacinth-blue eyes and strawberry-blonde hair. Perhaps I saw a little of her every time I looked in the mirror, although I didn't think about her as often as I used to. Sometimes, I forgot to miss her at all.

After tossing and turning for a while, Sprout crept into bed beside me. We often shared a bed, to keep each other warm, and to feel safe. We held hands in the dark as a light rain tapped against the window.

'What's bothering me is who will look after the sunflower when we're gone?' Sprout whispered.

I stared at the ceiling.

'It will have to look after itself now,' I said. 'In the end, I suppose we all do don't we.'

ELSPETH

The day of our move arrived with golden-syrup skies and the first hoarfrost of the season. I rose early, partly relieved that it had happened quickly, and that I hadn't had time to think about it too much, or dread it. There was only time for the practicalities of packing, and yet I felt a need to say a farewell to this place I'd called home.

I washed and dressed as quietly as I could, anxious not to disturb Minnie, who was still snoring away at her side of the bed. I pulled on my shoes and wool coat, and crept silently downstairs. We'd been blessed with bright clear skies, but a cool breeze whipped around the school and whistled at the eaves as I set off toward the bay. I imagined the school was singing a farewell.

Home Run was patrolling the grounds. He stopped me, as I'd anticipated.

'Where do you go?' he asked.

'For a walk,' I replied, smiling politely, even though my stomach turned cartwheels. Since the shock of Trouble punching Minnie in the face that first morning, the threat that it could happen again had been ever present, but thankfully there hadn't been a repetition of any physical cruelty. Even so, whenever I'd had cause to interact with one of the guards, I felt deeply uncomfortable. 'I want to say goodbye,' I added. 'I won't be long.'

He considered me for a moment. 'You are sorry to leave?' he asked.

I nodded, surprised by the exchange. 'I am sorry that any of this ever happened.'

He nodded toward the beach. 'Ten minutes.' As I turned to walk away, he added, 'I am sorry, too.'

The sun had not yet fully risen, and the bay was cold and steeped in shadow. I didn't mind. I was alone and undisturbed, like the quiet December morning in the chapel doorway when I'd watched snowflakes tumble from the sky and finally felt confident about my decision to leave. Just as I had then, I drew strength from the quiet beauty.

The ocean was a calm grey-blue. Gentle waves lapped at the shore as I closed my eyes and imagined the merry squeals of the children captured in the water. I drew comfort from the thought that the tides would carry their laughter on, until it lapped at some other shore and mingled with the laughter of children at liberty to play where they wanted, watched by adoring parents whose arms waited to enfold them in a loving embrace.

I thought of Lillian Plummer, and how she'd pressed her gratitude into my hands when I'd offered to keep a special eye on Nancy during the journey from Shanghai. 'You're very kind to offer, Miss Kent. It's never easy to let your children go, especially not your youngest, but it will be a little easier now, knowing she's with you.' I recalled the delicate scent of her perfume, and the way she'd turned her face so that Nancy couldn't see how upset she was. I'd known Lillian Plummer for all of ten minutes, and yet I'd felt her beside me ever since; reminding me of my promise, encouraging me to be the mother she couldn't be.

The Bird in the Bamboo Cage

I'd often felt angry with her over the past year; resentful that she, and the other parents, had placed such a huge responsibility on our shoulders, but now I only felt sorry for them. What a terrible waste it was to have children you never saw. Like the ebb and flow of the tides, these informative years came and went so quickly. The children were growing up; developing from young girls into young women, and their parents were missing it all. I wondered if it would ever be possible for women like Lillian Plummer to catch up with these lost years, or if the scars of separation would run too deep to ever truly heal.

Stretching my permitted ten minutes to fifteen, I picked a handful of shells from the sand and made my way back to the school. The seashells clattered in my pocket as I walked. A reminder that this gentle place had offered me shelter when I'd needed it most. A memento, so that I would never forget where I'd been, or how far I'd travelled.

I returned to my bedroom and pulled the steamer trunk from beneath the bed. While the sudden arrival of war had caught us all by surprise a year ago, I'd since made sure I was prepared for whatever might happen next. Over the past few months, I'd been quietly putting aside old school books and exam papers, reams of writing paper, poetry books, chalk, pencils and sharpeners, and other classroom supplies. It wasn't much when I looked at it now, but it was better than nothing.

As I sorted through my many skirts and dresses, blouses and cardigans, stockings and shoes, I wondered how I'd ever thought so much of everything was necessary. I dressed in as many layers as I could stand, limited myself to two items each of anything that remained, and one pair of shoes. Sacrificing clothes made room in my trunk for extra text books and exercise books, past exam papers, all the wool I could find, knitting and crochet needles, spools of cotton and embroidery thread, needles and scissors, safety pins, first aid supplies and all the Brownie and Girl Guide uniforms I could stuff inside. There wasn't space for all the books I'd brought from home, so I chose just two: my Girl Guide Handbook, and the Buddhist scriptures Shu Lan had given to me. I picked up the small cotton square containing the eight remaining sunflower seeds from Wei Huan, and placed it in my coat pocket. I remembered what he'd said that cold morning before he'd been marched out of the school. *We grow anywhere with strong roots.* Wherever we were going, and wherever we might go beyond that, I resolved that I would plant a sunflower seed at each place; a symbol of our strength and our determination to carry on. A reminder that we could thrive, even in the harshest conditions.

I was almost done packing when Minnie peered around the doorframe. 'Are you done? They're asking everyone to assemble outside.'

I pulled down the lid of the trunk and sank onto the bed. 'Yes, I'm done.'

She let out a long sigh as she sat beside me. 'I know it's silly to feel sentimental about a building, but I've been here so long and I'm ever so fond of the old place. It's my home, Els. It's where I belong.'

I'd often wondered what – or who – had brought Minnie to China, but I'd never directly asked. You could see the past in people though, and I'd caught occasional glimpses of hers, especially at the end of the day, when we'd sat on the bed together, backs against the wall, our shoes kicked off as we talked about our favourite books, or a special piece of music. A wistful sigh, a particular song, a name mentioned in passing – the tell-tale signs of everyone's pasts were there if you looked closely enough. Most of the time, we chose not to look. It was easier, somehow, to keep things hidden away.

I tucked my arm into the crook of hers. 'It isn't the bricks and mortar that make a home, Minnie. It's the people. Your home will be wherever you are. Wherever *we* are.'

She pulled a handkerchief from her sleeve and dabbed at her nose, waving my remark away. 'Don't be kind, Els. You'll only make it worse.'

I smiled, and leaned into her. 'I'm not sure things can get any worse than they already are.'

But we both knew they could. The longer the war went on, the worse things would get. It was only a matter of time.

NANCY

We clattered noisily along the corridor, bumping awkwardly down the steps with our heavy cases, pillows and favourite teddies and dolls stuffed under our arms. I'd tied brown string around my tea caddy so it was easier to carry, but I still struggled to manage everything.

'Why don't you put that in your case,' Sprout suggested. 'It'd be one less thing to carry.'

I told her I would rather hold onto it.

'What do you keep in there anyway?' Mouse asked.

'Special things.'

'Like a treasure chest?'

'A bit. Yes.'

'I wouldn't have anything to put in a treasure chest,' she said. 'I don't have anything special.'

'Of course you do, silly! You've all your Brownie badges for a start. They're special, aren't they.'

'I suppose so. Yes.'

I promised to help Mouse start a treasure chest as soon as we were settled into our dorm at the new school.

'I wonder if it will be the same,' I said. 'Eight beds, and bamboo blinds at the windows. Perhaps it will be even bigger. I hope we still get to share, anyway.'

At the bottom of the stairs, while we waited for everyone to catch up, Sprout grabbed both our hands. 'Quick. Come with me.'

'What are you doing?' I whispered, as she pulled us along the corridor. 'We'll get into trouble.'

'We're saying goodbye,' she said over her shoulder. 'If we're quick they won't even miss us.'

She took us to our classroom first.

As she pushed the door open, the three of us stepped tentatively inside. We stood quietly together, lost in our memories. I stared at the proud dragon of the school crest, and the school motto above the blackboard: 'IN DEO FIDIMUS' and 'NIHIL ABSQUE LABORE'. *Trust in God. Nothing without Labour.*

'Eyes on the horizon, that's the ticket,' I whispered.

Sprout looked at me. 'What did you say?'

I smiled. 'Nothing. Just remembering something somebody once said to me.'

It was sad to see the blackboard wiped clean of Miss Kent's writing, her chair pushed behind the desk, all our work taken down from the walls. I wondered if she'd kept the heart-shaped pebble I'd once left on her desk.

'It's like we've already left,' I said.

'It's like we were never here,' Sprout replied, smothering a cough behind her hand.

'But like part of us will always be here,' Mouse added. 'Even if we're not.'

We both looked at her. As ever, she'd said the last and most important thing.

'We'd best get back,' I said, 'before they send out a search party.'

I closed the classroom door behind us, and locked the memories away in my mind.

Deflated, we trudged back along the corridor, past the trophy cabinets full of silver cups and house shields, and for one last time we stepped into the assembly hall where we'd first heard the news that we were at war with Japan. So much had happened since, it was hard to believe it wasn't even a year ago.

From the hall, we were led out to the courtyard where we stood among the groups of teachers and children, our possessions strewn around us, our embroidered armbands placed over our coat sleeves. I reached up onto my tiptoes to search for Edward, but I couldn't see him, or Larry, anywhere.

'He'll be here somewhere,' Sprout said, guessing that I was looking for him. 'They won't leave anyone behind.'

'It would be just like Edward to be left behind on purpose,' I sighed. 'I hope he isn't planning to do anything silly.'

We'd been instructed to wear several layers of clothing so that there was less for us to carry. I was bundled up so tight I could hardly bend my arms properly, but I was at least warm, and there was a lot to be said for that. Along with some of the other girls, I wore a borrowed coat, mine having mysteriously gone missing during our first winter under Japanese guard. We were all neatly turned out in our uniforms, hands scrubbed clean, hair thoroughly combed, faces gleaming.

'You'd think we were part of a festival parade,' Sprout said, looking around. 'Not a group of enemy prisoners.'

'There's nothing wrong with being smart,' I replied. 'I'd rather be neat and tidy than scruffy and dirty. You know what Miss Kent says. "A tidy girl makes for a tidy mind."'

We repeated the words together, and smiled at each other, but my smile hid an awful lot of sadness and worry.

The teachers walked along our lines, taking a register for each year group, closely watched all the time by the guards. Connie had told Sprout that Commander Hayashi was staying at the school, but Home Run and Charlie Chaplin and some of the other soldiers would accompany us to the new school. I don't know how Connie knew these things. Perhaps it was because she was older than us.

Sleepy and sluggish after a restless night, we fussed and fidgeted while we waited for the off. I heard the occasional meow from Tinkerbell who was hidden in a plimsoll bag looped across Miss Butterworth's body, concealed beneath her overcoat.

'She won't suffocate will she, Miss?' I asked. We were all ever so worried about the tiny little thing.

'She'll be fine, Nancy,' Miss Butterworth assured. 'Nice and warm. I made lots of holes in the bag so she'll have plenty of air.'

She smiled her prim little smile, which always made me feel safe and sure, although I couldn't help noticing how Miss Butterworth flinched when the guards walked past with their huge dogs. Their paws alone could flatten Tinkerbell with one step.

Our mattresses and bed rolls and larger trunks had been brought down from the dorms, and were now piled high onto handcarts and rickshaws. Other carts were loaded with pots and pans, washboards and hot irons and other domestic equipment, as well as more suitcases stuffed full of books and school supplies.

I remarked on how little room they'd left for us on the rickshaws, but my assumption that we would be transported to the new school was quickly proven wrong.

'Now, children. We will be walking for quite a while,' Miss Kent announced.

'Walking, Miss?' Winnie Morris blurted it out, but we were all thinking the same thing.

'Yes, Winnie. Walking. If we keep up a good pace, we should

be there in just over an hour. Perhaps two, allowing for the luggage.'

We were all surprised to learn that we would walk to the new school. Winnie was downright disgusted.

'So now we're *really* being treated like enemy prisoners. This certainly wasn't what my mother had in mind when she sent me to the best school this side of the Suez,' she grumbled.

I wished she hadn't mentioned mothers. I tightened my grip on the string of my tea caddy as a cold breeze tugged at our hats.

Miss Kent ignored Winnie, although she didn't look very pleased. 'You must stay in your pairs, and leave a gap between yourself and the pair in front. We don't want anyone treading on our heels. And remember to smile and sing along the way.'

'Sing, Miss?' Now it was Sprout's turn to speak up.

'Yes, Dorothy. Sing! No Girl Guide worth her salt sets out on an expedition without a rousing song to keep her company. We'll march out of those gates with our heads held high and a song on our lips, because a Guide smiles and sings under all difficulties, doesn't she?'

'Yes, Miss. She does.'

'Jolly good. Then that's exactly what we'll do. Besides, singing will keep us warm.'

A whistle was blown to signal the off, and our group of over one hundred children, a dozen teachers, several missionaries, and three school nurses set off at a brisk march. I tried not to be sad or scared, and to remember what Miss Kent had said about always looking forward, never back, but no matter how much I forced myself to smile, my voice pitched and wobbled like a ship in a storm as we sang our way through the school gates.

'Off on an adventure we go,' Miss Kent called over her shoulder. 'Just like Livingstone, and Lewis and Clark, and Gertrude Bell.'

'It doesn't feel much like an adventure,' Sprout grumbled beside me. 'It feels more like a punishment.'

Beyond the school gates, the roadside was lined with people. It was such a long time since we'd seen anyone apart from each other and our Japanese guards that I couldn't help but stare. The women and girls were clothed in tattered dresses and trousers, the men in faded blue cotton jackets and trousers, patched-up straw sandals and bamboo hats. Their faces were gaunt from lack of food, and their clothes hung off their shrunken bodies, yet they smiled and waved their encouragement and clasped their hands together, as if in prayer. I suppose we must have been a curious spectacle, a group of schoolchildren and their teachers, marching away from the school, as if we were part of a parade and not under enemy guard at all.

I searched the crowd for Shu Lan, or Wei Huan, or any of the servants I might recognize, but I found only the faces of kind strangers. Something about them being there to wave us off made me feel a little better about where we were going.

As we marched away from Chefoo School, I took one last look at our beloved bay to the right, the junks and sampans dotted about on the water with their sails spread wide. I looked to the horizon, and then to the long road ahead, leading us towards a new school, and away from everything we knew. A cool breeze danced and swirled among us, tugging at our hats and blowing out our coats in time to our song.

We walked for a long time before we stopped for a rest. A line of first-year boys stopped in front of our group, and while Miss Kent and Master Harris had a long conversation about something or other, we sat on the smaller cases we each carried, glad to be off our feet for a while. I thought an insect had landed in my hair and brushed it away, only to feel something else land in my hair straight after. I turned around to see Larry Crofton picking up small stones from the road and flicking them at me. I scowled and turned away, but he did it again.

'Stop it,' I said. I stood up and folded my arms crossly.

He smiled. 'Or what?'

'Or I'll tell.'

He didn't seem particularly concerned. 'I thought you might like some help carrying that case. It's almost as big as you.'

I was tired, but I didn't want to appear weak. 'I can manage perfectly well. What about your own case anyway?' I asked. 'Who'll carry that?'

'I've two arms, haven't I?'

He smiled again, and I wanted to laugh because his ears moved up when he smiled.

I scowled at him instead. 'You can carry this case if you're so keen to help.' I told Sprout to quickly stand up, and passed her case to Larry. Sprout's cough was at her again, and she'd been struggling for the last while.

Larry took the case, pushed a strand of sandy-coloured hair from his eyes, and turned to face the front.

As we set off again, I picked up a small stone and threw it. With a perfect aim, it landed in the middle of Larry's neck. He didn't turn around, but I could tell he was smiling because the tips of his ears moved up.

'He's awfully handsome, isn't he,' Sprout whispered as she walked beside me.

I adjusted my grip on the handle of my case and winced as it banged off my shins.

'He's a boy, Sprout,' I replied. 'Handsome or not, they're all horrid.'

ELSPETH

Despite the autumnal chill, I soon began to perspire beneath my many layers. My suitcase, although smaller than the trunk I'd hefted onto one of the rickshaws, was still cumbersome and heavy, and banged painfully against my shins with every step. I tried to ignore it, focusing instead on the words of the children's song.

'*God is our refuge, our refuge and our strength. In trouble, in trouble, a very present help . . .*'

As their earnest little voices infused the air with bravery and hope, I thought about what we might be leading them towards. My courage faltered with every step.

From Charlie's radio, and the occasional letters from home that had made their way to us, we'd heard intermittent reports of British nationals, servicemen, and other western civilians being taken to large internment camps in Hong Kong, and on the islands of Java and Sumatra. Although we couldn't be certain, rumours suggested that these camps were under the control of the Imperial Japanese Army. If true, accounts of conditions there were horrifying. Reports of torture, slave labour, rape, and a high death toll from infectious disease were almost impossible to comprehend. It was simply too terrifying to think that we might be taking the children toward something similar.

'Is there nothing at all we can do?' I'd asked at our final staff meeting the previous evening, exasperated by how easily everyone had accepted the instruction to leave. 'No compromise to be reached? Nothing HQ can do to stop it?'

Mr Collins had answered me, his face full of empathy for my frustration. 'I'm afraid this isn't up for negotiation, Elspeth. We've been given our orders to leave, and that's what we will do. We may not know what lies ahead, but I *do* know that faith, routine and discipline are our best allies now. Of course, there will be challenges ahead, but the matter of how we approach those challenges is entirely in our own hands. Whatever weapons our enemy has, never forget that we possess the most powerful weapon of all: the ability to educate. With that knowledge alone, we should all walk through the school gates tomorrow with our heads held high.'

As I walked on, I wondered, truly, if our abilities as teachers would be enough to cope with whatever awaited us at Temple Hill.

As we passed the crowds who lined the road, eager to gawp at our rag-tag group, one of the women lunged forward, grabbed my arm, and pulled me roughly out of the line. I recognized her as one of the school cooks.

'Please let go,' I gasped. 'You're hurting me.'

The girls behind me bunched up like a concertina as I tried to pull away, but she gripped hard.

'Send doctor, Miss. Please! My son. Very sick.' She pressed a piece of paper into my hand. The despair in her eyes was unbearable.

I glanced at the paper, but I couldn't understand the writing. I didn't have time to process her rambling distress, or to cry out a warning to her as a guard raised his bamboo stick and cast a heavy blow to the back of her legs. I could only stare in horror as she fell to the ground like a pile of washday rags. The crowd around her peeled away. Not one person went to help her. I was too shocked to move until the same bamboo stick prodded me in the back and propelled me forward.

'You! March on!' the guard shouted. 'Go!'

The piece of paper fell to the ground as I walked on, horrified by what I'd witnessed, but urged on by some greater instinct for my own safety. Behind me, I heard Minnie encouraging the girls to keep singing, as if nothing had happened at all.

'*God is our refuge, our refuge and our strength. In trouble, in trouble, a very present help . . .*'

It didn't take long for the first of the stragglers to fall behind. Time and again we had to stop and wait for those at the rear to catch up. The younger children were soon exhausted, and those for whom physical exercise had always been a chore struggled to keep up with the pace. Several children who weren't in the best of health pressed on valiantly, despite their sniffles and coughs. Those who weren't concentrating trod on the heels of those in front. Unwieldy cases banged against legs. Hats and gloves were continually dropped and retrieved, and cross words were exchanged.

Winnie Morris refused to carry on after we'd taken a short rest.

'Come along, Winnie. On we go,' I said, as brightly as I could.

She stuck out her bottom lip, folded her arms, and kicked petulantly at the ground with the toe of her shoe. 'I'm too tired.'

I glanced at Minnie, who thankfully stepped in, aware that I was losing my patience.

'Come along now, Winnie,' she chirped. 'We're all tired, but we're almost there, and we can't very well leave you behind, can we?'

At that precise moment, I would have happily left Winnie behind, and anyone else who volunteered, for that matter.

Winnie huffed out a breath as she stood up. 'My father won't be pleased to hear about this. I was sent here to prepare for my Oxfords, not to go marching about from one school to another.'

'I should think your father won't give a fig about you marching about,' Nancy replied. 'There's a war on, Winnie, in case you hadn't noticed.'

I was tired and anxious, and in no mood for Winnie's petulance. Something in me snapped. 'You're quite right, Winnie,' I said as I organized the girls back into their pairs. 'Your father won't be at all pleased to hear that you were disobedient and lazy. I don't think he'll be very pleased at all.'

She stared at me, speechless for once, and picked up her case.

We walked on, our singing a little less cheerful.

Our little troop fell silent as we reached the Temple Hill area of town. The guards at the front brought us to a halt, and over a hundred pairs of weary feet came to a standstill.

Our new home loomed in front of us, a large compound of missionary houses that, like everything else in Chefoo, had been commandeered by the Japanese Army. Our exhausted silence was filled by a flock of birds that chattered in the blossom trees above our heads until a shrill whistle was blown to bring us to attention, and the startled birds took flight. I could have wept as I watched them fly away. How I envied their wings; their freedom.

Up ahead, our headmaster was deep in conversation with an official-looking man in uniform.

'Our new Commandant?' Minnie whispered.

'Possibly,' I replied. 'He looks officious enough.'

Whoever he was, he made Commander Hayashi look almost friendly in comparison. He was tall and angular, lean and healthy-looking, with an air of hard authority. He spoke in clipped, firm sentences that carried a tone of simmering menace. Even the other soldiers looked wary of him.

After standing about for an age, the children grew fidgety. I knew they were tired and hungry, but only a few grumbled. I admired their ability to adapt and change to each new and bewildering situation. Fortunately, their naivety prevented many of them fully comprehending what was happening. Easily distracted by a game or a song, they followed instructions and did as they were told, just as they did in the classroom. As I so often did when I found myself in a sticky situation, I drew on my Guiding experience and set the girls off in a memory game that passed along the line and kept everyone busy until we were instructed to pick up our belongings, and follow the guards.

We entered the compound through an elaborate gateway that resembled a traditional Chinese temple with a red pagoda-style roof. Ornate lettering and symbols decorated the tall columns on either side of the entrance. In different circumstances I would have stopped to admire it, but I had no energy for culture or architecture. All I could think about was getting to wherever it was we would now call home, making our beds, and getting a decent night's sleep.

The children trudged silently along as we were led down a narrow road, flanked on either side by colonial-style houses. They might have once been welcoming family homes, but now stood empty and neglected, and lent the whole place an uncomfortable air of melancholy.

'Not exactly Raffles Hotel, is it,' Minnie said as she joined me at my shoulder. 'I wonder what happened to the families who used to live here.'

'I'd rather not think about it,' I replied.

The boys and their masters filed off together into one of the houses. I wondered how there would ever be room for them all, especially with some of the older boys now as tall as the adults. The dozen or so very youngest children went with Amelia Prescott, Eleanor Yarwood, Nurse Eve and the other two Chefoo School nurses to another house. They would at least be a little less squashed on account of their being smaller in number and half the size of the boys. At the very end of the street, we reached the house where Minnie and I were to be accommodated with two dozen girls.

Minnie hesitated in front of the short pathway, which led to a black door. The glass panes were dusty and dirty. One pane was completely broken.

'Shall we?' I said, as we stared at the imposing building.

Minnie offered an anxious smile as she stepped aside to let me pass. 'After you, Miss Kent.'

I lifted my chin and pushed back my shoulders. Whatever degree of trepidation I felt, I was determined to look confident as I approached the unwelcoming door. It was already slightly ajar, the lock apparently broken.

I pushed the door open and stepped inside, avoiding a pile of broken glass on the floor which I kicked aside with my shoe before encouraging the girls to follow, carefully, one at a time. 'Come along, girls. That's it. Hurry up.' I touched the top of each head as they entered, counting to make sure we hadn't misplaced anyone on the way.

The girls crowded into the sparsely decorated downstairs room, which, I presumed, had once been a living room, but which now looked like a room for anything but the living. They whispered and speculated as they took in their new surroundings. Nobody quite knew what to make of it. There wasn't much in the way of furniture, just the odd chair and a few old packing crates. There was no table in the dining room. No curtains at the cracked windows. The floor looked like it hadn't been swept for weeks, possibly months. Blank rectangles and squares decorated the walls where family portraits and treasured artwork must have once hung. Bare light fittings dangled limply from the ceiling. Any remnants of furniture bore the now-familiar seals declaring them to be the property of the Great Emperor of Japan.

I took a deep breath, and held my head high. 'I know it doesn't look much right now, but we'll soon have it shipshape and cosy, isn't that right, Miss Butterworth.' I stared pointedly at Minnie for support, the shock on her face all too evident.

'That's right, Miss Kent,' she replied, playing her part admirably. 'We'll have it feeling like home in no time. For a start, I think a pair of curtains would help these windows look a bit happier.'

I sighed quietly. It was going to take far more than a few hastily thrown together curtains to make this hollow house feel anything like a home.

Dorothy Hinshaw stuck her hand in the air. Always the first with a question.

'Yes, Sprout? I mean, Dorothy?' I was so used to hearing the girls use each other's nicknames, I almost used them myself.

'Where will we sleep, Miss?'

'That is a very good question, and one I will answer as soon as I've taken a look upstairs.'

'You can call me Sprout if you like, Miss,' she added. 'Everyone else does.'

I offered a small smile. 'Very well. *Sprout.*'

The girls giggled, amused to hear me use her nickname.

Minnie stayed with the girls while I walked up the carpet-less stairs to assess the condition of the bedrooms. They were even worse than I'd imagined. The upstairs rooms were musty and cold, the walls riddled with mildew and damp. Apart from a single Queen Anne chair placed beside a window, there was not one item of furniture. Not one bed. Not one chest of drawers.

I walked quickly from room to room, but it was the same throughout. More broken windowpanes let in a cold breeze, and piles of mouse droppings in the smaller of the rooms offered evidence that we weren't the only occupants. I slumped against the doorframe, imagining what Alfie would say if he was standing beside me, his arms folded. 'Blimey, Els! Looks like you've got yourself into a right pickle this time. I don't think you're going to be able to sing your way out of this one!' I kicked at the wall in temper and frustration. I was angry with Alfie for being so bloody silly as to go missing; angry with Harry for being so bloody stubborn and going back down the mine to look for his friends after the first collapse; angry with my mother for never being proud of me; angry with the soldiers for invading our school and spoiling my plans to go back to England. Mostly, I was angry with a God I'd struggled, all my life, to truly believe in.

'*Why*?' I groaned, wringing my hands in despair. 'Why are you doing this to us?'

I pulled at my collar as I struggled to breathe, suffocated by my past, by the helplessness of the present situation, by the relentless pressure to be jolly and hopeful while feeling so utterly desperate and afraid.

Minnie arrived at the top of the stairs. 'Elspeth?' she called. 'Who are you talking to? Is everything all right?'

'I'm here,' I called. 'Everything's fine.'

'I wondered where you'd got to. I didn't want the . . .' She stopped talking as she reached the bedroom doorway and saw the state of the room. 'Oh, dear. Everything isn't fine at all, is it.'

I let out a long sigh. 'It's awful, Minnie. All of it.'

She placed an arm around my shoulder and gave it a firm squeeze.

'Now, now. I shan't be having any of that sort of talk. We'll grab a broom and some hot water and make the best of it. Besides,' she said, holding out the kitten who she'd brought upstairs with her, 'Tinkerbell is quite fond of the place. She says she'll take it.'

I smiled as I lifted the warm little bundle of fur to my face. Tinkerbell mewled and licked a tear from my cheek.

After climbing another flight of steps to a loft area, I settled on that being where we would all sleep. It was at least a little warmer and drier, and there was space for all of us to be together. I didn't especially want to relinquish the privacy of my own room, but nor did I want to have the children sleeping, unsupervised, in a separate room while there was a broken lock on the front door of the house.

I took a moment to compose myself before I made my way downstairs and clapped my hands to get everyone's attention.

'Miss Butterworth and I have carried out an inspection,' I announced, 'and we've decided to set up a dormitory-style camp in the loft. We'll roll out our mattresses, and make it jolly.' The girls didn't look convinced, their eyes straying from Minnie and me to the bare floorboards and mould-riddled walls. 'Rome wasn't built in a day,' I added, forcing a smile. 'The sooner we get started, the sooner we'll have the place looking shipshape. We might have left our school, but that's no excuse to let our standards slip. You'll be expected to keep your uniforms and hands and faces neat and tidy, as usual.'

'Will we all sleep in the same room, Miss?'

'Yes, Nancy. For the first few nights at least. Until we're settled. After that, we'll see.'

'Will we still have Guides?' she added.

'Of course! We'll have lessons and prayers, and Girl Guides, the same as usual. We can use one of the rooms downstairs as our meeting room. Now, more than ever, you must all remember your Guide laws and Promise, and try to do a good turn every day. There might be a shortage of furniture, but there will never be a shortage of ways in which you can be helpful.'

'We will all need to help with domestic duties,' Minnie added. 'Cooking and cleaning, washing and mending, so you'll all be earning plenty of points toward your Homemaker badges.'

The girls cheered up a little, happy to hear their beloved Girl Guide meetings would still take place and that they would still be able to earn new badges.

The prefects helped to organize the girls into an orderly line from the front door all the way up the stairs to the loft. In a human chain, we passed our possessions from one person to the next, and so on and so on, until I declared us moved in and closed the door. I tried not to think about the absence of a key.

Once all the children were occupied with various chores to make the houses more habitable, or sent off in groups to explore their new surroundings, Mr Collins called a staff meeting in the kitchen of the boys' house. It was no better than our own, a little worse even, if that were possible. For a home intended to accommodate a family of four, they really were dreadfully cramped. Charlie, Tom, Eleanor, Amelia, Nurse Eve and I nodded a rather grim greeting to each other. I offered a hopeful smile, but felt it fade before it had even reached the edge of my lips.

'There's no point pretending otherwise, so let me start by acknowledging that the conditions are rather, what one might call, lacking,' the headmaster said as he opened the meeting. 'The compound previously belonged to an American Presbyterian Mission, but has clearly become rather run down since it was abandoned. I'm confident we will all muck in and do our bit to have things looking much better sooner rather than later. Our priority, as always, must be the children's moral, physical and intellectual education. I've drawn up a number of activities and routines to address all aspects of their welfare.'

A stubborn part of me wanted to ask about the adults' welfare. I was exhausted, dirty, hungry and thoroughly wretched. As I listened to Mr Collins while he set out the daily routines – breakfast at seven-thirty, lessons at nine, tiffin at twelve, and so on – I looked around and wished one of us would be brave enough to admit how frightened we were, and how helpless we felt. But nobody said a word. We diligently volunteered for our share of activities and responsibilities, and carried on, just as we always did.

Charlie was put in charge of Physical Education. He'd already measured the distance from the compound gate to the Sanitorium, which Nurse Eve and her colleagues had been relieved to discover was in a reasonable condition.

'The distance is exactly one mile if repeated fourteen times,' Charlie explained as we walked back to our houses together. 'Perhaps we can award prizes for the boys and girls who record the most miles between now and Foundation Day. Give them something to work towards.'

Foundation Day was an occasion we celebrated to mark our founders' establishment of the China Inland Mission School. I liked the idea of retaining the anniversary, even though we'd left.

'But Foundation Day is months away,' I replied.

Charlie looked at me and offered a grim smile of resignation. 'Yes, Elspeth. It is.'

He didn't need to say anything else, but I saw the question in his eyes: how many miles would the children run before the war, and our ordeal, was over?

The day had started early and had offered more than its fair share of challenges by the time the low autumn sun began to set in the late afternoon. Our new home looked worse when stripped of sunlight, so I was relieved when two of the older boys knocked on the door and delivered several light-bulbs.

'Where on earth did you get them?' I asked. It was the one thing I hadn't thought to pack; hadn't at all considered we would require.

'From the Boys' School. Master Harris had us take as many as we could from the light fittings before we left.'

'Well, wasn't that wise! Thank you, boys. And please thank Master Harris for his foresight. At least we'll be able to see each other now!'

After locating a set of stepladders in an outhouse, I gave the girls an impromptu demonstration on how to attach a lightbulb to the fitting.

'You must make sure the switch is off before starting, and have someone hold the bottom of the ladder at all times.'

Of course, they were all eager to have a go, and the bulbs were taken in and out until everyone had taken a turn. When all the bulbs were in place, Minnie did a countdown from ten and the lights were switched on at the same time. The girls cheered as our dark unfamiliar home was lit up like a Christmas tree. It reminded me of our family trips to Blackpool to see the illuminations. For a brief moment everything felt a little better, but the front door suddenly flew open and the man I'd seen talking to Mr Collins earlier marched inside.

'I am the camp Commandant, Major Kosaka,' he announced, his voice loud and authoritative.

Three Consular guards flanked him as the door banged loudly off the wall. Minnie and I instinctively moved to shield the girls, who stared at our new ruler.

Major Kosaka's petite moustache reminded me of an illustration of Adolf Hitler I'd seen in a satirical magazine. A sword hung from a thick leather belt as he stalked around the room, intermittently prodding and poking at our belongings with a large bamboo stick.

'You,' he barked, pointing at me. 'Name?'

I was accustomed to the curt commands, and replied without hesitation.

'Miss Kent. Elspeth Kent.'

'How many here?'

'Twenty-six, in total. Twenty-four children, and two adults.'

One of the guards made a note on a piece of paper attached to a clipboard.

'Roll-call in compound square,' he continued. 'Tomorrow morning. Seven o'clock.'

As he made to leave, a ball of wool rolled down the stairs and landed at his boot, followed by Tinkerbell who batted at the wool with her paws before pouncing on Major Kosaka's boots.

Nobody dared move.

He bent down slowly, and picked the kitten up by the scruff of her neck.

I rushed forward. 'Please. Don't hurt her.'

He glared at me. 'No pets. Get rid of it.'

He dropped the kitten to the floor and kicked her out of the way with the toe of his boot. The girls shrieked. Minnie rushed forward and scooped Tinkerbell into her hands as Major Kosaka and his henchmen marched out of the house.

Several of the girls started to cry, and only calmed down when we assured them that Tinkerbell wasn't hurt, and that we wouldn't get rid of her.

'We'll find somewhere to hide her,' I said. 'A Guide is a friend to all animals . . .' I nodded to indicate that the girls should continue.

They diligently took my cue, and recited the rest of the law in unison.

'All Girl Guides take particular care of our dumb friends, the animals, and are always eager to protect them from stupid neglect or hard usage.'

'Very good. Which is why, despite the Commandant's instruction, we will hide her. We won't need to discuss the matter any further, will we?'

The girls all shook their heads.

As Major Kosaka made his way around the compound, reports trickled back to us of similar experiences in the other houses. He was clearly a deeply unpleasant man, and considered even our most basic requests to be indulgent extravagances. Worse still, my old adversary arrived that evening.

I was walking back from the San with an aspirin for Dorothy when I heard close footsteps behind me.

'Hello again, Elspeth Kent.'

I recognized Trouble's voice immediately. My stomach lurched with a familiar sense of dread as I took a deep breath and turned around to address him.

'If you'll excuse me,' I said, before walking on, heart thumping in my chest.

He laughed, sarcastically, but let me continue on my way.

I walked faster, my breaths coming fast and shallow as I stared straight ahead, and hurried on.

'I see our friend, Trouble, turned up like a bad penny,' Charlie said. He was helping me fix boarding over the broken windows while Minnie kept the girls occupied by reading to them from the Bible. 'I thought we'd seen the back of him.'

'Me too,' I sighed. 'I haven't told Minnie yet.'

'Best not. Not on the first night anyway. Give it a few days.'

I wanted to tell him about the threats Trouble had made to me, never mind Minnie, but I couldn't find the words, and besides, I was too embarrassed to say anything to a man.

'We'll have to keep Tinkerbell well out of sight of Major Kosaka and his dog,' I said, changing the subject. 'He makes Commander Hayashi look like Father Christmas.'

'Maybe, but I still think we're better off under the command of the Consular guards,' he replied. 'They're former diplomats, mostly. Well-educated family men. I don't think they intend to harm us, just cause enough discomfort to remind us we're the enemy and that they have the upper hand. It would be *far* worse if we were under the Imperial Army or the dreaded *kempeitai* – the military police. You know about the dreadful atrocities in other parts of Asia.'

I nodded. 'I wish I didn't.'

'And I'm sure we've only heard the half of it,' he agreed. 'I dread to think of the stories that will emerge after liberation.'

'Do you think the Allies will be victorious soon?' I asked, ever hopeful that Charlie had picked up some news on his little radio, which he'd managed to keep hidden from the guards during our relocation. 'It all seems to be going on for such a terribly long time.'

Charlie stopped his hammering. His shoulders slumped as he pushed his hair from his eyes and wiped dust from his cheeks with the back of his hand. 'Honestly?'

'Honestly.'

'I don't know. All I can be sure of is that we won't be here for just a few nights. If I were you, Elspeth, I'd start to make yourself at home and try to make peace with it. I think we could be here for a long time yet.'

Whether it was the kindness in his gaze, or the brutal honesty I'd craved for so long, I wasn't sure, but tears welled up in my eyes and I couldn't stop them spilling onto my cheeks.

'Oh, dear. I'm terribly sorry.' Charlie fumbled as he searched for a handkerchief from his pocket. 'I've upset you. I shouldn't have . . .'

'Yes,' I sniffed as I wiped my tears away with his handkerchief. 'Yes, Charlie, you should. I'm tired of all the false optimism.' I sighed and leaned against the wall. 'I'm just ever so tired of it all.'

He offered a reassuring smile and placed his hand on my arm. 'We all are. And you're doing remarkably well, you know. You're much stronger than you think. And the children! Goodness, how they look up to you.'

'To me?'

'Yes! To you. Don't sound so surprised!' He picked up his tools and stepped back to inspect his handiwork. 'That'll have to do for now. It's all any of us can do, Elspeth. Patch things up to make them better. You shouldn't be so hard on yourself.'

But despite Charlie's assurances, I lay awake in the loft that first night at Temple Hill, my mind turning over everything as Minnie snored beside me. Her hand was clasped tight around her hockey stick, just as mine was clasped tightly around mine. We were both painfully aware of the lack of protection they would offer should the soldiers decide to march upstairs but, somehow, they made us both feel safer.

I shivered as a full moon sent shadows dancing on the walls. I tensed at every unfamiliar creak and crack, and held my breath as the guards' boots crunched over the gravel beyond the windows. I flinched at the growls of their dogs, straining on their leads.

I only relaxed when the first hint of daylight tiptoed through the shutters. Only then did I let myself drift into a sleep of pure exhaustion. I dreamed of a child cradled safely in my arms, protected from some dark threat I couldn't see, but which I sensed with every fibre of my soul. And in the child's impossibly small hand, I held the trust of dozens of children, all desperate for a mother's protection, all longing for the reassuring touch of loving arms wrapped around them.

I slept for what felt like only moments before I was woken by Dorothy coughing and wheezing. I lay awake, watching her, wishing there was more I could do to help her, to help them all.

As the early morning light bathed the room in violet, the girls looked so peaceful, and yet they were so vulnerable. There'd been many moments in the past year when I'd been afraid for myself, but my greatest fear, when I dared to admit it, was losing one of the children. Not only would it have a profound impact on everyone's fragile emotional state, but I also worried deeply about how we would let the parents know. We were so cut off from the rest of the world. So completely alone. It made me fearful of liberation; fearful of what we might find waiting for us on the other side.

Charlie was right. I *had* done my best, and I would continue to do so until the end came. Until then, I was a lonely shepherdess with her flock of lambs. I knew it would be only a matter of time before I would lose one of them.

NANCY

None of us liked the new school.

It was horrid: uncomfortable, cold and unwelcoming, and our new Commander shouted even more than the last. Most of all, we hated the daily roll-call in the compound square. Sprout had picked up another cold as a result of being forced to stand around in all weathers. We sometimes had to wait for an age as we each called out our assigned number in Japanese, just so they could be sure nobody had escaped, which was highly unlikely with guards at every gate. We all wished we were back in our classroom at Chefoo School, with Miss Kent at the front in one of her pretty cardigans, ticking our names off the register.

The only good thing about Temple Hill was that our lessons became a bit more interesting. Master Harris knew a lot about the stars and planets and took us in small groups to the boys' house, where they'd set up a makeshift observatory in the loft. Edward and Larry had helped to make a Newtonian reflector – a small telescope made from the lens of a pair of binoculars, a mirror from one of the teacher's powder compacts, and various bits of wood and cardboard they'd found in an abandoned outhouse. They were very proud of it and let us take turns to look through it after dark. I found Orion's Belt, and the Plough, and what I think might have been Jupiter, although I wasn't sure if I was looking at the right thing. My head was soon full of light years and galaxies and the unfathomable size of the universe. It made me feel awfully small, but it also made me keen to learn more about it.

'Can girls be astronomers?' I asked, as I helped Miss Kent clean the downstairs windows one morning. 'Or is that just for boys?'

'Of course girls can be astronomers! Girls can do anything boys can, and often do it much better, although don't tell your brother I said that. Why do you ask?'

'I like learning about the stars and planets. Master Harris makes it all sound so interesting, but I think my father would prefer me to go into nursing.'

Miss Kent tutted and rubbed vigorously at a mark on the glass. 'I'm sure your father can be talked around when he sees how enthusiastic and clever you are. Fathers are funny things. They might seem all stiff and serious, but they're not so bad underneath. He might surprise you.'

'Is your father nice, Miss?'

Miss Kent's hand settled against the glass. 'He was, yes. Ever so nice. One of the kindest men you'd ever meet. He died in the last war. I was a few years younger than you when the telegram arrived.'

I didn't often think about my father and, when I did, I found that I mostly remembered him talking to Edward about cricket and football. Other than the occasional pat on the head, and a reminder to keep my elbows off the table, we'd never really had much to do with one another. The more I thought about him, the more I felt that I didn't know him at all. What *would* he say when I told him I wanted to be a scientist or an astronomer? 'Don't be ridiculous, Nancy. You'll be a nurse, of course.' I imagined Mummy would smile and say, 'That's marvellous, darling. Now, wash your hands for lunch.' It didn't matter anyway. My parents were as far away as the planets I saw through the telescope. They weren't there to encourage or discourage me from anything. That job fell to Miss Kent and the other teachers. We turned to them now, not just for advice about what we might do when we were grown up, but also for everything else in the meantime.

As we stepped inside to wash our hands, I said something I'd wanted to say for a long time.

'Thank you, Miss. For keeping a special eye on me. I know it made Mummy happy.'

Miss Kent paused for a second before she dried her hands briskly with a towel, and hung it neatly from a small hook beside the sink. She looked at me, searching for the right words, as she tucked a stray curl behind her ear.

'Well now, run along,' she said eventually. 'You don't want to be late for tiffin.'

As the first weeks at Temple Hill passed, 'Foxglove' (the name we'd chosen for our house at Guides) began to feel a little more like home. We swept, scrubbed, and polished every surface until it sparkled, and made patchwork curtains from old scraps of fabric Miss Butterworth had cleverly thought to bring with her. We snipped sprigs off the berry-laden bushes in the grounds and placed them in empty soup tins and old bottles we found lying around. Master Harris and Master Martin had the boys make the most wonderful lampshades from old kitchen colanders and discarded washing-machine drums, the machines themselves having been left to rust in a pile behind the houses. The light shone through the small holes, covering the ceiling with stars.

It was so pretty, especially when we spun the lampshades and the light danced around the room.

In many ways, life at the Temple Hill compound was strangely similar to life at Chefoo School. Our homes weren't as comfortable, or the setting half as nice, but we still had to learn boring Latin and algebra, Sprout still spoke when she wasn't supposed to, and Mouse was still the quiet one. We found fun wherever we could, worked hard, and dealt with any difficulties to the best of our ability, and on days when one of us was fed up, or feeling under the weather, we took it in turns to jolly each other along. Most of the time, the teachers kept us so busy that we didn't have time for moping about or feeling sorry for ourselves. It was only when the seasons changed, or someone's shoes suddenly didn't fit, or their skirts were too short, that it struck me how long we'd been under Japanese guard; how long it had been since I'd seen my mother. I didn't ache for her like I once had; the sharp pain of separation replaced by a sort of distant numbness.

Edward still didn't approve of my occasionally talking to Home Run, but even he admitted that the guards weren't half as bad as we'd thought they might be.

'I bet they never thought they'd end up guarding a group of schoolchildren and their teachers when they joined the army!' he said. 'We're not exactly high risk, are we!'

We were walking around the compound square where we had roll-call each morning, and where siblings now mingled on Sibling Saturday. Although we were both a year older (our eleventh and fifteenth birthdays having passed rather unceremoniously earlier that year), I still looked up to Edward, and he still tolerated having his little sister around. He also still liked to show off with bits of information he'd picked up here and there.

'We're actually very lucky we didn't end up in a missionary school somewhere in Malaya, like Father was planning at one stage. I overheard Master Harris talking to Miss Kent about the conditions in the camps there.'

'What conditions? Is it horrid?'

'Apparently they lock people up in solitary confinement, and torture them,' he whispered.

I didn't understand why he felt it necessary to tell me this, and very much wished he hadn't. 'That's awful, Edward. Don't tell me any more.' I placed my hands over my ears. 'How would Master Harris know anyway?'

Edward tapped the side of his nose. 'There are ways of getting information. I know it's not exactly pleasant here, but it could be worse. That's why I'm telling you. Even Major Kosaka isn't that bad.'

'He's a brute. Always barking orders and making roll-call go on forever, even when it's freezing.'

Edward shoved his hands in his pockets. 'I'd take roll-call and a bit of cold weather over torture and slave labour any day.'

Larry caught the end of our conversation. 'Thought I should come and save you, Nance. I presume Edward is crashing on about war again. *Did you know, Nancy, that during the Battle of Midway, Allied troops defeated the Japanese army?*'

'That would be the Japanese *Navy*, Larry,' Edward corrected. 'If you're going to poke fun at me, at least get your facts straight.'

Larry made me smile when he mimicked Edward. He often teased my brother about being a know-it-all, but they were good friends, and Edward didn't seem to mind.

Later that afternoon, Sprout started to tease *me* about Larry. He'd helped us carry a heavy pile of laundry to the outhouse, and she wouldn't stop talking about him as we put it through the mangle.

'Is he your boyfriend?' she asked.

'Of course not!' I blushed furiously. 'He's just being helpful.'

'Funny how he only seems to be helpful when you're around,' she said. Sprout had decided Larry Crofton liked me, and that was that, no matter how much I denied it. 'You can tell he likes you. He looks at you the same way Trouble looks at Connie.' She clapped her hand over her mouth.

'What do you mean? Sprout?' I pulled her hand away from her mouth.

She let go of her end of the bedsheet and grabbed my hands. 'Promise not to tell?' she begged. 'Guide's honour?'

I promised. I even did the Guide salute and secret left-handed handshake to show her I really meant it.

'He gives her chocolate and other treats. He told her he wants to be her boyfriend.'

'But she *can't* have a Japanese boyfriend. They're our enemy' It all sounded very dangerous. 'We should tell Miss Kent.'

'No! We mustn't! We can't.'

'Why not?'

'Because he made me promise.'

'Who did? Trouble?'

She nodded. 'He said if I told anyone there would be . . . consequences.'

'What sort of consequences?'

'I don't know. But I'd rather not find out. Forget I ever mentioned it.'

I promised again that I wouldn't tell anyone, but I couldn't stop thinking about it.

We finished mangling the laundry in silence.

After Tinkerbell had been discovered by Major Kosaka, Miss Kent and Miss Butterworth had agreed that she could sleep in the loft with us. We all had great fun with the kitten, laughing as she pranced around the room chasing threads of string and bits of wool that we dangled in front of her.

'Sprout,' I whispered, as we settled down to sleep that night. 'Have you seen Tinkerbell anywhere?'

She said she hadn't now that I mentioned it. 'I'm sure Miss Butterworth has her wrapped up in a blanket in a drawer somewhere,' she said. 'We'll find her in the morning. Sleep tight.'

I lay awake for a long time beneath my mosquito net, worrying about the kitten, but I must have eventually dozed off, because I woke in the middle of the night, disturbed by a tremendous commotion beyond the window: dogs barking, and a horrible sound like foxes fighting.

I turned onto my side, stuffed my fingers in my ears, and went back to sleep.

ELSPETH

Minnie and I awoke at the same time, disturbed by a dreadful commotion below the window. I pulled on my housecoat.

'Where are you going?' Minnie whispered.

'To see what's going on. You stay with the girls.'

'They'll be perfectly all right for a minute or two,' she whispered. 'I'm coming with you.'

Together, we crept quietly downstairs and made our way outside, edging around the side of the house in the direction of the noise. Whatever we'd expected, neither of us was prepared for what we saw as we peered around the corner and watched as Major Kosaka tugged roughly on his dog's lead and shouted a command in Japanese before it dropped something from its mouth.

I grabbed Minnie's hand as she let out a reedy gasp.

Major Kosaka looked directly towards us, although we were hidden by the dark.

'No pets,' he called. 'You obey orders.'

We watched in terrified silence as he pulled on the dog's lead and they loped off together into the shadows.

Minnie sank to her knees and wept like a child.

'Oh, Minnie. I'm so sorry. I . . . Don't look,' I urged. 'Please don't look.'

'How could he?' she sobbed. 'How could he hurt such an innocent little thing?'

I gave her a moment, too distressed myself to be of any use. When her tears had subsided a little, I placed my hand on her arm and encouraged her to stand up.

'I'll deal with it,' I said. 'You go back inside. Boil some water for tea and to . . . well. Boil a decent pan full.'

It was one of the worst things I'd ever had to do.

I scooped up the lifeless remains of the kitten with a garden spade, retching as I placed the ragged little body into a shallow grave beneath a plane tree. With the ground frozen, I couldn't dig deep and hoped the dogs wouldn't return for another go. I placed a sprig of winter jasmine on top of the disturbed earth and, with the boiled water from the kitchen, I scrubbed the stained ground, determined to remove any trace of the incident. It would be hard enough to tell the children without them discovering any signs of the kitten's violent demise.

I scrubbed the ground long after the mess had gone, washing away the injustice of what was happening to us, sweeping my frustration and fears into the weeds that choked the neglected flower beds. My tears weren't just for the kitten. They were for all of us, for the fact that life had brought us to this miserable abandoned compound, and left us to suffer at the hands of those whose cruelty knew no end. In the year since the soldiers had marched into the school and Trouble had punched Minnie in the face, I'd often wondered what would follow; what would break the veneer of optimism we'd created to protect the children. I knew we couldn't keep on smiling and singing forever. Nobody could, no matter how deeply rooted their faith, or how brave they were. And now, here we were, facing the aftermath of another act of needless cruelty.

The awful task done, I went back inside and slumped into a chair beside Minnie. For a long time, neither of us spoke. The cups of weak tea Minnie had made for us sat idle on their cracked saucers.

'Did you . . .?'

I nodded. 'Under the tree.'

'Thank you, Els. I couldn't . . .'

I placed my hand on her arm. 'It's done, Minnie. Let's not think about it any longer.'

'It's just . . . it reminded me of something that happened a long time ago.' She took a deep breath and picked at a thread on the cuff of her nightie. 'I've never told you why I came to China, have I?'

I shook my head. For all that we'd become good friends, we didn't talk about the past. We instinctively understood that whatever had happened before Chefoo wasn't something we wished to share.

'You can tell me if you'd feel better for doing so,' I prompted, too exhausted to keep up the usual façade.

'I was treated rather cruelly by my husband, you see,' she continued.

'Husband? I didn't know you were married!' I'd checked Minnie's ring finger the first time we'd met. It was something we all did, from habit. A quick glance to see if this woman or that woman had managed to snag herself a husband when there were so few to go around after the Great War. With Minnie's ring finger empty, like mine, it had never occurred to me that she might once have been married. She seemed so perfectly suited to life as a spinster, but then, didn't we all when there wasn't much choice in the matter?

'I'm not married,' she said. 'Not anymore. He's dead now.'

'Oh dear. I'm very sorry,' I offered.

'Don't be. I'm not. He drank a lot and was . . . rather rough, shall we say.' I let the words settle between us as I waited for her to continue. 'I should never have married him. Everyone warned me not to.'

'What happened?' I asked, but my question was met with silence as Minnie stared at the floor. 'You don't have to tell me,' I said. 'Some things are best left in the past.'

But, like a canal lock gate slowly opening, once she'd started, the words flowed out of her.

'The final straw came when I told him we were going to have a baby. I was several months along when I found out. It took me another month to pluck up the courage to tell him.' She took another deep breath. 'He'd made it very clear he didn't want children so I was afraid of how he'd react.'

'What did he say?'

'Not a great deal. He did all his talking with his fists.'

'Oh, Minnie.'

'He didn't want a child, so he made sure we didn't have one.'

I couldn't speak, unable to marry the things Minnie was telling me with the kind, gentle woman I knew. I put my cup and saucer down and took her hands in mine.

'I'm so sorry. I had no idea.'

'I lost the baby a few days later. On the bathroom floor.' She gulped in a great mouthful of air. 'Thankfully, he was out. I had to . . . deal with it.' Her grip tightened on my hand so that my nails pressed painfully into my skin. 'I wrapped everything up in a towel and buried it in the field behind the garden.' A hollow silence filled the room as Minnie's awful revelation settled over us. 'I didn't know what else to do.' She looked at me, her face etched with anguish. 'I didn't know what else to do.'

'Of course you didn't. You poor, poor thing. You must have been so frightened.'

'I hardly had time to think. All I knew was that I had to leave. Had to get away. I packed a small case and took the bus to Liverpool docks that evening. I bought a ticket for the next steamer, which happened to be bound for Shanghai. I didn't care where I went. It didn't matter. I met Amelia Prescott on that steamer, and, well, here I am.' She dabbed at her tears. 'My mother sent word several years ago that he'd been killed in a bombing raid.'

'Good riddance,' I muttered. 'And may God forgive me.'

'I think of that child every day, Els. I don't even know if it was a little boy, or a little girl. Isn't that the most dreadful thing? I call the child Georgie, because that could be a boy's name, or a girl's. The poor little thing deserved so much better.'

'And so did you.' I squeezed her hands tight. 'So did you.'

We sat in silence as the sky slowly lightened through the windows and the horror of the night faded a little. Minnie seemed a little lighter too, as if the burden of shame and guilt and secrecy she'd carried all these years had lifted from her.

Sounds of movement upstairs made us both stir.

I pressed my hands to Minnie's as I stood up. 'Take a few minutes to yourself. I'll see to the girls. I'll tell them about Tinkerbell after breakfast and prayers.'

They were all absolutely heartbroken. Nobody could understand how the kitten had got out in the first place.

'We were all so careful about keeping the doors and windows closed, and there were no obvious holes she could have squeezed through,' Nancy said as she wept inconsolably.

I was in no doubt that Major Kosaka had sent one of the guards into the house while we were in the school building to let the kitten out on purpose. I understood the message loud and clear. We were all disposable. We were all entirely at their mercy.

There were many tears and lots of questions, which I indulged for a few minutes before I encouraged the children to dry their eyes and put on their coats and follow me out to the garden where we performed a little funeral ceremony for Tinkerbell, and said our goodbyes.

We sang 'All Things Bright and Beautiful' which brought tears to my eyes, especially when Minnie made a funny little gasping sound behind me, and I thought of everything she'd told me and what she must be thinking as she looked at the small mound of disturbed earth. We said the Lord's Prayer, held a moment's silence, and that was that.

'It isn't fair, is it, Miss,' Dorothy said as we walked back to the house. 'Why does God let innocent creatures die? Why would He let Tinkerbell die when she's never done any harm to anyone, and yet the guards kick their dogs and do all sorts of horrid things? Why is the world so cruel and unfair sometimes?'

Not for the first time in recent months, I struggled to provide an answer. Instead, I reverted to what I knew best.

'Let's do something to cheer everyone up, shall we. How about a session of self-defence at Girl Guides later? You can apprehend Miss Butterworth with your best knots.'

To the best of my faltering ability, and summoning all my former years of unquestioning belief, I prayed for Minnie's lost child that evening, and for my missing brother, and for everyone facing the agony of another Christmas without their loved ones. I meant my Amen more than ever; felt it in every pulse and beat of my tired and shattered heart.

NANCY

Christmas Day was as merry as could be expected, our Christmas wishes exchanged without any sense of merriment at all until a surprise delivery of Red Cross food parcels gave us something to celebrate.

The parcels didn't come nearly as often as they should, or half as often as we hoped, and we gasped with delight as we inspected the contents of the little cardboard boxes: powdered Carnation milk, Spam, chocolate, jam, sugar, margarine, apple pudding, and a whole tablet of Lifebuoy soap.

'We wouldn't have looked twice at it a year ago, would we,' Sprout said as we marvelled at the treasures inside. 'I'll never complain about soggy cabbage again.'

'Me neither.' I felt ashamed when I thought of all the times in the school dining room when we'd grumbled about porridge and lumpy custard.

Those little parcels gave us such joy, and although Sprout insisted it was a coincidence that they'd reached us on Christmas Day, I desperately wanted to believe that our captors had saved the parcels especially for today; that the spirit of Christmas really could make enemies become friends, even if only for an hour or two.

Over lunch, Miss Kent told us all about Agnes Baden-Powell, our founder, and Olave, Lady Baden-Powell, World Chief Guide.

'They both sound marvellous,' I said. 'Do you think we might meet them one day? Perhaps at a jamboree, when we're back home.'

An awkward silence followed, as it always did whenever someone mentioned home.

'You should write a letter, Miss,' Sprout suggested, 'to tell Lady Baden-Powell all about the Chefoo Brownies and Kingfisher Patrol and everything we're doing here. I bet she'll be surprised to discover there are Brownies and Girl Guides all the way out here in China, stuck in the middle of a war!'

Miss Kent agreed that it was a very good idea, and she would do precisely that.

'It doesn't feel like Christmas, does it?' Sprout said later, when we were sent outside to play a game of Cat and Mouse. 'It feels like we're all pretending.'

Even the annual Chefoo carol concert couldn't cheer us up. We'd all assembled in the school building, and we sang our hearts out, but it wasn't the same with the soldiers at the doors. Home Run smiled and whispered 'Happy Christmas' as we all trudged wearily back to our house. I noticed that he stopped Miss Kent, and took her aside to talk to her. I wondered if he sometimes gave her humbugs, too.

We went to bed earlier than usual that Christmas night. Nobody complained.

It was dark when Miss Kent woke me with a gentle shake of the shoulders.

'Wake up, Nancy. We have a surprise for you all.'

'What time is it, Miss?'

'Nearly eleven o'clock. Come along. Quickly now.'

When everyone was awake, we were instructed to go quietly downstairs. The lights were kept switched off because it was after curfew. We tiptoed and whispered and bumped into each other as we sat in a circle around a table, upon which stood a wireless.

'We're going to listen to the King's Christmas message, children,' Miss Kent whispered. 'We can't listen for long, and the line will be very faint, so not a sound from anyone.'

She seemed rather twitchy and kept glancing toward Miss Butterworth, who stood beside the door. Although I couldn't be certain because of the darkness, I thought I saw Home Run through the glass, standing guard on the other side of the front door.

There was no time for questions, about where the wireless had come from, or who was standing where. However it had happened, we all sat absolutely rigid as the voice of our Sovereign came faintly through the crackly line.

'*The Queen and I feel most deeply for all of you who have lost or been parted from your dear ones, and our hearts go out to you with sorrow, with comfort, but also with pride. We send a special message of remembrance to the wounded and the sick in the hospitals wherever they may be, and to the prisoners of war, who are enduring their long exile with dignity and fortitude. Suffering and hardship shared together have given us a new understanding of each other's problems.*'

It was like magic. I'd always looked forward to the Christmas message, always felt that even though he was many thousands of miles away in Sandringham House, the King was speaking to each and every one of us; that he was talking directly to me, and to Edward, and Sprout, and Mouse and each of our teachers. We sat in perfect silence as we listened to our marvellous King, to every pause and stuttering breath. As he spoke, we held hands in the dark, and I'd never felt more certain of victory in the coming year.

The wireless had disappeared by the time we woke up the next morning, but I clung tight to the memory of those few precious moments in the dark, when our King had come to China, and brought with him a sense of home, and a reminder that we weren't alone, or forgotten, and that if we were very good and brave, we would see home, and our loved ones, again.

We'd been at the Temple Hill compound for two months when the new year arrived on a bright January day. We'd found our way back into the familiar school routine, despite having to sometimes use the larger trunks and cases as makeshift desks, and sitting cross-legged on the floor when there weren't enough chairs to go around. We'd learned to use the paper in our exercise books very sparingly, often reusing the pages over and over again, rubbing out old calculations and past lessons to make way for new. We learned not to press too hard with our pencils so they would last longer, and we kept the shavings from our pencils to help light the fires. Our chores were always used as an opportunity to learn, and Miss Kent insisted that we kept the house, and ourselves, clean and tidy. With the fresh sea breezes that blew in across the ocean, we fell onto our mattresses at night exhausted.

Despite being enemy nationals, we were permitted to observe important dates, and our Guide leaders were especially keen for us to celebrate World Thinking Day that February.

'Thinking Day is a special day on which we remember all the Brownies and Guides and Scouts around the world,' Miss Kent announced as she opened our little parade. 'It is a day when we show our gratitude for being part of the international Guiding movement.'

We were all turned out so neatly in our Guide uniforms. I always felt terribly grown up when I put on my smart blue shirt and skirt, and I was ever so proud of the kingfisher emblem sewn onto our pockets. I thought about how seriously we'd prepared for our flying-up ceremony and the excitement of our investiture. Miss Kent had said we would soon be ready to take the tests to become Second-Class Girl Guides.

It was a bright cold day, but some of the guards brought out chairs to watch. They seemed quite fascinated by the whole thing. Home Run and Charlie Chaplin were especially interested, clapping enthusiastically when we did our semaphore and gymnastics displays. It wasn't that they were friendly with us as such, but there was something different about the way they treated us. They smiled when we ran past them, giggling at something or other, and they turned a blind eye when we strayed too close to the compound wall, or caught us climbing trees to get a glimpse of the ocean. They gave us as much freedom, and showed as much kindness as they could, without getting us, or themselves, into trouble with Major Kosaka. Freedom and kindness were the things we craved as much as bars of chocolate and syrup pudding, and it was comforting to know that even in a world full of war, kindness was never too far away.

As the months and the seasons moved on, our bodies began to change, and with so many of us living together, there was never any privacy in which to try to make any sense of it all. It was hard not to stare as the older girls pranced around in their knickers and brassieres. I was in awe of their long legs and curvy hips and proper breasts. When they were off doing something else, Sprout stuffed rolled-up socks under her vest, and pretended to be her sister, Connie. We sometimes smoked imaginary cigarettes and talked about boys, copying the things we heard Connie and her friends whispering about after lights out. Sprout pretended to be kissing a boy, using a pillow, which made us all giggle and go red. Still, I wondered what it would be like to really kiss a boy, and with Sprout going on about Larry Crofton all the time, I couldn't even look at him without staring at his lips.

There was also the rather excruciating business of our monthlies. Winnie had got hers just before Christmas, and Mouse was next. She thought she was dying when she came running to me to tell me she'd found blood between her legs.

I calmed her down and told her she wasn't dying. 'It's just . . . you know.'

'What?'

'Your monthlies. The thing girls get, so we can have babies. I'll fetch Miss Kent.'

Miss Kent handled it all in her usual efficient way. She gave Mouse a supply of rags to use and explained how she should change and wash them.

'It's all perfectly normal and nothing to worry about,' she said. 'You can expect the same thing every month until you're in your fifties.'

'Fifty!' Mouse was horrified. 'But that's forever away.'

'Indeed it is.' Miss Kent laughed. 'Welcome to the joys of being a woman.'

My monthlies still hadn't arrived and I was worried there was something wrong with me. I asked Miss Kent about it that evening after supper.

'Your turn will come, Nancy,' she said. 'And trust me, when it does, you'll wish you could be eleven again and not have to deal with it at all.'

'It's not fair, is it?' Mouse said that night, reassured by her chat with Miss Kent and sure she wasn't dying. 'Boys don't have to worry about things like this. They just get taller and their voices go deeper.'

'They have to shave though,' I said. 'Imagine having all horrid prickly whiskers on your face.'

'What, like Miss Prescott?'

We laughed so much tears streamed down our faces.

I'd spent more time with Mouse since we'd moved to Temple Hill, and I'd discovered that I enjoyed her company. Sprout was in and out of the San more than ever, so it was nice to have Mouse to talk to when Sprout wasn't around, although I worried terribly about her and wished she could get better once and for all.

She'd improved a little during the warmer months of spring and summer, but as autumn arrived and the leaves began to turn on the plane trees, she began to complain of a sore throat, and then a headache, and eventually she'd stopped coming to lessons. I was especially worried about her as she lay on her mattress beside me one September night, tossing and turning and coughing horribly.

I drifted in and out of sleep and heard whispers and footsteps intermittently throughout the night until I eventually fell asleep and dreamed about the sunflower we'd left behind at Chefoo School. In my dream, I watered it and took care of it as best I could, but no matter what I did, it withered and wilted until its sunny face drooped to the ground where it shrivelled up to nothing, and the birds pecked at the seeds and flew away with them, dropping them over the school walls.

When I woke in the morning, Sprout's mattress was empty.

Pulling my coat around my shoulders, I crept downstairs to find Miss Kent and Miss Butterworth sharing a pot of tea, both of them pale-faced and still in their nightdresses. Miss Butterworth had rollers in her hair.

Miss Kent walked over to me. 'Is everything all right, Nancy? You're up early.'

'Where's Sprout, Miss?' I asked. 'I mean, Dorothy. She isn't in her bed.'

'She had a rather bad night, I'm afraid. She's in the San. Nurse Eve is taking good care of her.'

'Can I see her?'

Miss Kent looked at Miss Butterworth, who raised her eyebrows in an 'I don't know' sort of way.

'Let me check with Nurse Eve first thing after breakfast. If Dorothy is a little brighter this morning, I'm sure she would like to see you.'

I trudged back upstairs to the loft where Mouse was also awake.

'Where were you? And where's Sprout?' she asked. 'Is everything all right?'

I shook my head and sat down beside her. 'I don't think everything's all right at all, Mouse. She's in the San again. Miss Kent wouldn't say very much, but I think she's really quite poorly this time.'

Mouse looked at me, eyes wide as she spoke in a thin whisper. 'You don't think . . . You don't think she might die?' She stared at me as she held my hand. 'Do you?'

I nodded, unable to speak my worst fears out loud.

Without saying a word, Mouse wrapped her bedsheets around me, and then she wrapped her arms around me and we sat together, huddled in a tight cocoon as we watched the autumn sun rise over the distant mountains.

ELSPETH

September 1943

'I'm proud of us, Almena Butterworth,' I said as we walked back from chapel. The sun was shining and I was in an unusually optimistic mood.

'Elspeth Kent? Proud! Goodness! We must celebrate immediately.' Minnie smiled.

'I'm not that bad, am I?'

'Yes, dear Elspeth. You are. So what has you all cheery?'

'It's just that we're all still here, still making a good go of things; still talking to one another. I'd say that's worth admiring, wouldn't you?'

'Absolutely,' she agreed. 'And you're right, you know. We're doing ever so well, the children especially. They're really quite remarkable.'

They certainly were resilient little things. No matter what we threw at them, they got on with it.

'I envy their innocence sometimes,' I said. 'Their lack of understanding of what this all means.'

163

'I think they understand more than we know,' Minnie replied. 'But, you're right. Children don't deal in consequences. They have a wonderful capacity for living in the now, while we're forever imagining the worst, and "what-iffing".'

As we approached the end of our second year under Japanese oppression, I'd learned that there was little benefit to continually worrying about what lay ahead. What was the point? We had no control over our destiny. The best we could do was enjoy any brighter moments when they arrived, however brief they might be. I'd also learned that every situation, no matter how bleak it might seem, always had the potential to improve, and so it had proven to be with our move to Temple Hill. A year after our weary arrival, our group was managing well. The children had settled into the school routine nicely, and we had an efficient system in place for the day-to-day management of domestic arrangements. We'd made an unfamiliar, hostile place feel like home. We'd survived and endured, when everything had conspired to see us fail.

But my mood darkened as we passed the hospital.

'I think I'll check in on Dorothy,' I said.

Minnie placed her hand on my arm. 'I doubt there'll be much change from this morning. Why not leave it to the nurses and have a sit-down for once.'

She already knew my answer.

I made my way to Dorothy's room, but, as Minnie had predicted, there was little change.

'She's comfortable, but still running a fever,' Nurse Eve confirmed. She saw the concern on my face as I looked at the child who, mercifully, was sleeping and at least looked peaceful. 'Try not to worry, Elspeth. We'll make sure she's comfortable. Rest and kindness are the best remedies for her now.'

But I did worry. I worried all the way back to the house, where I found Minnie setting up the gramophone player.

'I thought it might take your mind off things,' she said as she took a record from its sleeve, set it onto the player and carefully lowered the needle.

Charlie had given us the gramophone player after finding it in the basement of the boys' house. Fortunately, Minnie had been silly enough to pack her collection of sixpenny records, bought from Woolworths before she'd left England, so we had everything we needed to add a little musical interlude to our days. The scratch of the needle as it connected with the grooves on the record made us both smile.

'See?' Minnie said as the first bars of music struck up. 'Music is the best cure.'

Since Charlie's discovery, we'd got into the habit of playing records for a precious hour of relaxation each week, an hour during which we forgot about everything else and let ourselves become gloriously lost in the music of dance bands and military bands. 'Goodnight Sweetheart', 'Easter Parade' and 'Cheek to Cheek' from *Top Hat* were our favourites. Our musical interludes beside the gramophone were a balm; a reminder that life was full of beauty, and that a gentle waltz or a rousing band number could do wonders for one's sense of hope and determination. Minnie was right. It did take my mind off things, if only for a little while.

But like a plaster placed over a grazed knee, show bands and symphonies only concealed the wounds of war temporarily, and the next cruel reminder that we were in a precarious and dangerous situation was never far away.

On a cool September morning, almost exactly a year after we'd arrived at Temple Hill, and after an especially grim breakfast of watery porridge, and even more watery tea made from six-day-old leaves, Charlie asked if he might have a quiet word. Alone.

I left the girls in charge of washing up the breakfast dishes, reminding them not to leave the soap in the water.

'We're down to the last few tablets of Lifebuoy,' I told Charlie as we stepped outside. 'And to think we used to rub naughty children's toothbrushes in it to wash their mouths out after being caught using bad language. It's far too precious now to waste on reprimands.'

I always talked too much around Charlie. Minnie was right when she said he made me come over all silly, and his easy brooding silence only made me natter on all the more.

Once we were safely away from prying young ears, he began to explain why he'd wanted to talk to me.

'I'm afraid I've had some rather upsetting news concerning a former servant at Chefoo School. The gardener. Wei Huan.'

It was such a long time since I'd heard his name spoken that I was a little taken aback.

'Wei Huan? Is he in difficulty?' I swallowed hard and prepared myself for the worst.

'Since leaving the school, he's been staying in the Temple Hill area with his family,' Charlie explained. 'He saw us arrive, and suspected we would be short on supplies. You might not be aware,' he continued, 'but Wei Huan has been working with some of the male staff to send additional food in to us.'

'Gosh. How brave of him.'

I smiled as I fondly remembered the kind gentle man who'd been so patient with the children and who had given me the parcel of sunflower seeds, but my smile faded as I thought about the haunted expression on his face as he'd stolen from the school supplies.

'It was indeed brave,' Charlie continued. 'An act of admirable loyalty, but not without risk.'

He paused.

'What is it? Charlie?'

'I'm afraid he was caught smuggling eggs and milk over the

wall. We believe one of the guards tricked Wei Huan into his confidence, and betrayed his trust.'

I felt sick to my stomach. 'What happened to him?'

'The guard who caught him has been promoted in rank. The one who calls himself Trouble.' I stiffened at his name. 'Wei Huan, I'm sorry to say, was beaten in front of his family and other local farmers,' Charlie continued. 'I don't know what his condition is now, but it is clear he was being used to teach a lesson to those who sympathize with enemy nationals.'

It was the most upsetting and awful news, a chilling reminder that those who disobeyed the rules would pay the price.

'And his wife? Shu Lan? Did you hear any news of her?'

He shook his head. 'All I know is that they were married in the spring, but she has already travelled north, to Weihsien, with other members of the family. Wei Huan's mother is unwell, so they couldn't make the journey together.'

Our conversation was interrupted by the headmaster.

'Emergency staff meeting,' he said. 'Quick as you can.'

I looked at Charlie. 'Whatever now?'

He shrugged. 'We'd better go and find out.'

We made our way to the school building where all the Chefoo School staff were already gathered.

'I'm just back from a meeting with Major Kosaka,' Mr Collins announced. He looked exhausted, and serious. 'I'm afraid it's not good news. We are to be moved again.'

A gasp of shock and disbelief passed around the room.

I clasped my hands together, my nails pressing into my skin. Minnie's hands fell to her sides. 'And just when we were making a good fist of things here.'

The headmaster's shoulders slumped as he continued. 'I know you'd all hoped we would remain here until we were liberated, but that is not to be the case.'

'Do you know where we're going?' Charlie asked.

'I wasn't told, but I have my suspicions.' Mr Collins paused. 'As you all know, large groups of enemy nationals have been moved to so-called Civilian Assembly Centres in Shanghai. Those further north have been taken to a centre in Weihsien. Without doubt, that is where we are going.'

'When?' I asked, my voice thin and strangled with shock. 'When will we go?'

He cleared his throat. 'We leave first thing tomorrow morning. I think it will be best if we tell our individual house groups, rather than a formal announcement coming from me. The children might take the news better if it is presented in a more matter-of-fact way.'

Whichever way we presented it, there was no avoiding the fact that the children would be dreadfully upset. I couldn't bear the thought of telling them; of disrupting and unsettling them again.

After more questions to which there really weren't any answers, we returned to our respective houses in a daze, all of us devastated by the news of another move, and terrified by the prospect of where we were being moved to. I felt as if we were teetering on the edge of a deep hole, waiting for someone to push us in.

I looped my arm through Minnie's as we made our way back to the house.

'I can't bear it, Min. How can I tell them? I just can't.'

'Of course you can. You'll find the right words, just like you always do.'

I let out a long sigh. 'I find words. I'm not entirely sure they're always the right ones.'

'I'll tell the girls if you'd really rather not, but I honestly think they'll take it better coming from you. They trust you, Els. We all do.'

I leaned my head wearily on her shoulder. 'Dear Minnie. Whatever would I do without you?' I pushed my shoulders back and closed my eyes, savouring the stillness and the golden glow of the autumn sun. 'I'll tell them,' I sighed. 'Somehow, I'll tell them.'

Once again, I found myself standing in front of dozens of eager young faces, ever more conscious that their well-being and safety rested in my hands. I calmly explained that we would be leaving Temple Hill, careful to erase any hint of worry or concern from my voice, and yet I heard the echo of my words from a year ago when I'd offered the same calm reassurances. How many more times would I do this? I drew strength from the girls in front of me, a year older, taller and wiser. Despite everything, they were doing what all children do: learning, growing, finding their way in the world. Even war couldn't hold back that which nature intended.

I fielded questions for which I didn't have any answers, and consoled Connie Hinshaw who was particularly upset to hear that we were leaving.

'Will my sister be able to travel with us?' she asked. 'We won't have to leave her behind, will we?'

'Nobody will be left behind, Connie. I can promise you that.'

When I'd addressed their immediate questions and concerns, I dispatched the girls to the loft to gather up their things. They were instructed to take down the pictures they'd drawn to make the place look a little more like a home, to pack away their clothes, roll up their mattresses, and sweep the floors so that anyone arriving after we'd departed would find the place clean and tidy and far more welcoming than we'd found it when we arrived.

'As Lord Baden-Powell once said, "Try and leave this world a little better than you found it,"' I remarked. 'And that applies to this house, too.'

Before I attended to my own belongings, I went to the hospital block to see how Dorothy was faring. Nurse Eve's diagnosis was not good.

'She's still very weak, I'm afraid. Tuberculosis is a cruel condition. Consumption, as we used to call it. It was a fitting name. It really does consume the person who suffers.'

I flinched at the word. It was the first time she'd officially diagnosed Dorothy's condition. I'd suspected for a while, but hoped I'd be proven wrong in my amateur diagnosis.

'Is she well enough to travel?' I asked.

'Not really. She needs plenty of rest and fluids, and clear fresh air. I'll keep doing my best. That's all I can promise.'

I thanked her and popped my head in to check on Dorothy. She was sleeping. I sat with her for a while, remembering all the times I'd asked her to stay behind after class, and all the curious questions I'd answered. Mostly, I thought about the potential I saw in her.

'Come along now, Dorothy,' I said as I held her hand. 'It's time to put up a fight. I know you can, and we'll hopefully find a doctor at the new place we're going, and there'll be all the medicine you need to get better.' I smoothed her bedsheets and straightened her blanket and touched my fingertips lightly to her cheek. 'One more big effort, Sprout. That's my girl.'

Before I returned to the others, I took a moment in the garden beside the hospital block, and stood for a while next to the patch of earth where Tinkerbell was buried. I took a sunflower seed from my pocket, and pressed it deep into the earth that had been warmed by the generous autumn sun. I watered the patch of soil, said a prayer for Dorothy, and made my way back to the house.

From the nine seeds Wei Huan had given me, I had seven left. One sunflower grew at Chefoo School, and one would grow here, at Temple Hill. I wondered how many more places we would call home, how many more sunflower seeds I would plant before the war was over.

Whatever happened, I was determined to keep one seed, to

plant when I was back home, in England. That one would be for freedom, and in its bright face I would see the hope and resilience of the children I'd kept in my care. From its seeds, I would plant many more sunflowers, until there was an entire field of them chasing the sun, and I would be gloriously free to walk among them; to go wherever I might choose.

But that was for the future. For now, I must follow orders and go where others instructed, no matter how great my fear of what awaited us there.

PART TWO: INTERNMENT

Weihsien Civilian Assembly Centre, Shantung Province

1943–1945

THE GUIDE LAW: A GUIDE OBEYS ORDERS

It makes no difference whether you are cleverer, or older, or larger, or richer than the person who may be elected or appointed for the moment to give you orders; once they are given, it is your duty to obey them.

NANCY

Oxford, 1975

Memory is a curious and maddening thing. People and places appear and fade as quickly as footprints in the sand so that no matter how desperately I wish to remember something or someone, I can't always grasp them or study them properly before they are washed away. My past is one of scraps and fragments. Perhaps it is the same for us all.

And yet there is a cruel irony in that the memories I would rather forget are precisely the ones that I recall most often. They bloom and form with ease, creeping up on me when I least expect it – while pruning the roses, or minding my own business along the riverbank – yet the moments and conversations I actively seek cannot easily be found. Do I imagine things, or did they actually happen? I can never be quite certain.

Of all the things I recall from those years, what I remember most is how desperately I missed my mother. Even when the soldiers arrived, and our lives were forever changed, being apart from her was the hardest thing of all. You see, our war wasn't one of battles and bombs. Ours was a war of everyday struggles; of hope versus despair, of courage against fear, strength over frailty. For all the time we spent under the control of the Japanese regime, without any certainty of when – if – it would end, not one of us could be sure which side would win. So we simply went on, rising and falling with each sunrise and sunset; forever lost, until we were found . . .

ELSPETH

September 1943

We left Temple Hill at first light, in a convoy of dirty trucks. The loose tarpaulin flapped at the sides, letting in a cold breeze as we rumbled along.

'Bunch up, girls,' I instructed as I buttoned the collar of my coat. 'Keep tight together. It'll help keep you warm.'

Their cheeks were pale, their eyes tired and confused. I couldn't even bear to look at Minnie who sat opposite me; couldn't allow any emotional cracks to seep through the fragile veneer of my resolve. I pushed my deepest fears far from my mind, fixed a reassuring smile on my face, and focused on the immediate needs of the children, which were thankfully plenty. Handkerchiefs, reprimands, and reassurance were dished out as and when required. Dorothy was transported under the careful watch of Nurse Eve who offered me a reassuring smile whenever I caught her eye.

After a mercifully brief but unsettling and uncomfortable journey, the trucks jerked to a stop. As I peered through the gaps in the tarp, I saw we'd arrived at the harbour.

'We're going on a boat?' I whispered to Minnie, horrified by the thought of leaving land.

'Apparently so,' she replied, peering through the tarp beside me. 'Charlie was right, then.'

He'd guessed that if we *were* being taken to the camp at Weihsien as we suspected, we would travel by boat, around the Shantung peninsula to Tsingtao, and, from there, be transported by road or rail to our destination.

A rising sense of panic washed over me as the soldiers barked orders at us. All was noise and confusion, and I could hardly think straight as they hurried us along, looking on sternly as we struggled to unload our trunks and smaller cases.

'Hurry up, Elspeth Kent.'

I flinched at the voice. Just as I'd feared, Trouble was coming with us, wherever it was we were going.

When the last of the children had collected their belongings, I helped Nurse Eve and the other two nurses with the most sickly children, several of whom were too weak to walk and had to be carried to join the others on the wharf. Poor Dorothy looked like death warmed up. I pulled her close to me and held her hand as we all huddled together and waited for further instruction.

'Not long now, Dorothy,' I said. 'We'll be on our way very soon and then you can rest again.'

Her silence was dreadfully upsetting. More than anything, I wanted her to ask one of her infuriating questions, or be too busy chatting to Nancy to pay any attention to me.

The worst part of being moved again wasn't leaving, but the empty void of not knowing our destination. Everything felt very different from the last time. We weren't simply relocating to another school in a different area of Chefoo; this time we were leaving the city entirely. The sight of the small steamer moored alongside the wharf made my stomach lurch. Even the usual chirp and chatter of our little flock was silenced by uncertainty and apprehension. Only the adults spoke in low voices, making sure we wouldn't be overheard as we took it in turns to speculate and reassure one another.

Despite the rush of our departure from Temple Hill, we'd made sure everyone was turned out as neatly as possible, but even so, in my patched-up skirt and threadbare cardigan, I felt more like a prisoner than ever. My shoes were scuffed, my coat was coming apart at the seams. Even my ugly red armband was faded by the sun and frayed around the edges. As I looked around at our rather forlorn group, it struck me that we were all rather frayed around the edges; one loose thread away from unravelling altogether.

The children did their best to be patient, but the youngest were tired, hungry and confused, and the older children were unusually sullen, their faces drawn. I knew they were lacking in essential vitamins, and it was starting to show. Their once plump cheeks had sunk into valleys. Their bright eyes lacked the lustre of full health. We'd done our best to shield them from the very worst of things, but they were old enough to understand that this wasn't a jolly expedition, but something far more serious.

After an age, we were finally instructed to board the steamer. I tripped over a stray suitcase as we moved forward, arms flailing as I fell awkwardly to the ground. The guards laughed.

Charlie rushed to help, taking my elbow to lift me up.

'Anything broken?' he asked, his eyes full of concern.

'No. I'm fine.' I stood up and brushed myself down. 'Rather embarrassed, but nothing broken.' I blinked tears from my eyes. *Don't be such a baby*, I scolded myself. *Pull yourself together, Elspeth.*

'Best hurry,' he urged as one of the guards blew a whistle and the ship's horns sounded for departure. 'We don't want to be left behind.'

'Don't we?'

We studied each other for a fleeting moment, and I knew he was thinking what I was thinking. What if we dared to make a run for it? How far would we run, and where would we go?

'Perhaps another time, eh?' he said, a smile of resignation at his lips.

'Another time,' I replied.

My knees smarted from where they'd taken the brunt of my tumble and my wrists ached from where I'd braced myself, but there wasn't time to make a fuss. The low rumble of the anchor being raised made the gangway shake as we stepped aboard and made our way down to the ship's cargo hold, where the entire Chefoo group was packed tightly together, like too many books wedged on a shelf, with hardly a gap between us.

'Well this will never do,' Minnie muttered, as she assessed the cramped conditions. 'I'm sure we can do better than this.'

I looked on wearily as she organized the children into neat rows, each child alternately sitting one way, then the other, so they faced each other with their feet beside their neighbour's bottom, rather than sitting side by side. It made a surprising difference and provided everyone with a precious few inches of extra room.

'Simple mathematics and spatial awareness,' Minnie said as she squashed into the spot beside me, her feet extending well past my hips. 'I really should have been a scientist, you know.'

But despite Minnie's problem-solving skills, there was still very little privacy to be found. For all that we'd lived and worked together for many years, the situation in the ship's hold presented an entirely new level of domestic entanglement. We quickly learned that hats were a nuisance, and that body odour was unavoidable, and that there was little we could do but accept the excruciating indignity of it all.

The ship's hold was dark, cold and horribly claustrophobic.

A nauseating stench of damp wood and saltwater laced the air. The portholes had been covered by sacking, presumably so we wouldn't be spotted and rescued by any passing American warships. A makeshift curtain of sorts divided the hold in two; girls and women on one side, boys and men on the other. It hardly made one jot of difference, but we were too tired to care.

'Take off your armbands and tie them around your mouths and noses,' I suggested when the children complained of the terrible smell. 'It might block it out a little.'

Our conversations were muted and muffled beneath the fabric. Eleanor Yarwood passed around a bottle of very expensive-looking perfume that still had a few precious drops of amber liquid inside.

'Shalimar,' she said. 'We might as well use it. I don't exactly have any special occasions to save it for.'

I tried not to think about how much it had cost as we passed the bottle around and each took a drop. The smell was exquisite. I closed my eyes and imagined I was on my way to a dance, dressed to the nines, my skin laced with the scent of fine perfume, but my temporary escape didn't last long.

Conditions during the journey were testing to say the least. We tried our best to be polite and considerate, but there simply wasn't enough room to prevent one's elbows from continually bumping into a neighbour's, and there was nothing to be done about an itch somewhere awkward, other than to scratch it, or grin and bear it. As the hours pressed on, I thought about the struggles we'd faced when the soldiers first arrived at Chefoo, and the struggles Temple Hill had presented us with. All of it had been manageable, but this . . . this was different. It was degrading, and demoralizing.

Despite being under Japanese control for two years, I'd never felt more like an enemy prisoner.

* * *

There was nothing we could do other than to somehow endure the cramped conditions and the relentless seesawing of the ship. We roused the children after a restless night, arms and legs wrapped around each other like a litter of puppies. Limbs that were so carefully restrained at the start of the night were splayed every which way come the morning, any politeness and embarrassment eventually replaced by the physical urge to stretch out.

During the daytime, we took it in turns to lead the children in hymns and Psalms and songs to bolster their spirits, and told them stories of difficult journeys and hardships endured. Shackleton's Antarctic expedition, dramatically recounted by Charlie, became a firm favourite. But the dark endless nights posed their own challenge, and I came to dread the setting of the sun. When the last of the children had finally fallen into a sleep of pure exhaustion, I curled up beside Minnie, and retreated to some other place in my mind, far away from the suffocating cargo hold I found myself in. I drifted in and out of sleep as the ship rocked and rolled. Sometimes, I dreamed about Harry. Other times, I worried about Alfie. Mostly, I clung tightly to whatever small scraps of hope and dignity remained.

Some of the children vomited endlessly. Others were pale and quiet. Nurse Eve kept a special eye on Dorothy, who, thankfully, slept most of the way, apart from when she was roused to make sure she drank water, or have her temperature checked. It was still on the wrong side of acceptable.

'How is she doing?' I asked.

Nurse Eve shook her head, despondently. 'The sooner we get to wherever we are going, the better.'

The terrible, unavoidable reality of the situation weighed heavily on my mind, so that I found it hard to breathe when I thought about it for too long. But the question nagged and nagged at me: what if Dorothy didn't pull through? What if, after everything we'd been through, we lost her?

'Any improvement?' Minnie asked as I returned to my space beside her.

I shook my head wearily. 'None. She's still running a fever. I wish it were me who was poorly. I wish I could take her fever away and see her back on her feet, bossing the others around and being her usual mischievous self.' There was no longer any point in denying my fondness for the girls. They'd become my family in the past year; the children I'd never had. 'I feel so helpless.'

Minnie sighed, and patted my hand. 'We all do, Elspeth. We all do.'

After three insufferable days, the steamer finally came to a stop, and we disembarked, blinking like moles as we emerged into the daylight at the port of Tsingtao.

'What now?' Minnie asked, yawning as we stared at a railway station platform on the other side of a dusty road.

'I don't know,' I sighed as I watched our Japanese guards assemble in front of us. 'And I wish, with all my heart, that we didn't have to find out.'

NANCY

'Wake up, Plum. We're here.'

A dusty breeze blew through the canvas tarpaulin of the truck. I blinked and rubbed grit from my eyes as Mouse shook my shoulder to wake me.

'Where are we?' I asked. I sat up and peered through a gap in the tarp as we passed through a tall gateway, decorated with Chinese writing.

'We're at Weihsien Civilian Assembly Centre, Nancy,' Miss Kent replied. 'Our new home.'

The motion of the truck rocked me from side to side. I was too exhausted to brace myself, hardly caring who, or what, I bumped into as Mouse shoved in beside me. Together, we looked out at the barbed-wire fences surrounding the high grey-brick walls, and gazed up at the tall watchtowers, patrolled by guards with guns.

'Who are all those people?' Mouse asked as the trunks lumbered along a sort of main road lined with acacia and juniper trees, and where people of all ages and races, sizes and shapes waved as our convoy of trucks rolled past. 'And what are they all doing here?'

'Whoever they are,' I said, 'they seem pleased to see us.'

Most of the people were westerners like us, with white skin, although their arms and legs had been deeply browned by the sun. The women wore loose-fitting dresses, and some of the men wore khaki shorts, with nothing on top. Their ribs poked through the skin on their bare chests, their arms as skinny as some of the Chefoo boys'. I'd never seen men look so thin, and couldn't stop staring. After spending the past two years with only the other Chefoo children and teachers, it was fascinating to suddenly see so many new and different people.

As the line of onlookers outside the truck gradually thinned, my gaze turned to the grey-brick buildings that ran in long rows off the main street, barrack-style with red iron railings at the windows. Between these smaller buildings were larger blocks with signs on the walls saying 'No.1 Kitchen', 'No.2 Kitchen', and so on. As a group of young children ran alongside the trucks, I stuck my arm through the gap in the tarpaulin and waved to them, calling out a tentative 'Hello!' to acknowledge their shouts of welcome.

'Nancy! Please keep your arms inside the truck.'

I jumped at Miss Kent's voice. 'I'm sorry, Miss. I just—'

'And don't talk to strangers,' she added, rather sternly.

'She looks ever so tired, and cross,' Mouse whispered beside me as we turned our backs to the tarp. 'Best do as she says.'

After taking a left turn and following the wall alongside 'No. 3 Kitchen', the convoy of trucks eventually came to a stop.

'We've arrived, children,' Miss Kent announced, clapping her hands to rouse those who were lucky enough to still be dozing. 'Here we are.'

Two by two, like a reverse of the Ark, we clambered out

into the sun, both relieved, and afraid, to have arrived at our destination.

'What now?' Mouse asked.

I shrugged. It was too big a question to answer.

We'd hardly been out of the trucks five minutes when a new Japanese guard directed us to a large parade ground, where we were ordered to line up in neat rows. Two very stern-looking men in uniform climbed onto a high platform in front of us. They exchanged a few words before the more senior of the two began to speak. We'd become accustomed to the way in which orders and instructions were shouted in clipped sentences, rather than politely explained.

'I am camp Commandant, Mr Tsukigawa. This is Chief of Police, Mr Nagamatsu. You will obey the rules of Weihsien camp.' Several other guards stood close by, guns at their hips. They kept their eyes on us as Mr Tsukigawa listed instructions about camp rules and regulations. 'Roll-call each morning. Meals three times a day. Curfew at ten.' On and on he went.

Little clouds of dust swirled in mini-tornadoes at my feet as I swatted at flies that buzzed annoyingly around my head. With Mr Tsukigawa's voice droning on in the background, my mind began to wander. I was hungry and tired, and swayed like a field of kaoliang blown in a summer breeze. I must have nodded off because one minute I was staring at the back of Miss Kent's head, thinking about my mother, and the next minute, Miss Butterworth was shepherding me back into line.

'Stand still,' the Commandant shouted. 'No moving.'

'Am I in trouble, Miss?'

Miss Butterworth shook her head and pressed a finger to her lips.

It was all terribly serious. Much more so than at Temple Hill.

I forced myself to stand perfectly still while the Commandant explained, in rather broken English, that there were nine camp committees, each in charge of Discipline, Medicine, Finance, Food, Education, Engineering, Quarters, General Affairs and Employment. When he finally finished his announcements, we were instructed to follow a group of guards along a road that ran parallel to Main Street. They left us outside one of two large buildings, signed 'No. 23' and 'No. 24', and left us to figure the rest out for ourselves.

'I don't like it here,' I whispered to Mouse.

'Me neither,' she agreed. 'I don't like it at all. Hopefully we won't be here for long.'

'Now girls, gather around.' Miss Kent clapped her hands and beckoned us toward her like a mother duck flapping her wings. 'I know you're all tired and hungry after our long journey, but there are lots of things to organize before we can eat and get some rest, so I need you all to be patient and show our new . . .' She paused, fishing for the right word. 'And show the people here how well-mannered and polite you are,' she continued. 'We'll no doubt be of great interest as new arrivals. Everyone will want to know where you've come from, and more besides. While there's no need to be rude, I'd encourage you not to engage in prolonged conversations. We Chefusians will stick together for the time being.'

When she'd finished, we were given permission to stretch our legs, but not to go too far. As the others dispersed, I hung back.

'Run along now, Nancy,' Miss Kent chided when she noticed I hadn't gone with them. 'Off you go.'

'Is there a hospital, Miss? You said there might be a hospital with doctors and medicine for Spr . . . Dorothy. She was so listless during the journey and I'm dreadfully worried about her.'

After we'd got off the train that had brought us from Tsingtao, I'd seen Sprout being lifted into a truck by one of the male teachers and Home Run, who'd offered to help. For a terrible moment I'd thought she was dead, she looked so pale and still, just like a piece of marble, but she'd opened her mouth to take a sip of water. I hadn't seen her since.

'There is indeed a hospital, Nancy. Dorothy has already been taken there. The nurses will make her as comfortable as possible. I'll let you know when you might be able to see her. Now, off you go.'

I caught up with the others as they trudged up a road toward a rather neglected-looking sports field. With a breeze swirling around us we were soon covered with a fine film of dust. Winnie Morris spat on her finger and drew the Girl Guide trefoil emblem into the dust on her leg. We all copied, carefully drawing the three leaves that symbolized the three parts of our Promise: Faith, Loyalty and Service. Soon, our arms, legs and cheeks were covered with trefoils. As the newest members of the Chefoo Girl Guides, and the founding members of Kingfisher Patrol, we were ever so proud of the Promise badges Miss Kent had pinned to our Guide uniforms. 'A reminder of the lifelong commitment you've made, to the Guide movement, and yourself,' she'd said during the Promise Ceremony. With our uniforms packed away in our trunks, we didn't know when, or if, we might have our next meeting of Girl Guides, so the trefoils we drew on our skin that first afternoon at Weihsien weren't just for fun, but a reminder of the promise we'd each made. Sprout had once said the three-leaved shape represented the three of us: Plum, Sprout and Mouse. Thinking about it again made me sad that she wasn't with us.

'I do hope Sprout will be all right,' I said, as Mouse kicked along beside me. 'It isn't the same without her.'

'I'm sorry I'm not more like her,' Mouse said. 'You must find me rather quiet and dull in comparison.'

'Oh, Mouse. You mustn't think that. I don't find you dull at all. I don't want you to be like Sprout. I miss her, but I like you for *you*. For who *you* are.'

'Really?'

I smiled. 'Really.' I grabbed her hand. 'Come on. We should probably head back before Miss Kent sends out a search party.'

We passed a tennis court and gardens, a large church, a school building and an enormous hospital, where I presumed Sprout had been taken. Behind the hospital, furthest away from the guard towers, was a leafy lane, lined with acacia trees. It was sheltered and secluded and, as we turned to walk down it, we saw a boy and girl kissing. We ran off, giggling, until we passed a large toilet block. The stench of sewage was impossible to ignore. We covered our noses with our hands and ran faster, eyes smarting with the effort not to retch.

We arrived back at the barrack-style houses hungry, thirsty and tired, but there was no time to rest.

'Right, girls,' Miss Butterworth chirped, rubbing her hands together as she always did when she was feeling industrious. 'We'll follow the same layout as we did at Temple Hill. The rooms are a little smaller, but we'll make it work.'

The basement room we'd been allocated was impossibly small. Reed mats appeared to be our beds, and the only protection from the bare floor and the cockroaches I saw scuttling about.

For our meals, we were each given a small tin container, a spoon and a tin mug. We'd missed the first two meals of the day, so by suppertime we were ravenous. We lined up, as instructed, outside Kitchen 1, where we were given a ladleful of a watery stew that looked like dirty dishwater, and a black-ened bread roll that was as hard as a rounders ball.

We joined the rest of the Chefoo group and sat together at the end of one of dozens of long wooden tables. The other tables were occupied by people who looked like they'd been in the camp for a very long time, and I tried not to stare at them.

Miss Butterworth said grace, thanking the Lord for all the good gifts around us and for providing food and shelter (at which I opened my eyes a fraction and stared at Mouse). We waited politely until the Amen before we tentatively spooned the grey stew into our mouths. It smelled like damp soil, and tasted worse. I imagined what Sprout would have said about it if she'd been there, but although it was disgusting, it was hot and it was food, and I didn't wish to be ungrateful or impolite. I tried to ignore the gritty bits that crunched against my teeth as I took slow steady mouthfuls, and tried my best to swallow. I was so hungry, but I retched with each mouthful. Even Miss Kent and Miss Butterworth were unusually quiet as we ate, each of us focused on the process of chewing and swallowing, despite every instinct telling us not to. Even though the food was terrible, and we were too tired to hardly lift our spoons to our mouths, our teachers didn't let up on their insistence on good table manners.

'Don't slouch, Nancy.'

'Elbows off the table, Joan.'

'Don't speak with your mouth full, Winnie.'

I hardly thought table manners mattered, given the situation. Winnie even said as much.

'Everybody else is slouching and resting their elbows on the table, Miss,' she grumbled.

Miss Kent put her spoon carefully down into her tin bowl. 'Which is precisely why we will not be doing the same, Winnie.

There is no excuse for poor table manners. We wouldn't tolerate it at Chefoo School, and we won't tolerate it here, either. In fact, we will tolerate it even less here.'

We ate the rest of the meal in silence.

Back at our dormitory, Miss Kent instructed us to all gather round.

'Once again, we find ourselves in a new and unfamiliar place, with new and unfamiliar people and rules. Things will be a little unusual until we find our feet, but let us not forget that we are resourceful Girl Guides, and can do anything we put our minds to.' She smiled her best 'We Will Be Brave' smile. 'There will be lots of ways for you to get involved in camp life,' she continued. 'You'll be required to help in the kitchens and the garden, and to collect water, and fuel for the stoves when it gets colder in the winter.'

Mouse raised her hand. 'Will we still be here in the winter, Miss?'

I very much hoped the answer would be no, because that would mean another Christmas without Mummy. I sometimes wondered if she would even recognize me after all this time. When she'd last seen me, I was only eight, and didn't even know how to tie my shoelaces properly. What if she didn't know who I was? What if, after all this time apart, we couldn't remember what to do when we were together?

Miss Kent fidgeted with a handkerchief as she answered Mouse's question.

'Hopefully not, Joan. But, if we are here for a while, then we will at least be prepared, and we will manage admirably.' She cleared her throat. 'There's a communal shower block, and latrines. We'll use chamber pots during the night, and empty them each morning.'

We stared at each other, horrified by the prospect of sharing toilets and showers with strangers.

'We're like proper prisoners of war now, Miss, aren't we?' Mouse said.

Miss Kent looked surprised, and didn't answer immediately. I was just as surprised to hear Mouse speaking up so often.

'We might not have the same liberties we once had, but freedom doesn't end with high walls and guard dogs,' Miss Kent said as she tapped a finger to her head. 'Freedom is here, girls. In the mind.'

I wasn't quite sure what she meant, but her words stirred a quiet surge of determination in my tummy.

'Now, that's enough for our first day,' Miss Butterworth announced. 'Everyone get ready for bed, and let's try and have a good night's sleep.'

We kept to our now familiar order of topping and tailing, mosquito nets suspended on an old fishing line above us, our smaller cases stacked neatly in one corner of the room. Mouse coughed and spat into a handkerchief as she got ready for bed beside me.

'You're not sick, too, are you?' I asked. I didn't want all my friends stuck in the hospital.

She shook her head and opened the handkerchief to show me a small grey lump of meat. 'I couldn't swallow it,' she whispered. 'But I didn't want to leave it in my bowl, either.'

I was both appalled and impressed that she'd kept the lump of meat in her mouth for so long.

'You'd better get rid of it,' I whispered. 'We don't want to attract rats.'

A trip to the latrines saw the end of the meat, but I knew we couldn't store food in our cheeks like hamsters, no matter how inedible it was.

As we knelt on our mats to say bedtime prayers (there wasn't room for us to kneel beside the mats, there being only eighteen inches between one and the next – Mouse had measured), I remembered my tea caddy. I hadn't seen it since we'd boarded the steamer in Chefoo.

My eyes flew open. 'My tin! My special tin! I don't know where it is!'

Everyone opened their eyes and turned to look at me.

Miss Kent didn't look very pleased. 'Goodness, Nancy. Whatever is the matter?'

I burst into tears. 'My tin. My special tin with Mummy's letters and everything. I've lost it.'

Within minutes, everyone was searching for it. The orderly pile of trunks was pulled asunder, each one opened to check that it hadn't somehow found its way inside, but it was nowhere to be found.

Mouse put her arm around my shoulder and patted my back and said not to worry.

'Someone will find it, Plum. It's most likely ended up with one of the boys, or something. We'll ask everyone in the morning.'

I bit my lip and tried to stay hopeful, but, despite Mouse's reassurance, I had the most awful feeling I'd left it on the boat, and would never see it again.

As the trunks were stacked neatly together again, and lamps were blown out, I curled up on my mat and tried to hold back the sensation that I was going to be sick. Mummy's words were the only thing I had to keep her near, and now I'd lost them, and it felt as if I'd lost her all over again.

I lay awake in the dark that first night at Weihsien. I listened to the familiar sounds of the other girls fidgeting and snoring beside me, and tried to ignore all the new and bewildering sounds beyond the barred windows: occasional shouting, men's laughter, the distant lowing of water buffalo. I shut everything out and focused on the bird that sang beside the window. Miss Kent had told me it was called a whip-poor-will, or a nightjar.

I was comforted by his strange little lullaby, in which he seemed to repeat his own name over and over. 'Whip-poor-*will*. Whip-poor-*will*. Whip-poor-*will*.'

It was the first of many nights when he would sing me to sleep.

ELSPETH

Our worst fears had been realized. Along with some fifteen hundred other souls, we were to be interned at Weihsien Civilian Assembly Centre. It was almost impossible to comprehend, impossible to accept that we'd been taken somewhere so primitive and so far removed from the comfortable lives we'd known not two years earlier.

From the outset, it was clear that life behind the high compound walls would be a very different experience to that which we'd left behind at Temple Hill. In addition to the hostile stares from the new guards, and the menacing barbed wire and strict rules set out by Mr Tsukigawa, Weihsien was far bigger, and populated by a bewildering variety of people.

'It's all rather . . . mixed, isn't it,' Minnie remarked as we reorganized our sleeping arrangements.

'That's one word for it, yes,' I agreed. I made no attempt to conceal the sarcasm in my voice. 'No wonder the children gawp and stare.' I gawped and stared myself. I'd already noticed several morally questionable women hanging around the men's shower block, and Minnie had discovered empty bottles of alcohol in the dustbins. 'When I think of all the effort we went to at Chefoo School to shelter the children from external influences. What a pointless exercise that was. Now they'll be exposed to goodness knows what.'

'At least the camp committees seem to have everything well organized,' Minnie said as we swept the floor and washed the windows to make our room a little more hospitable.

In a small way, I agreed that it was a relief to find routines already established, and elected chairmen and monitors in charge of the various committees.

'Yes. I suppose there is that to be grateful for,' I agreed, albeit half-heartedly.

There was really very little to be grateful for, but searching for positives in our situation had become as much of a habit as searching for bedbugs. They weren't always easy to see, but we knew we would find them eventually, if we could just summon the energy to keep looking.

After twenty-four hours, we'd experienced the full Weihsien schedule of roll-call, breakfast, tiffin, supper and curfew. Meals consisted of a millet-type porridge for breakfast, inedible stew for lunch, and a watery soup for supper, and everything was served with dry bread and black tea. Fresh milk wasn't available. We'd quickly discovered that the food committee kept any Red Cross supplies of Carnation powdered milk for the very young and elderly, who needed the calcium the most.

We were all very worried about the lack of calcium in the children's diet, aware that they needed it to develop strong bones and teeth. While they kept themselves reasonably clean and well-presented on the outside, we couldn't always tell what was happening to them on the inside; what damage their poor diet was doing to them, or what long-term emotional toll their prolonged separation from their parents would have on them. The children in our care had been brought up to believe that it was unmanly to cry if you were a boy, and silly and spoiled to cry if you were a girl, so they kept their feelings as tightly locked up as the great compound gates that had closed behind us.

As I lay awake on my mat during those first awful nights at Weihsien, I wondered which would prove to be the most harmful aspect of our captivity when – if – an end to it ever came: the physical deprivation, or the emotional.

It was just one more question to which I didn't have an answer.

At the start of our second week in camp, I woke with crippling cramps and pains in my stomach. I spent the day running back and forth to the latrines, and lay on my mat, groaning, between visits.

Apart from the insufferable tedium and indignity of daily roll-call, the latrines were one of the worst things about camp life. Without a reliable supply of running water, the cesspools were regularly overwhelmed, and the nauseating stench was unbearable. I pitied the so-called honeypot girls, local Chinese women who came into the camp several times a day to remove the stinking sewage. It was a stark reminder that however bad things might be, there was always someone suffering a greater indignity.

My fifth trip to the latrines in less than an hour happened just as the women arrived to empty them. I gagged and retched as the buckets of waste swayed on the bamboo poles suspended from their shoulders. One of the women seemed to be in some discomfort. From the roundness of her belly it was clear she was pregnant, but the other women, oblivious to her struggles, ignored her.

I covered my nose as I approached her, forcing myself not to look at the contents of the buckets.

'Here, let me help,' I said.

She flinched as I reached out a hand, but then she looked at me.

'Miss Elspeth?'

'Shu Lan?'

I was so surprised and pleased to see her, and yet horrified to see her at the same time. Her eyes were empty; her face tired and drawn.

Neither of us knew what to say. We stood in silence, floundering in questions and shame and uncertainty, and all the while the stench from the cesspool buckets engulfed us.

'You are alone?' she asked. She glanced anxiously over my shoulder, her gaze never straying from the guards on patrol nearby.

'We are all here,' I said. 'We arrived two weeks ago.'

'The children, too?'

I nodded. 'The whole school.' I had so many questions. 'How are you?' I asked. 'And Wei Huan? Is he with you?' I thought about Charlie's quiet concern when he'd told me about Wei Huan taking a beating from the guards at Temple Hill.

At Wei Huan's name, Shu Lan dipped her head. 'My husband is forced to work for the puppet regime.'

'Here? At Weihsien?'

She nodded again, and placed a hand on her swollen belly.

I offered an encouraging smile. 'When is your baby due? Wei Huan must be very happy.' I recalled how he'd once told me that flowers required patience and love and care, just the same as children, and that he longed for the day when he would become a father.

'Not his child,' Shu Lan said, her face set hard as she tipped her chin toward the guards patrolling the watchtower in the distance. 'Theirs.'

The horror of her words sent a shiver across my skin. 'I'm so sorry,' I offered. 'I'm so very sorry.'

'I do not need your pity, Miss Elspeth. I need your help.' She trembled as she spoke.

By now, the other women had gathered their buckets and were ready to leave. Our conversation had sent a ripple of concern spreading among them and they regarded me with disdain and distrust. One of them spoke to Shu Lan brusquely, clearly urging her to hurry up. Their raised voices caught the attention of Trouble, who was passing by.

He marched over to us, shouting something at Shu Lan as he poked her with his bamboo stick, before adding a particularly hard thrust to her stomach.

She cried out in pain and sank to the floor. I reached down to help her, but he pushed me roughly aside, sending me tumbling to the ground where I cowered beside Shu Lan, shielding us both with my arms.

'You again, Elspeth Kent.' He kicked Shu Lan's bucket of waste, deliberately sending the contents spilling over my clothes and hands. 'Clean it up,' he snapped as he pointed his stick at the honeypot girls. 'All of it.'

Some of the women rushed to fetch buckets of water and a broom as Trouble stalked away, leaving me sprawled on the ground in the filth. Two of the younger women scooped Shu Lan up from the ground and rushed off, half-carrying, half-dragging her between them. As I watched her go, someone grabbed my elbow and helped me to my feet.

'Not very pleasant, but nothing that won't come off in the wash, and at least he didn't strike you. Awful pig of a man. Come on. Straight to the shower. I'm Edwina, by the way. Edwina Trevellyan. Eddie will do.'

I could hardly keep up. Too shocked to say anything, I let Edwina Trevellyan take over. I managed to mumble a thank you as she led me to the shower block, where she announced to the dozen women already waiting that I was going straight to the front of the queue.

'And no complaints,' she announced, brusquely. 'I don't see anyone else covered in other people's shit.'

'Thank you,' I offered again as she waited beside me. 'I'm Elspeth Kent. I'm with the Chefoo School group.'

She didn't appear to care who I was, or what group I was with. She was already busy talking to one of the other women about the camp library.

Edwina Trevellyan was older than most of the women I'd seen in camp. Her hair, which she left to hang long and loose around her face, was pure silver, and her skin was as wrinkled as creased linen. She wore the most extraordinary collection of flamboyant clothes, none of which appeared to fit her properly, but she somehow managed to look elegant and stylish nevertheless.

'We don't talk to the honeypot girls,' an Australian woman beside me said.

'But I know the woman I spoke to,' I explained. 'She's a friend. Of sorts.'

She laughed. 'And you'll forget you ever set eyes on her, if you know what's good for you. If there's one thing the guards hate more than Chinese women, it's a British woman being friendly with one of them.'

The shower, which I'd avoided using until now, worked by pulling on a frayed rope which sent sporadic bursts of cold water over me and did little to make me feel in any way clean. I did my best with the rather meagre remnants of a tablet of soap, and rinsed off my skirt, which had taken the brunt of the spillage.

Edwina escorted me back to our basement room.

'What you did was admirable,' she said. 'And utterly foolish. I don't know where you were before they brought you here, but it seems to me that you need to wise up, dear.'

'How long have you been here?' I asked.

'Six months,' she said. 'And a lifetime.'

She left me as abruptly as she'd found me.

Cold, wet, deeply humiliated, and with my stomach still cramping, I stepped inside our miserable little room.

'You braved the showers then! How was it?' Minnie asked.

I didn't tell her why I'd taken a shower, too embarrassed about the entire incident, but as she held up a bedsheet to protect my modesty while I changed into clean clothes, I told her about Shu Lan.

'She told me Wei Huan is here, too,' I said. 'Forced to support the puppet regime. I suppose that was his punishment for trying to help us at Temple Hill.'

Minnie was as surprised as I'd been. 'It's a dreadful turn of events, but at least we know they're both alive.'

'Yes. At least there's that, I suppose. And there's something else.' I leaned closer to make sure the older girls couldn't hear. They had a terrible habit of eavesdropping. 'She told me the baby isn't Wei Huan's. She said it was . . . theirs.'

'Whose?'

'The guards'.'

'Which guard?' Minnie asked, keeping her voice to a whisper, not only to keep the children from hearing, but because it was so shocking and upsetting.

I tugged the sleeve of my cardigan and fiddled with a button as I took the sheet from Minnie. 'I got the impression there was more than one.'

We knew about 'comfort women' – Chinese women and girls, kidnapped by Japanese soldiers and raped, but such things were simply too awful to talk about.

Minnie's face paled as she sank onto the edge of a low stool. 'Oh, Elspeth.'

'She's clearly in a very difficult and dangerous situation,' I added. 'I need to find Wei Huan.'

'Do be careful, Els. I know you mean well, but this maybe isn't the best place for daring acts of heroism.'

'There's nothing heroic about it, Minnie. I simply want to help a friend. I'd hope anyone else would do the same for me. For any of us.'

She fussed with her hair. 'Of course. You're quite right. But still, do be careful. I rather depend on you, you know.'

We agreed not to talk about it again. For now, all we could do was pray for Shu Lan's safety, and that of the child.

After curfew, as I lay in the dark, my thoughts and fears strayed and swelled. Memories of home visited without warning, offering a tantalizing glimpse of the past, and beckoning to the future: Mother at the kitchen sink, the cat in a patch of sunlight, Alfie's bicycle propped against the gate, a rainbow after a summer rain shower, the smell of peat fires and malt from the brewery, Harry at the door with a bunch of daffodils. Small moments I'd taken for granted, and which brought such delight and despair in the remembering. How could I ever return to that life? How could I ever fully enjoy the spring sunshine when I'd known all this? Even if the war ended and we were liberated, I knew that part of me would always lie in this dark little room, waiting for the sun to rise. There would be no escape from these years of confinement. No liberation from the memories. My past was fractured. My present, uncertain. My future, shattered.

Around the room the girls tossed and turned, trying to get comfortable on their unyielding mats. They really were such resilient hardy little things, like the first snowdrops of winter and the first crocuses of the spring. For them, I tried to hide my knowledge of the atrocities such as those endured by Shu Lan. For them, I rose each morning, washed and dressed, and prepared to face another day in camp with humility and good grace.

For them, I found a room we could use for our Girl Guides meetings. For them, I sang, and prayed, and busied myself with the very practical matter of their education and welfare.

In this way, the long uncertain days passed.

For the children, I kept going. Without them, what reason did I have to wake up at all?

NANCY

'We won't be defeated by a few sheets of paper, and a lack of pencils,' Miss Kent said from the front of the classroom. Some of us didn't have writing materials, which we'd hoped would make it rather difficult for the lesson to continue. We should have known better. 'All you need to learn is a pair of eyes, a pair of ears, and an inquisitive mind. And, Lord knows, you all have those in abundance.'

The sun shone through the classroom window as Miss Kent tapped out adverbs and pronouns on the blackboard. If I closed my eyes, I could pretend we were back in our lovely old school, a fresh ocean breeze lapping at the windows, the servants rushing quietly along the corridors, the prospect of an excursion to the bay never too far away. If I closed my eyes, I could pretend that we were free to go where we wanted, when we wanted, and not kept behind high walls and barbed-wire fences.

'You might find it easier to work with your eyes open, Nancy.'

My eyes flew open. Miss Kent was watching me from the front of the room, arms folded across a lemon-coloured cardigan, an encouraging smile at her lips. I sat up straight and picked up the remaining stub of my pencil.

Since there were so many of us, it had been arranged that all the Chefoo School children would be schooled together in one building in the compound. Other children were taught in other buildings. We'd been instructed not to mingle with non-Chefoo children, or with anyone else.

'You may see some rather more . . . cosmopolitan people than you've been used to,' the headmaster had explained at our first Weihsien assembly. 'And while I'm sure you'll find our new neighbours quite fascinating, we Chefusians will stick together. We will abide by the same structure, routines and high moral standards we've always followed.'

Whatever else we might see going on around us was to be ignored, but that was easier said than done, especially when we saw the ladies who hung around the men's accommodation blocks. They wore clothes that were too small for them and showed their bosoms, and we ran away when they saw us staring at them.

Weihsien was unfamiliar and overwhelming, but it also reminded me how big and varied the world was; that it wasn't all white-skinned children, and starchy British teachers and Received Pronunciation, but a whole wonderful jumble of colours and shapes, languages and customs. It reminded me that I used to wonder about the world; that it used to excite me.

'I don't know why they're so strict about us mixing with the other children,' I grumbled to Edward on Sibling Saturday. 'I don't see what harm it would do to be friendly.'

'You're so naïve sometimes, Nonny,' he laughed as we strolled around the parade ground together. 'They don't want us to mix with the other children because they're not Protestants, like us. They don't want us to be influenced by other religions.'

'What difference does it make? We're all stuck here anyway,

just the same. What does it matter if we say different prayers at night?'

For once, Edward didn't have a clever answer to give me.

I really didn't understand why the teachers enforced our separation from the other camp children so strictly. When the other girls asked us to play with them, they thought us rude and stand-offish when we said no, and they didn't ask again. Some of the older Chefoo boys spoke to the non-Chefoo girls anyway, despite the teachers' instructions. Edward and Larry were two of the worst culprits.

'You really shouldn't,' I cautioned. 'You'll be in awful trouble if you're caught.'

'Not jealous, are you?' Edward teased. 'Don't like to see Larry talking to other girls?'

I went bright red and told him not to be silly.

Larry offered an apologetic smile. 'I didn't tell him to say that, by the way.'

'You're both ridiculous,' I snapped as I stormed off in a huff, mostly because Edward was right. I *was* jealous of Larry talking to the other girls, and didn't understand why.

No matter how much our teachers tried to enforce our usual principles and school routines, it was clear from the start that Weihsien was different to anything that had come before. Weihsien rules were stricter, and Weihsien guards didn't hesitate to hand out punishments. Failure to bow when a guard passed, or to stand to attention, led to a slap in the face, or worse. We watched in horror one morning as an elderly man was cruelly kicked for collapsing during roll-call.

'I hate them,' Mouse whispered when they'd left the poor man sobbing on the ground. 'I know it's wrong to say, but I really do.'

I hated them too, and was glad that Mouse had said it first.

After that, we all made sure to bow or stand to attention, as required.

Roll-call was one of the worst parts of our new camp regime. As soon as the bell rang, we had to stop what we were doing and assemble at our so-called 'district' where our supervising guard issued the command '*Bango*' and we began the long process of calling out our numbers in Japanese: ichi, ni, san, shi, go, roku, shichi, hachi, kyuu, juu, and so on. When the guards in each district were satisfied that everyone was accounted for, the warden rang a bell to signal that we were dismissed and could return to our chores or lessons. Sometimes roll-call took so long we couldn't remember what we'd been doing before it had started.

It was unbearably boring and we often had to stand in the rain or a cold wind, our teeth chattering and our fingers and toes numb. Miss Kent encouraged us to use the time to silently recite the Psalms or the Guide Laws or a favourite poem, but I used the time to leave Weihsien and go back to warm days in our garden in England, and memories of catching butterflies in my net. I'd always let them go after I'd admired their beautiful wings. There were too many butterflies pinned behind glass frames in my father's office. 'Sometimes we have to trap things to understand them, Nancy,' he'd explained when I said it was cruel. 'It's how all the great scientists and naturalists gather their knowledge.' It was impossible to disagree with Daddy. He was always right, even when he wasn't. Standing at roll-call, my stomach growling with hunger, I felt just like one of Daddy's butterflies, pinned behind a glass case.

As I yawned, an older lady beside me caught my eye and winked. She was dressed in an odd collection of clothes; mismatched and brightly coloured. She rolled her eyes at me in a way that suggested she was as bored as I was. I had to nip my wrists to stop myself giggling, and jumped as the warden rang his bell to signal the end of roll-call.

'Insufferably boring, isn't it,' the woman said. 'I swear I'll fall asleep one of these days.' She spoke with a sprightly Scottish accent. 'Edwina Trevellyan,' she continued. 'Eddie to my friends.'

I smiled back shyly, unsure if I was allowed to talk to her. 'I'm Nancy,' I said, not wishing to be impolite, and because she looked like terrific fun.

'Very pleased to meet you, Nancy. You're with Miss Kent, aren't you? With the Chefoo group? Kingfisher Patrol?'

I nodded, but didn't get a chance to say anything before she carried on.

'I was involved in the Girl Guides myself, back in the day. Captain of one of the first companies formed. The 1st Budleigh Girl Guides. We were quite marvellous.'

She really did talk an awful lot.

'And who is this quiet little thing beside you?' she asked.

'This is Mouse,' I said. 'Joan, actually. Mouse is her nickname.'

'Well, Mouse and Nancy, it is a pleasure to meet you. Come and see me sometime. I have a little job for you both.'

Our love of Girl Guides had followed us to Weihsien, and we were pleased when Miss Kent found a room for our weekly meetings.

'We want you to find ways to help others around the compound,' she said. 'The elderly especially.'

'Mrs Trevellyan is elderly,' Mouse said. 'We should help her.'

Intrigued by Mrs T, as we called her, and by the job she had for us, we went to find her the following afternoon after lessons and chores.

'Aha! You found me,' she said. 'Although, I am rather hard to miss!' She chuckled to herself. 'They all think I'm an eccentric old bat, but somebody has to add a bit of colour to this dreadful place.'

As well as helping with her domestic tasks, she asked if we

might like to help with a camp library she'd set up; sorting the books into alphabetical order, keeping a tally of who had borrowed which books, and going around the camp to collect them again when they were due to be returned.

'I can't pay you in money,' she said, 'but I can most certainly pay you in knowledge, and, of course, you can choose any books you like, at any time.'

We were almost as hungry for books as we were for a decent meal. It was an arrangement that suited us all.

Mrs Trevellyan was a breath of fresh air. She was mischievous and forthright and full of fascinating and shocking tales. She shared a room with some other ladies who she wasn't especially fond of. 'Ever so stuck-up,' she muttered, under her breath, 'and really quite useless, even at the most basic tasks. If you could eat airs and graces, they'd all be as fat as hippos. And they cheat at poker.' She was wild and unpredictable – everything our teachers weren't – and our visits to her quickly became a favourite part of the week, not to mention a welcome distraction from the everyday drudgery of camp life.

Even the simplest tasks took forever, and we soon began to dread them. Water had to be fetched and then boiled before we could drink it, and boiling the water meant making a fire, and that meant first making fuel balls from the dirt and coal dust scraped from the stoves. Our mats and bedsheets had to be searched each morning for bedbugs, which we always found, like an advancing army that would never be defeated. There was no end to it all, and without proper meals to give us any energy to do our tasks efficiently, we were listless and clumsy and tempers frayed as quickly as the hems of our skirts and cuffs.

While we sorted through the library books, Mrs T told us things Miss Kent would never have approved of. We lapped it up like thirsty kittens given a saucer of milk.

'What is it you want to know, girls? Ask me anything. Boys? Sex? Might as well get your money's worth.'

I stared at Mouse. We didn't know what to say. I couldn't even say the word 'sex', let alone ask questions about it, so I asked about the Great War instead, presuming that Mrs Trevellyan was old enough to have been in it.

She told us about her role working in the factories as a munitionette making bombs.

'They called us "Canary Girls" because the chemicals turned our skin yellow. Look at me!' She rolled up her sleeve. 'Yellow as a ripe banana.'

'Is that why you keep a canary?' Mouse asked.

Mrs Trevellyan kept a little bird in a bamboo cage that hung from a hook in the window frame of her room.

She chuckled. 'I suppose it might be why I keep a bird, but Churchill isn't a canary. He's a yellow-breasted bunting, known locally as a "rice bird". He – or possibly she – used to belong to my servant,' she explained. 'She was taken away by Japanese police when they came to round us all up. I presume she's kept in a cage now, too.' She looked sad, and shook her head. 'Awful business isn't it. War. We thought we'd seen the last of it in 1918, and look at us. Right back at it, and worse than ever. What a waste of all those beautiful young men.'

Mouse and I enjoyed listening to Mrs Trevellyan's stories while Churchill sang away in his cage. He sang beautifully, unlike Mrs Trevellyan, who sang opera, very badly. She especially liked to sing songs from *The Merry Widow* and something by a lady called Jenny Lind, known as the Swedish Nightingale. Mouse said it was like listening to cats fighting.

Mrs T took Churchill 'for a walk' every day. 'He can't be cooped up in that awful room all day,' she said. 'He'd go mad! *I'm* nearly gone mad.'

I thought she was quite mad enough already.

'Why don't you set him free?' Mouse asked. 'Then he wouldn't be cooped up at all.'

'Well, young Joan. Some creatures, when they've been in captivity for a while, don't adapt to freedom as well as you might expect. Churchill here is used to being fed and given water. He's only ever known this cage, so this is where he feels comfortable.' He started singing, as if to confirm that he absolutely agreed with her. 'Besides, he's a dear friend, and nobody likes to lose a friend, do they.'

I thought of poor Sprout lying in the hospital, and suddenly missed her terribly. No matter how much I prayed, she wasn't getting any better. I secretly worried if she ever would; if we would ever play skipping games again, or whisper and giggle after lights out, or if I would ever get to visit her in New England in the fall, like we'd agreed.

'How is your friend? Sprout, isn't it?' Mrs T asked, as if she could read my thoughts.

'No better,' I said.

Mrs T put her hand on mine and squeezed it before she stood up. 'Bloody wars,' she said. 'Dreadful business altogether.'

I couldn't stop thinking about Churchill, and mentioned it to Mouse that evening.

'Don't you think he would be much happier flying free with the other birds?' I said.

Mouse agreed. 'We could always leave his cage door open, by accident,' she said, which was exactly what I'd been thinking, but hadn't dared to say.

'We couldn't,' I sighed. 'Mrs Trevellyan would be heartbroken. Still, it would be lovely to set at least one of us free.'

Mouse wondered if we might be able to tie a message to Churchill's leg, like the carrier pigeons Mrs T had told us about, who'd carried important messages during the Great War, but I wasn't sure rice birds were good at flying long distances.

'How would Churchill know where to deliver the message anyway?'

We concluded that it was a bad idea, and that he was probably better off in his cage with Mrs Trevellyan singing to him.

Despite everyone's very best efforts to be helpful and organized, our first few months at Weihsien were a strange and, at times, frightening experience. We all put a brave face on things during the day, but when the amber sun set at night, I often heard the tell-tale sniff and snuffle of someone crying themselves to sleep. I wished our parents could see the horrid little room we slept in and the awful food we had to eat. I wished my mother could know that the frightened little girl who'd watched her disappear beneath a sea of paper parasols now slept in a room surrounded by barbed wire and high walls and armed guards.

I still missed her terribly, and without my tea caddy or her letters, I felt further away from her than ever. I hadn't seen her, or heard her voice, or felt her arms around me for four whole years now. How would she ever understand what I'd been through? At least my log books from Brownies and Kingfisher Patrol were a careful record of my progress. When I showed her – when I told her about all this – I knew she would be sorry she'd ever put me on a boat from Shanghai, and gone off into China to do her missionary work. Now, when I thought about her, I didn't always feel sad. I often felt angry with her for leaving me; for being so far away when I needed her to be close.

We'd now been under Japanese occupation for so long I could hardly remember what life had been like before. Like Churchill in his cage, life in captivity was what I now knew, and although I longed for the war to be over and for the Allies to be victorious, I also worried about what would happen then. What, and who, would be waiting for me beyond the gates?

Sometimes, when I thought about liberation, about leaving Mouse and Sprout and Miss Kent and everyone I knew here, it felt as if the cage was on the other side of the compound walls, waiting to trap me all over again.

ELSPETH

November 1943

I felt empty during our first months at Weihsien. Like a dish-cloth wrung dry, or a pen run out of ink, I was drained of all purpose; too exhausted to do anything but unquestion-ingly comply. I hadn't given up, but part of me had given in. We were surrounded by a thousand strangers and entirely on our own, cut off from the safe comfortable world we'd known. I was weak with hunger, and the immense effort of shepherding the children safely from Temple Hill had also taken its toll. I worried endlessly about Dorothy, who really was very poorly, and I felt Alfie's absence more than ever. The awful agony of not knowing what had happened to him, or where in the world he was, dragged along beside me, tripping me up without warning, nagging at me and interrupting me, so that I was liable to burst into tears at any moment.

'I know it's unbearable not to hear, Els, but try not to lose hope,' Minnie offered when I explained the reason for my sudden tears as we walked to the school building. I'd heard the Salvation

Army band playing a chorus of "Abide with Me", which was one of Alfie's favourites. 'No news is good news, after all.'

Minnie did her best to administer a regular dose of comfort and reassurance. I was grateful for it, although it really didn't make me feel any better.

'It's like everyone back home has just vanished,' I said. 'No letters, no telegrams. Just, nothing. Nothing at all.'

'I imagine they feel the same way about us,' Minnie replied. 'It must be agony for the children's parents, separated from them for so long. I just hope some of the Red Cross forms get through to them.'

The short Red Cross pro-formas, which allowed for basic personal details – in good health, going along nicely, missing you terribly – were filled in by the children now and again, but I doubted very much whether they ever left the Commandant's office. Even if they did, the chances of them reaching the intended recipients were slim.

As the mellow colours of autumn decorated the plane trees along Main Street, and the spectre of my lost wedding days came and went again, I felt more trapped than ever.

'I'm thirty-five years old, Minnie, and look where I am.' I waved my arms around, at our dismal little room, at the bars at the windows, at the guards patrolling the watchtowers. 'I came to China to find a freedom that had eluded me in England. And look at me. As captive as a mouse in a trap.' I sank into a chair. 'Maybe I should have married Reggie and settled in York. He really wasn't the worst.'

'Why didn't you marry him?' Minnie asked, sensing a rare opportunity to ask me about my past.

'I thought life would be boring!' I laughed at the irony. 'What I wouldn't give to be bored Mrs Elspeth Smith right now.' I sighed wistfully, imagining another me; another life. 'I woke up that morning and realized I couldn't give half of myself to someone I didn't love. My mother said love didn't come into it, and that I should marry Reggie and settle down. I think she was right.'

'Pish, Elspeth. One settles into a comfortable chair, not into the rest of one's life. We should leap enthusiastically into marriage, or not at all.' Minnie sat beside me. 'Coming to China wasn't a mistake, but marrying a man you didn't love most certainly would have been. Don't give up now, Els. Not after everything we've been through. The children need you more than ever. Keep going for them, even if you can't keep going for yourself.'

Although many things had changed over the past two years, Brownies and Guides had remained the one reassuring constant, every Thursday, without fail. The immense effort required to put the war aside for an hour and find the necessary enthusiasm for the meetings wasn't always easy, and increasingly felt impossible, but the reward of the girls' eagerness kept us going and our meetings of Kingfisher Patrol punctuated the long weeks. While we didn't know how many more weeks lay ahead, we always remembered to be grateful for the weeks that were now behind us.

Our Tenderfoot Girl Guides of Kingfisher Patrol had passed their Second-Class tests with flying colours, and were ready to become First-Class Guides. Before even trying for their badges, they were proficient in many of the skills required for the next stage of their Guiding journey. In the most peculiar circumstances imaginable, their internment had ensured they were capable beyond their years.

We designed tests for the girls to bring together their experiences of camp life, and to emphasize the importance of the new skills they'd learned. For a special award, which we named the Weihsien Star, they were tested on camp rules, camp danger spots, where the doctors lived, which wells were condemned for drinking water, and when and where distilled water could be obtained. For daily tasks, the girls took turns on shower room duty during children's hour where they helped to wash the little ones. They also carefully cleaned the eggshells from which we made calcium powder. Even fly-swatting was set as a serious task, since sanitation was one of our biggest problems and there were still regular outbreaks of dysentery, cholera and typhoid.

But the girls' development wasn't only measured in the number of Guiding badges sewn onto their shirtsleeves. The reedy young things who'd walked out of Chefoo with the wind in their plump little cheeks and a song on their lips were maturing into young women. There was no denying the physical changes. The older boys certainly noticed it and, more worryingly, so did the guards. It was subtle enough at first. A protracted glimpse at roll-call, a turn of the head as we walked past on our way to the sports field. But the attention increased as once-strange faces became familiar, and the girls' initial fear of the new guards dissolved into something more akin to a distant wariness.

Connie Hinshaw was a particular focus of the guards' attention. They whistled and called out to her whenever she walked past. Her deep discomfort and humiliation was clear to see in the flood of colour that rushed to her cheeks. She was an undeniably attractive girl who'd somehow managed to keep her curves when other girls had never developed any in the first place, or lost them to hunger. Connie was at an awkward age for any young woman, but the added complication of going through puberty beneath the gaze of leering men, and while worrying about her sister, was a lot for her young shoulders. I kept a close eye on her, especially when I noticed how Trouble acted around her. He stood uncomfortably close to her at roll-call and made no effort to conceal his desire as his eyes settled on her breasts.

Charlie Harris noticed it, too. We'd started to walk to and from Kitchen 1 together at mealtimes, sharing our concerns and observations about camp life. I wasn't sure who had first waited for whom, but it had become a pleasant arrangement. I enjoyed talking to a man for a change, rather than to Minnie. Terribly fond of her though I was, Minnie had a rather particular outlook on life that I couldn't always get along with.

'I would keep a close eye on Connie, and the older girls,' Charlie warned as we walked back from supper together. 'If they offer the slightest hint of encouragement, there could be . . . well . . . liberties taken.'

'Do you think I should mention it to the headmaster? Perhaps he could raise our concerns with the Commandant.'

'I wouldn't imagine it will make any difference, and might only make things worse. Retribution for a complaint made to their superiors may be far worse than a roving eye.' We walked on in silence for a moment. 'Anyway, that's enough about the girls. How are *you* getting on, Elspeth?'

'Me?'

'Yes! You!' He stopped. 'I know we all do our best and keep up appearances for the children's sake, but I also know how damned exhausting this all is. I also know your brother is missing. I just wondered how you're doing. I wondered, actually, if anyone had ever asked?'

I could have wept. I could have crumbled to the filthy dusty ground, right there beside the latrines, just to know that someone had thought about me as a person, not just as a teacher or a figure of authority.

'I'm doing okay,' I sighed. 'I think we're all doing remarkably well, considering.' I laughed lightly, but there was no real mirth in it. 'Thank you, Charlie.'

'For what?'

'For asking.'

He looked at me, a puzzled frown on his face. 'Would you mind awfully if I asked again? Not all the time, but every now and then. Just to check in? Make sure?'

I smiled, this time without effort, or force. 'I don't mind at all. In fact, I'd like that. Very much.'

Having thought further about the situation with Connie and the soldiers, and conceding that Charlie was probably right, I decided to tackle the situation head on and speak to Trouble myself before anything unpleasant happened. Given our history, it wasn't without worry or caution that I approached him, but the girls' safety was my utmost priority, and I knew I would never forgive myself if something happened to Connie because I'd been too afraid to speak up.

I steeled myself as I made my way to the guards' house after visiting Dorothy in the hospital the following afternoon. As I knew he would be, I found Trouble drinking tea and smoking with some of the other guards. I recognized Home Run and Charlie Chaplin, but if they recognized me, they didn't show it. They acted differently around Trouble. Everybody did.

'I wondered if I might have a word?' I asked, addressing nobody in particular. 'About the children.'

Trouble took a long drag on his cigarette and stared at me indifferently. I cleared my throat and tipped my chin. 'We would prefer it if you didn't stare or jeer at the older girls. The attention isn't appropriate, or desired.'

Trouble tossed his cigarette to the ground, and stood up.

'She is jealous,' he sneered, addressing the other guards. 'You are an old woman and get no attention from men!' He put down his cup and stalked over to me. I swallowed hard as he stood too close and looked directly into my eyes. 'You still have a gift for me, Elspeth Kent.' He flicked the hem of my skirt with his stick. 'Shall I unwrap it?'

I hoped he couldn't see how I trembled. Ignoring his remarks, I pressed on.

'I don't wish to cause any trouble. I am merely concerned for the girls' welfare. I am their teacher. They are my responsibility.'

He laughed in my face, turned around and walked back inside the guards' house, slamming the door behind him.

Nevertheless, he didn't stand as close to Connie at roll-call the next morning.

'What did you do, Elspeth?' Charlie asked as we walked to breakfast. 'I hope you didn't do anything silly.'

'Nothing silly. I merely asked them to stop leering at the girls. It would appear that they listened for once.'

I felt rather pleased with myself, but I should have known better.

The following evening, as I made my way back from visiting Dorothy in the hospital, I heard a kerfuffle near the guards' accommodation block, and went to investigate. As I turned the corner, I was horrified to find Trouble pressing Connie against the wall. She was clearly struggling, trying to push him away and begging him to stop.

'Stop!' I called as I ran toward them. 'Stop it! Leave her alone.'

As he pushed Connie roughly away, I noticed Trouble's trousers were unbuttoned, and there was a tear on the sleeve of Connie's blouse. She was trembling and pale-faced, her narrow shoulders heaving with sobs.

'It's all right now. Come and sit down.' I took the crook of her arm and led her to the steps at the back of the building. It took her a few minutes to compose herself as I passed her a handkerchief. 'It's all right. He won't be bothering you anymore.'

'He said he liked me, but he only wanted to . . .'

She sobbed, too ashamed and embarrassed to say the words. She stared at me with enormous frightened eyes and I wanted to wrap her up and take her far away. I wanted to take them all away. This was no place for children.

'It's my fault, Miss,' she continued. 'I should have ignored him.'

'It is most certainly not your fault, Connie. Not at all. You mustn't talk to him again. Do you understand?'

She nodded. 'I understand.'

Only then did I realize Trouble was still there, watching us, listening to us.

'You should not interfere, Elspeth Kent,' he snarled as he walked toward us, a hard look on his face. 'A man will have what he wants. A *soldier* will take what he wants from his enemy.'

'You're a bully,' I said, my anger getting the better of me as I grabbed Connie's hand and encouraged her to stand up. 'We are *not* the property of your Emperor.'

He turned to Connie. 'Go!' he snapped. 'Leave us, English bitch.'

She flinched at his words.

'Go, Connie,' I said, firmly. 'Do as he says.'

'But, Miss . . .'

I smiled to show her I wasn't worried. 'I'll be along in a minute. And not a word about this to anyone.'

She nodded and left the two of us alone.

I tried not to look at the knife that hung from Trouble's belt as he lunged toward me and took my chin roughly in his hands, his fingernails pressing into my skin. With a jerk, he tilted my neck, forcing me to look at him.

'You are a teacher,' he whispered, his breath warm against my ear. 'You will give me a lesson now, Elspeth Kent.'

He leaned forward and licked my skin, slowly, from my throat to my chin. I stood rigid, too shocked and repulsed to move as he pushed me against the wall, his hand fumbling awkwardly at his trousers.

Suddenly, he stopped and pushed me away from him.

I opened my eyes to see Home Run approaching us. He said something to Trouble.

'English filth,' he hissed as he spat at my feet and stalked away.

I leaned against the wall, head spinning as I tried to compose myself. After a minute or two, I set off in the direction of the accommodation block. With blood pumping through my ears, I ran, stumbled and staggered behind the trees where I retched violently, my hands braced against a trunk, my knees shaking beneath me as my body purged itself of fear and revulsion.

'Are you poorly, Miss?'

I lifted my head to see Joan watching me.

My heart sank. 'Joan? What are you doing here?' She stared at me. 'Just a bit of an upset tummy,' I said, righting myself as I offered a weak smile. 'Something I ate, no doubt.'

Her face was pale and concerned. 'Should I fetch someone?'

'I'll be fine. Nothing to worry about. Off you go now.' I waved her on. 'I'll be along in a minute or two.'

As I watched her walk away, I wondered how long she'd been there. I wondered how much she'd seen, and who she might tell. But mostly, I wondered when Trouble would come looking for me again.

NANCY

Sprout's condition hadn't worsened since we'd arrived at Weihsien, but neither had it improved as we'd all hoped. I was allowed to visit when she was feeling up to it, which wasn't very often, and even when she was, she was weak and sleepy and it didn't feel like I was visiting Sprout at all, but visiting her shadow. I didn't look forward to seeing her as much as I once had. Sometimes, I dreaded it.

I hesitated as I was shown into the ward and saw how pale she was.

Nurse Prune gave me an encouraging nod. 'She knows you're coming. She's looking forward to seeing you.'

I sat on the edge of the bed. 'Hello, Sprout,' I whispered, a little shy, even though she was my best friend.

'Hello, Plum.' She offered a weak smile, which made me feel sad.

I fidgeted with the hem of my skirt. 'Are you feeling better?'

She shook her head slowly. 'Not really.' She took a deep breath, and sank back into her pillows. 'But I'm happy to see you. Tell me about Kingfisher Patrol. Have you any new badges?'

I told her about the whip-poor-will that sang at my window every night, and about the dreadful latrines, and the awful food we had to eat, and how we were planning to start a vegetable garden in the spring. I told her all about Churchill and Mrs Trevellyan, and that we weren't allowed to talk to the ladies who, she'd told me, were called prostitutes.

'You'd like her ever so much,' I said, relaxing as we started to talk. 'She makes us tea made from all sorts of funny plants, and she has a wicked sense of humour, and a filthy tongue, but don't tell Miss Kent or she might not let us visit her anymore.'

Sprout asked me to tell her the swearwords Mrs Trevellyan used. So I did. I'd never said them out loud, and blushed as I did, and Sprout laughed until she made herself cough, and then we both went quiet again.

'You will come and visit me, won't you?' she said, eventually.

'Of course. Every day, if I'm allowed.'

'I don't mean here. I mean in America. In New England. We'll eat lobster rolls on the boardwalk, and you won't believe the colours of the trees in the fall. They look as if they're on fire.'

I smiled. 'I can't wait.'

'Guide's Promise you'll come.'

'Guide's Promise.'

Mouse sometimes came with me to the hospital, because Miss Kent said it was nicer to do these things in twos. I was glad of Mouse's hand in mine as we skipped up the road to the hospital together, and even more glad as we walked quietly back again.

The funny thing about Sprout being so poorly was that everything carried on as normal. The same routines, the same indigestible food, the same boring roll-call, the same excitement when we changed into our uniforms for Guides. I missed her terribly, but I also forgot to miss her just as easily.

'Out of sight, out of mind,' Mrs Trevellyan said when I admitted to her that I sometimes didn't think about Sprout for hours, and once hadn't thought about her for an entire day.

Me and Mouse were sorting through some of the returned library books we'd collected from around the camp. I'd put *Black Beauty* to one side, and Mouse had chosen a Sherlock Holmes mystery.

'It happens at your age, girls,' Mrs T said. 'In love with a boy one minute, in love with his best friend the next. And I should know all about that!' She passed us both a slice of orange, which was a rare treat. Neither of us asked her where she'd got it, although I had my suspicions. Edward had told me about a black market that operated in camp. It all sounded terribly dangerous.

'I feel so helpless, Mrs T. I wish I could make Sprout better.'

'You can't look after everybody, Nancy. Sometimes we just have to look after ourselves, and sod everyone else.' She saw the look of shock on my face. 'Although that doesn't apply to your friend, of course. I'm sure the nurses are doing their very best for her.'

'Do you think the same applies to parents?' I asked. 'Do you think we're out of their minds, too? I haven't seen my mother for such a long time. Do you think she forgets to think about me, the way I forget to think about Sprout?'

Mrs Trevellyan always told the truth, even if it wasn't the nicest thing to hear.

'I don't imagine it's the same for your mother at all, Nancy. It's different for parents. I would imagine she thinks about you every single day.' She dabbed at the corners of her eyes with the end of her sleeve. 'I think about my boy, Billy, all the time, and I haven't seen him since the sixteenth of May, 1915.'

'Did he move away?' Mouse asked.

'He went to war, dear, and never came home. I miss him as

much today as I did the morning I waved him off. You never forget your children, no matter how far away they might be.' She looked up, presumably to Heaven.

We didn't ask any more questions. Everything was difficult whenever somebody mentioned death. It wasn't something I'd ever thought about before the soldiers arrived at Chefoo. I'd only ever known one person who'd died – Granny Plummer – and she was ever so old. Three people had already died since we'd arrived at Weihsien. Although we didn't know them, news like that passed through the camp like wildfire. Two of them were elderly, but one was a young woman; a mother with two young children.

I thought about death and talked about death so often it became a habit, like picking at a scab. I knew I shouldn't do it, but I couldn't stop. At first, when I'd asked Miss Kent if Sprout might die, she'd said reassuring things like, 'Of course not,' and, 'Let's think about more positive things.' But her answers changed as the weeks passed, until she started to say, 'Dorothy is in the best place, Nancy.' I remembered Mummy saying the same thing about Granny Plummer.

Churchill sang in his cage as if he sensed the awkward silence and wanted to change the subject. It worked. Mrs Trevellyan sat up in her chair and came back from wherever she'd been to think about the past.

'Now, girls. How about a cup of nettle tea to cheer us up? It's no good sitting here all maudlin, is it.'

Mouse looked at me, and pulled a face. 'Nettle tea? Doesn't it sting when you drink it?'

Mrs Trevellyan laughed. 'Not at all! I make it from the leaves. Far nicer than suffering through a cup made from anaemic three-week-old tealeaves. You'd be surprised what you can use to make tea. Flowers, herbs, all sorts. You've to be careful not to use the poisonous ones of course, unless there's someone you want to dispose of!' She winked, playfully. 'I've been reading too many Sherlock Holmes books, girls! Come along. I'll show you.'

Our teachers made our days as interesting and comfortable as they could, but we all looked forward to bedtime, because when we were asleep, we weren't hungry. As the weeks had passed, we'd stopped talking about the ache in our bellies and the dizzy sensation we woke up with each morning. I couldn't remember what it felt like to sit down to a full plate of food, with sponge pudding for afters. I wondered if I would ever sit at a clean table and eat a proper cooked meal again. I almost felt sick at the thought of eating so much food in one sitting.

'Maybe we'll always eat like baby birds, pecking at grubs,' Winnie Morris said as we walked to the kitchen to line up for a breakfast nobody wanted. The awful kaoliang stuck to the roof of my mouth.

'I can't wait to eat an enormous bowl full of jam roly-poly and custard,' Mouse said. 'And apple pie with tonnes of cream. And roast beef and Yorkshire puddings.'

Winnie said Mouse would make herself sick if she ate all that.

'I'll even eat sprouts with Christmas dinner,' Mouse went on. 'I'll never turn my nose up at a sprout ever again. I'd eat a whole plateful of them right now and I'd ask for seconds.'

'Why were you always so quiet before?' I asked as Winnie went ahead with the other girls and Mouse and I walked on in our pair. 'You hardly said two words when we were at Chefoo, and now you hardly ever stop talking.'

'You were all so talkative in the dorm, there was never a chance for me to get a word in edgeways,' she replied. 'I often tried, but someone else always said what I was thinking before I could get the words out.'

I felt mean for not having included her more in our conversations back in the dorm in Chefoo.

'I'm sorry,' I said, putting my arm around her shoulder. 'I'm sorry for ignoring you.'

She shrugged and said it was okay and that it didn't matter now anyway because we were all much more friendly towards her.

'People talk too much anyway,' she added as we took our food and sat at one of the long tables. 'Nobody ever listens properly. You see and hear so much more when you're quiet.'

'Like what?'

'Nothing in particular.' She looked at me as if she wanted to tell me something.

'What?' I prompted. 'What have you heard?'

She leaned toward me. 'Not heard. Seen.' She glanced anxiously over my shoulder. 'I saw something the other day.'

'What sort of thing?' I asked. 'Mouse? What did you see?'

Miss Kent came over to inspect our hands and nails which she insisted we kept well-scrubbed and clean, despite the lack of soap and hot water. Cholera and dysentery soon followed those who were too tired or too lazy to boil water, or to wash their hands after a trip to the latrines. When she'd finished, and was, thankfully, satisfied with us all, I turned back to Mouse.

'Well?'

She shook her head. 'It doesn't matter. Forget I ever said anything.'

But I could tell from the look on her face that whatever it was did matter. Very much.

She went off on her own later that afternoon. When I asked her where she'd been, she told me she'd taken a library book back to Mrs Trevellyan.

'You were gone an awfully long time,' I said, a bit miffed that she hadn't asked me to go with her.

'Yes. Sorry. I didn't plan to, but you know what she's like when she starts talking.'

We looked at each other.

'Never shuts up,' we said at the same time.

We burst into laughter, and I was so pleased to have Mouse as a friend that I forgave her for going off without me, and I forgot to ask her what they'd been talking about for so long.

As we lay on our mats that night, and I listened to the whip-poor-will at the window, Mouse whispered through the dark beside me.

'Do you think God can hear when you have bad thoughts about someone?' she asked.

I thought for a moment. I really wasn't sure if God heard anything at all. If He was listening, He would have stopped the landslides and the bombing of Pearl Harbor, and Mummy would have come to collect me and Edward off the boat in Shanghai that Christmas, as planned. But I remembered the time when my pet rabbit died, and Mummy said we must trust in the Lord, even when we don't understand His actions.

'I think He can hear our thoughts, yes,' I whispered. 'I once wished Winnie Morris would get the measles so she would be sent to the San, and she *did* get the measles.'

Mouse was silent for a moment. 'Did you feel awful for wishing her poorly?'

'Not really. I was mostly glad to not have to put up with her showing off all the time. The dorm was much friendlier without her, wasn't it?'

'Yes,' she whispered. 'It was.'

'Why do you ask?' I added. 'Who do you hope will get the measles?'

The room was silent.

'Nobody in particular,' she whispered, eventually. 'Goodnight, Plum.'

THE GUIDE LAW: A GUIDE IS THRIFTY

This means that a Girl Guide is a girl who is wise
enough to know the value of things and to put them to
the
best use.

ELSPETH

December 1943

From sunrise to sunset, we met the puzzle of each new day, charging quietly on in a constant battle of despair and hope, frailty and strength. In that way, the months steadily passed, and the seasons turned, and the unfathomable reality of life under Japanese oppression somehow went on.

Incentive, reward and inventiveness were our best allies during those first unsettling months at Weihsien. The inevitable ebb and flow of morale among the children was addressed by turning problems and difficulties into games. Who could catch the most flies? Who would be king or queen of the bedbugs? Who could gather up the most coal dust and make the most fuel balls for the stoves, ineffective as they were? The strategy worked, although my heart broke as I watched their triumphant faces proudly count up their contributions.

'They should be calculating fractions and equations,' I sighed. 'Preparing for their exams.'

The prospect of sitting their Oxford Matrics – one of the

reasons the children had been sent to Chefoo School in the first place – now seemed like a distant dream. As the children of foreign missionaries, influential diplomats and important businessmen, they were expected to achieve the highest standards of education, and yet here they were, being congratulated for catching flies. I felt every one of the thousands of miles to Oxford's famous spires. I'd always wanted to see them, and wondered if I would ever have the chance.

Our once-daily staff meetings gradually settled into a less frantic weekly event, where concerns were addressed, reassurances offered, and plans made.

'No challenge is too great,' our headmaster encouraged. 'No situation too awful not to be improved with a little imagination and resourcefulness.'

As our leader, he said all the right things – encouraging, forthright things – but he carried a weariness now that hadn't been there before. As we approached the end of our second year under Japanese guard, there was a weariness to us all. Two years of indignity, depravity and continually dashed hopes of liberation had taken their toll, and there were increasingly prolonged spells when it was just too difficult to remain hopeful of ever being freed. Without regular or reliable news about Allied progress, we had no new reason to hope for liberation. Charlie's homemade radio hadn't been able to pick up any signal since the move to Weihsien, besides which, it was incredibly dangerous for him to try. It was bad enough that he still even had it in his possession. I was terrified of the consequences should it ever be discovered.

'If only we knew when it might all end,' I said. 'Even if we knew we had to endure another year, it would be a little easier to tolerate.'

We craved information from the world beyond the compound walls as much as we craved fresh meat and vegetables.

'Do you ever just want to run up to those big ugly gates and scream until you're hoarse?' I said at the end of morning lessons. Minnie and I were standing together at the classroom window, through which the compound gates loomed a short distance away; a cruel and ever-present reminder of our captivity. We watched in thoughtful silence as the guards patrolled the watchtowers at either end of the high walls. 'Sometimes I think I might burst if I stay here a moment longer, pretending every-thing's perfectly fine. Don't you ever want to just let out a great roar and scream at the absurdity of it all?'

I tossed my battered copy of Shakespeare's *Hamlet* onto the desk behind me, but missed the target. It fell with a clatter to the floor. I balled my fists and huffed out a breath.

'I'm not sure what good it would do to go about the place shouting and screaming,' Minnie replied, calm and unruffled as ever. 'You'd most likely get yourself shot.'

The awful truth of her words settled around us. The threat of the soldiers turning their guns on us was something we were all aware of, but didn't talk about. We'd heard rumours from some recent arrivals into camp that civilians had been shot in other locations. We held a very real fear that if the Allies won the war and Japan was defeated, the guards might turn their guns on us in a final act of power and control.

I turned away from the window, picked up the book, and perched on the edge of the desk. I'd spent so much time in Minnie's company, her habits were becoming my habits.

'To be, or not to be,' I sighed. 'That, Minnie, is the question.'

She offered a thin smile. 'To be,' she said, firmly. 'It's the only possible answer.' She looped her arm through mine. 'Right. Best get on. We have children to educate. Cockroaches to catch. Socks and stockings to darn. No rest for the wicked British enemy.'

We were certainly resourceful. Nothing went to waste and a use was found for anything and everything we could lay our hands on. Old editions of *The Chefusian* school newspaper (which someone had cleverly thought to bring with us all the way from Chefoo) were used again that winter as an extra layer, wrapped against our skin to absorb moisture from clothes that took forever to dry after being washed. We rustled like autumn leaves as we walked about, and newsprint patterned our skin when we undressed at night. Charlie remarked that we would have to read each other when we ran out of books, which made me blush furiously.

The lack of vitamins and minerals in the children's diet continued to worry us greatly. We talked about bones so often, and saw them, poking through everyone's skinny bodies, that I sometimes dreamed we were all walking about as skeletons and nobody batted an eyelid. We didn't need to show the children pictures of human skeletons to teach them about the human anatomy. Ribcages and sternum, shoulder blades and collarbones were right there, in front of their eyes.

Minnie had been supremely clever in suggesting we grind up eggshells and feed the powder to the children as a way of getting essential calcium into their diet. Of course, they all grumbled and gagged when we forced them to swallow a spoonful of the gritty powder, but we ignored their protests, pleased to be doing something positive and useful, and improvising for the greater good.

'Growing children need calcium for strong bones,' I nagged as I walked along the line of girls, their faces scrunched up in revulsion. They barely opened their mouths wide enough for me to get the spoon inside.

'It's worse than the cod liver oil Nurse Prune used to make us take,' Nancy groused, pulling the most tremendous face as I presented her spoonful.

'That's as may be, Nancy,' I remarked, 'but it's a small price to pay for the benefit of healthy bones when you're older. You'll thank me for it one day. It's eggshells now, or arthritis later. Which would you rather have?' She swallowed the eggshells. 'And, by the way,' I added with a wink. 'Your face will stay like that if the wind changes.'

I took a spoonful myself later that day, to see how awful it really was because I suspected the girls were making a terrific fuss over nothing.

'What's it like?' Minnie asked.

'Absolutely dreadful,' I winced. 'It's like falling at the seaside and swallowing a mouthful of sand.'

The grit stuck in my teeth all day. I delivered the girls' next dose with a little more empathy.

Thankfully, the children hated the powdered eggshells so much that it didn't occur to them to ask where the eggs came from. Charlie had first told me about the black market operating in camp. He told me in strictest confidence, as we'd walked back from breakfast.

'It's an extremely dangerous operation,' he explained, keeping his voice low. 'Not only for the local farmers providing the eggs and other essentials, but for everyone involved inside the camp.'

'Are many people involved?' I asked, surprised by how accepting I was of the idea. If it helped us to obtain food and medicine, and other essential information and supplies, I was all for it.

He nodded. 'More than you might think.'

'You wouldn't happen to be involved? Would you?' I kept my voice low and walked close beside him so he could hear me.

'Involved in what? I don't know what you're talking about.' He glanced at me, without any hint of irony or a smile.

'Do be careful,' I urged. 'I'd hate for . . .'

'For what? Anything to happen to me?' Now, there was a trace of a smile at his lips.

'Just be careful, Charlie,' I said, before I hurried on to catch up with Minnie and Eleanor.

But despite the secrecy surrounding it, rumours about the black market spread, the way so many rumours did as a result of living in such close proximity. The headmaster addressed the issue at the weekly staff meeting.

'Desperate times call for desperate measures, and yes, there is a black market operating in camp through which we have been able to obtain some essential supplies, and information. It is being run through a priest. As a man without family commitments, he believes he is best placed to shoulder the burden of risk. He is aware of the likelihood of harsh reprisals should he, or the operation, be discovered. We are also operating what's known as a "bamboo radio", a process by which secret coded messages are smuggled into camp. It's a vital lifeline to the outside world, and one through which we hope to hear if the tide of war is turning in favour of the Allies.' It was a lot to take in, and there were a great many questions and plenty of conjecture and speculation. 'I'd much rather none of you knew about it if I'm perfectly honest,' he continued. 'But some of you asked, and you have a right to know the truth.'

For the dangers involved in getting them, and the health benefit they offered to the children, we treasured our supply of eggshells more than the eggs inside. We stored them in an old tin box in our room, and couldn't have kept a more watchful eye over it if it had been filled with precious diamonds and rubies.

'Who would ever have thought it, Minnie. Watching over a box of empty eggshells as if we were warders at the Tower protecting the crown jewels.'

But danger was never far from necessity, and sometimes the balance didn't turn in our favour.

I was walking back from breakfast with Charlie when one of the guards approached us.

'Take off your shoes,' he shouted as he grabbed Charlie's arm and pulled him roughly aside, sending him stumbling to the ground.

I ran to help him, but the guard blocked my path.

'Stay back,' he ordered, waving his bamboo stick to indicate that I should leave. 'Go!'

Charlie looked up at me. His hand was cut and bleeding. 'Go, Elspeth. I'll handle this.'

I couldn't move. I stood, rooted to the spot, as I watched Charlie take off one shoe. He passed it to the guard who ripped off the sole and shook the shoe roughly.

'Other one,' he snapped as he tossed the first shoe to the ground.

Charlie took a deep breath, and looked at me, and my heart sank. In an instant, I knew he was hiding something, and there was nothing either of us could do to stop the inevitable discovery and punishment.

'Go, Elspeth,' he whispered. 'Please.'

Before he could say anything else, the guard raised his stick and struck Charlie's ankles with a sickening crack.

'Shoe! Now!'

I couldn't bear to stay; couldn't bear to leave him. Head spinning, I turned and pushed my way through the small crowd that had gathered to see what all the commotion was about this time. Tears streaming down my cheeks, my hands over my ears, I stumbled blindly on, not sure where I was going, only certain that I couldn't bear to watch them hurt him.

Only when I reached the hospital, did I stop and look back. In the distance, the crowd had started to disperse. As they did, I saw Charlie stagger to his bare feet, before he was pushed down again and dragged away, by his ankles.

I wiped tears from my eyes, and ran to tell the others; desperate to try and find someone who could help him.

Rumours circulated madly among the Chefoo group at meal-times and roll-call. It was believed that Charlie was being kept in solitary confinement, in a sparse stone building beside the Commandant's house. I couldn't sleep; couldn't bear to think of him out there, alone.

'He's strong,' Minnie offered by way of comfort. 'He'll take his punishment like a man. You'll see. He'll be back to us in no time.'

But he wasn't.

Charlie's absence made everything about Weihsien worse. The dirt was suddenly unbearable, the insanitary conditions unacceptable, the scraps of questionable meat and rotting vege-tables inedible. The fear and threat of reprisal that swarmed over the compound as rampantly as the cockroaches was more unsettling than ever.

'You're fond of him, aren't you?' Mrs T said as we walked to church together.

'I'm worried about him, as a friend,' I replied.

'Of course. A friend you've grown fond of.' She placed her hand on my arm and pulled me to a stop. 'It's quite all right, you know, to form a friendship with a man, even here. In fact, it's probably more important than ever. We need to grab onto anything that makes us feel human, Elspeth. Lord knows, they've stripped us of pretty much everything else. If we deny ourselves love in a place like this, then what the devil is the point of it all?'

I stared at my feet. 'You're right,' I conceded. 'I didn't realize quite how fond of him I'd grown until this happened.'

She raised an eyebrow. 'We never do, dear. We assume people will be around forever, that we have all the time in the world to tell them we love them, or can't stand the sight of them, and then . . . poof! They disappear, and it's too bloody late to say anything at all.'

She pulled a grubby handkerchief from her sleeve and dabbed at a tear against her cheek. She was always so forthright and strong, her tears caught me by surprise.

'Oh, Mrs T. I'm sorry. I didn't mean to upset you.'

She waved my apology away as we walked on. 'You haven't upset me. *I've* upset me, silly stubborn thing that I am. It's too late for me, Elspeth. Don't leave it too late for you.'

During the church service, I thought about what she'd said. I thought about Harry, and about Alfie and Charlie, and all the missed opportunities and lost words.

No more.

From now on, I would tell the truth. Just as soon as he came back, I would tell Charlie Harris that I was terribly fond of him.

Just as soon as he came back.

NANCY

Edward came to find me after Sunday prayers. I knew something was afoot as soon as I saw him running toward me, a grin on his face.

'What on earth's got into you?' I asked, as he grabbed my arm and pulled me after him. I'd given up hope of being liberated, so I didn't even ask.

'You'll *never* guess who's here, Nancy. Never!'

'Princess Elizabeth? The king?'

'Don't be silly. Eric Liddell! The Olympian! The Flying Scotsman! My hero! He's actually here!'

I couldn't remember ever seeing Edward so excited. 'He's here in the camp? Is he visiting?'

'Visiting? Why on earth would anybody be visiting this place? He's a prisoner, same as us. Come on. I'll introduce you.'

I could hardly believe it until I met the man myself.

'This is my sister, Nancy,' Edward announced when we found Mr Liddell at the sports field. 'Nancy, this is Mr Eric Liddell.'

He shook my hand. 'Very pleased to meet you, Nancy.'

I gawped at him, unable to find anything to say in reply. He wasn't at all what I'd expected an Olympian to look like. He was completely bald for a start, and dressed in faded khaki shorts and a rather unusual patterned shirt which, he proudly announced when he noticed me staring at it, he'd made himself, from an old curtain.

'I've been working as a missionary in China for so many years I've quite forgotten how eccentric I must look in my home-made clothes!' He laughed and did a twirl.

Edward couldn't wipe the grin from his face, but I felt shy in Mr Liddell's company. It wasn't every day you met a real-life Olympian. I wasn't sure whether I should curtsey.

'Are you a keen runner, too, like your brother?' he asked. 'Another budding Olympian?'

I shook my head. 'I want to be a scientist, or an astronomer.'

He smiled, and looked impressed. 'Very admirable. Then I'll look forward to having you in my science class, Nancy.'

'You teach science?' I couldn't hide my delight.

'I do now. We all have to do our bit to help out.'

Since our teachers had to take their turn with camp chores, several camp inmates with experience in a particular subject had joined the Chefoo School teaching staff. They had a rather unconventional, un-Chefoo way of teaching, which we all rather enjoyed. To think that an actual Olympian would be teaching me was beyond thrilling.

Word about Mr Liddell's arrival spread quickly around camp, and a small crowd of children soon gathered, eager to see him for themselves.

'Well, isn't this something,' he smiled. 'I'm delighted to discover such a lot of children in need of regular physical education. We shall keep each other very busy, no doubt.'

I was so pleased for Edward. Mr Liddell's unexpected arrival had given him a reason to smile again. I'd been worried about him recently because he'd grown at least another inch, and had also grown dreadfully thin. I tried to give him my portion of food sometimes, but he refused to take it.

'You need your strength, too, Nonny. Besides,' he added, lowering his voice and tapping the side of his nose, 'the black market will see me right.'

I didn't like Edward getting mixed up in such things, but I knew there was no point nagging him. He'd told me how the black market worked by people trading things they didn't want for things they did.

'A group of farmers who live outside the camp are in secret contact with people inside the camp,' Edward explained. 'They smuggle things in with the men and women who come to empty the latrines. According to the American man we share a house with, you can get whatever you want: cigarettes, tobacco, chocolate. One woman traded her wedding ring for some sugar and soap.'

'Is that what happened to Master Harris?' I asked. We'd heard about him being searched by the guards and taken away somewhere.

Edward nodded. ''Fraid so. Risky business.'

Although I didn't see him very often since the boys' accommodation block wasn't close to ours, I was glad to have Edward around. Whenever I did see him, he was usually with Larry and the older boys, and I was too shy to go over. Edward waved if he saw me, and Larry always smiled, but I couldn't be sure if he was teasing me, or really smiling, so I never smiled back, just in case.

Uncle Eric (as Mr Liddell soon became known by the camp children), quickly became an important addition to the compound. He told us he'd been captured in central China with a group of other missionaries, and brought straight to Weihsien. He hadn't, unfortunately, come across a Lillian or Anthony Plummer during his work. I'd secretly hoped he might know them, and might have brought a message from my mother to say she couldn't wait to be reunited with me. But he had no such message to give me.

'Try not to be too disappointed, Plum,' Mouse offered when I told her he didn't know my parents after all. 'China is enormous; it would have been rather miraculous if he *had* known them.'

Still, Uncle Eric brought plenty of other things to camp. He was a very kind and gentle man, always looking for ways to help out, even if it wasn't part of his assigned duties. He organized games of hockey, football and softball, and made up exciting PE competitions to keep us all fit and healthy. Mouse called him the Bald Piper because he never went anywhere without a group of children running alongside him. He was quite the celebrity, and we all adored him.

'If I train really hard, I might even be good enough to make the Olympic team when we get out of here,' Edward said, brimming with enthusiasm. 'Imagine it, Nonny! When they ask who coached me, they'll never believe it!'

I said that would be marvellous, because I didn't like to point out that, with his arms and legs having got so skinny, he'd do well to run to the latrines, never mind around an Olympic track. Still, it was nice to see Edward back to something like his old self, showing off with all the things he knew about Uncle Eric and the Olympics, and full of enthusiasm again.

If Edward and Larry couldn't believe their luck about having an Olympian as their PE teacher, I couldn't believe my luck about having such a fascinating science teacher. Uncle Eric knew much more than the Chefoo teachers. Best of all, unlike our own teachers, who didn't like us to ask too many questions and stuck strictly to the school syllabus, Uncle Eric encouraged us to question and wonder.

'It's the best way to learn, and the only way to really become a scientist,' he said, in his lovely Scottish accent that sounded like a song. 'We might never discover the answers, but the quest for knowledge drives discovery and invention. Always ask. You never know where your question might lead.'

Mouse shared my interest in science and the stars, and was as enthralled by Uncle Eric as I was. We talked about his lessons for ages after, and wondered about things together, in private. I'd started to realize I had an awful lot in common with Mouse and, with poor Sprout still confined to the hospital, I'd come to depend on her. We navigated our strange new life together, explorers mapping uncharted waters. But one thing that made us both feel rather lost and disorientated was the way our bodies were changing as we grew up, or how they didn't change, in my case. I still hadn't started my monthlies. Mouse said I must be a late developer.

We decided to take Uncle Eric's advice about asking questions, and plucked up the courage to ask Connie about boys and sex and things. We couldn't bear to ask Mrs Trevellyan, even though she'd offered. Apart from anything else, we decided she was much too old to remember anything about it.

'Why do you want to know?' Connie asked. 'You're still too young to be bothered about boys.' She wasn't the least bit embarrassed, even though Mouse and I squirmed.

'We just thought we should know,' I explained. 'We've seen the women with their big swollen bellies, and we know it isn't true that you get a baby from kissing, or from touching someone's belly button. Uncle Eric says scientists should always ask a question, rather than guess. So, we're asking you, because you're the oldest girl we know.'

Connie told us to sit down and to prepare to be shocked. Both of us were too horrified to ask any questions at all.

There was rather a lot for Mouse and I to talk about afterwards.

'I'm never having children,' she said.

'Me neither,' I agreed. 'I think I'll just have lots of cats instead.'

Having just had 'the conversation' with Connie, we both looked at the pregnant ladies in camp rather differently, but one woman in particular caught my eye as we made our way back to the accommodation block.

I tugged at Mouse's sleeve as the so-called honeypot girls walked past us on the way out of the compound. Large buckets of waste swayed from the bamboo poles they carried over their shoulders. We both covered our noses to block out the awful smell.

'Look, Mouse. Isn't that . . .'

'Shu Lan,' she whispered. 'Yes, it is!'

Without hesitating, we ran over to her.

'Shu Lan! It's us! Nancy and Joan! From Chefoo!'

She glanced over her shoulder toward the guards, and took a few steps towards us. She looked dreadfully tired. Her belly was swollen, like some of the women around the compound.

I smiled at her, surprised by how pleased I was to see her; to see part of our past from Chefoo School. I thought about our last day before the soldiers arrived, when we'd made paper snowflakes and Shu Lan had told us about the kingfishers trapped in the metalsmiths' nets. I'd thought about that story so often since. It was why I'd chosen Kingfisher for the new Guide patrol name.

'Hello!' I said, full of enthusiasm. 'It's ever so nice to see you.'

But Shu Lan didn't seem as pleased to see us. She looked nervous as she pulled a tiny piece of folded paper from beneath her hair. 'For Miss Elspeth.' She kept her voice low and glanced anxiously behind me as she held her hand at her side. 'Please. Take it.'

I stared at her hand and thought about how Master Harris had been taken away for apparently smuggling notes inside his shoe. I wanted to help, but I didn't know if I should. I wished Edward was there. He would know what to do.

Mouse nudged me. 'Go on,' she whispered.

I reached for the little piece of paper, but my fingers were hesitant and clumsy, and it fell to the ground. As we both bent to pick it up, Shu Lan's hand found mine and, for what could only have been seconds but felt like much more, she held my hand and looked at me, and there was such fear and sadness in her beautiful eyes that I felt afraid and sad. And in that moment, I understood what Miss Kent meant when we'd watched Shu Lan from the principal's office and she'd told me to think differently about the servants. Shu Lan was somebody's daughter and somebody's friend, just like me. She was also soon to become somebody's mother. However dangerous it was, I wanted to help her.

I grasped the piece of paper between my fingers.

A nervous smile flickered at Shu Lan's lips as she stood up. 'Thank you, Nancy,' she whispered, and it was like a breath of wind had spoken for her.

I watched as she joined the other women, and the gates were locked behind them, and as me and Mouse hurried back to our accommodation.

Miss Kent studied the note on the piece of paper before folding it up again and slipping it into her pocket. She asked a lot of questions. 'How did she look? Was her belly very big? Did anyone see her give the paper to you?'

We gave her as much information as we could.

'Are we in trouble, Miss?' I asked.

'No, Nancy. You're not in trouble. You did the right thing by coming to tell me. This isn't a place to keep secrets. It's always better to tell someone.'

Mouse stared at Miss Kent, as if she wanted to say something, but she remained silent.

'Actually, I'm glad you came to find me, Nancy. I have something to show you.' Miss Kent bent down so that her eyes were level with mine. She wasn't much taller than me now. Her grey eyes looked kinder close up. I could see the patterns and joins in her irises, like strands of wool knitted together. 'Hold out your hands,' she said, with a smile.

I closed my eyes and waited until she placed something in my hands.

My eyes flew open. 'My tea caddy! Oh, thank you, Miss! Wherever did you find it?'

I hugged it tight to my chest, so relieved to have it back.

'Don't thank me. Larry Crofton found it.'

'Larry?'

'Yes. Somehow it got mixed up with the boys' luggage when we left the train from Tsingtao. He found it when they were having a tidy up earlier.'

'How did he know it was mine?'

'He must have seen you carrying it from Chefoo to Temple Hill. Apparently, he was quite adamant it was yours. He said it was very special and that you'd be ever so pleased to have it back. I suggest you put it into your trunk for safekeeping.'

'Oh, I will. I'll do it right away.'

When we saw Larry at supper, Mouse said I should go over and say thank you.

'Must I?' I said, feeling suddenly shy.

'He did something kind. And he keeps looking over.'

I wished she hadn't noticed, and I wished Larry wouldn't stare.

After we'd eaten the awful watery soup, I walked over to where Larry and Edward were standing with a group of friends.

Edward ruffled my hair. 'Boys' talk over here, I'm afraid!'

I scowled at him, smoothed my hair, and stared at my feet.

Hazel Gaynor

Larry shoved my arm. 'Glad you got your tea caddy back?'

I glanced up at him from under my fringe, which had grown rather long, and was good for hiding behind. 'Yes. Thanks ever so.'

'What do you keep in it, anyway?'

I shrugged. 'Silly things, really.'

He grinned. 'You're a silly thing, really.'

I grinned back. 'So are you.'

I was so glad to have Mummy's letters and special things, but having them back also made me miss her more. When I re-read her letters and looked through all the little treasures I'd kept, it almost felt as though another child had collected them, and that another woman had written all those words. I wondered if she'd changed as much as I had. Would I still call her Mummy when I saw her, or was that too babyish? Should I call her Mother now?

After lights out, I turned onto my side and stared at the space where Sprout should be sleeping, and I wished it was possible to keep special people in a tea caddy, to keep them safe. I listened to the whip-poor-will singing his song beyond the window, closed my eyes, and waited for morning.

ELSPETH

'What did the note say?' Edwina asked. 'Did Shu Lan ask for your help?'

'She wants me – us – to look after her baby when it's born,' I explained. 'She says she's terrified the soldiers will take it from her.'

Edwina looked at me. 'I see. And will you?'

'I was hoping you would help me find the answer to that.'

I'd gone to Edwina for advice before even telling Minnie about Shu Lan's note. From experience, I'd learned that the fewer people who knew about camp secrets the better, and while I trusted Minnie, I didn't want to give her another reason to worry. We certainly had plenty of those already.

I slumped into my chair at the front of the classroom, and leaned my elbows on the desk.

'How on earth can I look after an infant here? I can barely look after myself. Quite apart from which, the guards would be suspicious. I don't exactly look as if I'm expecting, do I? Or look Chinese, for that matter. I wish she'd asked someone else to help her.'

'But there *are* babies here, Elspeth. And there are Chinese mothers, too.' Edwina leaned against the edge of the desk. 'I would have asked for your help, if I was her.'

'What do you mean?'

'If I were Shu Lan. If I had to think of someone to help me, to entrust my child to, I would come straight to you.' She placed her hands on her hips in a manner that reminded me of my mother when she was vexed. 'You really should try to like yourself a lot more than you do. You might have made a mess of things in the past but, from what I can see, you're making a damn good show of things now.' She ran her fingers over her hair, sending stray silver strands drifting to the classroom floor. 'You've done a fine job with the children, Elspeth. I do hope you realize that.'

'I've been their teacher, as I was appointed to be,' I replied, dismissing her compliment.

She raised a knowing eyebrow. 'You've been *far* more than their teacher. Teachers instruct. You have nurtured and comforted.' She leaned forward, her hands on the desk, her eyes full of intent. 'You, dear girl, have cared.'

I didn't tell Minnie in the end. I threw the note into the stove and tried to forget about it, while wishing there was some other way I could help Shu Lan. Schoolgirls I could just about handle, but a baby was a different matter entirely. I was a childless spinster, without nieces or nephews. What on earth did I know about any of that?

As the weeks passed, food and medical supplies continued to dwindle, and health and morale deteriorated. Malaria, typhoid and dysentery were as commonplace as measles and influenza had been in England. The hospital was kept at full tilt as winter temperatures fell below freezing and there wasn't nearly sufficient fuel to heat the inadequate stoves in our rooms. With increasing frequency and heavy hearts, we heard of another death in the camp. The old and the weak were especially vulnerable to diseases that spread easily in the insanitary conditions. Death was never far away, and I dreaded the day when it would knock at our door.

I checked in on Dorothy at the hospital every day, only to be greeted with the same grim report from Nurse Eve.

'She's very weak now,' she whispered as we stood beside her bed.

The poor child looked like a porcelain doll, so pale and still, only the threadbare hospital blanket rising and falling to signal that there was any sign of life at all.

'I've tried to prepare the children,' I said. 'Connie and Nancy especially. I don't offer the same reassurances I once did. Much as I can't bear to think about . . . the worst, neither can I bear to give them false hope.'

Nurse Eve patted my arm lightly. 'It's only a matter of time now.'

I sat with Dorothy for hours at a time, unable to bear the thought of her being alone or afraid. I read to her from the Girl Guide Handbook, slowly reciting the Promise and laws.

'A Guide's honour is to be trusted. A Guide is loyal. A Guide's duty is to be useful and to help others. A Guide is a friend to all and a sister to every other Guide. A Guide is courteous. A Guide is a friend to animals. A Guide obeys orders. A Guide smiles and sings under all difficulties. A Guide is thrifty. A Guide is pure in thought, in word and in deed.'

The laws took on a particular poignancy, given our present situation. Everything took on a different meaning; the words of the most familiar passages heavy with importance, demanding to be really understood.

'*It is no fun to them to walk by easy paths, the whole excitement of life is facing difficulties and dangers and apparent impossibilities, and in the end getting a chance of attaining the summit of the mountain they have wanted to reach. Well, I think it is the case with most girls nowadays. They do not want to sit down and lead an idle life, not to have everything done for them, nor to have a very easy time.'*

I let the words settle around us before I continued. With every page I turned, and every passage I read, I glanced at Dorothy, and wondered if I would ever get to the end.

I started my Weihsien diary that month; part account of camp life; part exorcism of the demons and fears that tormented me. I was nervous about documenting precise events, or my personal thoughts about our captors, aware of the punishments that might be dealt if they ever discovered it, but I added sufficient detail to form a record of camp life. Perhaps I would look back on it one day. Perhaps it was just a way for me to try to make some sense of everything that was happening to us.

'What are you writing about now, Miss Brontë?' Minnie teased.

'I'm writing about eggshells,' I replied as I hunched over the page. In an effort to use as little paper as possible, given our limited resources, my handwriting was so small it was barely legible, and my eyes were dry and tired from straining to see properly in the dim light.

'It's funny, isn't it,' Minnie mused.

'What is?'

'When you think about what we used to consider valuable. Pots of face cream, a well-lined winter coat, freshly laundered bedsheets.' She sighed, wistfully. 'I'd give up a lifetime of all that for a decent meal, and a hot bath. In fact, if we ever get out of here, I will eat my evening meals *in* the bath.'

It might have been an amusing idea had it not been prefaced with, 'if we ever get out of here'.

'Do you remember when Edward Plummer used to go

crashing on about the Navy and heroic rescue efforts?' I remarked wryly. 'And you were just as bad.'

'We were rather on the optimistic side, weren't we!'

'I wish we still were. We seem to have nothing to look forward to, Minnie. Nothing to celebrate.'

'What about your letter to Lady Baden-Powell?' she said, as I picked up the stub of my pencil to continue writing. 'I imagine she'll be very keen to meet you when she hears about the Chefoo and Weihsien Brownies and Girl Guides. That's something to look forward to. You are still writing the letter, aren't you?'

'Yes. I add a few lines now and again. Perhaps she will be interested, if I ever get to post the damned thing.'

I planned to finish the letter with the postscript we all hoped for. I pictured myself walking to the end of Rowan Terrace, back home in York, and dropping it into the postbox.

'Either way,' Minnie said, 'you should keep writing it all down. If it's good enough for our Girl Guides, it's good enough for us.'

We'd encouraged the girls to keep log books as a way of documenting their achievements. Minnie had worried that creating a record of their experience here wasn't a good idea, and that they might prefer to forget all about it after – if – we were liberated, but I'd disagreed.

'They'll never forget, Minnie, whether they write it down or not. War and internment are part of their lives now; part of their story, part of who they are.' I put my pencil down and closed the exercise book. 'I actually think life is meant to have its share of difficulty and struggle. That's when we find out who we really are, what we're really made of, not when everything's going along all jolly and straightforward and terribly nice. We come alive in the dramatic bits, don't we; in the moments that make us gasp and cry.'

Minnie was as surprised by my little monologue as I was. She stood up and threw her arms around me and we stood for an age, finding comfort and courage in the simple act of a friend's embrace.

Sometimes we needed remarkably little to see us through another day.

Sometimes, we needed far more.

Dorothy's deterioration weighed heavily on my mind as another Christmas approached and preparations were made to make it as special as possible for the children. All around the camp, groups of inmates pulled together to play music and sing carols, and the headmaster made a rousing speech about the true meaning of Christmas and the lasting value of the gifts of friendship and kindness. If the younger children still hoped Father Christmas would find them, and leave a stocking stuffed with toys at the end of their mats, they never said. War had taken the magic and innocence of childhood from them far too soon.

But a gift of my own arrived with the return of Charlie.

Minnie first alerted me. 'He's back, Els. He came back!'

I didn't need to ask who she meant.

He was shockingly thin, and his face was dreadfully hollow, but he managed to smile as he told us how he'd been kept in solitary confinement for around two weeks – he couldn't be sure – and had then been taken to see the Commandant.

'They interrogated me for days,' he said. 'They were planning to send me away, to a camp near Peking, from what I could gather.'

'Why didn't they?' I asked.

'As luck would have it, I noticed the Commandant's radio equipment was broken. I offered to fix it for him – and did a bloody good job of it, too. He decided I would be more use to him here, so . . . I'm staying. Albeit under very close watch. I used the situation to my advantage, of course.'

He explained that while he was fixing the radio, he'd taken

the opportunity to switch to the shortwave transmission bands, and had picked up the BBC Overseas Service.

'I couldn't listen for long,' he explained. 'But I did hear some encouraging news of Allied progress in the Pacific. US bombers have caused significant damage on the Japanese-occupied island of Tarawa in the Gilbert Islands. There have also been air attacks on a Japanese base in Rabaul.' It was the first time in months that we'd heard any news at all from the outside world, and we all listened intently to Charlie's account. 'Hopefully, my "repairs" were temporary enough that I'll be asked to look at it again.'

I couldn't hide my delight, or my relief, to have Charlie back with us, although it was difficult to come to terms with the fact that he had clearly suffered.

'Anyway, that's enough about me. How have *you* been, Elspeth?' he asked when everyone else had dispersed and we had a moment alone while I tidied some books in the classroom. 'You look tired.'

I smiled. 'And there I was all morning, creating perfect waves with my irons. I thought I'd never looked better, and it turns out I look like I've been dragged through a hedge backwards. Really, I don't know why I bother.'

He returned my smile. 'You look perfectly lovely to me.'

I folded my arms across my cardigan and told him to stop being so silly.

'You do,' he insisted. 'Tired, but lovely.'

'I've been dreadfully worried about you,' I admitted. 'It's good to have you back.'

'It's good to *be* back,' he said, and we smiled at each other without hesitation, or embarrassment, because it was a ridiculous thing to say, even if it was true.

As I made to return to my accommodation, Nurse Eve pushed open the classroom door.

'I'm sorry to interrupt.' Her face was heavy with concern. 'Could you come, Elspeth.'

I stared at her, and then at Charlie as I swallowed a knot of dread. 'Is it . . .?'

She nodded. 'It's Dorothy.'

NANCY

I was dreaming about my first winter in China, and a perfect December morning at the China Inland Mission HQ in Shanghai. 'It's snowing, Nonny!' Mummy whispered as she gently woke me. 'Come and see.' I could still feel the warmth of her arms around me as we stood together at the window; could still see the bright dazzle of the sun that scattered diamonds on the snow and turned the branches of the gingko trees to gold. It was all so vivid that, for a wonderful moment, I thought it was Mummy's hand on my shoulder, gently shaking me awake.

'Nancy, wake up.' But it was Connie's face I saw when I opened my eyes. 'Miss Kent says you're to come to the hospital,' she whispered. 'To see Dorothy.'

By the light of her hand lamp I could see that her eyes were red and swollen.

Half-asleep and bleary-eyed, I followed Connie from the accommodation block and trudged along beside her in my nightie toward the hospital. I knew something was horribly wrong because she was ever so quiet and held my hand tight in hers.

Miss Kent was waiting for us outside. 'Hello, Nancy. I'm sorry to wake you.'

'That's all right, Miss.'

'I need you to be especially brave, Nancy,' she said as we walked along the corridors towards Sprout's room. 'Dorothy is feeling very poorly tonight, but she asked to see you.' She smiled one of her encouraging smiles as she opened the door and we stepped quietly inside.

Sprout was in bed, but she was awake. Connie sat down in a chair while I perched on the edge of an empty bed beside Sprout's. The room was dark, but moonlight peered through the bars at the windows so that I could see Sprout quite clearly.

'Hello, Plum.' Her voice was a tiny whisper.

'Hello, Sprout.'

She reached for my hand. 'It's nice to see you.' Her words were so faint I could hardly hear her.

I didn't know what to say. Everything I thought of felt silly and unimportant.

'Dorothy wanted you to sing to her,' Miss Kent whispered. 'To help her fall asleep.'

'What shall I sing?'

'It doesn't matter. Anything.'

'One of our favourites,' Sprout whispered.

In the silence of the hospital room, I felt shy and tongue-tied and couldn't think of a single song, but eventually the words came and I started to sing, softly at first, and then a little louder, and Connie joined in. We sang and sang, one song after another – 'All Things Bright and Beautiful', 'This Little Light of Mine', hymns and rounds, our Six Songs from Brownies, the haunting words of 'Taps', on and on through the night until eventually the words became a tired jumble on my lips, and I fell asleep.

I dreamed of a field full of sunflowers, their bright faces turned toward the sun.

Nurse Prune woke me at first light with a gentle shake of my shoulder. Without a word, she took my hand, and led me quietly from the room. Connie wasn't in her chair. Sprout looked dreadfully pale, her bedsheets horribly still.

Still half-asleep, I followed Nurse Prune to a little office, where she wrapped a blanket around my shoulders and gave me a cup of hot black tea. I was glad of the warmth of both.

After a few minutes, Miss Kent stepped into the room. She closed the door quietly behind her. Everything was so quiet; so still. She crouched down in front of me, and pulled the blanket closer around my shoulders. Her eyes glistened, so that I could see my reflection in them. She seemed to be searching for the right words; for the best way to tell me what I already knew.

'She's dead, isn't she, Miss?'

She gave the smallest nod of her head and gently squeezed my shoulders. 'I'm so sorry, Nancy.'

I'd known from the moment Connie had woken me in the middle of the night. I'd known by the way that Miss Kent had smiled encouragingly at me. I'd known, and yet I couldn't bear it to be true.

Miss Kent brushed a tear from my cheek. 'She won't be in any pain now, Nancy. She's with God, in Heaven. Shall we say a prayer for her?'

'Will she hear it?'

'I'm sure she will. Yes.'

I closed my eyes and placed my hands together and listened to every word of Miss Kent's prayer. After the Amen I kept my eyes closed, because Sprout was dead, and I didn't want to open my eyes to a world without her.

Miss Kent sat beside me and held my hand. For a long time

we didn't say anything, but quietly watched the sky grow lighter beyond the window, and listened as the first birds began to sing.

'I'm afraid I'll forget her,' I said.

'You won't.' Miss Kent squeezed my hand. 'The people we love the most are always with us.'

I wanted to go back to the first time I'd met Sprout on the boat from Shanghai, and spend every moment together all over again. I wanted her to tell me all about New England in the fall. I wanted to really listen to her when she chattered on, so that I would never forget her lovely American accent, so free and loose. I wanted to give her my last humbug, and my best marble, and the heart-shaped pebble I kept in my tea caddy. I wanted to run with her across the bay at Chefoo School, tripping and stumbling in the sand as the wind blew our laughter up into the clouds. More than anything in the world, I wanted my best friend to always be there, because I didn't know what I was going to do, or how I was going to be, without her.

Sprout was buried the next day, beneath a blossom tree in a quiet corner of the cemetery, behind the guards' house. Master Harris made a headstone from a piece of wood to mark her resting place. He engraved it with the Girl Guides trefoil, and a kingfisher. It was the most beautiful headstone I'd ever seen.

For the first time since arriving in Weihsien, the whole Chefoo School group gathered to say goodbye. The girls of Kingfisher Patrol stood together, hand in hand. I stood at the end of the line, my right hand held tight in Mouse's. My left hand hung idle by my side.

Tears streamed down our cheeks as the final prayers were said. Poor Connie was inconsolable. Sprout was my best friend, but she was Connie's little sister. I reached for Connie's hand. What else could I do? Even Miss Kent and Miss Butterworth couldn't hide their distress. Every one of us wept for our dear brave friend.

As the low winter sun settled over the distant rice fields, we sang 'Taps', our voices captured in misty breaths that drifted slowly up to the heavens. I closed my eyes and sang as clearly as I could, so that Sprout would hear me. 'All is well, safely rest, God is nigh.'

Miss Kent asked me to wait when everyone else began to leave.

'There's something I'd like to do, Nancy. Could you help me?' She pulled a small square of folded cotton from her pocket, and opened it up. Seven sunflower seeds were inside. 'Take one,' she said.

I stared at the little seeds and thought about the sunflower at Chefoo School; how we'd diligently watered it and measured it, and how disappointed Sprout had been to leave it behind.

'Should I plant it?' I asked as I chose a seed.

Miss Kent nodded. 'A sunflower for Sprout. Perhaps just in front of the headstone.'

I took the seed and pushed it deep into the earth. Miss Kent did the same.

'Who is your seed for, Miss?'

'For all of us, Nancy. So that we'll always be with her.' She smiled a thin smile, and I smiled back, because it was such a nice thing to have done. 'Oh, and before I forget, I thought you might like to have this. I checked with Connie, and she agreed you should have it.' She put her hand into her pocket and pulled out a brass trefoil Promise badge. 'It was Dorothy's. I thought it would be fitting if her Promise was kept by her best friend.'

I took the badge from her and traced the tip of my finger around the three leaves: Plum, Sprout, Mouse. We'd promised we would be friends forever.

'Thank you, Miss. I'll keep it safe. Always.'

She looked at me in a funny way and took a step toward me. 'Nancy, I . . .' She held out her hand and let it rest against my shoulder a moment before gently pulling me to her, and holding me in an embrace.

I held my arms stiffly by my sides as my cheek pressed against her coat. I closed my eyes and remembered Miss Kent making her promise as I'd clung tight to Mummy's hand, afraid to let go among the chaos and clatter of rickshaws and hand-carts, and the shouts of beggars and fishermen on the wharf in Shanghai. 'How about I keep a special eye on Nancy until we get to Chefoo? We'll be the new girls together, Nancy. How about that!' It was four years since Miss Kent had made that promise; four years since I'd watched my mother become a small blue dot in the distance. Now, surrounded by Weihsien's high walls, I pressed my cheek closer to Miss Kent's wool coat and she tightened her embrace in response, I felt as if a thousand arms were wrapped around me, enfolding me in kindness, keeping me safe.

Too soon, Miss Kent pulled her arms away. She smoothed her cardigan beneath her coat, even though it didn't need smoothing, and straightened her spectacles even though they were already straight.

'Best catch up with the others,' she said. 'Run along now.'

I pulled my socks up and set off at a sprint, the winter wind whistling through my fingertips as I imagined Sprout running beside me.

ELSPETH

1944

O ur tight little group of girls was deeply affected by Dorothy's death, and the ripple of shock and grief spread beyond the wider Chefoo community to the rest of the camp. Any death forced us all to face our own mortality, and doubt and guilt tormented me as I wondered if I should have written to Dorothy's parents before we left Chefoo, or insisted she was too ill to travel, and remained behind with her at Temple Hill. I stumbled into the gaping hole of her absence every morning, her death the first thing I thought about when I woke up.

Poor Connie walked around like a ghost, and the rest of the Chefoo children were sullen and subdued. Bad dreams, and the painful cracks of broken hearts, disturbed us all in the difficult days and weeks that followed. Nancy and Joan were especially inconsolable. They asked if they could paint a sunflower on the wall of our sparse little room, 'So that she'll still be with us.' Their unceasing capacity to endure the most harrowing events was quite beyond my comprehension. Watching them remember their friend in such a touching and beautiful way broke my heart all over again.

Dorothy's death was also a stark reminder of the terrible conditions we were living in, and the silent dangers of poor nutrition and inadequate medical supplies. We'd already discovered that Weihsien winters brought chilblains and pneumonia, and had been warned that dysentery and tropical diseases were rife in the summer months. Our war became one of small daily battles, as we shared out the precious eggshells and looked wearily at the charts we'd drawn up to record the girls' victories in the various challenges and competitions we'd fabricated from the most awful tasks. We'd pressed on with the familiar and the routine. We even held our meeting of Kingfisher Patrol in the week of Dorothy's death. The girls voted unanimously to go ahead because it's what she would have wanted.

'It isn't enough, Minnie, is it,' I sighed as I sank down onto my mat. 'Encouragement and distraction, Guide patrols and semaphore displays, ground-up gritty eggshells. It will never be enough, will it?'

'It's all we have,' Minnie said, her voice unusually firm. 'Guide patrols and semaphore displays can go a long way when you have as little as we do.' She took my hands and pulled me to my feet. 'We promise to do our best, don't we? If our best isn't enough, then so be it.'

Had I truly done my best for Dorothy? It was hard to know.

I visited her grave every day.

Trouble watched me from a doorway of the guards' house as I made my daily vigil. I felt his eyes on me, like an insect crawling over my skin, but avoided making eye contact, and kept my head down.

'You will miss curfew,' he called, after watching me for several nights. 'Go back.' He pointed his stick in the direction of my accommodation block.

'I will visit the child,' I replied, defiant. 'Then I will go back.'

I was too exhausted to care about the consequences of disobeying him, but the fact that he let me carry on worried me. I knew he was biding his time; waiting for the right moment to finish what he'd started when I'd interrupted him with Connie. It was the continual threat that it might be today, that afternoon, that evening, that was so unbearable. And he knew it. Like the kingfishers Shu Lan had told us about, he had me trapped. He was waiting for the perfect moment to pluck his feather.

After Dorothy's death, we all felt the importance of new life, and encouraged the older girls to help the women who'd arrived in camp already pregnant, and who had to face the terror of childbirth without the usual medical interventions or sanitation. Thankfully, internment had also brought several midwives to Weihsien, but they weren't equipped to cope with the worst complications, and we all prayed for everything to go smoothly whenever anyone went into labour. There was little we could do to prevent the howls and deep moans drifting between the thin walls of the accommodation blocks. I laboured with every woman, breathing a sigh of relief when a plaintive cry signalled that the infant had been safely delivered, and offering a prayer for the fragile souls of those who never found their voice.

But despite the girls' interest in the babies once they were born, they were rather less enamoured with the process of how they got there in the first place. Their bodies seemed to mature overnight, and our cramped living quarters left no room for any privacy in which to get used to their new bumps and curves, and the onset of their monthlies. I lost count of the number of times I had to reassure another horrified girl when she showed me her bloodstained bedsheets.

Minnie and I did our best to handle it all as matter-of-factly as we could, but it wasn't always easy. Supplies of sanitary items were severely lacking, and we had to resort to torn-up towels and bedsheets as sanitary napkins, which the girls washed and reused as necessary. Their initial squeamish embarrassment at the pink-tinted water they poured away outside was soon replaced by a numb indifference. Exhaustion, hunger, and the menacing presence of guards with guns didn't leave much room for prudery or embarrassment, but it was those whose monthlies hadn't arrived that I was most concerned about. Poor nutrition had left many deficiencies, and some of the young bodies had simply stalled. I worried about the long-term damage being caused to girls like Nancy Plummer, one of those left behind.

'I hope there won't be any lasting issues down the road,' I said as I changed into my uniform for Guides.

'Let's hope not,' Minnie agreed. 'There's no pain greater than the ache in your arms for a child you'll never hold.'

'Oh, Min. I'm sorry.'

'Don't be. Look at all the children I've been blessed with in the end.'

She smiled, but the pain was evident in her eyes.

It was a pain I felt myself. Harry had always said I'd be a wonderful mother. It was one of my greatest sadnesses to have never discovered if he was right. As I tied my scarf, my thoughts drifted back to my old jewellery box, with a ballerina that danced to 'The Blue Danube' when you lifted the lid. I smiled as I remembered dancing around the front room with Harry, '*One* two three, *one* two three,' as we dipped and rose on our toes and heels and whirled around and around until we fell onto the sofa in a tangle of love and laughter. It seemed impossible that I had ever known such simple, happy times.

'Elspeth Mary Kent? Are you even listening to me?'

I turned to Minnie, and held my hands out in apology. 'I'm sorry. Miles away. As per.'

'You look as if you've seen a ghost,' she said as she buttoned her shirt and adjusted her Promise badge. 'Whatever were you thinking about?'

'Ghosts,' I said as I pushed a few loose curls into my bun and put on my hat. 'I was thinking about ghosts.'

'You were thinking about Harry, weren't you?' she added, softly.

I nodded, and straightened my skirt. I'd already taken it in at the waist a number of times and yet it was still loose enough to fall to the floor as soon as I undid the zip.

There were no secrets between us now. We'd shared every painful memory, every happy moment, every favourite song and book and film star. Hunger, weakness and exhaustion left little room for secrets and shyness. Besides, as Edwina Trevellyan had said in her usual forthright way, 'We might all be dead tomorrow. We might as well talk now, because we won't be much good to each other when we're rotting in a ditch.'

'Shu Lan's baby must be due soon,' Minnie added as we set off to the meeting room together. 'I wonder how she is?'

I'd thought a lot about Shu Lan since Nancy had given me her note. I hadn't seen her since, nor Wei Huan, who seemed to have disappeared, if he'd ever been here at all. Perhaps it was too dangerous for him to come and find me. Perhaps something else was keeping him silent. I asked the honeypot girls about Shu Lan whenever I could without drawing the attention of the guards. After what had happened the first time I'd spoken to Shu Lan, they weren't keen to talk to me. 'No news,' was the best I got.

As the weeks and months passed, I found myself watching and waiting, never quite sure which I should fear the most; Shu Lan's baby being sent to me, or not.

* * *

The long hard winter eventually released its grip on north-eastern China, and spring arrived with a welcome burst of warmth and blossom on the trees. We stumbled into the gentle sunshine like the eager green shoots that poked through the soil in the vegetable garden; desperate for warmth and light. Even with the help of the Red Cross food parcels, which occasionally found their way to us and caused great excitement among the children and enormous relief among the adults, food and medical supplies were still worryingly low. We were so desperately isolated, cut off from the rest of the world, and reliable information about events happening beyond the compound walls was hard to come by. I was still desperate for any news of Alfie, or his battalion. Minnie didn't ask about him anymore, and I didn't mention him. It was like he'd disappeared all over again.

Only occasional scraps of news reached us through Charlie's careful 'tinkering' with the Commandant's unreliable radio equipment, and through the 'bamboo radio' that operated inside the compound. Despite the dangers involved in relaying the information through the farmers to the secret operatives inside camp, the secret chain of communication was a vital lifeline to the outside world. We were desperate for good news, desperate to hear that the tide was turning in favour of the Allies. By spring, the feeling was that the war wasn't going as well for Japan as it once had, and reports of more Allied victories in the Pacific brought fresh hope of liberation. But that, in turn, brought fresh fears about what our captors would do in the event of Japan's surrender. I swayed between celebratory visions of going home, and horrifying visions of mass execution, and somewhere in the middle I got on with the next chore, the next lesson, the next meal.

It was a relief when someone else took over for a while and, more often than not, that person was Uncle Eric. He was such a marvellous and valued addition to the compound and put the rest of us to shame with his relentless quest to help others, and to entertain the children. His 'Sports Days' were always eagerly anticipated, and although the dusty pathways we'd christened 'Main Street' and 'Sunset Boulevard' were poor substitutes for an Olympic running track, he never once complained and always set up his races with the same care and passion as if they were being held in a stadium.

'He's quite remarkable, isn't he,' Charlie said as we watched Uncle Eric set off, full pelt, with a crowd of excited children racing behind him.

'The children adore him,' I agreed. I felt unusually relaxed as we sat in the dust, bathed in spring sunshine. 'He exudes goodness, and hope. And he works so hard around camp. I don't know when the man ever rests.'

Uncle Eric really did put in the hours. Whether chopping wood or cooking, sweeping up leaves, or giving a classroom full of spellbound children a lesson in science, he was a relentless workhorse.

'Where on earth do you find the energy?' I'd asked him recently when we'd crossed paths in the school building. He was making a model of the solar system from things he'd found around camp: discarded tins and punctured tennis balls and rusting wire he'd found beside the guards' house.

'I get my energy from being busy, Elspeth. I don't know about you, but I find the idler I am, the worse it all is. If I keep going, keep working, I don't have time to think too much.' He tapped his bald head with his finger. 'Thinking is the real war, isn't it? It's our minds that will ultimately determine whether we win or lose; whether we survive.'

I'd thought about those words many times since.

The crowd cheered and whooped as the racers reappeared in the distance.

Hazel Gaynor

I stood up to get a better look. 'Oh, look, Charlie. Edward Plummer's in the lead.'

'Gosh. So he is.' He laughed as he stood up beside me. 'Perhaps all those lessons of mine have paid off after all.'

Edward crossed the finish line first and raised his arms in victory. Uncle Eric, only just beaten, shook his hand, and all the Chefoo children watching rushed around to offer their congratulations. It was a rare moment of celebration; a moment of unity and joy.

'It might not be so bad if we could be sure of a month of days like this,' Charlie remarked. 'Funny isn't it, how little you need when you have nothing.'

'We won't know what to do with ourselves when we're back home,' I said. 'Three full meals a day and all the soap you can lay your hands on. Imagine!'

'Where is home, exactly? I don't think I've ever asked.'

'Yorkshire. A little village outside York.'

Charlie studied me as he shielded his eyes from the glare of the sun. 'I've never been to Yorkshire. They say it's very pretty.'

I adjusted my sunhat and pushed my hands into my skirt pockets. 'Then you must visit.'

'Yes,' he replied. 'Yes, I must.'

270

NANCY

March 1944

'**B**ooks are a feast for the imagination,' Mrs Trevellyan announced as she wafted around her room like a will-o'-the-wisp. 'Who cares if there's barbed wire around the walls. *This* is our escape. Right here, in all these glorious words. Between these pages, we can be as free as the birds. We can go anywhere we please!'

I wasn't sure what Churchill would have to say about that, but I understood what she meant. Books took us far away from Weihsien. We ate them up as ravenously as if they were beef stew and dumplings, and jam roly-poly and custard.

Mouse and I enjoyed helping Mrs Trevellyan with the camp library. As one of the first arrivals into the camp, she'd had the idea of pooling all the books anyone had brought with them, so that everyone could share. We'd help to arrange the books into alphabetical order by title (because nobody could ever remember the name of the author), and made weekly trips around the compound to collect books from people who'd forgotten they'd ever borrowed one, or were too poorly to return them, or wanted to keep the book for themselves. Plenty of people denied ever taking a book in the first place, but Mrs Trevellyan was meticulous about keeping a list of borrowers, so we knew they were being what she called 'Economical with the Truth'.

From Shakespeare's Sonnets to the *Reader's Digest* and a much-loved edition of *The Hound of the Baskervilles*, people held onto their favourites as if they were loaves of freshly baked bread. I couldn't blame them. Books really were our escape from Weihsien. Between the pages we walked beside blue oceans, solved murders in English country houses, ate sticky buns beside crackling log fires, and travelled the world from Paris to Nepal, Africa to New York.

The best part of helping was that we always got first pick of the books as they were returned. Mrs Trevellyan said we were only allowed to borrow one book at a time because there weren't nearly enough to go around, but we found ways to make one book last an age, savouring each delicious chapter, and often reading it twice, just to make sure. Mouse read books from back to front, and then by reading every odd-numbered chapter and then every even-numbered chapter. Best of all, I forgot to miss my mother while I was reading. In the middle of a really good story, I forgot I was in China, in the middle of a war, at all.

Sometimes, we found scraps of paper in the books, or little tokens people had used as bookmarks and forgotten to take out. Mouse found a tiny strip of folded paper tucked inside the sleeve of a book called *The Thirty-Nine Steps*. The paper had Chinese writing on it, and a picture of a lotus flower. She put it in her pocket.

'What are you keeping that for?' I asked. 'You're getting as bad as me for collecting things. You don't even know what it says!'

'It's pretty,' she said. 'And I want to learn Chinese when I'm older. I'll use it as a bookmark until I can understand what it says.'

We sometimes found corners of the pages turned down, and passages marked and underlined. Mrs Trevellyan didn't seem to mind, although I thought it spoiled the books.

'I'd never write in a book,' I said. 'It makes them look messy.'

'It does if you look at it one way,' she clucked as she put some books back onto the shelves we couldn't reach. 'But it also makes them look loved. It means that someone stopped and thought about that sentence, or that paragraph. Books aren't museum pieces to be admired from a distance. They're meant to be lived in; messed up a little.'

When our work was done, she made tea. As we'd both come to expect, it wasn't any normal tea.

'Hibiscus,' she announced. 'Made from flowers I found at the far end of the compound. There's an entire garden down there. Somebody's obviously looking after them. Perhaps some of the soldiers have a heart, after all.'

Mouse was fascinated by the different types of tea Mrs Trevellyan made, and she mostly liked the flavours. I would have much preferred to have an ordinary cup of Lyons, but I drank the hibiscus tea anyway to be polite, after which I excused myself and left them chatting about the dangers of rhododendron, and pink oleander, and the medicinal properties of ginseng and ginger.

I could never get used to Weihsien being my home, no matter how long our internment went on. Every day, I looked at the armed guards at the watchtowers, the locked gates and barbed wire, the ditches dug beside the walls to prevent escape, and it felt as if we'd only just arrived, and everything was unfamiliar and strange.

It wasn't terrible every day, but it was often difficult, and it was always fraught with danger. I felt it in the air, as clearly as

I felt the autumn mists and the coming of the winter snows and summer rains, and although we had each other, and our teachers, and Kingfisher Patrol, I felt horribly alone, and envied the children whose mothers were with them.

'Do you wish you could swap places with her?' Mouse asked as we watched a little girl play skipping with a frayed piece of rope while her mother looked on and clapped her encouragement.

'I'd just like to see my mother,' I said. 'Even if it was only for a little while, and then she had to leave again.'

'What would you say to her? If you could see her?'

I thought for a moment. 'I don't think I'd say anything. I'd be happy just to feel her arms around me.' I took my shoe off and tipped out a stone that had been bothering me. It was nice to wiggle my toes in my socks. My shoes were too small for me now and nipped at my heels. 'I'm sorry for always going on like an awful bore, Mouse. I know it's much worse for you.'

'But it isn't. Not really,' she said. 'I don't remember my mother. You have memories and feelings to miss. I just have a blank space.'

'I don't think you have a blank space at all,' I said. 'I think your mother is with you all the time, encouraging you, just the same as that mother over there.'

'Do you really think so?' She smiled, pleased by the thought. 'I do. Yes.'

Without our parents, we looked after each other, and squabbled with each other, and shared secrets and stuck together. In a funny way, my Chefoo family was more like a family than my own had ever been. My parents had become wispy memories, so that I almost felt shy when I thought about them. Who were Lillian and Anthony Plummer? What made them laugh, and cry? What were they afraid of? Sometimes I felt as if I didn't know my parents at all.

* * *

Almost worse than being constantly hungry was having to go to the latrines. Several of the Chefoo children and teachers had caught dysentery, and the cesspools and latrines were almost unbearable as the infection spread through the camp.

'Block your nose, and go in backwards,' Miss Kent advised when we complained about how awful it was. 'And be thankful you're not the ones who have to empty them,' she added.

Even in a place like Weihsien, where everything was awful, there were still people worse off than us. We felt especially sorry for the local women who came in to the compound to take away the waste from the latrines.

'If we really felt sorry for them, we would do it for them,' Mouse said as we stood a short distance away and watched. 'It's no good pitying someone and not doing anything about it. Come on.'

She grabbed my hand and dragged me over to the group of women.

'Mouse, I really don't think we should,' I cautioned, looking over my shoulder toward the guards. 'We'll get into terrible trouble.'

'Then let's get into trouble,' she said in a rare moment of defiance and determination. 'What would Sprout do if she was here?'

'She'd get into trouble,' I replied. I missed her so much. Her sense of fun and adventure; her wild unpredictability. I missed the confidence I felt when I was with her.

'Exactly,' Mouse said. 'So let's get into trouble for her!'

I imagined Sprout giggling beside me as I followed Mouse's lead.

'We've come to help,' Mouse said as we reached the women. She picked up one end of a pole, and indicated that I should take the other end. The stench from the buckets swaying beneath was so overpowering that I retched and had to breathe through my mouth as we walked toward the gate.

We were nearly there when Home Run rushed over to us.

'Put it down!' he urged. 'You must not do their work.'

'We're earning points for our Guide badges,' Mouse said. 'We only want to help.'

'Let us just go as far as the gate,' I pleaded. 'That's all.'

He looked over his shoulder and nodded his consent. 'Hurry. Before Commandant sees you.'

We reached the compound gate and took the heavy pole from our shoulders. The two women who were supposed to carry the buckets had caught up.

'We must all help,' Mouse said. 'We wanted to help you.'

They looked at each other and then the younger of the two leaned toward us.

'You are kind,' she whispered. 'Very kind.'

It was the closest we'd been to the gates since we'd arrived. I stared up at the Chinese writing along the top of the gates which I now knew said 'Courtyard of the Happy Way'. I took a step forward and pressed my hand against the solid wood.

'It's just through there, Mouse,' I whispered. 'Freedom. The world. The rest of our lives. It's so close.'

I peered through the wood to see if I could catch a glimpse of the other side, but the camp Commandant had been alerted to us and stalked over.

'You! Go back!' he barked, waving his stick at me. 'Children not allowed here.'

'Go,' Home Run whispered. 'Quickly.'

I grabbed Mouse's hand and we ran, as fast as we could, away from the Commandant and his great bamboo stick. As we ran away from the gates that led towards freedom, the wind whipped around our legs and ruffled our hair, and I caught the scent of English lavender on the breeze and I was sure I could hear my mother, calling out to me, 'Run, Nancy! Run!' For the first time since we'd been under Japanese guard, I understood that freedom wasn't something I had to wait for, but was something I could choose. In my mind, in my imagination and my memories, I could be as free as the birds that raced the wind; as free as the clouds that chased the sun far above me.

ELSPETH

Our remarkable Girl Guides passed their Weihsien Star tests that month. Minnie insisted we have a celebration to acknowledge their hard work, and although our enthusiasm for celebrations was rather lacking, her relentless enthusiasm was infectious.

The guards were surprisingly tolerant of entertainment in camp. From the raucous rehearsals and performances of the resident amateur dramatic group, to the beautiful harmonies of the Weihsien choir (an unlikely group of camp inmates who'd found companionship in their shared love of choral singing), a defiant spark of creativity seemed to always linger in the air. From Shakespeare to Chekhov, to operatic arias, and the innocence of our girls' own voices, it was wonderful to hear. Music held such beauty and hope, and had a wonderful ability to connect us all, whatever our language. Even the guards stopped to listen whenever music played. It was as if we'd all taken in a collective deep breath, and let out our differences in a long sigh.

As more bewildered souls had arrived, Weihsien had grown

to the size of a small town and, like any town, it had its share of reprobates and hooligans, courtesans and prostitutes, as well as those whose lives had run a gentler course. It was a dizzying concoction, but one that somehow worked. The sheer variety of people interned at the compound never failed to astound me, so I wasn't surprised to discover that a dozen members of the Salvation Army had been brought to Weihsien in one of the first waves of civilian internment. They were part of a band, and had brought their instruments into camp with them. Charlie told me they were secretly rehearsing the British and American national anthems, to play in the event of liberation.

'They rehearse silently,' he explained, 'because although the guards tolerate a bit of classical music or show tunes, they won't permit the playing of patriotic national anthems.'

'How are they rehearsing then?' I asked.

'They're learning the pieces on pretend instruments: an old tennis racket for a guitar, a broken shovel is a violin, a rusting piece of metal is a flute. It's quite something to see. They follow the sheet music and stay perfectly in time.'

'Do you even think about liberation anymore, Charlie?' I asked as we made bunting from leaves and spring blossom the children had gathered from around the compound. 'I used to think about it all the time. How it would happen. Who would come to our rescue. What I would do in my first moments on the outside.' I threaded a rusting piece of wire through the stalk of a leaf. 'I don't do that anymore.'

Charlie studied me from beneath his sandy fringe, which was in need of a good trim. 'You *should* think about liberation,' he said. 'You must. Otherwise it means you've given up.'

'Maybe I have.'

He put down his leaf, and took my hands in his as he gently pulled me to my feet. We stood, face to face, his eyes smiling at the corners.

'Elspeth Kent give up? Never! How about tea at The Ritz when we get back to England?'

I turned my face to hide my blushes, and my smile. 'Don't be silly.'

'I'm serious. I'd like to take you for tea at The Ritz. Maybe a little dancing to end the night? That's got to be worth looking forward to, hasn't it?'

'I have two left feet, and absolutely nothing to wear,' I protested.

'And I have two right feet, so we'll make a perfect pair. And who cares what anyone wears. We've seen the absolute worst of each other. We've worn newspaper vests for goodness sake.'

I smiled. 'I suppose we have seen rather the worst bits!'

The familiar strains of 'The Blue Danube' drifted toward us from the school building, where the Salvation Army band were rehearsing for our celebration.

'Aha! A waltz. *An der schönen blauen Donau*,' Charlie said with a smile. 'Shall we?'

He placed his hands at my waist and shoulder, leading with confidence. Although my instinct was to protest and tell him to stop being silly, for once, I didn't. I closed my eyes and listened to the familiar rise and fall of the music as we moved in time to the beat, and it was thrilling, and beautiful, and desperately sad all at the same time.

'I can't remember the last time I danced,' I whispered.

'Me neither,' Charlie replied as we bumped into each other and apologized and then laughed nervously as the music came to a stop. 'I don't think we'll forget this dance in a hurry.'

We returned to our bunting, but something had changed, and a distant neglected part of me, the part of me that was once full of hope for the future, flickered tentatively back to life.

* * *

With the Salvation Army band accompanying the girls' singing, we drew quite a crowd for our celebration. Even some of the guards who came to watch gave an enthusiastic round of applause at the end.

Mrs Trevellyan rushed over to me as I was packing away the chairs.

'Well, that was marvellous,' she gushed, as she pressed her hands into mine. 'Thank you so very much.'

'Whatever for?'

'For what you've brought to the compound,' she said. 'When those lorries rumbled through the gates and you all stepped out, I knew we would be all right.'

'Why?' I asked, a little taken aback by her unexpected show of emotion.

'Because you brought hope, dear. Over a hundred children! And as neatly turned out as I ever saw. You brought a glimpse of a future we'd all but given up on. You should be very proud of what you're doing with those girls. No mother could be prouder.'

I didn't quite know what to say. I thanked her, and as I made my way back to the accommodation block, I gave myself permission to feel a little proud. Just for a moment or two.

I offered to cut Charlie's hair that afternoon. My hands trembled as I combed and cut. I hadn't touched a man's hair for over seven years and had forgotten how close one must get; how intimate an experience it was. The rather lopsided end result was a testament to my nerves, but he was gracious enough to thank me all the same.

'You have improved me, Miss Kent.' He smiled as he studied his reflection in the bottom of an empty tin of powdered milk that he used as a mirror. 'Indeed, I believe I have never looked better.'

I scolded him for being flippant. 'It's terrible. I blame the scissors. They're awfully blunt.'

He laughed. 'You're right. It is absolutely terrible, but you, dear Elspeth, are a tonic.'

With 'The Blue Danube' waltz, and the girls' proud faces and Edwina's kind words in my mind, it was with a rare sense of peace that I fell asleep that night, but I couldn't have been asleep for long before I was disturbed by a persistent tapping at the window.

I pulled my nightdress around myself, opened the door, and peered out into the darkness.

'Who's there?' I whispered, part dreading, part hoping it might be Charlie Harris.

My heart stuck in my throat as Wei Huan appeared around the side of the building, a bundle of rags in his arms.

'Miss Elspeth! Oh, Miss Elspeth.'

'Wei Huan! My goodness. Look at you.' He was so desperately thin I couldn't suppress my shock. 'Whatever are you doing here?' I whispered. 'It's far too dangerous. You'll be in terrible trouble.'

Disturbed by the commotion, Minnie had also woken and joined me at the door. 'Elspeth? What on earth's going on? Oh! Wei Huan . . .'

The poor man's distress was evident. 'Take her,' he pleaded as he pushed the bundle of rags into Minnie's arms before he fell to his knees. 'Please. Keep her safe.'

Tears spilled down his cheeks as I stared at him, and then I turned to look at Minnie and the bundle in her arms. A baby.

'I can't take her . . .' she stuttered. 'I don't know how . . .'

Yet even as she tried to form the words to explain all the reasons why she couldn't take the baby, I already knew that she would. As the child began to whimper, she instinctively rocked and soothed her.

Wei Huan grasped my hands. 'She is called Meihua – named

for the plum blossom. My wife said to bring her to you. That you will keep her safe.'

'Shu Lan? She is well?'

He shook his head. 'She bleeds heavily. We send for the doctor.' He stood up and kissed the infant on her forehead. 'I must go,' he said. 'Please. Keep her safe until we are free.'

Before either of us could say anything, he turned and hurried away into the night.

All the questions I wanted to ask – about Shu Lan, about how he had brought the child into the camp, about how the guards would ever let us keep her – fell from my lips as he disappeared and left Minnie and me alone with the baby.

'Gosh, Els. Whatever do we do now?' Minnie whispered.

'We should get her inside, out of the cold.'

'But how will we explain her arrival to the children? And whatever will we tell the guards? They won't let us keep her if they suspect we're helping the enemy farmers. What if they take her? Surely he'll come back for her when Shu Lan recovers?'

I had agonized over all these questions since Nancy had given me Shu Lan's secret note.

'If anyone asks, we'll tell them she's the twin of another baby born to a Chinese mother in camp. We'll say we're helping to mind her because twins are too much for the mother to manage on her own.'

It was, at least, a plausible explanation and might, if we were lucky, allay any suspicions.

'I suppose it's as good an explanation as any,' Minnie conceded, her gaze fixed on the child as she started to fuss and flail her little fists around in a temper. 'Come along then, little one. That's all right. Shush now.'

I looked at her impossibly perfect little face and wondered, just briefly, what would have happened if Minnie hadn't woken up; if Wei Huan had placed the child in my arms instead of hers? Would I have taken her so willingly, eager to feel the feathery weight of her, or would I have hesitated, insisted he take her back, even? As if she knew what I was thinking, the child gazed up at me, intense black eyes studying mine for a moment, before they flicked back to Minnie and stayed there, as if she knew which one of us needed her the most.

As Minnie soothed the infant, I felt an emptiness in my arms; the absence of a light ache where a child should have been.

I wrapped my arms around myself and followed Minnie inside.

NANCY

The baby had arrived in the middle of the night.

I woke to the sound of her squalling, and thought a bomb was being dropped on us. Nobody knew where she'd come from, but I did know she hadn't been delivered by stork, like Winnie insisted.

Mouse rolled her eyes. 'Honestly, Winnie. That's an old wives' tale. You should ask Connie Hinshaw where babies come from.'

'Why?' Winnie asked, sniffing out gossip and scandal. 'It's not hers, is it?'

'Of course not.'

'Then what . . .'

'It doesn't matter,' I sighed. 'Let's just say the storks brought her.'

We all wanted to hold the baby, and held out our fingers for her to grasp.

'She smells like almonds,' Mouse said as she cuddled her and sniffed the top of her head.

'As you can see – and hear – we have a new arrival,' Miss Butterworth explained when we were all awake. 'This is little Meihua. Her name means plum blossom. Unfortunately her parents aren't able to look after her themselves, so Miss Kent and I have offered to help. And I know you will all be willing to lend a hand, too.' She went on to explain that they would prefer it if we didn't talk about the baby to other people.

'Is it a bit like when we kept Tinkerbell hidden in the loft at Temple Hill?' I asked.

Miss Butterworth smiled a sad sort of smile. 'It is, Nancy. But a little more complicated.'

The baby was soon forgiven for all her noise. It was as if she'd always been there, and we doted on her as if she was a new doll to play with.

That afternoon, while we were helping Mrs T, I asked her if she thought the baby might be Shu Lan's. Mouse and I suspected that Shu Lan's note must have been to ask Miss Kent to look after the baby when it came.

'I suppose it makes sense,' Mrs T agreed. 'Shu Lan's husband was your school gardener, wasn't he?'

I nodded. 'She was a servant at the school, too. But why wouldn't she be able to look after the baby herself?'

Mrs T looked at me, her head tilted to one side. 'There are many reasons why, dear, and even more, given that we're in the middle of a damned war.' She frowned and folded her arms. 'Best not to ask too many questions. As long as the child is safe, that's all that matters.'

We both agreed with that.

'Now girls. I don't suppose either of you happened to find a piece of paper inside one of the library books?' She held out a copy of *The Thirty-Nine Steps*. 'This one?'

I stared at Mouse, but she kept her eyes on the book and wouldn't look at me.

'No,' she said. 'We didn't find anything.'

Mrs T muttered something to herself. 'Well, never mind then. Off you go. I can't be sitting around talking all day.'

'Why didn't you tell her about the note we found?' I whispered as we walked back to our side of the compound.

Mouse shrugged her shoulders. 'I'm not sure really. I thought I might be in trouble for taking it out.'

'Well you'll definitely be in trouble now that you've lied about it.'

'It's only a scrap of paper,' she said. 'It can't be that important.'

'Maybe not, but if you still have it, I really think you should give it back to Mrs T.'

Since the move from Temple Hill to Weihsien, we'd encountered lots of new guards, most of whom were sour-faced and serious, but Home Run continued to be quietly friendly whenever we saw him. I often thought about how carefully he'd lifted Sprout from the truck and carried her to the hospital when we'd first arrived. Sometimes, when he was certain nobody was looking, he would slip an apple or a Chinese gooseberry into my hands. 'Shh,' he would whisper, his finger to his lips. 'Secret.' I always shared with Mouse, and we stuffed that fruit into our mouths as fast as we could, juice spilling down our chins. Even Edward didn't mind me chatting to Home Run as much as he once had. With so many guards being horrid to people, it was nice to know they weren't all the same inside, even if their uniforms tried to make them all look the same on the outside.

Home Run had been especially kind after Sprout died. He told us he'd left flowers at her grave.

'All death is very sad,' he said. 'But a child. That is the worst.'

He took a photograph from his jacket pocket and showed us his children. 'Two girls. Like you!' he said. He told us he missed them very much, and showed us another photograph, of his wife outside their family home.

'Where do you live?' Mouse asked.

'Hiroshima. On Honshu island. It is very beautiful.'

I told him his wife was very beautiful, too.

He put the photographs away. 'It is very bad,' he said, 'what we do here. I am the shame.'

'Do you mean, ashamed?' I asked.

He nodded. 'Yes. Very ashamed.'

'Then why are you a soldier?'

'I make my father proud. But this . . .' He gestured at the compound, and the sword at his waist, and the guards on top of the watchtowers. 'This is not proud. This is wrong.'

'Why does your Emperor want to control China?' Mouse asked.

'Men are greedy,' he said. 'They want to be rich and powerful, to take what isn't theirs.'

'Don't you want to be rich and powerful?' I asked.

He shook his head. 'I want to see my wife and children. I want to go home. Like you.'

The next time we spoke to Home Run was an unbearably hot afternoon in late summer. Lessons had finished early because of the tremendous heat in the classroom, and we were told to sit in the shade. Me and Mouse were dispatched to the well to fetch water.

As we made our way slowly back to the others, struggling with the heavy containers of water, I heard a 'Psst', and turned to see Home Run sheltering in a doorway at the foot of one of the watchtowers. He beckoned for us to go over to him.

I glanced up at the high walls. There were no guards on patrol.

'You want to go over?' Home Run said. 'The guards are inside. Commandant says it is too hot for anyone to escape.'

We looked at each other in shock. 'Go over the wall?' I said.

He nodded. 'You run in the field, and come back. I lift you over.'

'But, we can't!' Mouse whispered. 'We'll get into awful trouble!'

'Nobody see.' Home Run smiled. 'Come. Quick. You promise not to run away?'

'We promise,' we said, together.

Where would we run to anyway? We didn't know where we were, or where we would go.

I knew we would get into the most awful trouble with the guards, not to mention with Miss Kent if she ever found out, but the temptation to step outside the compound walls, even for a moment, was too great to resist.

We put down the container of water, and I carefully climbed the wooden steps that led to the top of the watchtower. I gasped as I reached the top. I'd never been so high up. Green and golden fields stretched out on every side, as far as I could see. The compound was like an island in a sea of fields. I'd always imagined we were in the middle of a town, like the compound at Temple Hill, but this . . . this was a wilderness.

'No wonder nobody has come to save us,' I gasped as Mouse climbed up beside me. 'How would they ever find us?'

'Go now,' Home Run said, an urgency to his voice as he pointed to the field directly in front of the school gate, across a dusty road. 'When I wave, you come back.'

We promised again.

Using a rope that we clung to for dear life, he lifted Mouse down first, then me. We stood together for a second, our backs to the wall, and then I grabbed Mouse's hand and we ran together across the road into the kaoliang field, my heart racing madly with excitement and terror. The grass was so high it went above the tops of our heads so that in seconds we would have been invisible to anyone looking out from the watchtowers.

'We're free, Mouse!' I whispered, gripping her hand tight in mine. 'We're free!'

It was delicious. The air smelled so sweet and fresh and I

gulped in great mouthfuls of it. The earth felt soft and rich beneath my feet. The sky was endless and blue. Without walls around us, the world felt suddenly enormous.

'I can't believe we're outside the compound!' Mouse whispered, even though there was nobody to hear us. It was just us, and the birds. 'Winnie will never believe it!'

'We mustn't tell her,' I urged. 'We can't tell anyone, Mouse. This has to be our biggest secret ever.'

We walked through the grass for a moment, and then ran through it, letting our fingers brush against the stalks, just like we used to do on Miss Kent's field trips at Chefoo. We laughed and stumbled and ran wildly on until we reached a dry riverbed, and came to a stop.

'We should go back,' I said, suddenly nervous, and unsure of what to do next.

I turned back to face the compound. Home Run was waving his arms above his head.

We obediently ran back through the long grass toward him.

Home Run lowered the rope and lifted us up, one at a time, until we were back over the wall, and it was as if nothing had changed at all, and yet everything was completely different. The walls and watchtowers looked smaller, somehow. Less intimidating.

He smiled as we brushed grass seeds from our skirts and socks.

'The fields will wait for you,' he said. 'You will run in them again.'

We hid our smiles and our secret for the rest of the afternoon but in our basement room that night, I smiled into the dark. I smiled because I had tasted freedom, and because Home Run was right. The fields, the birds, the sky . . . they would all wait for me.

ELSPETH

1945

It seemed almost impossible to me that while we remained so dormant and trapped in our small corner of China, the earth took another full turn around the sun, and another year crept over the distant mountains in a palette of apricot and rose.

'The world can be so beautiful, even when it is at war,' I said as I watched the dawn of the new year with Minnie at my side, as always. 'I suppose we should take comfort in that.'

'We should indeed,' Minnie agreed. 'Take heart, dear Elspeth. One day, that same sky will bring an American aeroplane and brave Allied soldiers parachuting through the clouds.'

We knocked our tin mugs together in a toast as I said, 'Amen to that.'

'I'm going to check on Uncle Eric,' I added. 'Wish him a happy New Year.'

'How did he seem yesterday?' Minnie asked.

'The same,' I replied. 'Melancholy, and muddled.'

Even Olympic gold medallists couldn't protect themselves from the relentless waves of sickness that washed around the compound like a spring tide. Typhoid followed dysentery followed influenza, around and around, until there was hardly anybody who hadn't been touched by some form of sickness or disease. The strong became weak and the weak became weaker. That was how it was at Weihsien. People became clouds. One minute they were there, the next they'd evaporated into thin fragile wisps and then, nothing.

I'd first noticed Uncle Eric acting a little strangely around Christmas time. Usually so enthusiastic about marking occasions and important dates, he was silent and withdrawn, and often forgot what he was doing. He complained of severe headaches and removed himself from the more boisterous evenings of entertainment, complaining that it was too noisy, and that he found it too tiring.

When I got to his room, I found him sobbing on his makeshift bed. I apologized for intruding and made to leave, but he asked me to stay.

'Sit with me a moment, will you, Elspeth. I don't want to be alone.'

We all went through phases of low morale, or worrying about those at home, but Uncle Eric never had. Until that day.

'I feel uncommonly tired,' he explained, in his gentle way as I sat beside him. 'I'm afraid I just don't have the energy for it anymore.'

'Nonsense. Of course you do. It's perfectly all right to have a little wallow every now and again. I'd say we'd all be better off if we did it more often rather than going along being all jolly and courageous all the time. *That* makes me feel uncommonly tired.'

He smiled weakly. 'But this is different. I feel tired in my brain, Elspeth. Tired of thinking, and being.' He sighed a heavy sigh.

'And I feel so desperately sad about not seeing Florence, and the girls. I have nightmares that I'll never see them again, and when I wake up I feel so lonely and afraid. Did you know I've never seen our littlest? I don't even know what she looks like. Isn't that frightfully sad?'

It was, and I couldn't think of a single thing to say to make it any less sad.

'You'll see her soon,' I offered eventually. 'When the war's over. And what a tale you'll have to tell her then! There's talk of Allied victory coming in from the outside every day. It's coming, Eric. Soon. You just need to hold on a little longer.'

Even I heard the weary echo of dashed hope in my words.

He nodded, and pressed his hands to mine. 'You're right, of course. And I cannot tell you what a wonderful job you are doing with the children. You're truly remarkable – you, and Almena and everyone in the Chefoo group. What you have done for them is quite extraordinary, and when you lead them back out of that gate, I hope you'll hold your head high and know that they are walking out because of you.'

'You are very kind to say so, but we do nothing that anyone else wouldn't do in our situation. Now, I must leave you to get some rest. Send word if you need anything.'

He promised he would.

It was the last conversation I had with him.

He struggled bravely on for several weeks, until he fell into a coma, and passed onto the next life on a bright February morning.

'He never once complained, or blamed, or resented,' I said when Charlie told me the awful news. 'Did you know he once told me he forgave them – the soldiers? He believed there was good in everyone. Even here, when he'd seen some of the worst of humanity, he still believed in universal goodness.'

Charlie offered me a scrap of what had once been a hand-kerchief to wipe my tears.

'He was the best of all of us,' he said. 'He was what we should all aspire to be.'

Uncle Eric's funeral was attended by almost the entire camp. Nobody could believe that such a vital vibrant soul had been taken from us. We'd thought him invincible; immune to such things as disease. He was everyone's friend, father, brother. A dear uncle to us all.

So many people wished to pay their respects that there wasn't room in the church, and many of us had to stand outside during the short service. His simple wooden coffin was then carried down Rocky Road to the cemetery beside the guards' house. A guard of honour was formed and his coffin interred as a silence descended over the mourners, the only sound that of the birds singing in the branches above us.

I wept for this good gentle man, taken too soon. I wept for his wife and children. I wept because he had lived the last of his years here, in this place, and because part of him, part of us all, would forever be interred here, inside the compound walls, looking for a way out.

When everyone else had dispersed, I took the little parcel of sunflower seeds from my pocket and pushed one into the fresh earth of his grave. New life, to remember that which had been lost.

'Another sunflower?'

Startled, I turned to the familiar voice. 'Minnie! I hadn't realized you'd waited for me.'

'How many are left now?' she asked as she linked her arm through the crook of mine.

'Four,' I said. 'And I hope it stays that way.'

Despite the hunger that gnawed in my stomach, and the melancholy that hung over the compound that evening, I felt the need to add a few lines to my diary. I wanted to capture my thoughts while they were fresh. I wanted to document the facts: that we lived and struggled, cherished the arrival of new life, and mourned that which was lost.

We go on, I wrote. *We wake up each day and find some way to make it bearable. The baby gives us immense joy – her precious coos and grasping little fingers thankfully know nothing of war – yet it breaks my heart to know that her mother is missing her, aching for her. I take comfort from nature: from the birds; the sky. They offer a glimpse of life beyond the compound walls, and remind us that there is beauty in its dramatic sunsets and gentle sunrises. I look to the sky for hope, for a future I have to believe is out there. I ask myself if it will ever end, if we will ever walk through the compound gates? It is impossible now to be certain of the answer.*

Rumours that two men had escaped spread quickly along the line at roll-call the following morning. The numbers wouldn't tally and the guards, growing increasingly frustrated and then angry, wouldn't dismiss us until everyone was accounted for.

Hour after hour, we repeated our numbers, until it was eventually established that the missing numbers belonged to two men from Block 35. The Commandant was furious. Dogs were sent snarling toward the nine other men who shared the same room. They were marched off to the church to be interrogated.

News of the escape was both shocking, and thrilling. That someone had successfully avoided the electric fences and barbed wire and the ever-watchful eyes of the guards long enough to get a good distance away sent a ripple of hope around the camp. We talked about nothing else all day.

'Did you know anything about it?' I asked Charlie, keeping my voice low as we walked to the kitchen.

He assured me he had nothing to do with it. 'Believe me, Elspeth, I have no desire to go back to solitary.' He had, however, heard that the escape had been arranged with the help of Chinese guerrilla soldiers hiding out in the fields outside the compound. 'The two men got out at a pre-cut gap in the barbed wire,' he explained. 'Just after the guards changed their watch, around midnight.'

It reminded me of the daring food drop we'd arranged at Chefoo. It seemed so innocent now compared to the dangers here.

'Are they going to fetch help?' I asked.

He nodded and checked over his shoulder for anyone listening. 'It's hoped they'll gather reliable intelligence and stay close enough to send coded messages into camp,' he explained. 'Information is our best weapon now. With information, we can prepare.'

'Prepare for what?'

He took in a deep breath and let out a sigh. 'For whatever's next.'

But the escape meant the guards had been deeply humiliated, and those who'd been on watch while it happened were punished. I was terrified of reprisals, and of the inevitable scrutiny and forensic searches we would be subjected to. Charlie assured me he had already dismantled his little radio and disposed of the component parts. Everyone was suspected of being involved, and those with a record of insubordination, like Charlie, would surely be first on the guards' list. The response from the rest of the guards was to reassert their authority with a renewed hatred of their enemy prisoners.

Later that morning, the men who'd shared accommodation with the escapees returned from their questioning and were forced to dig a second deep trench along the entire length of the compound walls. A tangled mass of electrified barbed wire was placed on the other side of the trench, making it virtually impossible for anyone to attempt escape. It was also announced that a second daily roll-call would take place every evening. Recreation time was banned. Curfew was brought forward an hour. To Edwina's dismay, all books were also confiscated, and the men and women who came to empty the latrines were thoroughly searched at the compound gates every time they came in, and again, when they left.

Only two days after the escape, one of them was found to have a message concealed in the hem of his jacket. We were all summoned to the parade ground and forced to watch his beating.

'Look away, girls,' I urged. 'Find a cloud, or a tree, and look at that instead. Recite the Psalms or your favourite songs silently in your heads. Whatever you do, don't look.'

They looked anyway.

Again and again the bamboo sticks rained down on the poor man's body. Verse after verse of 'Rule Britannia' circled through my mind, but still the beatings came, until eventually he lay in a motionless heap on the ground. He was then dragged away, bloodied and bruised, and surely dead.

We gathered the Chefoo children and prayed for him.

'I wish the men hadn't escaped, Miss,' Nancy said. 'I don't think the guards will be very kind to the rest of us now.'

I did my best to reassure her, to reassure them all, but my own fears echoed hers, even as I told her we were perfectly safe.

I'd always been an early riser, waking before everyone else. I liked to sit alone and watch the sun come up over the church, and listen to the birds. There was something necessary and restorative about that time of day; time when I could think and try to make some sense of things that made no sense at all. But it was also the time when I faltered; when I let myself wonder. What would happen if I walked away from our dark basement and placed a ladder against the compound walls and started to climb? What if I ran, screaming, at the gates, and demanded they let me out? Even in the gentle light of early morning, there were dark moments, a sort of madness, when I found myself willing to accept the punishment rather than continue with this passive acceptance. But I sat just long enough for the sun to rise, and the darkness to pass, and Minnie or one of the girls would stir. That was when I stood up, brushed the dust from my skirt, windmilled my arms, and got on with it.

Several days passed, and there was still much discussion about the escape. Our accommodation was searched repeatedly, (thankfully, the guards weren't remotely interested in baby Meihua, focused instead on discovering hidden messages or means of receiving communication from the outside). We were also summoned to an impromptu roll-call in the middle of the night. Tensions between inmates and guards were higher than they'd ever been, and I felt the latent threat of Trouble's presence around every corner.

I was making my way back from visiting Dorothy's grave when I saw him, lurking beside the barracks.

He stepped forward to block my way.

'Excuse me,' I said, as firmly as I could. 'I'd like to get past.'

'What do you know, Elspeth Kent? About the escape?'

'I don't know anything,' I said. My heart thumped. Blood rushed to my ears. I knew he didn't believe me.

'British all lie,' he snapped. '*You* lie.' He waved a small scrap of paper in front of me. 'This is a secret message. You know it.'

I took it from him and looked at the writing, and an illustration of a lotus flower, the lettering and symbols swimming about on the page. My head was dizzy; my stomach sick with fear.

'I've never seen it before.'

He snatched it back from me. 'Your friend, the library lady, she passes secret notes around camp, hidden inside her books.'

'Mrs Trevellyan? You must be mistaken.'

'We searched. We found. She will be punished.' He took a step closer so that his nose was almost touching mine. 'Your girls help her. I see them, delivering the books.'

I couldn't comprehend what he was saying. 'No! You're wrong. The children have nothing to do with it.' Fear and panic swelled within me. 'They're only children!'

For a moment, I thought he was finished; that he would send me on my way, but he suddenly grabbed my hand.

'It is time. *Teacher.*'

He pulled me into a small shed where he pushed me roughly against the wall. He held one hand against my mouth as he undid the buttons on his trousers.

I struggled and grabbed at his arms. I kicked at his shins and tried to scream but his hand muffled the sound. With his other hand, he pinned my arms against the wall. I was too weak with hunger to fight and struggle for long.

I shut down. Separating my mind from my body, I mentally peeled myself away from the hard brick wall that pressed painfully into my shoulders, picked up my dignity and the contents of my heart, and ran out of that damp dark room. I didn't stop running until I'd climbed the camp gates and disappeared into the rice fields where nothing, and nobody, could hurt me.

Silence was my self-defence; a refusal to give him anything of myself. Not the tremble in my voice. Not the agony of my pain. Silence was my protection, while my mind was a riotous clatter of Psalms and songs, and the ballerina twirling in my music box. I filled my mind with noise so there was no way in for this monster who took more from me in those few frantic moments than a starving farmer ever had. I searched for Harry amid the horror. *He can't touch your soul, Elspeth*, he whispered. *He can't touch your heart.*

Outside, the birds sang in the trees; their gentle beauty so at odds with the brutal violence below, and in the middle of it all, a deeply private part of me wished he had closed the door behind us.

I don't know how long it lasted, but with each terrifying, sickening minute, I thought of Connie Hinshaw, and how much worse it would have been for her. I had promised to protect the girls. I had promised to keep them safe.

A Guide's honour is to be trusted. A Guide smiles and sings under all difficulties. A Guide is thrifty. A Guide is pure in thought, in word and in deed.

And then, as suddenly as it had started, it stopped.

Relieved of his anger and frustrations, he pushed me to the floor like a discarded rag, and stepped outside as casually as if he'd only been looking for something or other, but couldn't find it.

I sat for a while to gather myself; to straighten my clothing and hair. My body shook as I hunched against the wall. I hugged my knees to my chest and stared blankly up at the rafters, at a swallow's nest, where the mother was brooding her clutch of chicks, and I felt so ashamed to know that she had watched; that she had seen everything. And she wasn't the only one. As I left the shed, I saw Joan duck behind a tree, from where she quietly watched me walk away.

When I returned to the dormitory, I told Minnie I was feeling unwell and curled up on my mat in the far corner of the room.

I clasped my hands around my knees and lay like a discarded alabaster vase. Empty. Cracked. Irreparable.

I wrote only a short entry in my diary that week.

Two inmates escaped.

NANCY

The rumour that Mrs T had gone missing spread along the line at breakfast, and was confirmed when me and Mouse went to look for her. I went straight to Edward, hoping he might know something about it.

'We can't find her anywhere,' I explained. 'The guards have taken all the library books, and she's disappeared.'

Edward didn't say anything for a moment, and then he took my hand and led me toward the sports ground.

'Look, you might not like to hear this, but I heard that she was involved in the escape. It seems that she was hiding coded messages inside the library books.'

I couldn't believe it. 'But she can't have been. Not Mrs T?'

'It's very clever when you think about it,' he said. 'She's the last person you would suspect. And to think it was all going on right under the guards' noses.'

'But, Edward. We helped her with the library! Me and Mouse. What if we get into trouble, too?'

He ruffled my hair. 'You won't. As long as you didn't know

anything about it?' He looked suddenly very serious. 'You didn't, did you?'

'Of course not! Oh, Edward. It's just awful. Poor Mrs T.'

'Clever Mrs T, more like.'

'What do you think they'll do to her?'

'I wouldn't worry too much,' he said. 'If anyone can handle those guards, Mrs T can.'

But I worried terribly. It felt as if all my friends, and everyone I cared about, were being taken away from me. First Mummy, then Sprout and Uncle Eric, and now Mrs T. Who would leave me next? Tears pricked my eyes as I rushed back to our basement room to find Mouse, and tell her everything Edward had told me. It all came out in a frantic jumble.

'Do you still have that piece of paper, Mouse?' I whispered. 'The one you found in *The Thirty-Nine Steps*?'

'No. I gave it back to Mrs T, the day before the men escaped.'

We stared at each other, shocked to think that Mrs T had somehow been involved in the escape.

'She did seem rather anxious to find that note, didn't she?' I said. 'What if Edward's right?'

'I wish I'd thrown it into the stove,' Mouse sighed. 'Then maybe she wouldn't be in trouble.'

'You don't think they'll hurt her, do you? An old woman?'

Mouse looked at me. 'I do, I'm afraid. Remember poor Miss Butterworth?'

I was even more worried then. 'Poor Mrs T. I can't bear to think of anyone being cruel to her.'

'Would you do something about it?' she asked. 'If you knew that one of the guards were treating Mrs T badly? If he was hurting her?'

'I would want to, but what could I do? None of the other guards would care, except Home Run, perhaps. Maybe I'd tell him.'

Mouse was quiet for a moment. 'Yes. Maybe I'll tell him.'

'Tell who what?'

She shook her head and stood up. 'It doesn't matter. I'm talking nonsense. Come on. Let's ask Miss Kent if we can bring Churchill to our room. He'll be ever so lonely on his own.'

Miss Kent agreed that we could bring the bird to our accommodation. 'But only until Mrs Trevellyan returns, which I expect will be very soon.'

I could tell by the way she said it that she wasn't sure Mrs T would come back at all, but at least Churchill was happily rehomed. We put his cage beside the window so that he could see out, although Winnie pointed out that he would see only more bars.

'It's like being in a cage, within a cage. The best thing you could do is let him out.'

'Oh, do be quiet, Winnie,' I snapped. 'Don't you ever have anything positive to say?'

'I'm only telling the truth.'

'Well, don't. The truth isn't always very helpful.' But her suggestion to let Churchill out of his cage nagged at me, because I'd been thinking the same.

For days we wondered and worried about Mrs Trevellyan. Even Churchill didn't sing as much as usual. Mouse said we should ask Home Run if he knew anything, but all he could tell us was that she was being questioned by the Commandant.

'I cannot tell more,' he said.

'Couldn't, or wouldn't,' Mouse said as we trudged wearily back from another awful meal of Same Old Stew. 'He might be friendlier than the others, but he's still on their side.'

Our questions were partly answered when, a week after the escape and interrogations, Mrs T returned. Although, she was a very different Mrs T; a less colourful version of herself.

Edward and Larry came to find me after lessons to share the news.

'Your friend is back,' Edward said. 'Mrs T. We've just seen her.'

'Really? Oh, thank goodness for that.' I called out to Mouse, who was practising a new knot for Guides. 'She's back, Mouse! Mrs T is back. Hurry up. Let's go and see her.'

'There's just one thing,' Edward added, putting his hand on my shoulder. 'She's had a bit of a rough time of things by the look of it.'

I stared up at him. He really had got terrifically tall. 'What do you mean?' I looked from him to Larry. 'What's wrong?'

'She's a bit black and blue,' Larry said. 'Bruised.'

My hand flew to my mouth. 'Badly?'

They looked at each other and nodded.

'Perhaps you shouldn't go to see her,' Larry said. 'Or, if you do, be prepared for a shock.'

Whatever I'd imagined, the reality was worse.

Mrs T was lying on her mat when we arrived at her accommodation. She looked terribly pale, and had the most awful bruises on her face and arms. She waved us away when she saw us and turned to face the other way.

'Not yet, girls,' she whispered. 'Not like this. Go. I'll be much better in a day or two.'

I reached for Mouse's hand as we both stood in silence, afraid and upset and unsure of what to do.

'We took Churchill to our room,' I said. 'Shall we bring him back?'

'Keep him,' she said. 'He's yours now.' She waved her hand over her shoulder. 'Off you go.'

Her favourite china teapot and cups sat on the windowsill. The hook where Churchill's cage had once hung was now being used to dry somebody's smalls. There was something terrible about seeing someone so loud and playful reduced to the shattered person in front of us.

'Come on,' Mouse whispered. 'We should go.'

Neither of us said anything for a long time as we walked back along Main Street.

'Stupid war,' I said eventually, unable to stand the silence. 'I hate it. I hate what it makes people do to each other. We're supposed to be helpful Girl Guides, and there's not a thing we can do about it.'

Mouse reached for my hand as the guard we called Trouble, and who we were all the most afraid of, walked past us, his lips set in the familiar cold sneer we'd grown so accustomed to.

'I hate him the most,' Mouse whispered. 'And maybe there is something we can do about it.'

'What?' I asked.

She looked at me for a moment before she shook her head. 'It doesn't matter. It would never work. Forget I ever said anything.'

We didn't visit Mrs T again that week. We got on with the usual things – school, chores, church, and Guides – but she was never far from my mind. The threat of the same thing happening to one of us lurked in the shadows at night and marched through my dreams.

'Would you mind helping me with something after class, Nancy?'

Miss Kent peered over the tops of her spectacles.

'Yes, Miss.'

Mouse raised an eyebrow at me. I shrugged and mouthed, 'I don't know?'

'I believe it is your birthday today,' Miss Kent said as we walked together along Main Street.

I nodded. 'Yes, Miss.'

'Your fourteenth.'

I nodded again. My birthday should have been a day to

celebrate, but birthdays didn't matter like they once had. Besides, it was another birthday without my mother, or Sprout, and it didn't feel right to celebrate without them.

'And to think you were only a little girl of eight when we first met.' Miss Kent smiled. 'You probably don't remember.'

'I do. I remember you stopped to ask Mummy the time, and you told us you were starting a new post as a teacher at Chefoo School.'

'You remember! Well I never.'

'You gave me your handkerchief as I waved goodbye to my mother, and you told me to pull my socks up, and that we must always look forward, never back. Eyes on the horizon.'

Miss Kent laughed lightly. 'Gosh! My brother used to say that to me. It's nice to be reminded.' She let out a long breath and smiled at me. 'Do you still have the handkerchief?'

I pulled it from my pocket. 'It's rather grubby now, I'm afraid. And some of the stitching has come undone.'

'Do you mind?' She held out her hand.

I watched as she ran her fingertips over the embroidered letters. I noticed that her wrists were bruised, but I didn't mention it.

'Does EK stand for Elspeth Kent?' I asked.

'Yes. Stitched by myself many years ago. Although it was all much neater back then.'

'So, if you're EK, who is HE?'

She looked up at me. 'That's Harry,' she said. 'Harry Evans.' She ran her fingertips over the stitches again.

'Is he your brother?'

'No. My brother is Alfie.' She let her hands drop to her lap. 'Harry was the man I was going to marry, but things don't always work out as we want them to, do they.' She folded the handkerchief carefully and handed it back to me with a small nod. 'Anyway, we can't be getting all maudlin. We have a birthday to celebrate!'

She produced an apple from her pocket and led me around the back of the hospital, where she lit a small fire inside a tin-can stove.

'Have you ever seen apple blossoms?' she asked.

'Of course. They look so pretty on the trees in the springtime.'

'Ah, but have you ever seen an apple blossom *inside* an apple?'

I watched as she took a knife and carefully cut a wafer-thin slice of apple and held it up to the sun.

'See? Apple blossom.'

In the centre of the translucent slice of apple was the perfect five-petal shape of a blossom.

She cut more slices and placed them on the hot metal where they curled and crisped until they were golden.

'Now, let's see how they taste.'

I closed my eyes and let the apple sit on my tongue, where it softened and melted. It tasted of summer orchards, and harvest festivals, and kindness.

'Do you miss England?' I asked as we enjoyed the apple slices and a few rare moments away from everyone else. 'I can't remember much about it, other than the fact that it rains a lot.'

'I miss the people there the most,' she said. 'But I miss the rain, too. And the smell of smoke from the chimneys in the autumn. It's all quite lovely really. Well, it is when I'm sitting here being all wistful about it. England has its difficulties, too.'

'I want to travel when I'm older,' I said. 'Visit lots of different countries, like Isabella Bird, and Gertrude Bell, and the pioneering women you've read to us about. I'd like to see the real China, one day.'

She smiled at me. 'You will, Nancy. One day.' She stood up suddenly and smoothed her skirt. 'We should be getting back to the others before they think *we've* escaped, too. Happy birthday, Nancy. I know it's not the way you would have chosen to celebrate, but we make the best of things, don't we?'

I couldn't find the words to thank her; to tell her that it was the perfect celebration, and the loveliest gift. Not just the delicate apple slices, but the sense of occasion; the sense that I mattered. For a few lovely moments, as the sun spread its fingers between the trees and painted us with bands of gold, Miss Kent wasn't just my teacher, or my Guide Captain. She was the mother I'd craved all these years; the mother I could hardly remember, and wondered if I would ever see again.

As we walked back to find the others, and before she became Miss Kent again, I thanked her once more. 'It's been a lovely birthday, Miss. I'll never forget it.'

She pushed her spectacles onto her nose and said she was pleased and that I should run along now. But despite her stiffness, I knew she understood how much it had meant to me.

And I knew we would never talk about it again.

ELSPETH

In the year since Wei Huan had placed Meihua in Minnie's arms, the infant had stubbornly bloomed, thanks to the invaluable help of a new mother in camp who had agreed to nurse the child. Babies, it turned out, were of no particular interest to the guards, and, thankfully, no awkward questions had been asked. Like the winds that blew across the fields that spring, she became a whirl of vibrant energy, and when our own demands left us without enough time to devote to her, a group of missionary women stepped in to help. But for all that we loved her as our own, we still hoped to reunite the child with her mother, and I was prepared to take the occasional risk to ensure that happened.

The church held its breath as I stepped inside, my footsteps the only sound as I walked to the pew toward the centre. The light never fully reached this part of the church, and one side was partially concealed by a large stone column. It was the perfect place for a brief clandestine reunion.

I was relieved to see Wei Huan already there.

'How is she?' he asked.

We were both too nervous to bother with any formalities.

'She is well. Thriving!'

Relief and joy lit up his face as I pulled back the blankets from the bundle in my arms. He brushed his fingertips over her cheeks and let his hand rest a moment on her soft-as-velvet hair before he took her from me.

'She looks like her mother,' he whispered. 'She is beautiful.'

Through a series of discreet enquiries, assisted by Charlie and the guard the girls called Home Run, who I now knew by his real name of Yuuto, I'd managed to send occasional messages to Wei Huan and arranged for us to meet after evening roll-call. It was the best time to slip away, while everyone returned to their respective parts of the compound. It was also the time when little Meihua slept, and I could be confident her hungry cries wouldn't give us away.

'How is Shu Lan?' I asked.

'She is well. She is strong.'

'She is a very brave woman,' I said. 'I think of her often, and all she has endured. I try to be strong, like her.'

Wei Huan's gaze was fixed on the child who slept on, oblivious to the dangers that surrounded her. We were both anxious and afraid. Yuuto had agreed to act as lookout, but we were still twitchy and uncertain.

After just a few minutes with her in his arms, Wei Huan passed her back to me. 'Thank you, Miss Elspeth, but we cannot meet again. It is too dangerous.'

I nodded; understood. 'I will find you when we are liberated,' I said. 'I will bring her to you then. I promise.'

He offered a nervous smile, pressed his hands to mine, and stood up. 'Soon, Miss Elspeth. Freedom soon.'

Afraid of being caught with every minute that passed, we left the church as quickly and as silently as we'd arrived. Wei Huan went first, and I followed a few moments later, only to find

Trouble talking to another guard directly in the path I needed to take.

I turned around and started to walk quickly in the opposite direction. The child fussed and whimpered in her little bundle of blankets. I begged her not to cry, and walked as quickly as I could, shushing and soothing her beneath my breath.

'Elspeth Kent!'

I glanced over my shoulder. Trouble was following me. He staggered a little as he walked, as if he had been drinking saké.

As dread and fear took hold, I put my head down, and rushed on. Not looking where I was going, I stumbled into Charlie, who appeared from the men's accommodation block.

'Elspeth! What's the rush?'

'Charlie. Thank goodness. I need to get back to my accommodation.'

He saw the baby peering out from the blankets. 'I see you have a rather precious load. Come along. I'll walk you there.'

Trouble called out as he watched us pass. 'Soon,' he shouted. 'I will have my next lesson soon.'

'What was all that about?' Charlie asked. 'You're not teaching the guards now, are you?'

'Of course not,' I said, a little too brusquely. 'Ignore him. He's drunk.'

I knew I'd had a narrow escape. I was rattled and restless and Minnie knew something was wrong. She saw it in my face when I returned with the infant.

'Did he come?' she asked.

I nodded and passed the baby to her.

'How was he?'

'The same. It was worth the risk to see his joy, but we've agreed it is too dangerous to meet again.'

I slumped down onto a chair and rubbed an ache in the small of my back.

'Is everything all right, Els? You're very quiet recently.'

'I'm fine. Just a little tired.'

She wasn't convinced. 'If there's anything you'd like to get off your chest, I'm a good listener.'

I smiled thinly. 'You're the best listener, Minnie. And if I could tell you, I would.'

I so desperately wanted to confide in her, but I couldn't find the words; couldn't bear to speak the awful shame of it all. As it was, I was certain everyone could see in my face what had happened; that everyone knew, but was too polite or afraid to say.

'They're coming to get us, Els,' she said, a smile at her lips as she patted my knee reassuringly. 'Soon.'

The echo of Trouble's words sent a shiver over my skin.

I sighed and leaned my head against Minnie's shoulder. 'Do you remember the first night we topped and tailed back at the school?'

She chuckled. 'I do. You snored like a hippo, but I didn't like to say.'

'And your toes were cold, and you fidgeted dreadfully.'

I felt the smile in her cheek. Dear dependable Minnie. I loved her like a sister. Perhaps I would tell her, one day, what she meant to me. For now, I wrapped my arms around her and let her hold me, like a mother holding her child, and for a few rare and precious moments, I felt safe.

'The Allies are getting closer,' Charlie whispered as he stood beside me in church that Sunday. Not long after our arrival at Weihsien, we'd decided that the safest place to share information was during our regular church services, our whispers and reassurances passing along the pews as we sang hymns and Psalms. 'We've heard reports of victories, and ongoing battles in Guam, Manila and Okinawa,' he continued. 'Liberation is coming, Elspeth. I can feel it.'

I so desperately wanted to believe him; to believe that I would soon be sailing back to England, and that Alfie would be waiting for me at the back door, and that Charlie and I would go dancing together at The Ritz. I feared false hope almost as much as I feared the heightened mistrust between us and the guards. The slightest hint of insolence, or the slightest delay at roll-call, now resulted in physical punishments. The guards' intolerance and cruelty seemed only to increase as our ability to endure it diminished.

Since the two men had escaped, impromptu searches had become more frequent, and the dangers associated with the bamboo radio became even greater so that ever more ingenious methods of smuggling messages into camp were being devised.

Coded messages were written onto silk, concealed in a pellet, and hidden up nostrils or inside the mouths of the local farmers who came in and out of the compound. The pellet was then ejected with a sneeze or a cough once the messenger had safely evaded the guards' inspections. Those involved in the operation inside the compound would stop to tie a shoelace, or to pick up a dropped item of clothing, subtly retrieving the pellet in the process, and taking it to the translator. It was fraught with risk and danger but, in this way, we learned vital news about Allied victories; news that sustained us for a little while longer. Without such messages, life inside Weihsien's walls stretched endlessly on in an increasingly desperate cycle of roll-call, filthy latrines, sickness and suffering, and the tired shuffling lines of starving people waiting for inedible scraps at mealtimes.

The challenges of life in the compound meant that gratitude was found in the smallest of ways, and I was pleased to see Edwina back on her feet and attending church again. After the discovery of the notes concealed in her library books and her subsequent disappearance and interrogation, she'd returned in such a dreadful state, badly bruised and shaken, her spirit broken.

Unsurprisingly – and not without consequence – she'd stubbornly maintained her ignorance of any escape plan, insisting she was an old woman who merely wished to share her love of books, and had nothing whatsoever to do with it. Without specific evidence of her involvement, and being subjected to her singing operatic arias day and night, she'd been released on the agreement that she was to report to the guards' house twice a day. 'They would have sent me to another camp,' she'd said, 'but I think they were afraid I would stir up anarchy there, too. Besides, they're all in disarray; bickering and squabbling among themselves. I think they're starting to fall apart.' With time and care, she was more like her old self again, although the twinkle in her eye had been put out.

After we'd seen Edwina safely back to her accommodation after the church service, Joan and Nancy walked with me to school.

'Miss Kent, do you remember the flowers Wei Huan used to grow at Chefoo?' Joan asked. 'Tall pink flowers that grew against the wall of the San?'

'Yes. Chinese foxglove. Deadly poisonous as far as I can remember.'

'That's right,' she said. 'I'd forgotten which ones they were. Did you know the leaves of the oleander are also poisonous?'

'I didn't, Joan. Who's been teaching you all this? You're becoming quite the horticulturalist!'

'Mrs T,' she said. 'She's taught me all sorts of interesting things. Plants that are good for headaches, and to cure vomiting and what-not. I wish we could have found a cure for Sprout and Uncle Eric.'

'So do I, Joan. So do I.'

She was a pleasant child who was growing into a confident young woman, and I was pleased to see her find her voice at last. And yet, I couldn't forget the look of shock and fear on her face when she'd seen me stumble away from the shed. I wondered if she understood what she'd seen and heard, and whether I should talk to her about it. But how could I when I could hardly comprehend it myself? Some things were simply too difficult to talk about. Besides, there were no words for what he had done to me. There was only a dark terrible silence.

But all Joan's talk of medicinal plants made me wonder if Edwina might know of something to prevent an unwanted pregnancy. My monthlies had arrived, much to my enormous relief, but if we were to stay here much longer, and if Trouble kept looking for me . . . I couldn't bear to think of the consequences.

The terrifying act of being violated hadn't only left physical scars, but psychological ones, too. The constant threat that it might happen again today, that afternoon, that evening, was utterly unbearable, and Trouble knew it. He circled me like a hawk hunting his prey, waiting for the perfect moment to swoop. I recalled the passage from the Buddhist scriptures that Shu Lan had marked for me: *The price of freedom is simply choosing to be; liberation is in the mind.*

'Are you all right, Miss?' Joan asked as we reached the classroom. 'You've gone ever so pale.'

I'd noticed how she watched me closely since that awful day. I think she understood, too, that Trouble was merely biding his time.

'I'm sorry, Joan. I was just thinking about something. Go and sit down now.'

As she took her seat behind her desk, it struck me how much she had changed from the shy quiet girl at the back of the classroom at Chefoo. I had a feeling that Joan Nuttall might yet turn out to be the most remarkable of them all.

'Open your books, girls. Page forty-nine.'

The Bird in the Bamboo Cage

I carried on, bolstered by the precious stability of routine and discipline, as the shadow of Trouble's threats settled in the seat behind me.

He found me the next day.
The second time was worse.
The second time, he closed the door.

MOUSE

I was always known as the quiet one; the one who never joined in, or spoke up, or stood out. But what I didn't say, I made up for in watching and listening.

I noticed things the other girls didn't. I understood the dormitory hierarchies long before they understood it themselves. They were always too busy bossing each other around and showing off, or giggling and whispering secrets to one another while I stood at the edge of it all, looking on. They thought I was minding my own business, but I was actually minding theirs.

I saw the way Larry Crofton looked at Nancy during our Girl Guide displays and ceremonies; how he always sat where he could see her. I saw the anxious glances between Miss Kent and Miss Butterworth when they took our monthly measurements and saw how thin we'd become. I heard the quiet sobs Miss Kent tried to muffle beneath her bedsheets at night. Worst of all, I had seen what Trouble did to her in the abandoned old shed, and I saw him pull her inside a second time, before kicking the door shut behind him. I didn't fully understand it, but I understood enough to know that he was hurting her in the most unimaginable way, and I hated him for it.

I couldn't keep it to myself any longer, but I couldn't bear to tell Nancy either. She was ever so fond of Miss Kent, and I knew it would upset her dreadfully to hear what was happening.

So, I told the only person who could help.

Mrs T wasn't easily shocked, but even she was horrified when I told her. She asked me to tell her precisely what I'd seen, and where, and how often.

'I wish he was dead, Mrs T,' I said when I'd told her everything I could remember. 'Truly, I do. I know it isn't Christian to think that, and that we must forgive our enemies, but I wish he would catch the typhoid, or whatever killed Uncle Eric and Sprout.'

'And you're quite sure about this, Joan?' Mrs T asked. 'About what you saw? This is very serious. It isn't something to be exaggerating, or making up.'

I promised on Guide's honour that I was telling the truth.

She looked at me and, for the first time since she'd returned from her 'holiday with the Commandant' as she called it, she looked like the Mrs T I remembered. The Mrs T who wouldn't put up with anybody's nonsense and would always lend a hand.

'Well, in that case, you did the right thing by telling me.' She narrowed her eyes. 'But now you must forget all about it.'

'I'll try,' I said. 'I just wish there was something I could do to help Miss Kent.'

'You already have,' she said. 'You leave the rest to me, dear.' She stood up, suddenly all action as she rubbed her hands together and rummaged through a pile of handwritten notes until she found what she was looking for. 'Now, how about a cup of tea? I've been experimenting with some new plants.'

Mrs T always made a fuss of serving tea, insisting on doing it properly and using her proper bone-china tea set with pink hand-painted English tea roses. The teapot had a cracked lid, and one of the cups had a chip on the rim, but I always thought it looked so elegant and refined among all the dust and dirt.

'Finest Wedgewood that,' Mrs T said as I lifted the handle. 'It belonged to my mother. She always kept it for best. For special and important occasions.'

'What's special about today?' I asked.

'We're having tea, dear, and nobody is bothering us. That's special, wouldn't you say?'

I tried to do as Mrs T had said and forget about Miss Kent and what I'd seen, but I couldn't help noticing how dreadfully tired Miss Kent looked, or how nervous and twitchy she seemed. Even at Guides she wasn't as enthusiastic as usual.

'You don't think Miss Kent's poorly, do you?' Nancy asked as we washed our socks that evening. 'She's ever so quiet.'

I said I hadn't noticed, and felt awful for telling fibs.

A few days later, as I was walking back from visiting Sprout's grave, Trouble stopped me as I passed the guards' house.

'You. Girl. Take this.' He held out Mrs T's special teapot and the cup with the chip. 'Tell her Japanese tea is better.'

I didn't ask any questions, but took the teapot and cup and hurried to Mrs T's accommodation.

'Trouble asked me to give you these,' I said.

'Did he say anything?' she asked as she grabbed them from me.

'Not much. Only that Japanese tea is better.'

We looked at each other for a moment before she lifted the lid of the teapot, and peered inside. 'Well, it can't have been that bad. He drank almost the full pot.'

'Was it one of your own recipes,' I asked. 'A special recipe?'

She nodded, and tipped the last few drops into the bushes beside the window. 'Your friend, Home Run, took it to him. He had a bet with Trouble as to which tea was better: Japanese, or English. Probably best not to mention it to anyone else,' she added.

'I won't even tell Nancy,' I said.

She smiled. 'Good girl. Now, I'd best go and wash these.'

'I'm very glad he liked your tea,' I said as we walked together to the pump.

Mrs T stopped, patted my arm lightly, and squeezed my hand. 'So am I, young Mouse. So am I.'

News reached us the next morning that one of the guards had become gravely ill.

'Home Run told me,' Nancy whispered. 'He says it's Trouble.'

I hardly dared breathe. 'Does Miss Kent know?' I asked.

'I'm not sure. Why?'

'It doesn't matter. I just think she might like to know.'

'Well, there she is now. Come on. Let's tell her.'

She dragged me toward Miss Kent who was drawing water from the pump.

'Did you hear, Miss?' Nancy said, all excited to share the shocking news.

'Hear what?'

'About the guard? Trouble? He's been taken ill. He's in a very bad way, apparently.'

Miss Kent's hand stilled on the pump handle as she seemed to sway a little. 'Are you quite sure, Nancy?'

'Yes. Home Run told me.'

'It must be a tropical fever,' I added.

Miss Kent looked at me for a moment, before excusing herself. We watched her as she walked quickly toward the school building. When she reached the wall, she leaned forward, her palms placed against the red bricks. Even from a distance, I could see that her shoulders shook violently. I felt the tremors of her pain and relief news beneath my feet.

* * *

As we lined up for Same Old Stew that evening, Mrs T joined the line behind us.

'Hello, girls,' she said. 'Ready for a feast? I hear it's roast swan tonight, with a fried ostrich egg.' We usually laughed at her imaginary menus, but I just stared at her. 'Dramatic news about that young guard, isn't it?' she added as she fussed with her earrings. 'Although I can't say I'm one bit sorry to hear it.'

'I hope none of us catches whatever he's got,' Nancy said. 'Edward said it's probably a tropical fever.'

'I don't think there's any need to worry, Nancy,' Mrs T replied. 'Not all fevers are infectious. Not this one, anyway.'

My tin bowl slipped from my hand and fell to the floor with a clatter. As I bent to pick it up, Mrs T reached for it at the same time, and our hands found each other.

I looked at her as she wrapped her fingers around mine, and I smiled.

Elspeth

May 1945

Trouble's sudden illness became a turning point around which everything else began to pivot. Like a tightly coiled rope being slowly unwound, I felt myself loosen. I could breathe properly again.

'I heard he had some sort of seizure or heart attack,' Minnie said, eager to talk about the event that had most of the Chefoo group speculating and gossiping. 'According to Charlie Harris, he's been sent back to Nagasaki for medical treatment. Good riddance to bad rubbish, I say.'

She trilled on and on until I had to ask her to stop talking.

'Please, Minnie. Can we talk about something else? I have the most dreadful headache.'

I couldn't share in the joy Minnie and many others took from Trouble's departure. His violence stuck to me like a dark spreading stain. No matter how far away he was, I would never be free of him, or what he'd done to me.

'I wish you would tell me what on earth's the matter,' Minnie said. 'I'm sure you would feel an awful lot better for getting it off your chest.'

I came close to confiding in her, but couldn't find the words. It was my secret; my burden to bear. I told her she worried too much, and went to bed early.

Alone on my mat, I folded in on myself, and wept for the life I'd lost; for the quiet life I should have been living with Harry in a pretty Yorkshire village, instead of fading away in this terrible unimaginable place. When I eventually fell asleep, I dreamed of birds kept in cages and kingfishers trapped in nets, and morning came before I could set any of them free.

As I'd seen so often since our internment, our primary concerns and problems changed quickly, and our fortunes fluctuated as drastically as the seasonal temperatures. Without the threat of Trouble lurking around every corner, I was able to focus on the infant a little more. I apologized to Minnie for having left her to take the brunt of the responsibility.

'Gosh, Els, I don't mind at all. You've enough on your plate with Alfie missing and what-not.'

Neither of us had mentioned Alfie for many months, perhaps for the best part of a year. His name stung my conscience.

'I'm sorry for bringing it up,' she offered, sensing my discomfort.

I told her I didn't mind. 'I should talk about him more,' I said. 'Say his name.'

'Do you think about him often?' she asked.

'As often as I can,' I replied. 'But there's no point driving myself to distraction, is there? I can't very well send out a search party.'

'I suppose not.' She placed a hand on my arm. 'Stay strong, Els. Don't give up on him yet.'

The child cooed in her arms, adding her own voice of encouragement.

The blossom on the plum trees, and the baby named for them, were the only things capable of bringing a smile to my face that spring. Like the sunflower that had grown at Chefoo, Meihua stubbornly thrived, despite the impossible conditions she'd been born into. We spoke to her of her parents; told her their names, and how brave they were, and I told her stories of beautiful ladies who wore jewels made from kingfisher feathers. Her innocence and resilience gave me strength. Her tiny little shoulders bore the weight of so much hope, and she buoyed us up as surely as a hundred barrage balloons. I adored her as if she were my own. But it was Minnie's face she smiled at; Minnie's voice she turned her head toward.

Wei Huan sent secret messages to us whenever he could. We were relieved to hear that Shu Lan had managed to escape from the soldiers who'd occupied Wei Huan's uncle's farm. She was now hiding in the hills with others. *I find her when we free*, he wrote. *I take Meihua to her.*

The world was broken beyond all recognition, but the child gave us a reason to believe – to hope – that it could be healed, and that we might heal with it.

'Elspeth. Psst. Elspeth. Wake up.'

I stirred and opened my eyes to see Charlie's face at the window.

'Charlie. Whatever are . . .' I wrapped my blanket around myself and pulled at my hair to smooth it down.

'Come outside,' he whispered.

I stepped from the room as quietly as I could, and pulled the door shut behind me. It was still dark, but the moon was bright and the first streaks of light were visible in the east. Charlie was already fully dressed.

'What time is it?' I asked, still half-asleep.

'Early. And I'm sorry to wake you, but I wanted to be the first to tell you.'

'Tell me what?'

'Germany has surrendered.' A broad smile spread across his face. 'The Allies have declared victory in Europe. We've won, Elspeth! We've bloody well won!'

I couldn't believe it. 'Are you sure?'

'Yes! I'm sure. A message was sent in from a reliable source, and the guards are twitchy. The war in Europe is over, and it won't be long before Japan surrenders, too.' He grabbed my hand. 'We're nearly there, Elspeth.'

After six years of unimaginable horror, it was almost impossible to believe that the Nazis had surrendered. I didn't know whether to laugh or cry. In the end, all I could do was stand in shock, my hand in Charlie's. My thoughts turned immediately to Alfie. If, as I'd chosen to believe, he'd been held as a prisoner of war, surely this would mean he was a free man.

News about the Allied victory in Europe spread quickly across the compound, and yet, for all our quiet relief, the fact remained that while one part of the war was over, another part wasn't. Our war continued.

We tried not to make too much of it when we told the children, careful not to raise their hopes of imminent release. We'd fallen into a rhythm at Weihsien, carefully navigating our day-to-day existence. It had kept the children safe and educated and in reasonable spirits for two years. Like a carefully balanced weight, we were all aware that too much emphasis on one thing or another could send everything crashing to the ground.

So, we pressed on; quietly hopeful of a change to our situation while we followed the now-familiar patterns of daily camp life. Roll-call and prayers. Lessons and Girl Guides. Sunset and sunrise. Routine and discipline sustained us once more as the gentle warmth of spring gave way to the suffocating heat of summer, and the heightened threat of disease returned.

Early August brought a fresh outbreak of dysentery that spread quickly and saw the hospital inundated with patients, several Chefoo children – including Nancy Plummer – among them. Losing Dorothy had been one loss too many. After all we'd come through, when we believed we were so close to being liberated, I prayed desperately for the children to make a full recovery.

Victory cannot come soon enough, I wrote in my diary. *Each new day feels like one too many.*

My diary entries had shortened over the months. Once-detailed accounts had given way to a few scant lines. Some days, and occasionally for entire weeks, I'd written nothing, unable to find the energy or the pencil lead necessary. But August brought a flurry of news, and I reached for my diary at the end of each eventful day.

America has dropped atomic bombs on the Japanese cities of Hiroshima and Nagasaki. Tens of thousands are dead. All expect Japan to surrender.

I wrote the words with a mixture of hope and horror.

'I can't bear to think of all those innocent people, killed,' Minnie said at the weekly staff meeting as we discussed the latest developments. 'Many children among them, no doubt. It's simply too terrible to think about.'

'War is a terrible thing, Almena,' Charlie said with a deep sigh. 'On that, I think we are all agreed, whichever side we are on.'

'Nagasaki? Isn't that where Trouble was sent when he fell ill?' I asked.

Minnie looked at me. 'I believe it was, yes.'

His name was never spoken again.

While the gathering rumours of imminent Allied victory over

Japan brought real and sustained hope, it also brought new concerns about retaliation, and what the guards would do with us if their leaders surrendered.

'There is a very real possibility of the children being used as hostages,' our headmaster warned. 'Or local farmers mounting some sort of mutiny and stealing what little food we have. Or, worse still, that all enemy prisoners will be killed.'

Set out so starkly, it seemed that, victory or not, there would be no easy end to this.

I had terrifying dreams that night in which the children were forced to dig a long ditch, which we were then all lined up alongside, our backs to the guards whose guns were carefully trained on us. On the command, they fired. Not all at once, but one at a time, so that those at the end of the line had to witness the execution of every other person before their turn came. I was the last in line.

I woke in a cold sweat and watched the guards' bayonet drills that morning with a heightened sense of dread. Would liberation – the very thing we'd hoped and prayed for every day since that snowy December morning at Chefoo – become the very thing that would see us all dead in an unmarked grave, our families never to know what had become of us? I couldn't believe it. Wouldn't believe it. Too much had already been lost; too many voices silenced for it to end that way. I stubbornly pulled on the tangled threads of the latest Allied victories, and stitched them into a shield of hope.

Before supper that evening, I walked alone to the imposing compound gates and imagined British and American soldiers breaking through, and the great cheers that would go up from the children. I'd already decided I wouldn't lead them out in an orderly manner, as I'd once thought I would. I would encourage them to run out of the gates in an unruly swarm of delight, arms windmilling wildly, their thin little legs hardly able to keep up with them. Routine and discipline had been our glue, but I wanted the children to understand that the best part of routine was the pure exhilarating joy that came when the rules were torn up and the gates of possibility flung wide open.

I took a step forward and placed the palm of my hand against the dark wood. With every ounce of strength I had left, I pictured myself turning the lock and pushing the gate open. Without fuss or drama, I would walk away from the camp, across a dusty road, until I stood at the edge of a field of ripe kaoliang.

And then I would take a deep breath, open my eyes wide, and run.

PART THREE: LIBERATION

August 1945

THE GUIDE LAW: A GUIDE'S HONOUR IS TO BE TRUSTED

A Guide's standards of honour are so high and sure that no one would dream of doubting her simple statement of a fact when she says: 'This is so, on my honour as a Girl Guide.'

NANCY

Oxford, 1975

It is easy now to set an end date; to mark an anniversary on the kitchen calendar, but when we were living through it, there was no guarantee that it would ever end. If a war could rage on for six years, what was to stop it raging on for six more? Of course, we hoped. We always hoped. But it became a jaded, fragile hope. We had no energy for certainty.

It has often struck me, in the years since, that while we changed so much during our time in Weihsien – our limbs grew longer, our skin was browned by the sun, our bodies discovered the shape of adulthood – our surroundings, our circumstances, and those around us, hardly changed at all. Our teachers were the one true constant. From Chefoo, to Temple Hill, and Weihsien, they were always there. I remember Miss Kent and Miss Butterworth especially.

As an adult with my fair share of inadequacies and failings, I've often wondered how on earth they managed to remain so forthright and composed. We didn't realize it at the time

– children never do, do they? – but the women and men who carefully steered us through those years were giants. I should like to thank them if I ever get the chance; say all the things I wasn't able to say as a child. Perhaps that is the cause of the regret I feel whenever I think about it. There is a melancholy deep within me, you see. An ache for what, and who, I left behind in China.

I'm often asked what the experience taught me, and my answer is always the same. Weihsien taught me kindness. Although I was in the worst place in the world, I remember moments of joy, and love, and a tenderness that had no right to be in a place like that. The teachers and strangers who guided me, and the friends who supported me – they taught me everything when my mother wasn't there to teach me herself. They, like her, are very much missed. Freedom, you see, came at a price.

I still remember that glorious summer's day. I remember the sound of the aeroplane's engine, faint at first, and then louder, to match the giddy thump of my heart . . .

NANCY

17 August 1945

At first, I thought the noise was one of the great hornets that often flew around the camp. It was an unbearably hot day and the flies were awful, even in the hospital where I'd been sent to recover from a mild dose of dysentery. I reached for the fan Mouse had made for me from leaves she'd gathered and tied together with half an old shoelace. I fanned my face wearily, but the drone grew louder; closer. The hospital room was hot and still. I pulled at the buttons on my nightie to get some air as I stepped out of bed and pulled back the curtain at the window.

The sky was the most perfect blue; the ground shimmered in a heat haze. I shielded my eyes from the sun and blinked away the brilliant dazzle. My mouth was dry and my head thumped as I rubbed a fine layer of dust from the window and stared up at a plane circling above the compound.

My hand stilled as I saw the flag painted onto the tail. I'd learned the flag's history; knew the national anthem of its country, and there it was, right above me. The stars and stripes. It was like seeing the face of a dear friend.

My heart raced beneath my thin cotton nightdress as one word fell from my cracked lips. 'America.'

The Americans were here.

For a moment it seemed as if the whole compound had fallen silent, each of us holding our breath as a hatch opened at the side of the plane. And then, one by one, great parachutes drifted down through the blue, twirling and dancing like dandelion seeds, until they disappeared into the fields beyond the compound walls.

I ran across the room and peered down the hospital corridor, desperate to ask one of the nurses if it meant what I thought it did, but nobody was about.

'The Americans are here!' I called. 'They've come to rescue us!'

I rushed back to the window.

By now, people were running through the compound, punching the sky and cheering madly. Men pulled off their shirts and circled them above their heads. A group of women skipped wildly in a circle, holding hands and hugging each other. Behind them, another woman sank to her knees in the middle of the road and wept uncontrollably.

My illness forgotten, I ran from the room, dashed along the corridor, and raced outside in my bare feet. Mouse was already running down Main Street toward me.

'Plum! Plum!' she shouted, waving her arms wildly above her head. 'They're here! The Americans! They're really here!'

I ran toward her, and grabbed her hands. 'Is it really them?' Tears pricked at my eyes. My words came out in little gasps.

'Yes! It's really them.' We looked at each other for a moment before she threw her arms around me and we both burst into tears of joy and relief. 'We're free, Nancy!'

Others ran past us, their cries of, 'They're here!' and 'God Bless America' ringing through the dusty air.

'Come on,' Mouse said, laughing. 'Let's follow them.'

She pulled me along after her, down the long road we'd driven up two years ago.

My nightie flapped around my legs and sent a lovely breeze against my skin. 'We're free!' I cried, as I tipped my head skywards and spread out my arms and twirled around and around in circles until I was dizzy. 'We're as free as the birds, Mouse!'

The huge compound gates already stood wide open, a stream of half-crazed people running through them, out into the kaoliang fields beyond. I remembered the few delicious moments Mouse and I had spent in those fields and, as we reached the gate, I stopped. I'd never seen fields look so lush and green, or skies so perfectly blue. It was like seeing the world for the first time, and I didn't know which part of it I wanted to discover first.

'Look,' Mouse said. 'Over there.'

To our right, a group of men in American military uniforms were laughing and smiling. There were seven of them in total. They were all so big and tall and suntanned; their arms so full of muscles that they looked like giants. Two of the men scooped up a couple of the smallest children and sat them on their shoulders. The men danced up and down, making the children squeal with joy. I couldn't believe what was happening. I couldn't believe they were really here.

The guards stood quietly to one side, looking on as some of the stronger men in camp hoisted the American airmen onto their shoulders and carried them in a procession along Main Street. We ran alongside, reaching up to touch their hands. The men from the Salvation Army band played the American national anthem. The patriotic rumpus of 'The Star-Spangled Banner' and the proud notes of 'God Save the King' made us all cry.

But the music and cheering melted away as the camp Commandant approached one of the airmen and stood in front of him, blocking his way.

'We surrender,' he said, as he held out his sword. 'Japan surrenders,' he repeated.

We surrender. The words we thought we would never hear, now so clear and wonderful.

The man who seemed to be in charge of the American airmen, stood up straight and proud. 'I don't want your sword,' he said. 'I want your word that you will protect the compound from looters and Communists. I have your word?'

The Commandant nodded, solemnly. 'You have my word.'

Mouse tightened her grip on my hand as we looked at each other. Without a single word being said, a thousand thoughts and conversations passed between the two of us.

It was over.

At last, it was over.

I'd always imagined that when the enemy surrendered, we would jump into the trucks and be on our way home to England right away. But it didn't happen like that.

Miss Kent gathered us together to explain what would happen next.

'Now, girls. Settle down! I know it's all very exciting. The Americans will airdrop food and medical supplies over the next few days, so we'll have plenty to eat, and clean water to drink. I know you're all especially eager to be reunited with your parents but there's lots to organize before we can be on our way home, so just a little more patience.'

The whip-poor-will didn't sing at the window that night. It was as if he knew that I didn't need his lullaby anymore.

'Perhaps he's flown away,' Mouse said. 'Gone to some other place to keep a lonely child company.'

I hoped so.

But Churchill remained locked up in his bamboo cage. 'I'm going to ask Mrs T if we can set him free,' I said as I watched him hopping about on his little perch. 'I do hope she says yes.'

To my surprise she did.

'I didn't tell you, Nancy dear, but I'd always promised myself – and Churchill – that I would set him free when I was free.' Mrs T said as she picked up the handle of the cage. 'Would you help me?'

We walked together to the compound gates at sunset, when the air was a little cooler and the flies and insects swarmed in small clouds. We walked to the edge of the fields where Mrs Trevellyan put the cage down.

'You lift the latch, dear,' she said. 'You be the one to set him free.'

I turned the latch, and the cage door swung open.

'You can go now, Churchill,' I encouraged. 'You're free. Just like us!'

He didn't fly straight out. He hopped about in his cage for a while and peered outside, uncertain, and unsure. For several minutes we stood and watched as he made up his mind, or plucked up his courage, I wasn't sure which. He turned his black eyes to me before he hopped onto the edge of the door, then launched himself forward, stretched out his wings, and flew away, over the fields. It was as natural to him as blinking and breathing. I shielded my eyes to follow him, until I couldn't see him anymore.

Mrs Trevellyan took a deep breath and picked up the empty cage.

'You looked after him ever so well,' I said as we walked back inside the compound gates together.

She couldn't reply. She was too busy dabbing tears from her cheeks.

Later that evening, I asked Miss Kent if she thought Churchill would be all right in the wild. I'd remembered what Mrs Trevellyan had said about his cage being his home, and it worried me a little.

'I think he'll be delighted!' Miss Kent said. 'It's where he's meant to be. Among the other birds. Free to go wherever he chooses.'

'He wasn't sure at first,' I said. 'He seemed a bit afraid. A little hesitant.'

'And that's perfectly understandable, Nancy. It will take us all a little while to find our feet, to remember how to live freely again and leave our cage behind.'

'We will though, won't we?' I asked, seeking her reassurance once more, as I had so often over the years. 'We will be all right?'

She smiled. 'Yes, Nancy. We will be all right. Guide's honour.' She took my hand, and wrapped her fingers tight around mine. I looked up at her as she gave my hand an encouraging squeeze. 'Always look forward, Nancy, never back. Eyes on the horizon. That's the ticket.'

My heart soared as I felt my wings unfurl, and start to beat.

ELSPETH

'That's it then,' Minnie said as we stood together at the edge of the fields. 'After all these years, it's over as quickly as blowing out a candle.'

I placed my arm around her shoulder, and pulled her toward me. We watched the children as they ran and skipped through the long grass in front of us; a perfect unruly jumble of excitement.

'Thank you, dear Minnie,' I whispered. 'For everything. I honestly couldn't have endured it without you.'

'Pish, Elspeth. It's me who should be thanking you.'

'Well, let's settle on having been a rather good team,' I said.

'Yes,' she agreed. 'I rather like that.'

Despite all our words of hope and encouragement to the children and each other, we'd never known when, or if, our ordeal would end. We'd existed in a seesaw of hope and disappointment until we'd become too broken and hungry to think about the future. Life had distilled down into the smallest actions required to survive, so when the end did finally come, we weren't entirely sure how to respond.

There was relief and joy, mostly, but there was also fear and uncertainty, and sadness for those who hadn't seen the spectacle of the parachutes drifting through the sky. Many of the prisoners ran straight out of the open compound gates, skipping through the kaoliang fields like wild creatures, whooping and hollering in hysterical joy. But there were others, like me, who first reacted with stillness and silence, and for whom liberation was our final cue to collapse.

All the worry, all the pain and loss, all the exhausting effort to remain optimistic poured out of me and I sank to my knees and wept, not just with overwhelming relief, but with a profound sadness for what we'd each lost in very private, and public ways.

'So, what do we do next?' Minnie asked when I'd composed myself a little and we began to walk back to the others.

I knew she meant what would we do in the next minutes and hours and days, but her question reached much further than that. What *would* we do now? We knew nothing of the world beyond Weihsien's walls. We knew nothing of our loved ones back home. What was waiting for us there? *Who* was waiting for us? Liberation brought as many questions as answers. The freedom and future we'd all longed for suddenly felt strange and unfamiliar.

'Will you go back to Lancashire?' I asked.

She shook her head. 'There are only bad memories for me there. My sister and her family are in Devon. I'll go and stay with her for a while. It's ever so pretty there. You must visit.' She stopped walking, and grabbed my hand. 'You *will* visit, won't you?'

'Of course! I hear the clotted cream is delicious. Mrs T told me all about it.' I fished in my pocket for the parcel of sunflower seeds. I had four left. 'Will you take one, for your sister's garden?'

'That would be lovely. What will you do with the others? Keep one for yourself, I hope?'

'Yes, and I'd like to give one each to Nancy and Joan. It's silly and sentimental of me really, but these little seeds have become quite important over the years. I'd like them to have one.'

Minnie patted my arm. 'I think it's a terrific idea.'

I hadn't forgotten my promise to find Wei Huan when we were liberated, and he and Shu Lan were on my mind that afternoon. They were free to return to their homes now, as a family, with baby Meihua.

'I never thought I'd have another chance to be a mother,' Minnie said when I delicately raised the matter. The infant slept in her arms. 'I know she was never mine to keep, but I wouldn't change it for the world.'

My heart broke for her. 'You took her without a moment's hesitation, Minnie. It isn't everybody would have done that. You've cared for her as well as any mother would care for their child. Wei Huan and Shu Lan will forever be grateful.'

I left her alone with the child to organize her things, and to say her goodbyes in private. It would, no doubt, be the first of many difficult farewells we would see in the coming weeks.

Over the course of a rather chaotic day, the American airmen told us about the atomic bombs that had been dropped on the cities of Hiroshima and Nagasaki, and that it was those events that had led to Japan's surrender. A little later, we gathered to listen to a speech from our King, played out clearly on the airmen's wireless.

'*Three months have passed since I asked you to join with me in an act of thanksgiving for the defeat of Germany. We then rejoiced that peace had returned to Europe, but we knew the strong and relentless enemy still remained to be conquered in Asia. No one could then tell how long, or how heavy would*

*prove the struggle that still awaited us. Japan has surrendered.
So let us join in thanking Almighty God that war has ended
throughout the world.'*

A great cheer went up as the national anthem played. It was,
perhaps, the moment when I finally believed that the war was
over. That we really were going home.

'I'll just be a moment,' I said, turning to Minnie as we made
our way back to the accommodation. 'There's something I need
to do.'

The day of our liberation was a sultry summer day when all
the air seemed to have been sucked out of the sky and the sun
stuck to my skin. I would usually have withered and wilted in
the heat, but I stood proud and tall as I walked away from the
excited conversations and talk of going home.

I took a moment, alone, to look around the compound. I
walked to the school building and the hospital, and along
the lines of low buildings we'd slept and eaten and cooked in
– the places where we'd kept our greatest fears silent and clung
onto hope with the tips of our filthy fingernails. I'd always shrunk
away from the substance of the place, afraid to look at it too
closely, refusing to let it define me. But I looked now, and what
I saw was just bricks and stone, trees in the full livery of summer,
dusty roads and abandoned watchtowers. There was nothing to
be afraid of anymore. Like the fledglings we'd watched leap, so
bravely, from the branches that spring, the children would soon
leave us to return to their families, our responsibility no more.
Our part in their story was done.

China had changed me in more ways than I could ever have
imagined. I wasn't the same person who'd arrived with a letter
to confirm my appointment as a teacher at Chefoo School. I
wasn't the same person who'd written eight versions of her letter
of resignation before settling on the right words to express my
regret and gratitude to the place that had given me a purpose

when I'd had none. I wasn't the same person who'd urged the children along on our daunting walk from Chefoo School to Temple Hill, nor was I the woman who'd pinned the trefoil Promise badge onto the shirts of the girls of Kingfisher Patrol in a solemn ceremony. Elspeth Mary Kent was so many things now, the sum of all these parts, and I liked her far more than the person she used to be. Like a treasured vase carefully repaired, nobody would ever see the cracks and flaws these past difficult years had left me with, but they would always be there, on the inside.

There was, however, one last part of the Weihsien compound that still held me captive.

I made myself go there, to the shed beside the guards' house. I knew I had to confront it before I could leave it behind.

The door was slightly ajar. I took a deep breath and pushed it open.

Sunlight fell in shafts through the window as I pulled the shutters open. I made myself breathe in, long and deep. The smell was still there, that particular stench of sweat and arrogance and disregard. I swallowed hard, pushing back the waves of nausea and fear that threatened to overwhelm me. *He's not here, Elspeth*, I told myself. *He can't hurt you.* Whatever had caused his sudden illness and led him back to Nagasaki shortly before the atom bomb fell, Trouble had got what he deserved, and yet death was an escape for him; a way out. I would forever carry the memory of what he had subjected me to. What had happened in this room had forever changed me, but I refused to let it define me. I had a choice. I could let it consume me, or I could leave it here, in this room, and walk away.

I took a deep breath, walked back out into the sunshine, closed the door behind me and turned the key in the lock. I walked to the compound wall, closed my eyes, pulled my arm back and threw the key as far and as high as I could. I watched it sail over the wall and disappear from view, lost forever among the fields beyond.

I pushed my shoulders back, turned to the west, and began to make my way back to the others. As I walked, I pulled out the pins securing my bun and let my hair tumble to my shoulders, a tangle of auburn curls, loose and wild and free.

NANCY

October 1945

People left Weihsien in dribs and drabs in the weeks that followed liberation so that tearful farewells became an almost daily event. Envoys from different embassies made arrangements for the repatriation of their citizens and, gradually, the lines for meals became shorter. Winnie, Connie, and our headmaster were the first to leave from the Chefoo group. Everyone from Kingfisher Patrol signed their names on a page in my log book. We promised to never forget each other.

One of the hardest goodbyes was Home Run.

'I go home,' he said, although there was a sadness in his eyes. 'I do not know what is waiting there, but I hope. You go home soon?'

'We leave next week. We will go to a hotel in Tsingtao first, and then make the long trip back to England.'

'Roast beef and Yorkshire pudding?'

'Yes!' I smiled. 'And jam roly-poly and custard.'

He saluted, and I gave my best Guide salute in return. I knew I would never see him again, nor ever forget his kindness.

When it was finally our turn to leave, me and Mouse went to the cemetery together to say goodbye to dear Uncle Eric, and Sprout, and the many others who had died here. The freshly turned earth was a reminder that some had lost their fight just a few days too soon.

'It doesn't seem right to leave Sprout here, alone,' I said as we stood beside the spot where Sprout was buried.

'She isn't here though,' Mouse said. 'She's in Heaven. With God.'

I wasn't entirely sure Sprout would have made it all the way to Heaven, but the thought of her asking God lots of difficult questions made me smile.

A bird settled on a branch above us. His cheerful song made it a little easier to leave.

The same trucks that had delivered us to Weihsien two years earlier, took us away again on a bright October morning. We'd arrived as boys and girls, and left as young men and women, our childhood toys and memories packed away in our cases and trunks. Some of the children cheered as we rumbled through the large gates, but I quietly stuck my arm through a gap in the tarp and let the breeze drift between my fingers. I watched the landscape slip by and made a silent promise to return one day, to see China properly and not just from behind dormitory windows or through barbed-wire fences.

In Tsingtao, we said goodbye to dear Mrs T, who invited me to visit her in Devon for a proper cream tea. She gave Mouse a rather prolonged hug, and told us we must keep in touch with each other.

'You've both made a friend for life,' she said. 'Nobody will ever understand all this, apart from those who were here. Don't forget each other.'

She dabbed a tear from her cheek as she waved goodbye, and drifted away in a muddle of colour, like a rainbow fading after a rain shower.

From Tsingtao, we travelled on to Shanghai, where Larry was being met by his parents.

He wished me the best of British as he said his farewells.

'Yes. And you,' I replied. 'Have a safe trip home.'

We stared awkwardly at each other for what felt like an age, before I leaned forward and planted a kiss on his cheek.

'Goodbye, Larry Crofton.'

He was too surprised to say anything, but his smile said enough. I didn't even mind Edward teasing me about it during the long sail back to England.

'I'm fourteen now, Edward,' I said. 'I can kiss who I like.'

Those of us who were left didn't really talk about what had happened. It was as if we all knew it was better to forget. Even Edward was much quieter than normal.

We slept and ate as much as we could. To be warm and clean, to have flushing toilets and warm running water was sheer luxury. Even the ship's food rations were far nicer than anything we were used to. I took my time with the simplest of tasks: brushing my teeth, washing my face, peeling an orange and bursting each segment between my teeth. There was so much joy in the everyday things I'd once taken for granted, and I promised I would never take anything for granted again.

I was glad that Miss Kent and Miss Butterworth travelled the final part of the journey with us. They, too, were quiet and reflective, no doubt thinking about what had been, and what was to come at the other end of the journey, like the rest of us.

Miss Kent joined me at the railings as we sailed into port at Southampton.

'It seems like an awfully long time since we stood together on the boat from Shanghai to Chefoo, doesn't it,' she said.

'A very long time,' I agreed. 'Do you think we'll ever forget what happened, Miss?'

She thought for a moment as she sniffed in a deep breath and closed her eyes. 'No. I don't. And I'm not sure we should. It's part of who we are now.'

I held my hat against the breeze as a light rain began to fall. There was so much I wanted to say to this woman who had kept me safe and taught me so many things, but I couldn't find the words, so I just said, 'Thank you, Miss. Ever so much.'

She buttoned her coat and pulled wrinkles from her gloves as she stared at the coastline ahead, and smiled. 'You won't understand this until you're older, Nancy, but really it is me who should be thanking you. Ever so much.'

They were the last words we exchanged.

I didn't see her again after we docked. Just as unexpectedly as she'd walked into my life on the wharf in Shanghai and promised to keep an eye on me, Miss Elspeth Kent walked right back out again. Miss Butterworth too, and Mouse.

'Look after yourself, Mouse,' I said, as we hugged among the crowded harbourside. 'I'll never forget you.'

'And I'll never forget you, or any of it. I'm going to write it all down in a book one day. I'll send you a copy.'

I smiled, and laughed through my tears. 'Will you put Sprout in it?'

'Of course. It would only be half a story without her.'

I watched as she walked toward a well-dressed man. She wasn't even halfway toward him when he pulled his hat from his head and rushed toward her, his face beaming as he scooped her into his arms, and I knew she would be all right.

There was a great deal of noise and confusion as dozens of children searched the faces in the gathered crowds, looking for their parents, hoping they would recognize them after all these years. Edward and I stood together, peering into the crowds.

'I don't see her,' I said, my gaze intent on finding my mother. 'I don't see them, Edward.'

Suddenly, he grabbed my hand. 'There! There's the old man! Come on!'

He led me in the direction of a tall man who weaved his way through the crowds, stepping to the left and then to the right, until he broke through the melee and ran the rest of the way toward us.

I hardly recognized my father. He was much taller than I remembered, and not at all as stern-looking. He had a moustache which I couldn't remember seeing before, and was dressed in a smart three-piece tweed suit and a navy-blue hat with a brown ribbon trim. He looked very much like Edward.

His hands flew to his mouth as he reached us. I stood to one side as he shook Edward's hand and then gripped Edward's elbow and then pulled him into an embrace and held him for several minutes. I thought, perhaps, he'd forgotten that he also had a daughter, and had mistaken me for a schoolfriend of Edward's, but then he released Edward from his grip and turned to me.

'Nancy. My dear dear little Nancy.' His voice cracked as he said my name.

He threw his arms around me and held me so tight against him I could hardly breathe. His arms were warm and strong, and he smelled of tobacco and hair tonic, and family. Like a flood, my memories of him returned. I remembered the little scar above his left eye, and that he took two sugars in his tea, and wrote with his left hand – like me – and that he always said White Rabbits for luck on the first day of a new month. The stern and distant stranger I'd imagined in my head was none of those things at all. He was my father, my daddy, and by some invisible bond that had connected us through all these missing years, I knew that I loved him, and that he loved me.

'I can't believe it,' he said, over and over again. 'I can't believe you're here.' He released me from his embrace and touched his hands to my face. 'Look at you! So tall and grown up!'

I peered over his shoulder, searching for Mummy in the crowd. 'Where's Mummy?' I asked. 'I can't see her.'

There was a moment, a pause.

'Where is she?' I asked again. 'Daddy? Where's Mummy? Where is she?'

When he pulled me close to him again, I could hear his heart thumping beneath his shirt. I felt the lurch and heave of his shoulders, and I froze.

'I'm so sorry, darling,' he sobbed. 'I'm so sorry I couldn't keep her safe.'

I hung like a ragdoll, suspended in my father's arms as I stared numbly into the crowd behind him, into the space where my mother should have been.

I couldn't keep her safe.

His words swam around and around in my mind, so that I couldn't quite grasp them; couldn't understand how Mummy wasn't there. She wasn't waiting for me in her blue dress. The air wasn't scented with English lavender.

My arms hung limply at my sides, as I felt the shudder and shake of my father's sobs.

'Don't cry, Daddy,' I whispered. 'Please don't cry.'

I sat quietly in the back of the car, my tea caddy clutched in my hands as we began the long drive home. Mile after mile, I watched the landscape slip past the window, and yet I saw nothing at all.

'What's that?' Edward asked as I took a small square of cotton from my coat pocket.

'A sunflower seed,' I said. 'Miss Kent gave it to me.'

'Why don't you plant it in the garden when we get home?'

he suggested. 'Mother liked sunflowers. She thought it was very clever the way their faces followed the sun.'

'I didn't know she liked sunflowers.'

'I bet you didn't know she liked cricket, either,' Daddy added from the front. 'And the occasional glass of stout.'

We talked about her all the way home, where nothing had changed and everything was different, and the scent of English lavender laced the air along the garden path. As I stepped inside the house, I caught my reflection in the mirror and gasped, shocked by how much I'd grown, and how like my mother I'd become. She had, and would, always be with me. She was there in the shape of my eyes, and the colour of my hair, and the way my nose crinkled when I smiled, and she would always sit in a special place in the very centre of my heart, reminding me to be strong; encouraging me to be brave.

ELSPETH

Nobody knew I was coming home. I hadn't written ahead, partly because I couldn't quite trust that I would ever arrive, and partly because I didn't want Mother to make a fuss or arrange any sort of welcome home party. It didn't seem appropriate with Alfie missing, and so many people unable to welcome their loved ones home. I just wanted to slip quietly in by the back door, hang up my coat, and put the kettle on.

From Southampton, I took a series of buses and trains, each one propelling me further away from China, and closer to home. I kept my head down, avoiding the glances and whispers. My skin was the colour of the conkers that decorated the horse chestnut trees, my gaunt cheeks and lightened hair offering more than a hint of the story I tried to conceal beneath my many layers of clothes. I'd been away, that much was clear, and, unlike so many others, I'd returned. There was more than a degree of guilt and shame in that.

I walked the last mile, up the hill and along the lane. The sun broke through the clouds now and again, as if it was afraid to shine too brightly. Birds sang from telegraph wires and chimney pots. A perfect patchwork blanket of fields stretched out to the horizon with their dry-stone wall hems and hedgerow seams. It was all so vibrant and alive. The smell of cut grass and malt from the brewery beckoned me home.

The back gate still squeaked when I lifted the latch and pushed it open, the gravel stones still crunched underfoot. Late-blooming pink geraniums danced in pots on the step, and sweet peas clung to their canes, decorating the grey walls with shades of powder-blue, rose and lavender. I stopped to inhale their sweet fragrance. More than anything else, the familiar scent of the flowers I'd known since I was an infant, told me I was home.

I was glad to find the house empty. Mother was no doubt collecting eggs from the farm, or visiting a friend. I savoured the silence of the kitchen, the gentle hum of the refrigerator, the steady tick of the carriage clock on the mantelpiece in the front room. Like a ghost, I wandered through the downstairs rooms, before climbing the stairs to my bedroom.

It was just as I'd left it. My blanket was still folded on the foot of the bed from when I'd taken it out of my trunk at the last minute to make space for more books. It was as if I'd only just left, as if the many years in between were merely minutes.

I washed and changed, and walked the short distance to the church. There were many more graves than when I'd left. Too many. A stark reminder that the war had left its mark on this quiet corner of Yorkshire, just as it had left its mark around the world. I took a moment to read the headstones, the years between the dates of birth and death too few by far. I bowed my head in silent respect, and walked on, toward the small headstone beneath the lilac bush, where I set down my posy of sweet peas on the freshly cut grass.

'I came back, Harry.' I brushed my fingertips across the lettering on his headstone. 'I came all the way back to say goodbye.'

It had taken a trip halfway around the world and back again, and the hardest years I would ever know, to finally accept that he was gone, and that I had to let him go.

I felt in my pocket and pulled out the last sunflower seed. I pushed it deep into the earth beside Harry's headstone, drew a can of water from the pump beside the churchyard wall, and gave the seed its first drink as I thought of Wei Huan's words. *We grow anywhere with strong roots.*

I stood for a long time. Thinking, remembering, listening to the whispers of my past, and the gentle call of my future.

The afternoon sun was high in the sky when I returned to the house. The gate stood open; the kitchen window ajar. Mother was home. She must have seen my trunk in the hall, and wondered so many things.

'Hello!' I stepped inside. The cat rushed past on the doorstep as if she'd never even noticed I was missing. 'Mother? Hello?'

But it wasn't my mother I found sitting at the kitchen table. It was Alfie.

I couldn't speak; could hardly breathe.

'You're here!' I said, laughing through my tears. 'You're here!'

A broad grin spread across his face. 'And so are you!' The arms that had carried me home when I'd sprained my ankle, and had carried Harry's coffin into the church, wrapped themselves around me, and all the years of anguish and fear, despair and hope, lifted from me so that I felt light-headed. 'And so are you.'

Like a pendulum reset, everything clicked back into place and time began again.

We didn't ask questions or offer answers. There would be time enough for that. We shared a pot of tea on the back step, just as we'd done as teenagers and young adults finding our way in life, and it was the most natural thing in the world. Family was what held us all together in the end.

The Bird in the Bamboo Cage

That afternoon, after Mother had recovered from the shock of my return, and I'd told her as much as I could, I took my letter to Lady Baden-Powell from inside the pages of my Girl Guide Handbook, took a pen from the writing desk, and added a postscript, detailing our liberation and the journey home, and my final thoughts.

Without the children, I don't think I would have coped as well, I wrote. *Their innocence brought moments of lightness to the most serious situations. Their willingness to try decorated the bare walls. Their squabbles and giggles brightened the dim electric lights and fading lanterns. Their natural curiosity and unstoppable instinct to play and learn gave me the determination to keep going. They were my food and my fuel, my light in the darkest moments.*

I will sign off with your own words, as written in my Girl Guide Handbook, which sits beside me now, and has been a source of tremendous faith and inspiration all these years.

'As a Guide your first duty is to be helpful to other people, both in small everyday matters and also under the worst of circumstances. It has been said that women can never be the same after the great events of the last few years, and we must never forget that the Girl Scouts of today are the women of tomorrow.'

Elspeth Kent, Guide Captain, 1st Chefoo Girl Guides

I sealed the envelope, added a stamp, and set off for the post box. A breeze whipped my hair around my cheeks as I made my way down the steep lane. As I walked, my feet picked up the pace of their own will, propelling me forward, until my walk became a jog, and then I started to run, and I ran and I ran and I ran, because I could, because I was free, and it felt wonderful.

PART FOUR: REMEMBRANCE

1975

THE GUIDE LAW: A GUIDE IS A FRIEND TO ALL AND A SISTER TO EVERY OTHER GUIDE

The Girl Scout finds a special comrade in every other Girl Scout, it goes without saying, and knows how to make her feel that she need never be without a friend or a meal or a helping hand as long as there is another Girl Scout in the world.

NANCY

St Hilda's College, Oxford University, June 1975

The last day of Trinity term delivers a much-needed downpour of warm summer rain. I push open the sash window and inhale the ripe earthy aroma. Petrichor. The scent of summer.

But summer rain isn't the only thing the day brings.

I've often wondered when my past would catch up with me, but in all my ponderings I'd never imagined it would arrive by second-class post from Scotland. I'd rather hoped it would be sent with a little more urgency for a start.

'Edinburgh? Who do I know in Edinburgh?' I push my reading glasses onto the bridge of my nose and scrutinize the address on the envelope. *Professor Nancy Crofton (née Plummer)*. I don't recognize the writing, although there is something rather admirable about the bold flourish of the N.

The grandmother clock beside me ticks away the seconds as I slice through the top of the envelope and remove a single sheet of Basildon Bond. It carries the scent of menthol cigarettes.

361

Consulate. Larry's favourite. And there he is, smiling at me through the candlelight, the tip of his after-dinner cigarette glowing red as we sit through another damned power cut. I grumble and call them a nuisance. He smiles and calls them romantic. I linger a moment in the memory before I drag myself back to the present and unfold the page. The groundsman cuts the engine of the lawnmower outside. Everything pauses, even the drone of a bee on the honeysuckle falls away.

10th June, 1975

25 Willow Lane
Edinburgh
Scotland

My dearest Plum,
  Surprise!
  I do hope this finds you well, and that you remember me! It really has been <u>such</u> a long time. Too long by far, and yet I can still see you as clearly as if you were standing beside me at assembly, all dimpled smile and Shirley Temple curls. I remember you very fondly, despite the many years and miles and all the curiosities of life that have passed between us since I last saw you.
  The thing is, dear Plum, I have embarked on a rather ambitious project to write an account of our internment to mark the 30th anniversary of our liberation. To that end, I'm inviting members of Kingfisher Patrol and the 1st and 2nd Chefoo Brownies to attend a reunion luncheon in London this summer. Finding everyone has proven to be rather tricky, and you, dear girl, are my last discovery, so I write this feeling rather triumphant. Of course, having found you, I have absolutely no idea of your personal circumstances, bar the obvious

acquisition of a husband somewhere along the way – Mrs Crofton. Professor Crofton, nonetheless! If your present situation makes a trip to London at all possible, do you think you might be able to join us? 17th August at the Chinese Embassy, 12 noon. It really wouldn't be the same without you.

I tracked down dear Miss Butterworth, who is delighted to join us, but sadly Edwina Trevellyan (do you remember her?) died quite a few years ago. We'd kept in regular contact over the years so I was desperately sad to learn of her passing. There's one other thing I must tell you. Miss Kent (or rather, Mrs Harris as she is now) is not at all well I'm afraid. Her family aren't sure if she'll be able to travel to the reunion, or, indeed, whether she might prevail that long. I'm dreadfully sorry to be the bearer of such sad news, but I thought you might like to know, since you were always especially fond of her.

I do hope to hear from you!

Fondest regards,

Joan Nuttall (aka Mouse!)

P.S. Do you still have the patrol log books? I would very much like to see them again, for old time's sake. I've also enclosed something I found recently, which I believe belongs to you.

I sink into my chair like a slowly deflating balloon.

'Well I never. After all this time.'

Amid the shock of the dreadful news waiting for me back in England following liberation, we'd lost touch. It is one of my greatest regrets in life. To see Joan's name, to hear from her after all these years, stirs a well of emotion that I've kept hidden, deep in my heart.

The heat of the wood-panelled office presses in on me as

distant names and places jump from the page. Like the magical pop-up books I'd loved as a child, my memories spring up in stark detail: the guards in their uniforms standing to attention on the parade ground as we begin the daily roll-call: *ichi, ni, san, shi, go . . .*; the clipped English vowels of our teachers; the thrilling drone of the American B-25 as I lay in my hospital bed; the kaoliang that stuck to the roof of our mouths; the terrible foul stench of the latrines. The years fall away as I imagine them all beside me – Sprout, Mouse, Miss Kent, Miss Butterworth, Larry, Wei Huan, Shu Lan, Mrs Trevellyan, Home Run – each of them tugs at the rusted buckles of the old steamer trunk that I'd locked and packed away nearly thirty years ago.

I read the letter several times and shake the envelope to see what she's enclosed. I unwrap the lilac tissue paper carefully. A Girl Guide proficiency badge tumbles into my palm. I run my fingertips over the careful embroidery, so many memories captured in the neat lines of running stitch. It was the one badge I hadn't completed before we were liberated, and she'd remembered.

For the first time in almost thirty years I let myself go back to China, combing over my memories, careful not to miss any strands. Like an echo carried over the years, I can still hear the chatter of the girls in the dorm, the hum of crickets and cicadas, the whip-poor-will singing me to sleep during sticky summer nights, the steady *click click click* of the ceiling fan that promised to cool us down and never did. But one memory stands out much clearer than the rest: the memory of waving to my mother from the deck of the boat that would take me away from her.

As a child, I'd wept with the agony of being parted from her. As an adult, I still ache with the pain of knowing that the distant flash of a kingfisher-blue dress was the last I ever saw of her. As my father had driven me and Edward home, he'd explained that Mummy had contracted the typhoid, and had died on February 22nd, 1943, after a short illness. While I was celebrating World Thinking Day at Temple Hill, my mother had slipped quietly away.

I write and post my reply to Mouse that afternoon to confirm that I will, indeed, attend the reunion, and to offer a small alteration to her plans.

> *I was so sorry to hear that Miss Kent isn't well. Of all the people who were with us at Weihsien, I think of her the most. I hate to interfere, but I wonder – since she isn't able to travel to London – might it be possible for us to travel to her? It would be a jolly adventure, as she would say. Her girls on the march once again. She did, after all, do so much for us. It only feels right that we do something for her in return.*

To have the chance to thank my teacher properly feels suddenly terribly important. I lock up the office, say a hasty farewell to my colleagues, and cycle the short distance home in a hurry.

The letter from Mouse has all but unbuckled the latches of the old steamer trunk so that it isn't so much a matter of *if* I'll open it, but how long I'll put it off. I decide to get it over with quickly, rather than prolong the agony of wondering.

It is hidden at the back of the wardrobe, gathering dust and mildew among a few old suits of Larry's. He can't fit into them anymore but he refuses to admit that his fondness for cheese and wine has any impact whatsoever on the size of his waist. Also, we never throw anything away. Camp Fever, we call it. The inability to waste a single thing, forever looking for an opportunity to reuse it.

Moving the suits aside, I grab the handle of the trunk and drag it forwards. It is surprisingly weighty, and just as cumbersome and bulky as I remember. I can still feel the pain as it banged against my shins on the long walk from Chefoo School to Temple Hill. I can still hear us all singing, so jolly as we marched off into the abyss. I wonder if our teachers knew what was waiting for us, or if they were as surprised by it all as we were. With the benefit of hindsight, I've often replayed the whispered conversations and furtive glances between our teachers, and wondered how many horrors they'd protected us from. The entire Weihsien experience looks rather different when considered from an adult's point of view.

The trunk topples forward as I wrestle it out of its hiding place. It lands on the carpet with a thud. I pull a pillow from the bed to save my knees and hunker down in front of the trunk. The old luggage labels are still there. *Nancy Plummer. China Inland Mission School. Chefoo.* I run my fingertips over the black and white school emblem of a Chinese dragon and the lettering on the Chinese seal which, I remember, translates as 'Chefoo's Old Scholar's Association'. Funny how little details come back to me.

Everything is still in its place, perfectly preserved like a museum exhibition. My Girl Guide uniform and Promise badge, our patrol flag with the kingfisher crest stitched neatly onto both sides, my log books for Kingfisher Patrol, and my old tea caddy, full of little trinkets and mementoes.

For a long time I sit quietly, surrounded by this strange museum of memories. Some happy. Some sad. Some poignant and indefinable in their own way. But it isn't the items spread on the floor around me that give me pause, it is the heart-clattering absence of the things, and the people, that aren't.

The last thing I remove from the trunk is the letter my father had given to me when we'd returned to the family home. A letter from my mother, written in the final stages of her illness. I take a deep breath as I unfold the page for the first time in many years, and read her words again.

My darling Nonny,
When you read this, I will have already slipped away. I want you to know that I am not afraid, or in pain, and that I am smiling as I think of you. You will always be the world to me. I am looking at photographs of you and Edward as I write this, and my heart is full.

We heard about the occupation of Chefoo School, and your transfer to Temple Hill. Mission HQ managed to send word that you are all faring well and being terribly brave, from which I have taken much strength and hope. I know you will be missing me very much, and that you may be afraid of what is happening, but I also know that you are a very capable girl, and that you will make the best of it and go on to do many incredible and admirable things when the war is over.

Don't be sad, darling. Remember that I will always be with you, just as I have been every day we've spent apart. You must spread your wings now and fly, and what marvellous things will be waiting for you!

With all my love to you, darling.
Mummy

With the passing of time, I've understood that it was my desire to see my mother again that kept me going on the very darkest days. Even without being there, she'd walked every mile with me, stood beside me at every roll-call and tucked me in at night. In the end, I'd survived without her, learned to stand on my own two feet. For all my Oxford exams, and distinguished university degrees and doctorates, that has been the most important lesson of all: to trust myself, to cherish myself as much as I cherish others.

I'm still sitting on the floor of the back bedroom when I hear the key rattling in the lock. I glance at my wristwatch, surprised to discover it is already five o'clock and I've been sitting here for three hours and there isn't a potato scrubbed or a carrot chopped.

I stand and wince at the pain. I still forget about my osteoporosis – Weihsien's lasting legacy – staunchly denying the fact that I shouldn't kneel on cold floors for hours on end. I hear the radio being switched on, the sound of the tap filling the kettle, something being muttered to the cat.

'Hello, love,' I call. 'That you?'

'No. It's Elvis Presley. Where are you?'

I smile. 'Upstairs.'

'Are you coming down, or should I starve down here on my own?'

'I think you should come up.'

It still surprises me that I'd married Larry Crofton, that we'd found each other again after many years. Edward brought us back together, or perhaps it was fate. Either way, it makes sense that we are together. Nobody else would have ever understood. We know that look in each other's eyes.

He puts his arm around my shoulder as he walks into the bedroom. 'I see. Moving out, are we?'

I kiss him on the cheek and hand him the letter.

'From Mouse. Do you remember her? She's organizing a reunion of the Chefoo Brownies and Guides and wants me to go.'

He doesn't need to ask if I will. He already knows the answer.

'Take your time,' he says as he squeezes my shoulder.

It has been thirty years, and suddenly I'm in a rush. Miss Kent is running out of time, and there is still so much I want to say to her.

NANCY

August 1975

Nine of us manage to make the journey to St Columba's Hospice in Windsor. We gather in a small waiting room, embracing and admiring each other in turn; amazed to see the girls we'd once known now grown into women.

The nurse in charge of the ward steps into the room to tell us that although visiting is usually restricted to two at a time, the family members have agreed that we can all go in together.

'She might not be very responsive, but she's fully aware of what's going on, so please do talk to her,' the nurse explains. 'She especially likes people to sing to her.'

We walk along the quiet corridors, politely acknowledging the other visitors and nursing staff who bustle past and take a second glance. What a spectacle we must make in our matching blue hats, scarves tied neatly at our necks, our Promise badges pinned to our blue shirts.

Mouse holds the door open as we tiptoe into the dimly lit room. A bunch of sunflowers stands in a vase on the windowsill. The window is open slightly, allowing a light breeze to wash through the room and play at the lace curtains that flutter gently. A handsome young man and an older man smile warmly and thank us for coming.

The older man takes my hand and kisses me lightly on the cheek. 'Hello, Nancy.'

'You recognize me?'

'I'd recognize those curls anywhere. You look exactly the same.'

I smile. 'It's lovely to see you, Master Harris.'

'Charlie will do. We're not in school now!'

He introduces the younger man. 'This is our son, Harry.' He turns to the bed then. 'And this marvellous woman needs no introduction at all.'

And there she is, as fragile as melting snow, the hospital bed enormous around her narrow frame. She was always petite, but there is so little of her left. She is a bird with broken wings. Our beloved Brown Owl. Our dear Guide Captain.

Mouse sits on the chair beside the bed and patiently explains who is there, and all about the book she is writing, and the reunion she's organized, and how she found the girls from the 2nd Chefoo Brownies and Kingfisher Patrol and that we all insisted we come and see her.

It takes a moment for her to open her eyes. Her gaze flickers around the room like a guttering candle, taking us all in. We step forward one at a time, take her hand, and tell her how lovely it is to see her again.

I wait until last.

'Hello, Miss Kent. It's me. Nancy Plummer.'

Her grip tightens a little as she turns her face toward me, and in her eyes I see a glimmer of recognition. Her lips are dry and cracked, but she manages a brief smile.

'Dear little Nancy. You've grown.'

I smile. 'A little. Yes.' There's so much I want to say; so many things to thank her for. 'I wanted to say thank you. For being a mother to me when mine wasn't there. For keeping us safe, and giving us hope.'

She shakes her head. 'You gave *me* hope. All of you. My children.' She studies me, her grey eyes softened with age. 'I remember you,' she whispers. 'I remember it all.'

For decades I've fought against Weihsien, blocking it out, turning away, a part of my past that I refused to rake over. Only now, I understand that it is also my present, and my future. Weihsien is part of the young girl I was, and the woman I've become. Those years took so much from all of us, but our teachers gave us everything we needed to carry on: an education, a family, a home, hope.

It seems fitting to sing 'Taps'. One by one, the others join in, our voices linked in perfect harmony, soaring back across the miles and the years to the little meeting room we'd called our own, and where lost and frightened little girls had learned how to become strong and brave young women.

'*Day is done / Gone the sun, / From the lakes, from the hills, from the sky! / All is well, safely rest, / God is nigh.*'

We lower our voices as the song reaches its gentle end and we hold the final note, just as we always did.

I close my eyes and squeeze Miss Kent's hand.

'Goodnight, Brown Owl.'

The silence that follows breaks my heart, and yet I hear her, as clearly as if she were standing beside my bed in the dormitory at Chefoo School, the moonlight casting patterns against the floor, the smell of peach blossom settling over us like silk. Mouse is already asleep in the bed to my left, Sprout is fidgeting beneath her covers in the bed to my right, and Miss Kent steps from the room, turns out the light, and whispers into the dark.

'Goodnight, Brownies.'

EPILOGUE

NANCY

December 1975

It is only now, many years later, when stitched back together with the threads of hindsight, that I can try to make some sense of what happened all those years ago in China. I'm still trying to understand how it happened to me; to a group of innocent schoolchildren and their teachers. Perhaps I never will.

What I do know, however, is that when you spend enough time somewhere, it becomes your home, and the people you share it with become your family. There were times – awful though it was – when it was enough; when we simply forgot that any other life was possible. Weihsien was our present and our future until that glorious summer day when it became our past; something awful and fascinating that had happened to us once upon a time.

And yet the further away from it I go, the more I understand that it isn't over at all. In each retelling of our story, I remember something new: a shared moment of despair and joy, unexpected kindness and unfathomable cruelty, the faces of enemies and friends. The war will always be there, even as I listen to Larry pottering about in the kitchen, making tea and toast. I savour the simplicity of such unremarkable moments, moments I once thought I would never know, and within which I feel so very safe and loved.

Now that we have found each other again, Mouse plans to visit once a month for lunch at Browns and, despite my better judgement, she has also encouraged me to start a local company of Brownie Guides. I now find myself a rather frazzled Brown Owl in charge of a boisterous group of girls. They give me a thumping headache, and the most enormous sense of joy.

I kept my promise to Sprout and finally visited New England in the fall. We stayed with her sister, Connie, and her husband and family. We ate shrimp and lobster rolls on the boardwalk. The trees really did look as though they were on fire.

Life is full, but I find time, once a week, to be alone; to reflect and remember. I especially enjoy long walks beside the Cherwell where, if I stay very still, I sometimes see a flash of iridescent blue and orange dart across the river, and I smile; so grateful for my freedom, and for those – loved, living, and lost – who taught me how to fly.

Mouse's finished book arrived two weeks before Christmas, along with the first of the season's snow. An end to our story, or a beginning? Perhaps it is a little of both.

AFTERWORD TO THE
PAPERBACK EDITION

Six months after *The Bird in the Bamboo Cage* was published, I received the most incredible email from Maida Harris Campbell. Maida was one of the children at Chefoo School during the years I have written about, and with her permission, for which we are enormously grateful, we have included extracts from her emails below.

Dear Hazel

I was one of the children in the Chefoo Weihsien story.

I am now 90 years old and was 11 on Dec 7th 1941 when the Japanese walked in to our compound and politely came in to our house and took my father's radio. Both my parents taught in the Chefoo schools, so I was one of the lucky ones never separated from my parents.

As teenagers we loved both playing and watching baseball games especially the British against the Americans and we adored Eric Liddell, especially when he told us it was OK to play on Sunday while we were in the camp.

I loved all your things about Guides and Brownies and that was so true. Also your portrayal of the teachers – they were strict but in most cases their kindness came through. I don't know if you knew that Bobby Grandon, who happened to be my sister's boyfriend, rang the bell in Block 23 in the middle of the night of VE Day to celebrate. The guards panicked and brought us all out to our roll call sites and that was scary, as they pushed us around with the searchlights on, and our neighbour said we are all being taken out to be shot. The only prisoners that had escaped was the year before.

You have opened a flood of memories.

The memories of the day we were liberated still bring tears to my eyes. Seven men parachuted down on August 17th including a Japanese American and a Chinese interpreter and many internees rushed out of the gates to the fields to meet them. Pamphlets rained down from the sky including instructions not to overeat or over-medicate. One of the party was an alumnae of the Chefoo school who asked to be sent on the mission. The liberators were greeted by the camp band playing all the national anthems of the internees. They had practised omitting the first line so the Japanese would not recognize them. It took many weeks to get us all on our way to wherever we wished to go paid by our respective countries.

You might well ask why the Mission allowed a boarding school to stay in an area that had been occupied by the Japanese in the late 1930s. My mother told me that there had been a vote and that my parents had voted to move the school to a part of China not occupied by the Japanese. I read in the mission archives years later that the British government, when asked, answered that the Japanese would never touch British citizens. And my father brought up in the heyday of the British Empire, they could totally not believe that Japan could immediately almost walk into Hong Kong and Singapore.

Thanks again that you have really opened up this little bit of history for our family. Thank you so much for telling the story so well. Soon those of us left with a living memory will all be gone. My father, Reg Harris, was Vice Principal of the Chefoo school.

Maida Harris Campbell

Hearing these memories from Maida is so powerful and moving. It really feels as if the story has now come full circle. To read more about other fascinating contact I've had with ex-Chefoo School pupils since writing the book, please visit my website at www.hazelgaynor.com.

Author Note

When my agent first introduced me to the remarkable events surrounding a group of schoolchildren and their teachers, taken to a Japanese internment camp in China in World War II, I knew instantly that I wanted to know more. The NPR podcast she directed me to started out as an amusing story about waylaid Girl Scout cookies, but quickly developed into an incredible story about a school caught up in the war following the events of Pearl Harbor. I was fascinated. The story also stirred fond memories of my years as a Brownie Guide, and of Sunday evenings with my mum, when we watched a BBC drama called *Tenko*, about a group of British, Dutch, and Australian women taken to a Japanese PoW camp in Singapore. The cogs began to turn and, as has been the case with each of my books, I knew this was a story I wanted to write.

Writing about war inevitably comes with very difficult stories of human suffering and grief. It is impossible for anyone other than those who lived through those years to truly know what the experience was like, and I approached my interpretation of these events with the greatest respect and care. Many of those interned at Weihsien have bravely shared accounts of their experience on the website weihsien-paintings.org, without which we would know very little about this part of the war. My characters are drawn from accounts of internment I discovered during my research and, of course, from my imagination, and while none of the actual children or teachers from Chefoo School were used in my book, I am very grateful to those men and women whose stories I read. The Chefoo School archives, held at the School of Oriental and African Studies (SOAS) in London, were also an invaluable source of information.

In writing the book, I kept picturing my own children faced with the same circumstances: What would they have done? How would they have coped? How would I have felt as a parent separated from my child? What especially struck me during my research was how many of the children recalled parts of their experience with a sense of fondness. That, despite the terrible circumstances they were faced with, those who led, cared for and inspired the children, managed to create a sense of safety and unity among their group. But there were also more harrowing accounts from children whose lives were deeply affected by the experience, particularly of being separated from their parents for so long. They talked about how they had struggled, in adult life, to form lasting relationships, and how they could never forget the sense of abandonment. Physical complications caused by poor nutrition during those years also affected many of them in later life.

The words of those who so bravely and stoically endured the privations and suffering at Weihsien, and those writers who have documented stories of other children caught up in the war in the Pacific, offer a vital record of this period of history. Although, as adults, the children wrote widely about their experiences, I found comparatively few accounts from the teachers themselves.

Clearly, they would have been more alert to the inherent dangers, and seen things the children were protected from. I imagine there was far more to the adult experience of internment which they felt unable to talk about, or which they preferred to remain locked behind Weihsien's high walls. It is within these gaps in the historical record that I have drawn on my imagination, and on my own life experience. No matter the time or the distance from an historical event, the universal themes of love, grief, hope, friendship, regret and resilience are what connect us all across the decades. As a daughter who lost her mother, as a sister, as a friend, as an ex-Brownie Guide (a Pixie, no less, although sadly never a Sixer – I gave that accolade to Nancy!), and as a mother, there are many aspects of both Elspeth's and Nancy's stories that I understand inherently.

What I've learned in researching and writing historical novels over the past eight years is that hope and kindness are always present during times of uncertainty and hardship, and that incredible stories of bravery and selflessness sit alongside those of pain and loss. It is impossible to write about one, without the other. The Chefoo teachers were so incredibly innovative and resourceful in keeping the children's spirits up. Their determination to keep the children safe, healthy and well-educated is, quite simply, astonishing. I hope to have captured their resilience, courage, and bravery in Elspeth, Minnie, and my fictional cast of teachers who were also inspired by the teachers I encountered during my school years.

As we commemorate key anniversaries of World War II – Dunkirk, the liberation of Auschwitz, VE Day, the Battle of Britain, the liberation of Weihsien and Japan's surrender – the memories and experiences of those involved are being shared with a new generation. These events were on such an enormous scale and magnitude, involving so many people around the world, that we are still trying to understand them. Incredible stories continue to emerge as forgotten letters, documents and mementoes are discovered in dusty attics, and as those who were there feel an urgency to tell their story before it is too late. I hope, in some small way, that by writing this particular story of World War II, and by following in the footsteps of those remarkable girls and boys, women and men who lived these years, that their experiences will become more widely known and their story will live on. We owe them all an enormous debt of gratitude.

That part of this story involved a group of Brownie and Girl Guides added an extra layer of intrigue and nostalgia for me. Brownie Guides was a very significant part of my life as a young girl growing up in a small Yorkshire village. I remember, so vividly, putting on my uniform every Thursday for our meetings in the school hall. I remember working hard for my badges (I peeled an enormous number of potatoes for my neighbour for my House Orderly badge!), and always wanting to Lend a Hand and do good deeds. I remember the songs, especially 'Brownie Bells' and 'Taps'. I remember the women – Brown Owl and Snowy Owl – who were our leaders, and from whom parts of Elspeth and Minnie are drawn. I also remember envying my older sister's Girl Guide uniform. While I was writing this book, I found a copy of the 1974 edition of *The Brownie Guide Handbook* on eBay. It is the same handbook I had as a young Brownie and every page is familiar to me, which just shows how often I must have read it. I've written more about the history of Brownies and Guides in a separate section of this book. I hope you enjoy it, and that it sparks the same fond nostalgia for many of you ex-Brownies, Guides and Scouts.

Finally, I would like to mention my grandma, who celebrated her one hundredth birthday while I was finishing this book. She received her letter from the Queen, and quietly celebrated with family. For a while, it was a milestone we didn't think she would reach (we should have known better – she is made of tough

Yorkshire stuff!), and when she did, it made me stop and think. Born just after the Great War, she grew up to watch her youngest brother and husband head off to fight in World War II, leaving her at home with her two young sons, including my dad. Her brother, Jack, never returned from the war. He was reported as Missing in Action, in October 1942. The anguished letters my great-grandmother continued to write to her dear son are utterly heartbreaking. Reading them gave me a very real sense of the desperation and agony felt by those separated during the war. Our grandparents and great-grandparents are our touchstone to a past that might sometimes feel too distant to be relevant to us and to our lives today. And yet, the older I get, and the more I learn about the world wars, they feel more important and more relevant than ever. I hope we will keep discovering; writing, reading, and sharing these stories. They are part of all our pasts, and we must never forget them.

When I was writing *The Bird in The Bamboo Cage*, I often wished I could speak to some of the survivors, but I didn't know how to find them or, indeed, whether they might want to be found. I was profoundly moved, then, when they found me. There are many reasons I write historical novels, but the urge to tell these forgotten stories from our past, to add colour where we only see black and white, to hear the voices of those whom history has silenced, is the strongest motivation for finding the right words to put on the page. I have always believed that ideas for books find the writer, rather than the other way around. I am so grateful and humbled that this story, and these very special readers, found me.

A final note on the text. Romanization is used throughout for Chinese place names and character names, consistent with Wade-Giles.

READING GROUP QUESTIONS

- The book opens with Nancy reflecting on her experiences of the war. Do you have family members who were involved in World War II? What memories have they shared?
- Did the book give you a better understanding about the war in the Pacific, and life under Japanese occupation and internment during World War II?
- The sense of routine and unity and optimism provided by the girls' involvement in Brownies and Girl Guides is key to their ability to endure life in the internment camp. Were you ever a Brownie, or a Guide or Scout? What do you remember from that experience?
- The book is narrated in alternating points of view between Nancy and Elspeth. Why do you think the author chose to do that?
- Nancy feels a strong urge to see Elspeth one last time and to thank her for all she did for her. If you could meet any of your school teachers now, what would you say to them?
- What will you remember most about the book? Would you recommend it to a friend?

A Brief History of the Girl Guides

'Remember, it is not what you have, but what you give
that brings happiness.'
Olave Baden-Powell

It was over a century ago, in 1909, when a group of girls
first appeared at one of Lord Robert Baden-Powell's Boy
Scout rallies at Crystal Palace in the UK, and asked to join
as Girl Scouts. Six thousand girls were already registered with the
Boy Scouts and practising their own version of Scouting, but
they wanted a movement of their own, comparable to the boys'.

Agnes Baden-Powell, Robert's sister, strongly believed that girls
should benefit from something similar, that 'girls must be partners
and comrades, rather than dolls'. A pamphlet was written, titled
*Baden-Powell Girl Guides – a Suggestion for Character Training
for Girls*, which set out instructions on how Girl Guides would
work and a list of the efficiency badges girls could earn. The six
thousand girls already registered as tempo-rary Scouts became

known as Girl Guides and, a year later, the Girl Guide Association was officially established in the UK under Agnes's leadership. The handbook *Scouting for Boys* was adapted for girls in a book called *How Girls Can Help to Build Up the Empire*, and was published in 1912.

Baden-Powell's movement encouraged spiritual, moral, physical, mental, social, intellectual and emotional development. All these aspects were part of the principles of the guiding movement, and key to the Original Promise and Law.

ORIGINAL PROMISE

On my honour, I promise that I will do my best:
To do my duty to God and the King (Or God and my country);
To help other people at all times;
To obey the Guide Law.

ORIGINAL LAW

- A Guide's honour is to be trusted.
- A Guide is loyal.
- A Guide's duty is to be useful and to help others.
- A Guide is a friend to all and a sister to every other Guide.
- A Guide is courteous.
- A Guide is a friend to animals.
- A Guide obeys orders.
- A Guide smiles and sings under all difficulties.
- A Guide is thrifty.
- A Guide is pure in thought, in word and in deed.

Groups of Girl Guides were established in Australia, Canada, Denmark, Finland, New Zealand and South Africa, and by 1912 there were also groups in Ireland, Portugal and Norway. Juliette

"Daisy" Gordon Low founded Girl Scouting in the USA that same year after assembling eighteen girls for a local Girl Scout meeting in Georgia. Like the Baden-Powells, Low believed that girls should be given the same opportunity as boys to develop physically, mentally and spiritually. In 1915 a charter was granted to the Girl Guides Association. The movement continued to grow, and today there are Girl Guide or Girl Scouts Associations in 150 countries.

When Baden-Powell married, his wife, Olave, was very keen to become involved in Girl Guides. In 1918 she was appointed Chief Guide for Britain and, two years later, she helped to form an International Council which went on to become the World Association of Girl Guides and Girl Scouts. Olave spent her married life promoting Guiding and Scouting, making many trips overseas (including 648 flights), and visiting many countries to promote the work, which she loved. Following Lord Robert Baden-Powell's death in 1941, Olave continued to lead the movement as Chief Guide.

Before her own death, Olave left a message for her family in which she expressed 'how greatly I rejoiced over the way in which you have all carried out your share in the work of the movement that my beloved husband invented for the advancement of boys and girls of all countries, years ago . . . I trust that you will continue fully to use the system of work and play that our movement provides, keeping up the fun and friendships made at your meetings and camps, abiding by the Promise and upholding the Laws that you undertook to live by when you joined up. In that way you will not only advance yourself in body, mind and spirit, but you will affect those around you, in doing what is honourable and right and wise, and in giving out kindness of thought and action, thus striving against all ills and helping to make the world a happier and better place in which to live.'

The Guide Movement continues to thrive today as an essential youth organization for young girls, offering a place for them to practise teamwork and leadership skills, to explore a wide range of interests, and to develop a sense of confidence and belief in their potential. In a world in which we still strive for equality for women, Girl Guides is perhaps more important and relevant than ever.

As Juliette Gordon Low once said, 'The work of today is the history of tomorrow and we are its makers.'

FURTHER READING

The following books and websites were invaluable to me during my research. I hope you might find them interesting if you wish to read more about the war in the Pacific during World War II, and/or about the history of Girl Guiding.

Empire of the Sun – J.G. Ballard
Dragon Seed – Pearl S. Buck
The Good Earth - Pearl S. Buck
How the Girl Guides Won the War – Janie Hampton
Girl Scouts Handbook: The Original 1913 Edition – W.J. Hoxie
The Story of the Girl Guides – Rose Kerr
Forgotten Ally: China's World War II, 1937–1945 – Rana Mitter
China's War with Japan, 1937–1945 – Rana Mitter
From Sprites to Dark Horses: A Girlguiding Journey – Avril Stouse
Stolen Childhoods: The Untold Story of the Children Interned by the Japanese in the Second World War – Nicola Tyrer
weihsien-paintings.org